AN OLD EVIL

OTHER BOOKS BY JACQUELINE AULD

MASSEY AND SPARKS

BOOK 1: The Children of Gaia

AN
OLD EVIL

A Massey & Sparks crime thriller

BOOK 2

JACQUELINE AULD

AN OLD EVIL

ISBN: 978-1-7385390-2-4

Published worldwide by Jacqueline Auld
under her Shuffle Books brand

Copyright © Jacqueline Auld 2024

The right of Jacqueline Auld to be identified as the author of this work has been asserted in accordance with the Copyright, Designs and Patents Act 1988.

All rights reserved. No part of this book may be reproduced or distributed in any form without prior written permission from the author, with the exception of non-commercial uses permitted by copyright law.

This book is a work of fiction. Names, characters, organisations, places, events and incidents are either the products of the author's imagination or used in a fictitious manner. Any resemblance to actual persons, living or dead, or actual events is purely coincidental.

SHUFFLE

For Kevin.
What would I ever do
without you?

CHAPTER 1

Friday 29th December 2023

'Moonlight Sonata' played while the curtains closed, so his loved ones couldn't hear the mechanism trundling, or see his coffin being carted away to be burned. It was what he'd asked for, but Ellie Morgan would far rather they'd played something like 'Another One Bites the Dust'. Something to make people laugh. Because that's what he did in life. That's how he'd reeled her in that first time, when he'd almost killed her and her son.

The funeral director came forward and whispered a few words she didn't hear. James touched her arm. 'Time to go, Mam.'

Megan took hold of her other arm and steered her into the aisle, James and Alex on either side, like bodyguards to someone famous, which she wasn't, of course, although she'd have to face being the centre of attention at least for a while longer. So that all these people – good heavens hundreds of them, lips moving, hands reaching out to touch her – could all witness her devastation. Like ghouls. But could she tell them all she was glad he'd finally gone? Because she did feel glad.

Not happy – she didn't think she could ever be happy again – but glad, certainly. Glad he had no pain now. Glad he didn't have to carry on through his agony trying to make her laugh one last time. Until it really was the last time and she wished she could remember what it was he'd said to make her crease up so.

Outside, the cold nipped her cheeks but with her phalanx of family in formation to protect her she hardly noticed. They took the brunt of the assault by well-wishers, shaking hands, thanking people for coming, listening to the odd anecdote. She played her part too though, simply by being there for people to talk at. But, when it came down to it, she couldn't tell them how glad she was he'd gone. She could barely even speak. Instead, she nodded and shook her head, with no idea at all of whether she'd nodded when she should have shaken or shaken when she should have nodded.

And then she felt the pressure of James's arms as he bundled her into the limousine. Back seat, Megan and Alex on either side, holding her hands. Megan's husband and James' wife opposite. James just about to get in, then pausing as a woman in a red coat filled the window, one hand on the glass.

'Ells? Ellie Crewe?'

'Step away,' James said. His best minder impression. As if she really were someone famous.

'Ells? Please. Just one word.'

Something about that voice.

James loomed large over the woman, holding his palms out in front of him to keep her at bay. 'I said step away.'

Then he climbed in, and the limousine moved off, with the handprint of someone Ellie felt sure she should know still cooling on the window. Like a ghost from her past.

***

The King's Arms. Their favourite pub, but her first visit without David. Just family and close friends today. She couldn't have coped with all those people from the crem around her. Not here. She couldn't even recall who they all were. She'd noticed several youngsters there though, all in school uniform. David's class at school, she supposed. GCSE students. And she'd seen a different sort of uniform too. Air Force Blue with the pilot's wings badge. Some senior officers from his old RAF squadron no doubt, accompanied by some of his old fellow-retired comrades.

'Another G & T, Ellie?'

'Please, Mark.'

Megan had got herself a good one in Mark, and at least he wasn't treating her as if she were a fragile old lady. This would be the third drink he'd brought her already. Doubles too. They'd have to carry her home.

'Oh God,' Megan said. 'Here's that woman again. In the red coat.'

'Ells Bells!' the woman cried. 'As I live and breathe. It is you.'

CHAPTER 2

Monday 1st January 2024

'A woman walks into a police station carrying a cool box—'

'Not another one, Flossie. Did your kids buy you a new joke book for Christmas?'

'No joke. Come see for yourself; she won't talk to me.'

'Why not?'

'Wrong gender. If I'm allowed to say such a thing these days. Insists on speaking to a female officer, i.e. a non-man. Someone without a bloody penis. And right now, DS Sparks, you're all we've got.'

'Ha bloody ha! Are you serious? A tool box. Maybe it's a bomb.'

'Not tool, I said cool. A cool box. She'd have left it here and done a runner by now if it were a bomb.'

'Unless she's suicidal.'

'Good point. So, are you coming down or what?'

DS Christine Sparks glanced at the clock on the wall, pinched the bridge of her nose and groaned, seeing the promises she'd made to her mother disappear, again. Not that her mother would remember her promise anyway. It probably hadn't even sunk in that today was a special day.

Hartington Police Station was deserted save for herself, a couple of male PCs who were on a break from the icy blast outside, and Desk Sergeant Bob Fossey – AKA Flossie on account of the strawberry-blond candyfloss frizz that had once adorned his now polished scalp. Less than an hour ago, other members of the flu-depleted shift – including two female PCs – had responded to a call for assistance from colleagues on patrol in the town centre who'd come across a horde of Hartington's finest, all tanked up on more than a week's worth of season's cheer and spoiling for a fight. Even if they returned in the next five minutes, they'd be stuck dealing with the fallout for the foreseeable.

Sparks was only here herself, well past her shift end, to wrap up the paperwork on a case she'd been working out of here so she could start the new year off back where she belonged at Area Command. The last thing she needed was to get caught up in something new, but she couldn't deny her curiosity had been piqued.

'This is shit, Flossie. I'm just about to leave; it's New Year's Eve.'

'Yeah right. Like you've got a social life. You just need a little motivation.'

She heard a dull rattle on the other end of the line.

'Got a brand-new tub of Quality Street down here that won't last five minutes once the crew gets back. And anyway, it's New Year's Day now. You've already missed the main event.

What? She looked at the clock on the wall. 11.25 pm. Then at the one on her Fitbit. 12.20 am.

Shit.

She closed her eyes and pushed a huge bubble of guilt back into its box. Her mother would likely be asleep now anyway. And if not, she'd just get tetchy, and it would take an age to calm her down.

'Alright sweet talker. Give me five minutes. And the fudge ones are mine.'

***

Viewed on the security screen, Sparks judged the young woman to be around twenty to twenty-five years of age. She looked calm. And sober. On New Year's night?

Despite the snow and ice outside, she wore flimsy party clothes, with ballet pump shoes nowhere near suitable for the icy conditions, and no coat, so maybe she had a car outside. Or else she'd been dropped off, by a taxi perhaps.

'She doesn't look suicidal,' Sparks said.

'She's too calm though, don't you think? As if she's made peace with herself and is prepared to leave this world.'

'Christ, Flossie. If she were going to blow up the station, she'd be wearing a big jacket with a bomb vest under it, or she'd have a sinister looking backpack. She wouldn't be done up to the nines and carrying a bloody cool box!'

'You're the one who mentioned suicidal bombers. I never thought about it until you said it. But look at her. Don't you think—'

'Put her in 3A. Let's see what she wants.'

Room 3A, she'd been told, had been referred to in the original plans of the building as a conference room. Fine if you wanted to confer with a concussed cat, but in reality it contained an oval table that could barely seat six people, very uncomfortably, and only then if the three smallest could manage to squeeze round the walls to the other side without mishap.

Up close, Sparks lowered her estimate of the girl's age to no older than twenty. She observed the nervous butterfly flutter of a pulse in her neck, heard the shortness of her breath, and could see that what she'd mistaken via the security camera for calmness was in reality no more than a brittle shell barely disguised beneath a mask of make-up and a sharp hair style.

She didn't get the chance to finish introducing herself before the girl took a huge breath, held it for a moment, and began talking.

'My name is Abigail Grant. Exactly three years ago tonight I was raped. I didn't report it at the time. I want to report it now.'

Sparks' pen made scratching noises on her notepad. 'Why now?'

The girl's nostrils flared, her chin jutted, and she touched her left ring finger to a small, jagged scar on her jaw. 'It's the anniversary. Three years. He attacked me. He hurt me physically, yes. But more than that. He has made my whole life a pile of crap for three whole years because he thought he had a God-given right to just... take...'

She paused, closed her eyes and clenched her fists to stop her hands from shaking before carrying on, her next words clipping the emotion before it could escape.

'It's New Year. I've made a resolution. I don't want to waste any more time. I'm sick and tired of seeing him, like a black monster in my dreams, every night. I can still feel his hands on me. I just... I need it to end.' She took in and released a huge breath. 'I need to do something to make it stop.'

'Why didn't you report it at the time?' Black monster, the girl had said. Could she be an early victim of Musk Man, who dresses in black and wears a ski mask? Over the past year, they'd had six reported rapes. But three years ago? Could this be connected?

'I... I was too frightened.'

'Did you know your attacker? Did he threaten you?'

'Oh God, no. I couldn't bear it if I thought it was someone I knew. He came at me from behind. From an alleyway. I was walking home from a party. There were four of us at first and I was the last one, because I lived furthest away. And... I never saw his face. He had some sort of hood on. I only remember the smell. Like sticking my nose in a donkey's armpit.'

Sparks grimaced, thrown for a moment. Did a donkey actually have armpits? And, if so, why on earth should this girl know what they smell like? Musk Man had been given the name by the press because all the current victims had reported their rapist smelling of musk, as if he'd been over-enthusiastic with a sickly aftershave. But no-one had ever mentioned a donkey's bloody armpits before now.

She paused before asking her next question – the one that had been bugging her since she'd picked up the phone to Flossie.

'So, what's in the cool box?'

'It's the clothes I wore that night. I put them in the freezer. To preserve DNA.'

'Seriously? You mean they've been in among your fish fingers and ice cream for three whole years?'

What the hell sort of personality could do that after having just been raped? Objective enough to preserve the evidence, and yet too frightened to report the crime?

Abigail opened the lid and fumbled four solid blue ice blocks out of the box, sending them skittering across the polished table. Then she lifted out a collection of crackling frost-encrusted objects as if they were fragile relics.

'They're perfectly safe. See. They're in zip-lock bags.'

CHAPTER 3

Sonia Wragg closed the study door to shut out the raucous sounds of their guests and set her drink on Ronnie's precious mahogany desk, spilling a little on the polished surface in the process. She yanked some tissues from a box on the filing cabinet and mopped up the spill, accidentally trailing the flared feathered sleeve of her black De la Vali mini dress in the liquid.

'Bugger.'

She grabbed more tissues to use as a drip mat then got herself comfortable on Ronnie's oxblood leather swivel chair and tapped the number she'd put into her phone just two days ago.

It took an age for Ellie to pick up, by which time Sonia had taken a deep swig of her drink, ice cubes tinkling, then set it back down on the pad of tissues.

'What do you want?'

'Is that a nice way to talk to your old friend?'

Ellie didn't sound sleepy, so she can't have woken her up. She didn't sound tipsy either, so she probably hadn't been partying. Hardly surprising. Recently bereaved and all that, and she had let herself go a bit, hadn't she? All that caring for the sick husband, no doubt.

If that ever happened to Ronnie, she'd be getting a nursing team in, or putting him in a private facility somewhere.

'Sonia, what do you want? It's half past midnight.'

'Yes it is. On New Year's Eve. Well, technically New Year's Day. You used to be such a party animal Ells.'

'Not now, Sonia. Good night.'

'No, wait. Please Ells. I'm sorry. You know me. I haven't changed. All the china shops still lock their doors when they see me coming. Anyway, the first thing I'm calling for. I thought you might be interested. Or not. I won't mind if you don't give a shit, but I had to tell someone. I have something to celebrate you see, I think, tonight. My son Nicky – can't remember if I mentioned him the other day because I was so distracted by that gorgeous hunk of a son of yours. God, it makes me feel so old. I remember changing his nappy and washing his little tinkle—'

'You never did anything of the sort. You couldn't stand babies.'

'And now he's eight foot tall and built like Adonis. And those eyes. God, I could drown in those eyes.'

'Crikey, Sonia. What have you been drinking? Can we get back to your own son? Nicky, did you say?'

'Ha. Yes, Nicky. My darling boy. Who has just gone and announced his engagement to a girl we'd never even met before he paraded her here tonight. I didn't even know she existed, yet already he wants to marry her. Nina, she's called. Nicky and Nina. Sounds like some crappy Eurovision pop duo, doesn't it?' She waited for a response. 'No? Come on Ells; that was funny.'

She heard a snort from down the line.

'Yes, alright,' Ellie said, 'that was funny. And now I'm never going to be able to forget it, am I? That's all I'll be able to think about if I ever get to meet them. So, is that all? Can I get myself off to bed now?'

'There is something else. It came to me after I saw you the other day. Hey, what a coincidence that was Ells? Me there doing my duty, having a look at my mother-in-law's flowers before they disintegrate. She died last month. Did I tell you? And you there saying goodbye to your husband. Serendipity, that's what it was. Anyway, back on track. The other reason I'm calling now. I just wondered if you'd remembered.'

'Remembered what?'

'Jools. It's forty years tonight since her murder.'

***

Fat tears sprang to Ellie's eyes and coursed down her cheeks. Tears she hadn't been able to shed since David died. Not even at the funeral, because she'd already cried so hard every day since his diagnosis. She looked at the phone in her hand, Sonia waiting at the other end for a response.

No, she hadn't remembered about Jools. Not this year.

She'd been so wrapped up in her own misery she'd forgotten to let anything else in.

Forty years. How could that be? And it took Sonia to remind her. Sonia, who could never be relied upon to remember anything. Who she hadn't seen nor heard from for nigh on thirty-five years. Until David's funeral.

A coincidence. Serendipity, Sonia had called it. A happy accident?

Maybe.

But forty years? Crikey.

The three of them, out on the town on a New Year's Eve. A pub crawl first, then on to JoJo's nightclub. Ells Bells, Sonic and Jools, best friends since nursery school, seeing the New Year in together. Until they all got separated by the street fight, and only two of them arrived back home.

'Ells?'

Ellie dashed tears away from her chin. 'I'm sorry Sonia, I can't talk about this now.'

CHAPTER 4

Sonia felt her feet going in different directions on a patch of black ice. Her arms flailed. She grabbed the fence post for balance and snorted a nervous laugh. These boots were definitely not made for walking. Not like Nancy's. Not in this bloody weather anyway. But the hooded red coat lived up to expectations. Lovely and thick and warm. Just as it should be, given the money she'd paid for it. It would take a hurricane for the cold to get through the layers, but she didn't intend to be out here for more than a few minutes, just long enough to call Ellie again and tell her.

Then she'd go back inside, plaster a smile back on her face, and drink until she couldn't stand up. Because that was the only way she'd be able to deal with what she'd heard tonight. Until she had the chance to decide what to do.

She took tentative steps until she reached the road at the end of the drive, hearing no sound other than the bass thump of the eighties music playing inside the house. Far enough away here not to be seen from inside, probably. Although if anyone so much as popped their head outside, she felt sure her voice would carry on the cold air. If someone wanted to listen.

But although she might be far enough from the house, she could never ever get far enough away from the words she'd heard spoken inside there tonight.

Words that had made her rush to the toilet to throw up.

Had they noticed that she'd noticed? God, she hoped not.

She tapped Ellie's number again and turned her back on her home, her prison.

She imagined Ellie looking at the screen, trying to decide whether to hit the green or the red button. But she'd already made up her mind to leave a voicemail if Ellie did reject her call, because she had to say the words out loud to someone, and Ellie was the only one who'd understand, and who might be able to tell her what she should do.

Because what she really wanted was impossible. She wanted to go back in time and unhear those words, to live the rest of her life never having to worry about how they changed... everything.

'What is it now, Sonia?' Ellie said. Forced politeness.

'Thank God, you picked up. I need to tell you something, Ells. You were there, you see. You know what it was like. You're the only one who could—'

She heard a vehicle behind her, driving far too fast for the conditions. She glanced over her shoulder. Kids out on a joy ride most likely. Or maybe someone behind the wheel after a skinful. But who was she to talk when she had two driving bans to her name? She stepped closer to the hedge, waiting for the vehicle to go past.

'Tell me what?' Ellie demanded.

'We're having a party tonight. You know, New Year and all that. I told you about it earlier, I think. And we've been talking about—'

The car's headlights glared on full beam, casting a shadow before her of an elongated version of herself. She heard the car's gears change and tried to turn round, but one high heel almost skidded out from under her. She grabbed the hedge for balance, speaking with more urgency than before.

'He said he was there, Ells. But he's always said he—'

The car engine snarled like a beast. She heard tyres mount the kerb. She sensed the driver's intention too late. No time to turn. The force of the impact snapped her shin bones and sent her high into the air. The vehicle rushed past below with no sign of slowing. Sonia landed on her head, her broken legs folding unnaturally to lie beneath her, snowflakes falling into unseeing eyes.

CHAPTER 5

Car fob in hand, Detective Inspector James Massey opened the front door of his home to a winter wonderland. When he and Helen had gone to bed after seeing in the New Year, the snow had been just a light sprinkle, and if he had any choice in the matter now he'd turn around and go back to bed. But he couldn't. A hit and run on New Year's morning, in Morpeth, in deep snow. Just the thing to start the year.

3.20 am, his phone had rung, a time most guaranteed to disturb Helen's sleep and ensure she wouldn't be able to nod off again. So she said.

'Why,' she'd demanded as she'd punched her pillow into submission, 'don't people have the decency to be killed earlier, or later, or through the bloody daytime like everyone else?'

He'd grabbed his clothes and his go bag and taken them into the spare room to get dressed, and when he'd stuck his head back into their bedroom to kiss her goodbye, he found her snoring her head off. Well okay, not snoring exactly, but there was definitely a little rattle there. He'd considered recording it on his phone and playing it back to her later to disprove her point, but thought better of it. It wasn't worth the risk of upsetting their fragile truce. Her truce. Her terms.

He cleared the snow from his car windscreen and from behind his rear wheels as quietly as possible and backed the car out of the drive onto the road. His phone rang again just as he was about to set off. Detective Sergeant Christine Sparks. Checking up on him, no doubt, as if she was the mentor and he the mentee rather than the other way round.

'Christine, Happy New Year.'

'Not for some poor sod lying dead in the road in Morpeth it's not. Where are you?'

'Just leaving the house now.'

'Good. Any chance you could pick me up? I doubt I'll be able to get the car back out of the street by the look of this lot. I can't believe it. I've only been home an hour or so. It was nowhere near this bad when I turned in. I'll walk down the bank and wait at the bottom by the Londis.'

***

'How did the funeral go?' Sparks asked, once she'd thrown herself into the passenger seat, bringing the cold into the car with her.

'As well as could be expected, for a funeral. Apart from a mad woman in a red coat, who accosted us as we were leaving the crematorium and then followed us to the pub.'

The satnav took them up Pottery Bank until they saw the flashing lights of two patrol cars parked across the road either side of a narrow right turn – an unnamed road, according to the satnav. From here they'd need to walk.

They trudged up the road. Hoods up to protect their heads, but snow still bleached horizontally towards them, making them duck their faces against the wind. To their left, a skeletonised hedge ran along the road, with dead beech leaves still clinging to its branches like copper baubles. On the right, a new estate of executive houses.

No forensic tent in sight yet.

They kept walking, past a turn off on the right, round a downward bend then up a steeper incline. Jesus, how much further?

'Do we know who's SIO?' Sparks shouted over the sounds of the wind and the swish of their coats as they walked.

'Sorry?'

'SIO. Who's SIO?'

Three months ago, after a period of enforced leave in the wake of the Children of Gaia child abuse outrage that had rocked the force, their regular Senior Investigating Officer, DCI Guy Keegan had been demoted to DI and shuffled off into a new cold case task unit. He'd been lucky to survive the cull, given the favours he'd performed for his now disgraced and imprisoned senior officer that had contributed to the scandal.

'Lou Portas, I think.' If he was right, this would be Portas' first investigation in charge for Northumbria Police. She'd transferred over from Cumbria after Detective Superintendent Oliver Hitchins was arrested, having served over there at the same rank for more than three years. She came highly recommended, so a simple hit and run death in icy conditions would hardly tax her. He'd met her a couple of times in the office, and he approved so far. Around ten years his senior, hailed as the force's latest golden girl, he hoped she had the courage to overcome the stigma Hitchins had left in his wake.

Massey's own application for the vacant post of DCI, now that Keegan had moved over, was still making its way through the process. He'd completed all the SIO training units even before Keegan's move had left a void that needed filling. Since applying, he'd sat the exam already and felt confident his professional development portfolio was up to scratch. It was the work-based assessments that might be the stumbling block, given everything that had happened last summer. Perhaps the whole Children of Gaia business would count against him rather than for him.

'You got here eventually then,' Detective Superintendent Portas said, her frozen breath whipped away by the cold wind. 'I thought two locals such as yourselves would have beaten me here.'

'Ma'am,' Massey said, puffing for breath. Walking uphill in heavy snow hadn't just taken it out of his legs. 'What have we got?'

Portas smiled at his discomfort and winked at Sparks, who in Massey's opinion had always been way too physically fit for her own good. 'We have a lone woman, hit from behind. Dead before she hit the ground I would imagine, although we'll need to wait for confirmation on that from Dr French.'

'Lorraine is here already?'

'She is. She came down from the Morpeth Northern Bypass, like anyone else with any sense. You know her personally do you, DI Massey?'

If he counted the fact that Home Office Pathologist Lorraine French had stayed with him and Helen for a couple of weeks last summer, sleeping in their spare room and eating at their table, while her own life was in disarray. 'I do, ma'am.'

'I see from the grimace on DS Sparks' face that there's a story there to be told. Is it anything I need to know about now?'

Massey shot Sparks a look. 'No ma'am, nothing at all.'

'Well then, let's get on. Here's what we know. The victim lives just here, in that house there. She'd come outside for some fresh air, or for some peace and quiet from the New Year's party they've had going on in there. For whatever reason, out she came onto the road in icy conditions – this was before the snow turned heavy, we believe – wearing just her glad rags, high heeled boots with no grips, and a thick designer coat. So whether she slipped on the ice and fell in front of the vehicle, or whether the driver just didn't see her standing out here, your guess is as good as mine for the moment. Either way, he or she didn't wait around to find out how badly hurt she was. Or perhaps they did, and when they saw she was dead they got straight back into their vehicle and buggered off.'

'And no-one saw anything?'

'Not that we know of yet. We'll get a house to house started as soon as we have enough bodies, but none of the family or guests in the house say they saw anything. They've been spoken to, very briefly, and they all say they had no idea she'd even gone outside. They'll need to be questioned a little more thoroughly before we can allow them to leave. But it's the husband and son I'd like you two to tackle.'

'Looks like this is a quiet road,' Sparks said. 'Who found her?'

'The husband. Ronald Wragg. Said Sonia is prone to doing daft things. When he hadn't seen her for a while, and he couldn't find her inside, he came outside looking for her. Says he saw her red coat first. Lucky the snow hadn't completely—'

Red coat? Sonia? Hell's teeth. 'What sort of age is she?' Massey asked.

'Fifty-nine, so I'm told. Why?'

'Ma'am,' Massey said. 'I think this could be someone I know. Well, someone my mother knows, and who I met for the first time two days ago. At least she was called Sonia and wore a red coat, and she'd known my mother from childhood.'

Portas stared at him for a moment, clicking her tongue against her teeth. 'Then DI Massey, I don't want you at my crime scene, or anywhere near this case until I say so.'

CHAPTER 6

He shook his head while he trudged. He shouldn't have opened his mouth, although he hadn't exactly had a choice. He'd done what he was supposed to do. He'd informed a senior officer as soon as he suspected he might know the victim. That was the right thing to do. But now he wouldn't have the opportunity to demonstrate his skills to Portas on this case, and he wasn't likely to get another opportunity before a decision was made on the vacant DCI position.

At least he had plenty of loose ends from other cases to keep him busy, including the one that had brought about the downfall of DSU Hitchins and two junior officers, as well as the demotion of Guy Keegan. There was still plenty of work to do to get that one ready for court.

Although less than half an hour had passed since he and Sparks had walked up the bank, already their footprints had disappeared. But still it was a lot easier walking back down, despite the blasts of wind against his back and the sheets of ice disguised by drifted snow under his feet.

Shit, Sparks has no transport now.

Nothing he could do about it. She'd sort something.

And what about his mother, should he tell her what had happened? Could she cope with this in her current state, after having just lost her husband? She seemed too fragile to cope with more heartache right now. She'd have to know though, but probably best to wait until he knew for definite that this was the same Sonia with the red designer coat that his mother knew from years ago. No point worrying her before then.

Not that there was likely to be another Sonia of a similar age running around in a red designer coat.

But what a coincidence. He hadn't even known the woman existed before his stepfather's funeral, yet she'd once been one of his mother's closest friends, and she'd even remembered him as a small child. And now twice in three days he'd come across her.

Although he'd rather not have come across her dead.

So, where to now? Technically, it being New Year's Day and so a bank holiday, and with his services now being surplus to requirements, he had the day off, but he didn't feel much like going home and listening to Helen's moans about being woken up again. Not now he was out and about. But he needed to eat. All the exercise had made him hungry.

***

Still half an hour before the Woodhorn Grange opened for breakfast, so he sat in his car, staring out at Queen Elizabeth Lake – the centrepiece of the QEII Country Park near Ashington – and took in the beauty of the snow-covered landscape.

The place had once been a working mine with the biggest colliery spoil heap in Europe, but had been restored now and reclaimed by nature to provide diverse habitats for wildlife, as well as being a centre for fishing and sailboarding.

Or so the internet said when he searched for it out of curiosity while waiting in the car.

This morning, with everything draped in a blanket of snow, the place looked magical.

He could see only a dozen or so other vehicles in the car park, so the hotel next door can't have had a busy night. And he knew what that meant. No all-you-can-eat buffet today. Only table service.

As soon as the doors opened, he took a seat by a window looking out towards the lake and ordered a full English breakfast. He'd got himself a third coffee and ordered a bowl of fruit and yoghurt by the time he felt his phone vibrate against his thigh.

A call from Lou Portas.

Had she changed her mind?

'Ma'am.'

'DI Massey, thank you for being so honest with me earlier. You did the right thing.'

'I know that, ma'am. I wouldn't have wanted—'

'As it turns out, I'd have found out very quickly anyway. We've just discovered that the victim was in the middle of a call on her mobile when she was hit. To a woman called Eleanor Morgan, who I have on very good authority is your mother.'

Shit!

'We found the phone in the hedge. And we only found it because it rang. It was your mother calling to check up on Sonia after they'd been cut off so abruptly. She'd already tried several times, but no-one had heard it ring.' Portas paused for a moment, waiting for him to absorb the information. 'She sounds like a nice woman, your mother. I broke the news to her myself. But it was only after I spoke to her that DS Sparks told me she's recently bereaved. I'm sorry. Your father. I didn't know.'

'How could you? And he was my stepfather, but the best father anyone could have.'

'I'm so sorry, Massey.'

'Ma'am.'

Portas went quiet for so long he began to think the call had dropped out, but then she continued.

'You do know that someone will need to speak to her. And it can't be you. I'm only telling you now because it would probably be best, given the circumstances, if she had someone with her as support when she's questioned. And again, that can't be you. But perhaps you could arrange something.'

'I understand, ma'am. Thank you. I'll speak to my sister. I'm sure she'll want to be there.'

'It's DS Sparks you need to thank. And by the way, I'm waiting for a call back on what to do with you for the duration of this inquiry. I'll let you know. As soon as.'

Massey put his phone on the table. When the waiter brought his fruit and yoghurt, he no longer felt like eating but he hated waste.

He glanced at his watch. Still a bit early to call Megan, and she'd want to know the far end of a fart anyway, which he could hardly talk about here now, especially now that the tables around him were filling up.

He'd give it another half an hour, then he'd call her from the car.

The sound of his phone vibrating on the table made him jump.

A text.

From Lou Portas.

'Report to DCI Flowers tomorrow. 8 am sharp. You'll be joining his team for the duration of this case.'

What? How is that fair?

DCI Raymond Flowers. SIO on Operation Bryony, investigating the serial rapist the press had christened Musk Man.

Flowers was a dick. The last person he wanted to work with.

CHAPTER 7

So this was the house Massey had grown up in. Sparks took in the details of the semi-detached property at the top of the leafy cul-de-sac. Edwardian maybe? Victorian? Not her strong point, architectural history, nor any other kind of history, to be honest. Brick built, with the upper half pebble-dashed and painted cream. Big bay windows on two floors and a dormer window in the roof.

Could that have been Massey's bedroom, up there in the attic?

The front door opened before they got out of the car. Massey's sister Megan Stock, she assumed.

If so, she looked nothing like him. She had his dark hair, yes, a big curly mop of it, but where Massey was tall with an athletic build, his sister – his half-sister – was average height and built for comfort.

A strange feeling of discomfiture washed over Sparks, and she hung back for a moment, leaving it to Detective Constable Andrew Donaldson – whose confidence had soared since his permanent promotion from uniform had come through a month or so ago – to make his way up the path first to shake the woman's hand.

Did she really want to know as much about Massey as she would surely discover inside this house? They'd developed a close relationship as colleagues, but this felt like an intrusion.

She gave herself a mental shake and stepped forward. His mother was a witness to a crime.

Up close, she could see that Megan's eyes were different to Massey's too. A rich chocolate brown, whereas his had a strange iridescent quality, like oil on a puddle, that seemed to change colour depending on the light. She could also see that Megan was pregnant, and judging by the size of her belly, she could be almost full term. Again, not her strong point.

'Come in,' Megan said. 'Mam's through in the kitchen. Coffee? Or tea if you prefer.'

'We're okay,' Sparks said. 'But thank you.'

The kitchen turned out to be a vast space that took up the whole width of the house at the far end of a wide hallway floored in ornate tiles that Sparks assumed to be original. Family photos in groups lined the pale yellow walls of the hallway. Sparks wished she could stop and look for any that might include Massey as a child or as a younger man, but instead she forced herself to continue past them. Now was hardly the time.

On the far side of the kitchen, huge sliding glass doors looked out onto a big garden that the snow had transformed into marshmallow mounds. Kitchen units took up only a third of the huge space. The rest accommodated a large oak dining table with mismatched wooden chairs, all painted in contrasting bright colours, and an arrangement of well-worn leather armchairs and settees around a huge, upholstered coffee table/stool type of thing, scattered with magazines.

Two enormous canvasses dominated the walls in here, clearly painted by the same artist and both featuring dramatic abstract seascapes in splashy greens, blues and gold.

As vast as the room was, it enveloped Sparks in a warm hug.

'Please, sit,' Megan said, as she claimed the space closest to her mother and held her hand.

Sparks could see Massey in his mother's face. The same strange eyes and high forehead, and something about the nose too, at least before Massey's wife had broken his six months ago – not that he'd ever admitted it was Helen who did the damage, although Sparks knew it must have been.

Eleanor Morgan looked slender to the point of emaciation. No doubt due to the protracted worry she'd have suffered while caring for her dying husband, who must have been very ill and in need of a high level of care for months before he died.

And, as she understood it, this woman had done the vast majority of the caring herself.

Massey had never said a word about his stepfather's illness at work. Not until afterwards, and then only the barest of details.

'Mrs Morgan, thank you for seeing us. I appreciate this is difficult for you, especially right now.'

'Please, call me Ellie. And it's fine. A shock obviously, but I'm alright. You have questions, of course you do. I hope I can answer them.'

The woman's voice sounded strong and clear. Perhaps she wasn't quite as fragile as she looked.

'Thank you, Ellie. As you know, we've discovered that the victim, Sonia Wragg, was talking to you on the phone at the time she was hit.'

Ellie closed her eyes and nodded. 'Did she suffer?'

'No, we don't think so. We believe she was killed outright by the impact.' Sparks saw the relief on Ellie's face. If it helped the woman sleep at night, she didn't mind sharing that much. 'But you understand I can't disclose any further details.'

'Yes, of course. Thank you.'

'We're hoping you can tell us what you heard when Sonia called. I appreciate it was late, well after midnight, and you were probably asleep when—'

'I wasn't. I'm not sleeping well at the moment.'

Sparks noticed tears in Megan's eyes as she gave her mother's hand a squeeze. This must be hard on her too. She'd just lost her father recently after all, and Sparks had first-hand knowledge of how that felt. And didn't pregnancy make women extra emotional?

'I was in here, sitting in this same seat,' Ellie said. 'It was around two I think, maybe quarter past. But you'll know the time if you have her phone. She said she needed to tell me something. Because I was there, she said, and I'd know what it was like. But I have no idea what she was talking about. Then she started telling me about the New Year's party they were having. I knew she was outside, although I'm not entirely sure how. Because I couldn't hear a party going on I suppose. And I heard a car engine, so I assumed she was near a road rather than out in a garden, unless she lives on a main road of course. Does she?'

'You don't know where she lives?'

'No idea. We only ran into each other again by chance at the crematorium, after David's funeral. I hadn't seen her for well over thirty years before that.'

'You say you heard an engine. Did she say anything about that? Did she see the vehicle coming towards her?'

Ellie closed her eyes again and put a hand to her mouth. 'No, she didn't say.'

'Could you tell by the sound of the engine what sort of vehicle it was? Did it sound like just your average car or something bigger and more powerful?'

Ellie closed her eyes and shook her head. 'I'm sorry, no. I'm not good at that sort of thing. I'm pretty sure I didn't hear it brake though, and I think I would've heard that if I could hear the engine. I might have heard a gear change though. Yes, I'm sure I did.'

'You're saying you think the driver hit her deliberately?'

'I don't know. I mean, why would he, or she? Perhaps he just didn't see her. It was very dark last night, wasn't it? Before the snow, I mean. I remember going over to stand by the window and looking out into the garden while I was talking to her. No lights on in here apart from the display on the fridge freezer. And all I could see was my own reflection.'

'Did she say anything else to you?'

'Yes, something about someone being there. He, she said. A man. He said he was there.'

'Do you have any idea what she meant?'

'No. I asked, but...' She drew in a shaky breath. 'I'm pretty sure she didn't mean that someone was there with her when... But then I heard an enormous loud bang, and... and then the line just went... dead.'

Tears trembled on Ellie's eyelashes then rolled down her face.

Megan pulled her in for a hug, muttering comforting words, as she would to a child.

Sparks nodded to Donaldson, who put away his notebook. 'I'm so sorry we had to put you through this Ellie, to have intruded at such a terrible time for you and your family. We'll leave you in peace now. Thank you both for your time.'

***

Ellie shivered as the detectives let themselves out. She'd worried about the questions they might ask, but Detective Sergeant Sparks had been nothing but sensitive and respectful.

And she hadn't pushed her on whether she knew the meaning behind Sonia's words, thank goodness.

At least it hadn't been James who'd come to interview her, because before the car hit her Sonia had been talking about the old days. 'You were there', she'd said. 'You know what it was like'. And since she and Sonia had no 'there' in common in the present day, other than their encounters at the crematorium and the King's Arms, she had to have been talking about their shared past. And that wasn't the sort of thing she'd be comfortable talking to her son about. Not now. Probably never.

Sonia had also talked about someone saying he'd been there when they'd always previously said something different. But who 'he' was, and where he said he'd been, she had no idea.

Had Sonia been talking about her husband Ronnie, or had she remembered something someone had said back then simply because she'd been reminiscing about Jools? And, if so, what could she possibly have remembered that was so important and so sensitive she'd had to leave a party to go out into the street in the dark, in the freezing cold, to make a phone call?

Ellie gave a big sigh. It was hardly worth worrying about it when there was nothing at all she could do about it.

'Detective Sergeant Sparks reminded me of myself at that age,' she said. 'Or at least the me I'd have liked to have been if I hadn't been running myself ragged with a house full of children.'

Megan patted her knee. 'You never had hair that colour though, surely.'

Ellie smiled. 'Mine was much wilder. She suits the red and the spikiness. I imagine she could be just as spiky as her hair if the mood took her.'

'That shade can hardly be within the regulations though. Aren't police officers supposed to keep their hair looking natural?'

Ellie lapsed into silence for a few moments and drifted again, while Megan straightened cushions. She'd been doing a lot of that lately, drifting. Crikey, what would she have been like if she'd agreed to take the medication the doctor had offered? Completely out of it probably. Comatose.

'I'd like to have had a career, you know,' she said. 'Like Detective Sparks.'

'You do have a career. You have your painting.'

'It's not the same thing. That's just a hobby.'

'There can't be many artists whose work sells as well as yours does, who'd still call it just a hobby.'

***

Sparks had asked Donaldson to drop her off at the bottom of her estate so she could walk up and dig her car out from the drive – she needed to be able to get herself to the mortuary under her own steam – but he'd volunteered to help her, and in no time she was mobile again.

The roads had all been gritted now. At least the main ones in built up areas had, but there'd still be lots of rural Northumberland and Durham under a couple of feet of snow.

It felt unnatural to be working without Massey, but she understood why he couldn't be involved in this one.

'Good New Year, Christine?' Dr Lorraine French's voice echoed in the large sterile space of the mortuary.

'Not so you'd notice.'

Lorraine laughed. 'Ditto. Getting called out for this one in the middle of the night didn't help.'

They got on a lot better now since all the hassle last summer. Sparks admired the pathologist's strength. There weren't many people who could have coped with everything that had been thrown at her and come out the other side so determined to make such a situation work.

'This lady is someone James knew, is that right?'

Sparks looked at the body on the table. Naked now. Almost sixty-years-old when she died. Battered. Both legs broken. But still with the physique of a much younger woman. She hoped she still looked as good herself when she reached that age. Without the broken legs, of course, or the death pallor.

'She was an old friend of his mother apparently, and so the SIO took him off the case. That's why you've got me this morning and not him.'

'I'm sure we'll cope without him. How awful for his mother though. And so soon after having lost her husband.'

'They hadn't seen each other for thirty odd years. They'd only just got back in touch.'

'I'm not sure if that makes it better or worse. All that time lost.' Lorraine glanced at the clock, and then at her new assistant, Dante Green. 'Let's get started then shall we?'

DC Paul Scott, as Exhibits Officer, had already taken custody of the clothing and jewellery Sonia had been wearing when she died. And now Sparks stood with him, silently watching Lorraine work, listening to her catalogue the injuries Sonia had sustained. Cervical spinal fracture, crushed skull, transverse fractures of the tibia and fibula in each leg.

'Hit from behind,' Lorraine said as she stripped off her gloves and face mask. 'Cause of death, cervical fracture. Her neck broke when she hit the ground, severing the spinal cord. Along with the simultaneous compression of the brain, death would have come quickly, if not instantaneously.'

'Can you tell us anything about the car that hit her?'

'Something low slung, judging by how her legs were broken. Don't expect to find any of her blood on the vehicle though. That was all contained within the high boots she wore, and her hood contained the head injury. Anyway, at the speed it hit her, the car would have been long gone before her head even hit the ground.'

CHAPTER 8

Tuesday 2nd January 2024

Massey looked around the room. Operation Bryony. Half a dozen detectives, all busy at their desks. Three desks empty. DCI Raymond Flowers visible through the open door of his little office cubicle, his feet propped up on his desk and mobile phone clamped to his ear. A personal call given the flirty tone of his voice, which carried right out to the door where Massey stood. He could see Flowers had spotted him too but had no intention of bringing his call to an end until he was good and ready.

Why the hell had Portas put him here? He understood absolutely that he couldn't work on a case in which he had a personal connection to the victim, however small, and on which his mother was a material witness. But he had bags of other work he could be getting on with over at MIT. Portas didn't need to have removed him so completely from the team.

Had he upset her in any way?

No, not that he could think of.

So, was this a sign his application for the post of DCI stood no chance?

Whatever the reason, here he was, and he'd just have to make the best of it.

But DCI Flowers, for Christ's sake.

He walked to the front of the room so he could read the screen and get an idea of what he'd be working on for the next however long. Six victims on the main screen – he'd thought there were only five. All between the ages of nineteen and thirty-two, and all home alone when attacked by a forensically aware rapist, who'd so far left nothing of himself on his victims or in their homes save for a few black fibres that were so generic it was impossible to pin them down to anything specific enough to be useful. On a separate board, with information only partially constructed, was the name of only one victim.

Abigail Grant, the girl Sparks had been telling him about on their journey to the hit and run crime scene yesterday morning. The one who'd come into Hartington station three years after having been raped, with all the clothes she'd been wearing at the time still frozen and packed into a cool box.

On the face of it, the crime against Abigail didn't match the others. She'd been grabbed outside on the street, on her way home from a party, by a rapist who'd evidently left his DNA behind in copious deposits.

The complete opposite of Musk Man's attacks.

***

'Massey. I've just found out this morning that we're getting saddled with you. We're only good enough for murder squad cast-offs now, it seems. Welcome to Operation Bryony.'

'Sir.'

Massey hadn't heard a sound as Flowers had crept up behind him. Only just found out, bollocks. He'd known about it himself since yesterday morning. Was it DSU Portas Flowers had just been talking to on the phone in his office? If so, the flirtatiousness he'd heard in the man's voice suggested they had something going on together.

Perhaps she did have some faults after all.

Flowers was an arsehole. If he paid as much attention to getting the job done as he did to the tailoring of his suits, then maybe he'd have made a decent DCI. As it was, the fact that Operation Bryony still floundered was more than likely down to his bad leadership.

'I see you're familiarising yourself with the victims. Good. Then grab a desk and I'll leave you in the capable hands of DS Brooks. She can bring you up to speed.'

Flowers didn't wait around to introduce him to DS Brooks or to any other member of the team, but returned to his office, closed the door and left them to it.

A compact fair-haired woman put her hand up. 'Hi. I'm DS Brooks. Kirsty Brooks.'

'Kirsty. Hi. DI Massey. James.'

Brooks' smile transformed her otherwise dour freckled countenance. 'I've seen you around sir. Welcome. Probably best to start by introducing the rest of the team.'

'Good idea. Thank you.'

'Over there,' Brooks pointed to a dark-haired man who Massey imagined got the lion's share of attention from his female colleagues, 'we have my fellow DS, Dan Lieb.'

Lieb raised a hand in acknowledgement, then dipped his attention back to his screen, renouncing any part of inducting the newest member of the team.

'And then we have DCs John Land, Natalie Clark, Robyn Moodie and Iain Johnson.'

Massey nodded to each of them in turn, trying to commit something about them other than just their faces to his memory to help him recall their names beyond the next five minutes. 'No other DIs?' he asked.

'Two sir,' Brooks said. 'DI Ange Roberts and DI Adam Poole, both on the sick. DI Poole has the flu, so I imagine he'll be back soon. DI Roberts has been away for a couple of months now. Stress and anxiety, I think, but don't quote me.'

'Okay, thanks Kirsty.'

They looked like a decent bunch. He'd seen a few of them around the building but had never had anything to do with any of them beyond that. With both DIs on the sick, perhaps that was the motivating factor behind his temporary – he hoped – transfer. Ange Roberts, he had worked with before, and now he knew why he hadn't seen anything of her recently. Stress and anxiety? Wow. It would take a lot to knock the stuffing out of Ange.

He looked at the screen and the board. 'Best bring me up to speed.'

'No problem, sir. So then, our victims. All attacked while they were home alone. Different times of day. Probably simplest if I go through them in order of them being reported.' She waited for Massey's nod before continuing. 'Okay, so, Sophie Robson. Aged thirty-two at the time of the attack in November 2022, early hours of the morning. She's an office worker and she'd recently thrown her boyfriend out. We looked closely at him, but his alibi is rock solid.

'And anyway, it was him who persuaded her to make the report. He'd found her in a distressed state later that same morning when he went to collect their dog. They'd agreed on joint custody you see. The rapist had locked the dog outside in the back garden during the attack. It had been going mad trying to get back in, but none of the neighbours investigated. He'd also laid out a polythene sheet, on which he make Sophie strip off and then... um... did the deed. He used a similar sheet with all the other victims too. Probably not the same one though, obviously. And he always takes it away with him. From what victims have described, we're assuming they're a sort of flimsy dust sheet. You know, the ones you get in multipacks at any DIY store, and online too.'

Massey nodded. He'd save his questions until he'd heard about the rest.

'Next we have Josephine Armstrong. Known as Josie. Aged twenty-three. The rapist entered her home late afternoon when her wife was still at work. Josie is an assistant chef at Noah's Nook in Jesmond. Do you know the place sir? Done out to make it feel as if you're in the belly of a ship.

'Never eaten there but I know where it is.'

'Josie had worked late the previous night for their Valentine's Day event and had been having a long lie-in before having to go back to work that evening, when the rapist dragged her out of bed by her feet and onto his plastic sheet. He didn't need to make her get undressed since she sleeps naked. He spent longer with Josie than he had with Sophie. Raped her multiple times, whereas just once with the others. We think he may have been in the house for some time watching her sleeping, and maybe that had got him more... excited.'

She blushed.

'Anyway, when she hadn't arrived at work on time for her shift, the manager started calling her mobile, and we think that's what eventually spooked the rapist into leaving. It was Josie's wife Sue who called the police and an ambulance after returning home and finding her.

'Number three, we have Jessica Elliot. She didn't report the rape until three months afterwards, making her actually the second victim and Josie the third. Lives alone. Aged twenty-nine. A nursery school assistant.

Attacked in the evening while watching telly. She's very closed off sir. Seems terrified it could end up affecting her job, although I'm not sure how. Says she can't remember much about the attack except the smell but kept getting panic attacks afterwards and so eventually went to a rape support centre. It was them who persuaded her to report it.

'Fourth, Nicole Selby. Works part time as a dog groomer. Aged twenty. Lives at home with her parents, who were out overnight celebrating their wedding anniversary when it happened. Her father, Robert Selby is what might politely be described as a bit overbearing. He's calling DCI Flowers two, three times a week every week demanding updates. It's been difficult to get anything out of Nicole because he's so over the top protective and she doesn't want to make him worse.'

'He even collared me out on the street, the idiot.'

Not recognising any of their voices yet, Massey glanced around and saw that the rest of the team had all gathered around to listen to Brooks' rundown too. Even Lieb. He noticed DC Moodie looking directly at him and assumed it had been her speaking.

'Really aggressive, he was,' she continued. 'Awful thing for any father to get his head around. I get that. But Nicole is definitely one of those who will be daddy's little girl forever, regardless of how hard she tries to escape.'

'What time of day did it happen?'

'First thing in the morning. He was waiting in the kitchen when she got up, with the plastic sheet spread out ready for her.'

'Okay,' Brooks said. 'Up next we have victim number five. Kayla Scott. Aged just nineteen. Our youngest victim. Studying psychology at Newcastle Uni. First year student from Leicester, sharing digs with two other female students, both of whom were out working bar jobs at the time. Attacked as soon as they'd both left for work, so we're working on the assumption he could already have been in the flat before they left, like with Nicole when he'd been waiting for her getting up in the morning. This was in October, so Kayla had only been up in the North East for a matter of weeks. First time away from home.

'And last but not least, Amber Pringle. This one is the most recent. Raped nine days ago, on Christmas Eve, after returning home from a night out with colleagues from the nail salon she works at. Twenty-one years old. Lives with her boyfriend in a one up, one down, upstairs flat in Heaton. He's a student and had gone home for Christmas to Edinburgh, so she was all on her own and planning to go to her own parents' house in the morning to celebrate Christmas there. Hers has been the most vicious attack so far. He beat her up pretty bad, possibly because she put up a fight. Once he left, she managed to crawl downstairs and alert her neighbour. She's still in hospital now. Broken rib punctured her lung.'

Another reason why Operation Bryony needed a DI. It looked like the rapist was escalating.

'The polythene sheet isn't the only thing he brings with him.'

The words came from the third female DC, chestnut hair up in a high ponytail. Natalie Clark? Was that her name?

'He wears condoms, and he brings wet wipes too and makes his victims clean themselves down when he's finished.'

Massey examined the six photos of six young women. No similarities he could see in the way they looked. If the rapist had a particular type, it wasn't anything to do with their physical appearance. 'Any touch points between them at all?' he asked.

'None we've found so far.'

'What about this one,' he said, pointing to the small board, unwilling to betray he already knew a bit about it.

'Ah yes,' Lieb said. 'Odd one this. Just got it in this morning. Abigail Grant. Says she was raped three years ago. Didn't report it at the time but put all the clothes she'd been wearing into her freezer, where they've been ever since, so she claims. Rocked up to the Hartington station on New Year's Eve to report the rape, with all her frozen party gear in a cool box. I'm going to call her Ice Cold Abbie.'

Ice Cold Abbie? Jesus.

'We're just putting the information together now sir,' Brooks said.

'Have the clothes gone off to forensics yet.'

'Waiting for the courier now. This could be the evidence we've been waiting for. If this is the same guy, then he wasn't forensically aware at all then. Not like he is now. Abigail reckons his DNA will be all over the clothes she was wearing. She says he spunked inside her and then made a show of wiping his dick...' Brooks screwed her eyes closed, her face growing redder under her freckles. 'Sorry, sir.'

Massey tried not to smile. 'How sure are you that it was the same guy?'

'Pretty sure. She described what sounds like the same smell. And if it was him, then maybe it was his first time and committed more on impulse than the more recent ones.'

'And if it was Musk Man,' DCI Flowers had crept up on them again. 'And if she'd come forward straight away, then we could have collared the bastard three years ago.'

'And none of these girls...' Lieb waved his hand towards the screen. '...would have suffered.'

***

Massey's first day on Operation Bryony had been a hard one. Hard in that he'd glued his backside to his seat – an unnatural state of being for him – and ploughed through all seven rape victim files from front to back, familiarising himself with the details of all of them. The work of the team had gone on around him, with Kirsty feeling obliged to check on him every now and then, even though he'd told her not to. It hadn't worked. She'd continued to offer to bring him coffee and include him in discussions. But he thought he had his head around it all now. Enough that after a good night's sleep to allow it all to percolate he felt sure he'd be on the ball tomorrow and ready to get stuck into actually investigating.

The snow had become piles of dirty, salty sludge at the roadsides now, playing havoc with the paintwork of his Hyundai Tucson Hybrid, which was still new enough for him to be bothered about keeping it looking good. His own street, where much of the road remained in shadow for most of the day at this time of year, still had sheets of ice in places.

Helen's car wasn't parked out front when he arrived home. She hadn't said anything about working late. At least not that he could remember.

She'd been acting a little weird lately since she'd got involved with a new group at church. Not that he'd listened much when she'd told him about it. Anything to do with the Catholic Church, or any other religion for that matter, set his teeth on edge. He had no time for any of it. He couldn't understand how people could believe such hogwash. They all preached love and compassion, but the vast majority of wars throughout history had been fought over religion in one way or another. But, if nothing else, at least Helen's involvement in the group was saving them a fortune on wine. She hadn't been drinking half as much lately because she needed to drive more, which could only be a good thing.

The house felt cold. He checked his phone for a text or a missed call from her. Nothing.

Oh well, dinner for one. He took beef biryani out of the freezer and stuck it in the microwave.

***

It had gone 10 before the headlights of Helen's car drifted over the walls of the lounge, and across Massey's eyes where he'd dozed off to sleep on the settee, the football match he'd been watching long finished.

He got up to meet her as she came in. 'Hi,' he said. 'Everything alright?'

She took her time locking the door before turning towards him. 'Of course it is. Why shouldn't it be?'

'No reason. Except I don't remember you saying anything about being late back like you usually do, so I was worried. That's all.'

And the fact there's a serial rapist on the loose.

'I told you the other day.'

'I don't remember.'

She rolled her eyes and tutted. 'Hardly surprising. You've been so concerned about your mother lately; you've barely bothered listening to me.'

'Whoa,' Massey held his hands up. 'Don't go there, Helen. What's all that about?'

She sighed. 'Nothing. I'm sorry. Look, I'm just going to go straight upstairs. See you when you come up.' She reached up to give him a quick peck on the cheek, but it felt as if she'd slapped him.

CHAPTER 9

Wednesday 3rd January 2024

Day two. Bright and early. Massey had expected to be the first one on Operation Bryony to start work this morning – he couldn't imagine Flowers being an early bird unless it was forced upon him – but when he walked into the office he found DS Brooks and DC Moodie already at their desks and discussing a new pattern analysis of the victims that included the information they now had on Abigail, plotting anything and everything the victims may possibly have in common.

Home address, places of work, daily commutes, routines, social activities – actual and online, hobbies, friends, family and significant others, all plotted in detail.

'Morning, sir,' Moodie said.

'Sorry if I've interrupted.'

'Don't be daft sir,' Brooks said. 'We're just getting this put together before everyone else comes in. We've been discussing Abigail and how awful it must have been for her seeing those bags in her freezer every time she went in there. Not allowing herself to forget what happened. We were wondering what made her decide after three years to report the rape. Robyn reckons something must have happened recently to spark something.'

'Must have,' Moodie said. 'She's been looking at those bags in her freezer every day for three years. So what's changed now?'

'Weren't they in a chest freezer in her garage rather than the one in the kitchen?'

As soon as he said the words, he remembered this was something Sparks had mentioned in the car the other morning rather than something he'd read in the file yesterday.

Brooks looked puzzled, clicked a couple of keys and scrolled down the information on her screen. 'Where does it say that, sir? Oh, right. Here it is.'

'Can we have less of the 'sir' please, while we're in the office?'

'It was Christine Sparks who took the initial report, wasn't it?' Moodie said. She's your sergeant usually, isn't she sir? I'd like to have seen her face when Abigail produced those freezer bags.'

Moodie must have noticed Sparks' name on the initial report on the system.

'Sorry for your loss, sir,' she said.

Now it was his turn to be puzzled. She couldn't have got that from her screen. But there was no time to ask her about it, for the door behind them opened and DCI Flowers strolled in. Sharp charcoal pinstripe suit and waistcoat this morning. White shirt and lemon tie. And a big smirk on his face. An early bird after all.

'Morning all,' he said. 'Alright Massey? Keeping your end up? Getting yourself bedded in, I see.' He didn't hang around to listen to any responses, but opened his office door and closed it firmly behind him.

Brooks and Moodie exchanged a look.

'Coffee anyone?' Brooks asked.

'He's been like that a lot lately,' Moodie said. 'Pretty much since the new DSU arrived in fact. So, you know. Just putting it out there.'

Which tallied with Massey's own thoughts yesterday about Flowers and Lou Portas.

'Is he married?' he asked.

Moodie laughed. 'Maybe not for much longer, the way things are going.'

***

Around eleven o'clock, Massey's phone buzzed, and Sparks' name popped up. It was the first time he'd heard anything from her since he'd left her and walked down that bank on his own in the snow on New Year's morning. As her mentor, he should probably have made the time to call her.

'Time for lunch somewhere?' she asked.

'Maybe. In an hour or so though, not right now.'

They met at Crusoe's in Tynemouth and ordered toasties, which they ate looking out over a sleet-swept Longsands.

'How are you coping without me?' Sparks asked, with a challenge in her eye.

'Oh, you know. DS Brooks is being very helpful.'

'Kirsty Brooks? I'll bet she is. Actually, that's not fair. She's alright is Kirsty. But mind, don't you go letting her get any ideas about riding your coat-tails back over to where you belong, with us.'

He felt touched. That was probably the nicest thing she'd ever said to him.

'How are you getting on with Lou Portas,' he asked.

Sparks shrugged. 'She's okay, I suppose. Except that she keeps watching me.'

'Watching you how?'

'I don't know, just every time I turn round there she is, watching me.

'Just getting to know her new teams through observation, I suppose. It won't be only you she's looking at. She'll be doing the same with us all.' Except that, given she was having to cover the vacant DCI role herself, she wouldn't have much of a chance to assess his own work while he was working on Flowers' team. Unless she and Flowers discussed that sort of thing while they were—

'James.'

'What? Sorry, what did you say?'

And anyway, when it came down to it, having only just arrived over here from Cumbria herself, Portas was unlikely to be given much of a say in the decision. She couldn't be expected to have formed enough of a positive or negative opinion of his work, or anyone else's, in that short a time to be qualified to make a decent assessment.

'I asked how your mother's doing?'

'She's doing alright. Considering. I spoke to her on the phone last night. She likes you. Said she found you...' He struggled to decide how best to paraphrase what his mother had said. '... interesting.'

'What the hell does that mean?'

'I have no idea. How's your own mother?'

'Away with the fairies half the time. But, you know, this is it now. Her doctor has said she's never going to get any better, only worse. And it's happening so fast. We've never got on well with each other though.' She bit her lip for a moment, then pasted a smile onto her face. 'And now we never will. So, another coffee? Then we can talk shop.'

***

Over coffee and chocolate muffins, Sparks told him where they'd got up to in the hit and run, which wasn't far. Nothing juicy from forensics. Paint flakes from the car on Sonia's coat would have been nice, but no such luck. No tracks on the road they could use because of the solid ice. And nothing on CCTV, since most of the cameras in Morpeth were further into the town centre and the snow had already started when Sonia was hit, which made identifying the car nigh on impossible.

'And as for home security cameras,' Sparks said. 'You saw for yourself before teacher sent you home that all the houses along that road are set back. Lots of cameras, but they're all set to watch over front doors and private driveways, not the road. As far as we can determine, all the family and party guests were where they say they were. And we've checked all the local garages for any damaged cars being brought in for repair, and there's nothing.'

'What's the next step.'

'You know what budgets are like. Portas doesn't make as big a song and dance about it as Hitchins did, but the pressure is the same. And the family are shouting about needing to organise a funeral. We'll end up going with the likelihood the car slid on the ice, mounted the kerb and killed Sonia. Case shelved, body released, and no-one will get to pay for the murder or manslaughter of a human being.'

Massey smiled. 'So, you may have me back sooner rather than later after all.'

Which, in a way, would be a bit of a shame. He'd have liked to be there when Operation Bryony brought in the rapist.

CHAPTER 10

He'd asked Kirsty to contact Abigail Grant while he was out to arrange for them to meet her later. By the time he got back, he found they had an appointment to see her that afternoon at four at her own home. It would take a little while yet for the DNA analysis of her clothes to come in, and even then there may be no matches in the system. So, given that the attack on Abigail looked like it could have been the first for the man the press called Musk Man, and he clearly hadn't been as careful with her as he'd become with subsequent victims, they needed to gather as much information as possible on what Abigail remembered of the rapist. Perhaps he'd even said something to her. Anything at all she remembered could be pivotal in solving the case and preventing other young women from becoming victims.

And it could also help Abigail herself to deal with it.

On New Year's night, Sparks had tried and failed to convince her to talk to someone with specific training in working with rape victims. Operation Bryony had two such specialists on call, and today he wanted Brooks to have another go at persuading Abigail to talk to one of them.

He also wanted to know more about what had prompted her to preserve potential evidence in her freezer and yet wait three years before going to the police. The contradiction had been nagging at him ever since Sparks had first told him.

***

Abigail lived on Avalon Place, part of the newish Filcher Estate on the outskirts of Ashington. They appraised the small semi-detached house as they pulled up outside. The garages on the unattached sides of Abigail's and her next door neighbour's house had been built so close together there was barely room for the tall fence between them, let alone room to carry out any necessary maintenance work along there. Massey wondered if the girl owned the property, and if so, how she managed to afford the mortgage as a student. If she had a mortgage. Perhaps she had generous parents. Or maybe it was a private rental.

They rang the doorbell.

The girl who answered wore a coat. Dark purple, quilted, with a fur trimmed hood.

'Sorry, come in.' She moved to the kitchen and picked up a teaspoon to resume scraping cat food from small ring-pull tins onto two saucers as twin white long-haired cats yowled and wove themselves around her legs. 'Just got in. The moggies go mad until I give them something to eat.'

While the cats got stuck in, their upright tails twitching with contentment, Abigail busied herself washing and drying her hands for far longer than she probably usually took, her eyes anywhere but on the two of them.

'Thank you for seeing us Abigail,' Brooks said. 'We appreciate how difficult this is for you.'

They'd agreed in the car that it should be Brooks who asked most of the questions and he'd only butt in if he thought she'd missed something, or he thought of something new.

Abigail picked up the kettle and moved to the sink. She still hadn't looked at them, and she hadn't yet removed her coat. 'Can I offer you a drink?'

'No, thank you, Abigail. We're fine.'

'I'm sorry. I'm really nervous. I don't even like thinking about... you know... let alone talking about it. But if three years haven't allowed me to get my act together, then I need to do something about it.' She rubbed a small, jagged scar on her jaw with a shaky finger. 'But I'm sort of... conflicted.'

Brooks gave a sympathetic smile. 'You know we have professionals we can call upon who have special qualifications in helping people in your position. I believe DS Sparks mentioned that to you when you came in to Hartington station the other night. So, if you prefer, we can arrange for you to talk to them instead of us. Or, if you'd rather not have a man present, I can ask Inspector Massey to wait outside in the car.' She shot him an apologetic look.

This wasn't something they'd discussed, but he understood.

'No, please, let's just get this over and done with. I'm not sure I could pluck up the courage again another time. Come through to the lounge.'

Massey didn't like to tell her that their talk today wouldn't be the end of anything. In fact, it would be only the beginning. Particularly if she had information that could help them snare a serial rapist. Giving evidence in court could prove even more traumatic for her than the hell she's been through already.

***

'And you're absolutely sure he said nothing at all?' Brooks asked.

'Nothing. Like I already told you. And like I also told that other detective on New Year's Eve. He said nothing. He just laughed.'

Laughing; something else that none of the other Musk Man victims had mentioned. They already knew he'd attacked Abigail outside in the street rather than in her home, and he'd tried to disable her first with a blow to the head, but he'd made a bad job of it, and she'd been able to fight back. Maybe it was his experience with Abigail that had taught him a few lessons he'd then carried over into attacks on subsequent victims. Or perhaps they were talking two separate rapists after all.

'What sort of laugh?' Brooks asked.

'Like a snigger. Like a child doing something he's not supposed to do.' Abigail put both palms on her cheeks, blinked away tears and sighed.

'You think he was young?'

Chin quivering, Abigail batted the suggestion away. 'No, he wasn't a little kid. He just giggled like a naughty boy. As if raping...' She took a gulp of air. 'raping me... was just a bit of naughty fun.' Her resolve crumbled then. She wrapped her arms around her body and dropped her head almost to her knees. 'I almost got away. I... I pushed him, and he fell. But I was wearing high heels and fell too, and I... twisted my ankle. And... then he dragged me... back into the alley and—'

'Abigail,' Brooks said. 'I'm so sorry we had to have put you through all this again. Is there anyone we can call? Anyone you'd like to have with you? Your mother perhaps, or a friend?'

'God.' She sniffed and wiped a hand under her nose. Her shoulders heaved. 'Not my mother. She's as much use as a chocolate fireguard. And she'd tell—'

'A friend then. Can we get one of your friends around for you?'

With her face contorting, Abigail wiped her tears away with the sleeve of the coat she never had got round to taking off. 'You don't get it, do you? I can't... I can't tell anyone about this. I shouldn't have come to you lot either. Because, if he... if he ever finds out—'

'We're going to get him, Abigail,' Brooks said, reaching over to pat her hand, abandoning all the guidance on never promising anything you may not be able to deliver. 'With your help, we'll get him, and we'll put him away. And then you won't need to worry.'

Abigail sniffed hard and gave a short, bitter laugh. 'I don't mean that bastard. I mean my dad.'

Massey and Brooks exchanged a puzzled look.

'Oh God, you have no idea whose daughter I am, do you?'

She was an adult. The subject of her parentage hadn't come up before now, as far as Massey knew. It hadn't been relevant.

'Stevie Grant. I'm Stevie Grant's daughter. So now you see why I can't tell anyone else about this, don't you? Can you imagine what my dad would do if he found out I'd been raped? I'm his only daughter, for God's sake. His only child. He'd go mental. He'd hunt the bastard down. And he wouldn't care who he hurt in the process. And not only that. My dad would never be able to look at me in the same way again. He'd probably disown me because I've been... What's the word they use in all those crappy historical romance things?' She shook her head in frustration and clicked her fingers. 'Sullied. That's the word. I've been sullied.'

***

'Wow,' Brooks said as they climbed back in the car. 'That's going to blow things apart a bit, isn't it, sir?'

'I think that's the understatement of the day.'

Stevie Grant, a vicious thug who thought that fear equalled respect. The main man responsible for the horrific rise in drug deaths over recent months across south east Northumberland, in a region already leading the field on that score. Peddler of the latest mix; heroin laced with the horse and cattle sedative xylazine, dubbed the new zombie drug because it rots the flesh of users.

And now, Stevie Grant, father of a girl who could very well have been the first ever victim of Musk Man. The one victim to give them a chance of identifying the pervert. Another co-incidence in a week full of them. But this time not so much a serendipitous one.

Abigail had been right. If Grant ever found out his daughter had been raped, he wouldn't hesitate to tear apart anyone who stood in the way of him finding and killing the man responsible.

If the rapist had known whose daughter Abigail was, then he'd knowingly signed his own death warrant.

CHAPTER 11

'Eddie, is that you? Where have you been?'

'No Mam,' Sparks said. 'It's me.'

The face of her mother glared at her from the living room door.

'Who are you? What are you doing in my house?'

Only just turned seventy, the woman who'd spent the last ten years or so feigning disabilities she didn't possess, marched towards her with not a trace of frailty.

'Get out. Get out of my house. How dare you come in here.'

Sparks sighed. Every day now, her mother had at least one episode when she completely forgot that her husband had passed away, oblivious to the fact she'd hounded him to his death with all her self-centred demands that had him running himself into an early grave trying to please her. And over the past couple of weeks or so, the episodes had become more and more frequent, with her mother reverting to a time when she and her husband were a young couple, Eddie and Sheila, just starting out.

'It's alright, Mam. It's me. Christine. Your daughter.'

'Liar,' her mother screamed.

Had she missed her medication today?

She'd definitely had her morning dose.

Best have a look under the settee cushions. That's where she'd found the stash of tablets last time. So, it wasn't that her mother was forgetting to take them. She was deliberately not taking them and then hiding the fact.

Although why she left them somewhere so obvious rather than flushing them down the loo, she had no idea.

'You're her, aren't you. You're Eddie's floozy.'

Spittle formed in the corners of her mother's mouth as she shrieked obscenities she would have never have tolerated to be even whispered in her presence before the last few months.

Shaking her head, Sparks took off her coat, hung it up in the understairs cupboard and walked towards the kitchen, another glorious evening at *chez* madhouse stretching out before her.

Her mother stomped along the hallway behind her. 'How dare you come in here as if you own the place. Have you no shame? You have no right to be here. This is my house. Mine and Eddie's.'

Sparks lifted the kettle and moved towards the sink.

Her mother caught hold of her sleeve, yanked it hard and the kettle flew across the room.

'Are you not hearing me?' She slapped Sparks across the face. 'Floozy. Get out!'

CHAPTER 12

Thursday 4th January 2024

'DS Sparks. A moment please.'

The voice had come from across the car park at Area Command. Bloody Superintendent Portas. Just what she needed this morning.

It had taken an age to get her mother settled last night but once she'd actually gone to sleep she'd been out for the whole night.

Unlike herself.

She rubbed her cheek and puffed a cloud of vapour into the frigid air, thinking about how long she'd lain awake in the early hours, running over in her mind what to do with her mother. Because the situation as it stood could not continue for much longer. And, as usual, when she'd called her brother Ian just to have someone to talk to, he'd abdicated all responsibility.

Put her in a home, he'd said, if she's too much for you.

And if he'd been in front of her when he said it, instead of on the other end of the phone, she'd have punched his lights out. She might still go round there and do it, right in front of that namby-pamby wife of his.

How could he think that removing their mother from everything she found familiar, everything that provided at least a little grounding in a world that must be feeling more and more alien every day, was the best thing for her?

And he his mother's golden boy, who'd never put a foot wrong in her eyes. Someone who, as far as their mother had always been concerned, Sparks had never been able to match in spirit, in generosity, in achievements, or in anything else for that matter.

'Everything all right, DS Sparks?'

'Of course, ma'am.' She rubbed her cheek again, feeling the imprint of her mother's hand like a brand, although her reflection in the mirror first thing had told her it had left no visible mark. Again.

'Good. That's what I like to hear.'

'You wanted to see me, ma'am?'

'Straight to the point. Excellent. Yes, I do, but not now. I have a half hour free at eleven this morning and I'd like us to get together and go over a couple of things.'

'Can I ask what they might be ma'am.'

'I'll let you know when you get there.'

'Ma'am.'

'Eleven sharp then. In my office.' Portas strode away, leaving Sparks standing with her mouth open.

***

Poised on the dot of eleven with her hand raised to knock, Sparks remembered the last time she'd been in this office, when it had been the lair of the now disgraced and imprisoned former DSU Oliver Hitchins. He'd kept the room stark and impersonal. Would it still look the same, or would Portas have injected some personality into the space? The new Superintendent's character had been hard to judge so far, as if she'd taken pains not to give anything of herself away, so perhaps not.

Sparks still had her hand in the air when the door opened, and the aroma of fresh coffee smacked her in the face.

'Don't just stand there,' Portas said. 'Come in. I take it you like coffee.'

A statement, not a question. As if a negative reply would result in her being labelled a grave disappointment.

The thought was reinforced when she noticed the vintage percolator that sat on top of a low filing cabinet, gurgling and hissing the coffee aroma into the air. Two cups sat alongside it next to a small milk jug and a sugar bowl.

Definitely a step up from the Hitchins era, and one that suggested a friendly chat rather than a dressing down. Although the coffee could just be a ploy.

'Milk? Sugar?'

'Just milk please, ma'am.'

'For goodness' sake, take a seat. Over there by the window. I don't often bite, and I'm not planning to do so today.'

Sparks accepted the coffee cup and took it over to a seat at a small circular table overlooking a secure parking area and the back of a huge DIY store.

Not as scintillating as the view across the main car park from the MIT room at the front of the building, but a view, nonetheless.

Portas took a seat opposite her and clicked her tongue against her teeth a couple of times. 'I understand you suffer from anger issues,' she said.

Sparks opened her mouth to speak but nothing came out.

Of course Portas would end up knowing about the mentoring arrangement set in place by her predecessor and HR as a form of support for her after her father had died so suddenly and unexpectedly.

Portas held up both hands. 'I'm not asking you to bare your soul here. I just want to have a chat about it. Because when I had DI Massey moved over to DCI Flowers' team I was unaware of the arrangement and, now that I do know, I need to make sure—'

'I get it, ma'am. You need to know I'm not going to go apeshit on you.'

At the time, she'd blown up at anyone. Everyone in fact. At the slightest provocation. So much so that she'd almost let it ruin her career. Not only had she been grieving the sudden loss of the father she'd adored, but with no warning at all, she'd found herself lumbered with what she'd seen at the time to be the completely unnecessary care of her selfish mother while her brother walked away scot-free. After all, he was his mother's darling boy, and nothing could be allowed to put a spoke in his vitally important career in the tax office. Whereas her job was of no consequence at all.

'I wouldn't have put it quite like that. But yes. Are you?'

'No, ma'am. Well, not at work anyway.'

Almost eighteen months on, she still desperately missed her father, and she did still feel a burning hot rage at times. But with the help of Massey, she'd learned how to lock it away in its box when she needed to.

'I'm not sure how reassured I am by that,' Portas said.

'Really, I'm fine. No-one is ever going to accuse me of being Zen-like, but you know, I'm cool. Honest.'

'Are you saying you no longer need the mentoring arrangement? You're happy not to be working day to day with DI Massey now? It hasn't had any negative impact on managing your anger issues?'

'That's three questions, ma'am.'

Portas raised one eyebrow, propped her elbows on the arms of her chair and steepled her fingers, waiting.

'Alright,' Sparks said. 'Do I still need the arrangement? No, I don't believe so. Am I happy not to be working with Massey now? Things move on, I appreciate that. It's not like we were welded together. Has moving DI Massey to another team negatively impacted my anger issues? Again, I don't believe so. I've never been the most patient person in the world, and I never ever will be. But, you know, it was a bad time for me back then. With my father dying and everything. And, well... things are different now.'

'I'm told you have caring responsibilities,' Portas said.

Jesus, is nothing private anymore?

'My mother. She has dementia. She was diagnosed some years ago, but my father kept it a secret from the family. And now he's gone, and she's getting worse...' Sparks gritted her teeth and shrugged. 'And *c'est la vie*. It is what it is.'

'You have a brother, I believe. Aren't you able to share the burden with him?'

Sparks laughed. 'No,' she said.

Portas opened her mouth to say something else, but Sparks jumped in.

'Look. I'm sorry, ma'am. Like I said, it is what it is. Lots of people have much worse challenges in their lives than I've had in mine and they carry on regardless. Yes, I went off the rails for a bit when my dad died. I admit that. But that was then, and this is now. I'm grateful for the support I've received. Really. I am. But I'm fine now.'

***

Stomping along the corridor back to the MIT room, Sparks ran over in her head everything that had been said, wondering if she'd shot herself in the foot. In hindsight, being so strident about how fine she felt and how well she was doing without Massey could have been a mistake. She'd let the anger she'd claimed to have controlled seep through. She'd handed Portas the opportunity to label her a liability and shuffle her over to another team, like she had Massey.

But on the other hand, if that's what Portas had intended, she could easily have probed a bit further to see how much more of the beast she could rouse. But she hadn't. Instead, she'd steered the conversation towards case specifics, asking for her opinion on whether the Sonia Wragg inquiry could be moved any further forward and for an update on how ready they were for the Children of Gaia inquiry going to court. And by the time Portas allowed her to leave, she'd formed no better idea of the new DSU's character than she'd had beforehand, other than the fact she enjoyed and was prepared to share rather fine coffee.

She bit her lip. For all she'd said she no longer needed the mentoring arrangement to continue, she wasn't quite so sure about that now she was out of there. And for all Hitchins had turned out to be a degenerate monster, she still felt she owed him for seeing that the potential in her still existed beneath the raging temper and persuading HR to offer her a lifeline, but most of all for hand-picking Massey to help save her from herself. For that, she would always feel grateful to Hitchins.

But not so much so that she could ever forgive the man for his actions last year that had led to the murder of the vulnerable woman whose childhood he'd already stolen.

She'd become accustomed to having Massey sitting at the desk opposite and in the driver's seat next to her, or at the end of the phone. Being there for her without being… patronising. By making the whole mentoring thing feel natural rather than something thrust upon him by Hitchins and HR. Like a normal friendship. Until that's exactly what it had become. Or at least in her own mind.

Could she really do without that?

Of course she could. It wasn't like they wouldn't still be friends.

If she couldn't deal with him working on a different team, then what did that say about their relationship?

Or what did it say about her own part in it?

Because Massey was… well, he was Massey. He was a mate. Whether they were working on the same team or not.

CHAPTER 13

As soon as Flowers had heard about Abigail being the daughter of Stevie Grant, Massey had seen the calculations behind his eyes and in his manner. Today the man was all over the case, pacing backwards and forwards across the room, shooting out questions as they occurred to him. No more hiding in his office. Sensing the potential for glory if he were to be the man leading the team that brought in Grant, he'd even loosened his Paul Smith tie and undone the top button of his Charles Tyrwhitt shirt. The last thing on his mind was the wellbeing of Abigail and the other victims. In his own little mind, bringing down Stevie Grant could earn him a lot more promotion points than identifying Musk Man and saving more women from the horrors of being raped.

And the worst of it? Massey could see already that some members of the team were being carried along with him. And not just the male members.

'If we're right that Ice Cold Abbie was the first one,' Lieb said, 'it's likely he already knew her from somewhere.' Arms folded across his chest, he swivelled back and forth in his chair, nodding his head at his own pearl of wisdom.

DC Natalie Clark scratched an itch under her high ponytail with the end of a pen. 'So maybe one of her dad's men?'

Flowers jumped on the theory. 'Three years ago. I want to know everything we have on his crew from that time. Did someone suddenly disappear?'

'But Abigail is certain her father doesn't know,' Brooks pointed out.

'Or perhaps,' Lieb said, 'Grant crossed someone he shouldn't have, and the rape of his daughter was a punishment.'

'Excellent suggestions everyone.' Flowers patted his inside breast pocket and pulled out his vibrating phone. Reading the name of the caller on the screen, he grinned and made for his office. 'Keep them coming, folks.'

'What about the other victims then?' Massey directed his question to Lieb. 'Are you suggesting they all have fathers who've upset the same someone?'

'Maybe doing Abbie gave him a taste for it,' Lieb bit.

Moodie shot to her feet. 'Doing Abbie? Seriously, Dan?'

Lieb looked round for support, but Kirsty Brooks and John Land looked like they agreed with Moodie, while Iain Johnson kept his head down and feigned concentration on his screen.

Lieb might have the looks, but he didn't have the respect of at least half the team.

'You know what I mean,' Lieb said.

'No, actually, I don't. Explain it to me, why don't you.'

'Why a wait of two years before the next victim?' Brooks asked, cutting off the spat.

Moodie clenched her fist on the desk. 'He had to have realised how stupid he'd been to leave all that evidence behind. Maybe it took that long for him to conclude that she wasn't about to report it, and so he was in the clear.'

Clark dug the end of the pen deeper under her ponytail and wiggled it around. 'Perhaps he didn't wait that long. Maybe there were others in between who we don't yet know about.'

Johnson lifted his eyes from his screen and addressed the room. 'If it was one of Grant's men who raped Abigail, then Grant couldn't fail to have found out. He'd have killed the bloke or had him killed. In which case Abigail can't have been raped by Musk Man, unless the others have been raped by a ghost.'

'Maybe he did,' Lieb said.

'Grant knows nothing about it,' Brooks insisted.

Massey looked around the room. 'DC Moodie could have a point. If Abigail really was the first of Musk Man's victims, and the offender showed no signs of being forensically aware at that time, then he can't have failed to realise later how stupid he'd been. So is it possible that he used the intervening two years to... train himself up, in a manner of speaking, before striking again? DC Clark's point is also valid. Given how prolific he's been over the past year, would he not have felt compelled to look for victims to practice on during those missing two years? Or, alternatively, maybe Abigail's attacker is a different person entirely?'

'But she described the smell, sir,' Brooks said.

'She described a smell. How did she put it? Like a donkey's armpit. That's a little different to what other victims have said about him smelling of a heavy musky aftershave or deodorant.'

'Same thing to me,' Moodie said. 'Musk smells disgusting. Like something from a zoo enclosure. And yet lots of men think it makes them smell irresistible.'

'How people feel about smells is very subjective though, isn't it?' Johnson said. 'I love the smell of motor oil, but my girlfriend hates it. I adore the smell of fresh coffee, but it makes her throw up.'

'What's she doing with you then?' Clark asked. 'Engines and caffeine, that's you in a nutshell.'

'So,' Moodie said, 'you're saying that there may be other victims, but they haven't reported being raped simply because they like the smell of musk? Fuck's sake, Iain. That's like that old joke about the prostitute who didn't know she'd been raped until the cheque bounced.'

'Don't be daft. You know that's not what I meant.'

'At least Abigail's rapist can't have been someone she already knew,' Brooks said, 'If the smell was so disgusting to her, she'd have noticed it on him before?'

'Not if she's never been physically close enough to him,' Massey replied. 'He could have targeted her from the periphery of her social circle. And isn't it likely anyway that he doesn't smell like that all the time? If he did, what with all the publicity there's been about the more recent rapes, surely someone would have talked to us about him. So perhaps the smell comes from something he wears specifically during an attack. A piece of clothing or an aftershave, for instance.'

'Something to get him in the mood, you mean?' Lieb said, waggling his eyebrows.

'We've looked at aftershaves and deodorants before sir,' Brooks said.

Moodie twisted her face and feigned vomiting. 'Have we not. That's a couple of days I'll never get back. Spraying different aftershaves onto pieces of card and waving them under our noses for hours on end at that perfume place. Enough to make anyone puke after a while. But then taking the cards round our victims and asking them if any rang a bell, while sort of hoping one of the cards would send at least one of the victims into meltdown, just so we'd have something to follow up. Not a nice thing to have to do. Plain soap and water girl I am from now on where my men are concerned.'

'And did they?' Massey asked. 'Did any of the aftershaves score a hit?'

'Not one. Although a couple came close.'

'Okay then, how far did you get yesterday with the new pattern analysis?'

'Still on it, sir.' Brooks said. 'Adding Abigail's data hasn't thrown up anything new yet.'

'Keep going. Something might still come up.'

Anything at all that could distance the inquiry from Stevie Grant. Although could they afford to discount the possibility of a link?

'I don't recall seeing anything about any blood tests carried out during examination of the victims,' he said. 'Do we know if the rapist used any drugs to subdue his victims?'

'Blood samples taken from just four of them sir.' Johnson's fingers rattled across his keyboard. 'Sophie, Josie, Kayla and Amber. Not Jessica because she'd waited months before making a report, and Abigail we know about. With Nicole, her father said no, and she did whatever he said.' He scanned the information on his screen, clicked and scrolled, then scanned again. 'Hold on, here's something I've never noticed before. I don't think any of us has.'

More clicking and scrolling.

'Well?' Clark demanded.

'Every one of the four we tested had at least one drug in their system. No date rape drugs though, which is what we were looking for. But Sophie and Amber had both used acid. Kayla had been smoking weed and Josie had taken speed. I don't mean immediately before, not for any of them, but recently enough for a certain amount to still register.'

They were all silent for a moment.

None of them had noticed before.

'They had to have got the drugs from somewhere,' Clark said eventually. 'What if they all came from the same source? Maybe even the same dealer?'

'Which leads us back to Stevie Grant,' Lieb crowed. 'Maybe we should see what Ice Cold Abbie has to say about that.'

'She can't help who her father is,' Brooks shot back. 'And most likely the rapist had no idea. Surely only a total nut job would deliberately sign his own death warrant by raping the daughter of the most evil villain around.'

'Maybe she was raped because of who her father is, not despite it. Either way, if she'd come forward sooner—'

'That's a ridiculous thing to say.' Brook's face turned an angry red, making her freckles barely visible. 'You know as well as I do the vast majority of rape victims don't report it at all. There could be hundreds of Musk Man victims too afraid to come forward for fear of having to deal with Neanderthal attitudes like yours. In Abigail's case, she was more scared of her father finding out about it than she was of us. That's why she didn't come forward sooner. And I for one applaud her courage in coming forward now.'

Moodie nodded and clapped her hands.

'What she said.'

The door of Flowers' office opened and closed, but he didn't join them, even though he couldn't have failed to hear the raised voices of his team.

Instead, he was out in the corridor and on his way out of the building before anyone registered he was leaving.

'There's a man on a promise,' Moodie said.

***

The disagreement deepened throughout the day, with the team finding itself divided into two distinct factions. Flowers did not return to the office, and eventually everyone started to drift off home around 6 pm. Massey and Brooks were the only ones remaining when Brooks' phone rang.

'It's Abigail. I'll put it on speaker.' She tapped the screen and laid the phone on the desk. 'Hi, this is DS Kirsty Brooks. Everything okay, Abigail?'

'No. No, it's not. Not at all.'

Her voice had a definite catch, as if she'd been crying.

'What's wrong?' Kirsty asked.

'Someone's following me. Everywhere I go, he's there. Just now. I had to run home. He's out there.'

'He? Who is it, Abigail? Have you seen someone?'

'Yes. Well... a shadow. I saw a shadow, but...' She sighed in frustration. 'Look, I'm not going mad. He's out there now. He's watching the house. It's him. It has to be...'

They both heard her lose it then. Kirsty glanced at the clock on the wall. 'I'm coming over, Abigail. I'll get there as soon as I can. Make sure all the doors and windows are locked. Stay inside and keep your phone with you. Don't open the door until you hear my voice.'

***

Massey drove while Brooks organised for a patrol car to park outside Abigail's house and wait for them there. When they arrived, Brooks went inside while Massey stayed outside to hear what the uniforms had to report. They'd seen no-one apart from a couple of neighbours arriving home from work and going straight into their own homes, but they promised to drive through the estate a couple of times during what was left of their shift and to alert the takeover crew.

Inside, although her tears had all but dried, Abigail still looked shaken. Whether someone really had been following her or it had all been in her mind, he could see she truly believed there had been someone there. He took a walk around the house, inside as well as out, mindful of the fact that the six more recent Musk Man victims had been attacked in their own homes, with the rapist believed to have been inside the property for some time before the attack in at least two cases. He found nothing. He spoke to the neighbours on both sides, but they'd seen no-one and noticed nothing.

By the time he returned inside, Brooks had persuaded Abigail to go and stay with a friend for a couple of nights, so they waited while she packed a bag, bundled the cats into a carrying basket and all their paraphernalia into another large bag, then gave her a lift to the friend's house. Massey wondered whether the friend was aware yet that she was about to be giving shelter to two moggies as well as their owner.

'What do you think, sir?' Brooks asked as soon as they had the car to themselves again.

'She's convinced someone was following her. And despite the trauma she's going through, I don't think she's one to get spooked easily. I believe her.'

'Me too. Maybe he knows she's finally reported her rape.'

'It's possible. But for him to be overly concerned about it, he'd have to also know she kept the clothes she wore that night in her freezer for all that time to preserve the evidence.'

'And since she swears she's told no-one else but us, that can't be.'

He admired Brooks' faith, but after the events of last summer when Hitchins was charged with murder and two junior officers with aiding and abetting, Massey knew things weren't always so clear cut. Sometimes, information had a way of getting out. But if that was the case here, then it was a miracle that neither the press nor Stevie Grant had got wind yet.

CHAPTER 14

Almost nine o'clock when Massey turned left into his own street and noticed Helen only just pulling onto the drive before him. She must have come into the estate from the other direction. 'You're late back again,' he said, when he joined her inside. 'You look bushed.'

She accepted a kiss on the cheek as she pushed a hand through her hair, which hung loose down her back, the way he liked it best but not usually how she wore it for work. 'I am a bit. Difficult times, you know?'

He did. Helen did a hard job these days, having changed career to something more challenging in the wake of last summer's events. Now she worked with families who were struggling to stay together after being made homeless, usually these days as a result of the cost of living crisis. And she'd also taken on the extra work with the church group she'd got involved with. It felt odd that he wasn't the only one now having to work late at the drop of a hat. Her old job with the council had been strictly office hours, with the option to work at home way more than most people. He looked at his watch. 'How about we order in tonight. What do you fancy? Chinese, pizza, tandoori? Or we could go to the pub if you like. If we go straight away, we should still make food service.'

'No thanks. Not tonight. I had something to eat earlier. You order in for yourself though.'

'You're sure?' Ordering and eating for one just wasn't the same. He'd find something in the freezer again instead.

As Helen disappeared upstairs to get changed, he noticed her weary tread and wondered whether the new career had been the right move for her after all, or if he shouldn't have another go at persuading her to take on less with the church. He'd hoped that doing a job she could get her teeth into and feel passionate about, rather than vegetating at County Hall, might have helped their marriage, which had been on the edge of breaking apart just six months ago. Instead, it felt like he was being slowly squeezed out of her life.

CHAPTER 15

Friday 5th January 2024

'Morning, Massey.' Flowers slapped him on the back. 'Getting you on board has certainly given Operation Bryony a shake-up. Has it not? I'll be sure to say a very special thank you to Detective Superintendent Portas for sending you my way.'

Good grief. The man might as well announce to the world he was shagging her. Portas would hardly be pleased if she found out he'd been boasting about it to the troops. He can't have stayed out all night with her though, since this morning he wore a different suit – a silver-grey three-piece this time, with a lilac shirt and co-ordinating paisley tie. So he'd obviously made it home at some point.

The man still wore the manic grin of yesterday though, and Massey had no idea if that was a result of getting his rocks off regularly with his new boss or because he'd convinced himself that he could be the one to achieve what Serious and Organised had failed to do and bring in Stevie Grant. Or maybe even both.

Massey wondered whether Portas was aware of what her new beau had in mind. He couldn't imagine she'd be happy about it. But what did he really know about her? He'd liked the way she worked until he'd discovered she had atrocious taste in men and showed such poor judgement in carrying on an illicit affair with a subordinate officer.

As far as his own situation was concerned she'd demonstrated a tendency for being a stickler for the rules, and yet she didn't seem to give two hoots about the conflict of interest she'd created herself by becoming involved with a married man under her direct command. So maybe she did know already what Flowers had going on in that egotistical head of his. Perhaps she too was happy to throw Abigail under a bus to achieve glory. It made Massey's blood boil. Abigail was a victim, not a tool to be wielded in bringing down her father.

***

Flowers clapped his hands, signalling the start of their team update. Once he had everyone's attention, he spent some time running through the latest developments, making special mention of Abigail's panicked call after most of the team had already left yesterday.

Johnson held up his hand. 'If he knows she's finally come to us, maybe he's concerned about what else she might be able to tell us and is keeping an eye on her.'

'She's paranoid, more like,' Clark said. 'How could he know she'd kept the evidence if she's told no-one else?'

'Maybe she did tell someone.' DC Land spoke slowly and deliberately, the most circumspect of the team so far since Massey had joined. 'And if the rapist is someone in her circle, even if she doesn't realise that yet, then he could also know she preserved his DNA.'

'How far have we got on chasing up Grant's crew from three years ago?' Flowers asked.

'Pretty much the same as now sir,' Lieb said, 'if we're just talking faces. Couple of extra in the mix, but no-one's disappeared. And Nigs Bowen was his right hand man back then too. It's going to take a lot more time if you want to get down to all the street dealers and runners. Unless we bring Serious and Organised in on this.'

'And we're not doing that, are we Lieb?'

'No sir.'

'So we need another angle. I want the girls talked to again. Face to face. Find out if they all had the same supplier. If that's the case, we'll have somewhere to start. And I mean talk to all six, not just those who had blood tests done immediately afterwards. But not Abigail. I have something else in mind for her once we have some ammunition.'

Ammunition? As if Abigail were a target, not a victim. The man had no shame. Did he really intend to use a rape victim as a lure to trap her own father?

'DI Massey, get all that organised first, and then I want you to personally chase up the lab for a DNA profile from Abigail's clothes.

Massey gritted his teeth but nodded his head. He'd be surprised if the lab had anything for them yet.

'Sir,' Brooks said, 'we talked yesterday about the possibility of other victims in the two years between Abigail and Sophie who Musk Man may also not have been so careful with.'

'So I see. Good shout. That needs to be chased up too, Massey. Any unsolved files that haven't been previously linked to Bryony. Oh, and I want Lieb to stay on Grant and his gang.

***

With a good idea now of which side of the debate everyone fell, Massey wanted to make sure that each team of two he sent out to reinterview the victims was as balanced as he could make it in terms of their point of view, and then he divided the victims in terms of their geographic location. He teamed DC Robyn Moodie with DC Natalie Clark to interview Sophie, Kayla and Amber and sent DS Kirsty Brooks with DC John Land to interview Josie, Jessica and Nicole. That arrangement gave Brooks and Land the two most difficult ones to deal with, which were also the two who hadn't had blood tests taken at the time of their rape. Childcare worker, Jessica Elliott, aged twenty nine, who'd taken three months to report being raped and then appeared to wish she hadn't. And dog groomer Nicole Selby, aged just twenty, who had the over protective father. If anyone could get information out of those two women, he'd bet on Kirsty Brooks to be the one.

DC Iain Johnson would stay in the office to look for other victims of rape or assault during Musk Man's missing two years and, at Flowers' insistence, DS Lieb would continue working on the structure of Stevie Grant's operation.

Flowers – having locked himself in his office for thirty minutes following the team meeting – had now disappeared, leaving no information on where he'd gone, which Massey gathered was par for the course with him. He planned to be out of the office himself for most of the day, but at least everyone would know where he'd be.

CHAPTER 16

The Forensics Services building in Peterlee, shared by both Northumbria and Durham forces, was the lair of CSI Manager Rosalind Dimeter. Pale, slim and softly spoken, Dimeter had a fresh pot of coffee brewing when Massey arrived and a tin of Christmas shortbread open on her desk. 'Got three tins as gifts this year,' she said. 'They're my favourites but I have no-one at home to share them with, so I bring them in here. Mostly so I don't end up looking like a house end by eating them all myself.'

It would take a ton of shortbread, Massey thought, to add any significant inches to Dimeter's spare frame.

'I'm pleased you called me today,' she said as she filled their cups, offered him milk and sugar and nodded towards the biscuit tin. 'I was on the point of having to call your DCI Flowers to give him the news, and I'd much rather not have to do that. How on earth did you end up working with that man anyway? You're usually on the MIT, aren't you?'

'I had a personal connection to the victim in the hit and run inquiry our team is working on, so the new DSU transferred me over to Flowers' team. Temporarily, I hope.'

'Ah yes, I remember now. And Zafar said something about one of the witnesses being your mother, I believe. How awful. Is she alright?'

Zafar Davani was the crime scene manager he'd worked with most often and, before having been so ignominiously dismissed from the hit and run scene following Sonia's death, Zafar had expressed his condolences on the loss of his stepfather.

'She's as well as can be expected, thanks. Flowers asked me to chase up the forensics on this and I fancied a drive, so here I am. I didn't really expect you to have anything for us yet, but I take it you do.'

'We do.' Dimeter patted the file in front of her. 'Abigail Grant and her frozen party clothes. That's a new one for the training sessions, by the way. I always like to keep a couple of weird anecdotes handy, and this one fits that bill. What's she like, Abigail, is she a strong person?'

Strange question.

'She's a contradiction. On the one hand she's been too terrified to report the rape for three whole years, for more than one reason. On the other, she preserved evidence to help catch the bastard, which couldn't happen of course unless she reported it.'

'So what prompted her to come forward now?'

'A desire for closure, I think, as well as all the reports in the news about so called Musk Man and the smell that gave him his name. She remembers a similar smell.'

He paused.

Dimeter sat with a thoughtful look while she crunched on a stick of shortbread.

He waited until she was about to take another bite before speaking. 'Are you going to put me out of my misery then?'

Dimeter smiled and took a moment before replying. 'We got a hit.'

Massey sat up straight. He'd gathered that already but there was never anything quite like hearing the words. 'Come on then. Don't keep me in suspense. Who is it?'

'It's not a direct match. It's a familial match to DNA that has only recently been added to the system.'

So no name to solve the case immediately. He tried not to show his disappointment. 'We can work with that.'

And they could. Whoever's DNA it matched to, then Abigail's rapist was a relative. They could find him from there.

'I have to warn you, it's not going to be as simple as you imagine. It was quite strange actually. Brodie had just finished working on one lot of samples when the very next thing he's allocated turns out to be this one. He recognised the similarities in some of the sequencing straight away because the previous one was still so fresh in his mind. It's not a full match, you understand. It's not even a fifty percent match.'

'It has to be better than we have now. Whoever you've got in the system is related in some way.'

'I'm sorry, you misunderstand me. What I mean is that the DNA from the clothes brought in by Abigail Grant has thrown up a familial link with another case, yes. But it's an unsolved murder inquiry.'

'Oh.' That threw him for a moment. 'It can't be a Northumbria case, then. I'd have heard.'

'It is. Newcastle city centre.'

'But I'd know if there was anything on the go.'

'Not this one you wouldn't. This one is forty years old. A cold case.'

Forty years and unsolved? Jesus.

'And this one belongs to Operation Casper.'

Dimeter bit her lip to prevent a laugh from escaping but he could still see the mirth in her eyes. Operation Casper. Named after Storm Casper that had devastated parts of the region last summer and caused flooding at a storage facility used by the force to store the paperwork from old unsolved cases that hadn't yet been digitised. Operation Casper had been set up to salvage as many of the old paper files as possible and get them onto the system before they disintegrated to mush.

Massey laid his head back in his chair. 'And that's—'

'Yes.' Dimeter couldn't suppress a bark of laughter this time. 'Guy Keegan. He was the second person I was going to have to contact today.'

CHAPTER 17

'Flash! Welcome to the swamp. Operation Putrid – sorry, Casper. To what do we owe this displeasure?'

Flash? Massey thought he'd left that unwanted nickname in the past, but he might have known that the man who gave it to him in the first place wouldn't forget it in a hurry.

Detective Inspector Guy Keegan sat perched on top of what looked like an archive box encased in a black plastic binbag on the far side of the room. His knees stuck out to either side of him with his beer belly hanging between as his nitrile-gloved hands handled the contents of a second archive box with a delicacy he'd no idea the man possessed. If it weren't for the full dark beard that bristled on all sides of the blue surgical face mask he wore, Keegan would look for all the world like a swamp toad sat on a rock.

The beard was a new development since the last time they'd seen each other. Massey decided to reserve judgement until he saw it without the mask.

Previously a Detective Chief Inspector, and until six months ago Massey's immediate boss, he wondered if the man would have felt so grateful to have received just a demotion instead of the chop if he'd known this was to be his punishment. Banished to a dingy old station that had been closed down eight years ago – the closest slice of the force's redundant estate to the storage facility that had flooded last summer – all so that none of the upper echelons at HQ would need to be subjected to the stench.

And Christ, did it stink. Putrid was an apt word for the miasma emanating from the sludge-coloured documents in piles on the floor around him.

Massey held a hand under his nose. 'Jesus wept.'

'A bit whiffy, isn't it?' Keegan said. 'Can't do with any more than two of these bloody boxes in here at a time!'

'How far have you got with it all?'

'Not far enough. It's never bloody ending. Drying things out, scanning documents, trying to decide which bits of evidence are still worth holding on to and which have been damaged beyond redemption. I need to have a shower at HQ when we finish every day before I can go home. The wife threatened divorce if I walked through the door with this smell on me again. Anyway, don't just stand at the door. Come in. You might as well suffer too. Have you met Lonnie?'

To Massey's right, half hidden now by the open door, sat DS Lonnie Burke, the man who had responded to his banging on the front door and allowed him access to the building.

Burke's grizzled hair formed a nest for the pair of funky turquoise blue spectacles perched on top.

'I have,' Massey said. 'Thought you'd have retired by now, Lonnie.'

'I nearly did. Last summer. Then this happened and someone remembered I have no sense of smell and so I was asked to stay on for a while.'

'And anyway,' Keegan said, 'his wife had already pissed off because of his cheesy feet. So he doesn't have the same issues at home as I have.'

'Just the two of you?'

'They lend us a couple of PCSOs every now and then if we're lucky. But they can never wait to get away again. Anyway, what brings you here?

'You got time for lunch or a coffee?'

Keegan stared at him for a moment, weighing up the possibilities. 'The problem with that is that this lot smells a lot worse if I go out and come back in again.'

'It'll be worth it.'

Dimeter had promised not to contact Keegan before Massey had broken the news himself, so he knew that what he had to say would come as a complete surprise. And an extra hour or so after a wait of forty years would hardly make much difference to the deceased.

'It had better be.'

***

They sat at a table right at the back of the café, the swamp stench still emanating from Keegan's clothes easily dissuading any other customers from occupying the two tables closest to them. Without the mask, Massey decided the beard suited him. Strangely, it made him look younger.

With a cheese and onion pasty poised half way to his mouth, Keegan stared at him. 'You're saying they've found a DNA match between the 1984 Probert inquiry and Musk Man?'

'A partial match,' Massey replied. 'To an unidentified rapist who may or may not be Musk Man.'

'How partial?'

'Twenty-five point something percent.'

'So that makes it what? Grandparent, grandson?'

'Or uncle and nephew, or half-brothers.'

Keegan dropped the pasty onto his plate. 'Well slap me stupid with a wet haddock.'

Massey watched the thoughts scroll through the man's head. With his mouth still hanging open, it looked very much as if someone had already done just that.

Keegan shook his head and said nothing while they both concentrated on finishing their lunch, then Massey ordered more coffees.

'Have you told Flowers?' Keegan asked.

'Not yet. Just come back from seeing Dimeter. Thought I'd find out what you know first. So are you going to tell me about Julie Probert?'

But Keegan wasn't ready to play ball yet. 'Tell me again how you ended up working under that prat.'

Massey sighed. *How many more times?* 'Because I have a personal connection to both the victim and a witness in the hit and run we caught on New Year's morning, and so DSU Portas shuffled me over to Operation Bryony, Flowers' team.'

'How personal?'

'The witness is my mother, the victim an old friend of hers.'

'Jesus, that's personal. But why move you to Flowers' team? The hit and run can't be the only thing you were working on.'

'It wasn't, but both DIs on Operation Bryony are on the sick, one of them long term.'

'Even so. If I was still... you know... I wouldn't have moved you.' He sniffed and changed tack. 'She's a bit of alright though, Lou Portas, don't you think? A big improvement on Hitchins.'

'Anyone would be an improvement on that bastard.' Massey looked down at his hands and sighed. 'I thought she was okay. At first. Until I saw the other side of her. When I told her about knowing the victim and the witness, straight away she did the right thing regulations-wise in taking me off the case. She couldn't have done anything else. It was too close of a conflict. But then, well, it appears she's not averse to a bit of a conflict of interest herself when it comes to the people under her command.'

Keegan barked a surprised laugh. 'She made a pass at you?'

'No, not me. She obviously has a taste for a sharper image.'

'Christ's sake. Not Ray Flowers.' Keegan shook his head slowly. 'No. I don't believe it. She's way too smart for that.'

'I'm telling you. They've been sneaking around together, and he might as well have shouted it out loud for the whole team to hear this morning.'

'In his wet dreams. He's not her type at all.'

And how could Keegan know what Lou Portas' type was, he wondered. Time to get the conversation back on track. 'So, are you going to tell me about Probert then?'

Keegan scratched his beard and gave a lop-sided smile. 'Why not. If it keeps me away from the swamp for a while longer. But I'm warning you, it's very basic so far. Julie Probert, aged nineteen, raped and murdered on a night out on New Year's night 1983/84, after she and her friends had become separated when a huge fight started outside JoJo's nightclub in Newcastle.

'And?'

'That's it. So far. We haven't finished drying out and deciphering all the paperwork on it yet. We haven't even found any of it yet. I only sent her clothes off to the lab as soon as we found them to prevent them disintegrating any further before being tested. And as a favour to Lonnie. He was there at the time, you see. Young lad on his first case. It's the one that still haunts him. You know how it can get.'

Massey did know. Every cop had at least one case that still woke them up at night years later. Especially the unsolved ones.

'JoJo's, did you say? My mother has mentioned that place a few times. Used to go there regularly apparently. Wouldn't it just be typical if she was there that night and I got kicked off this case too?'

'You're not on this case.'

'If it gets pulled into Operation Bryony, I will be.'

'So then,' Keegan said, slapping his palms on the table top. 'That's all I've got. As I said, this is Lonnie's last ditch attempt before he retires to catch the bastard, and I'm just along for the ride. Now it's your turn. Tell me how Julie Probert links to Musk Man.'

Massey told him about Abigail turning up at Hartington station with her frozen party clothes in a cool box on New Year's night, three years after having been raped. 'And because he left behind so much evidence, we think she may have been Musk Man's very first victim. "May" being the operative word. It's only Abigail's description of the musky smell that really links her case to the other six. But perhaps, with her, the attack was an impulsive one. She could have been what set him on the road and made him want more, so he took the time to learn from that first mistake before striking again. And now he plans his attacks meticulously.'

'Why now though? Abigail, I mean. What changed her mind about reporting it now?'

'Perhaps she just needed to free up some freezer space. Or maybe, as she claims, she's just had enough of allowing the experience to ruin her life and wants to take positive steps to get over it. I think she's having second thoughts now though. She's trying to be brave, but she's terrified of what her father will do if he finds out.'

'Her father? Why? I'm damned sure if that happened to one of my daughters, I'd—'

'Because of who he is.'

Keegan raised his eyebrows. 'And?'

'Her father is Stevie Grant.'

Keegan's mouth dropped open again. 'Bloody hell, there's a bloodbath waiting to happen.'

CHAPTER 18

Flowers paced the room. This meeting was going down about as well as Massey could have predicted, except that Superintendent Portas had decided to drop in at an inopportune moment. Inopportune for Flowers anyway, who saw the revelation of the partial DNA match as a threat to his vision of glory, because it seemed she didn't share his views after all.

'But forty years, ma'am,' Flowers said, straightening his tie and jutting his chin. 'I mean, come on. We've got no chance of chasing down a murderer from that long ago if he's not already in the system. And it's not like the DNA connects to all the girls, is it? Abigail, yes. I'll grant you that, but I'm not convinced her attacker was the same man. We have the drugs link now between the other girls. That's where we need to concentrate our resources.'

'Between two of the victims, I believe you said, DCI Flowers.' Portas perched on the corner of Flower's desk, blocking his access should he want to sit back down there.

'Two who are now confirmed to have used the same dealer, but four of them who had taken drugs before being attacked. All six may have done for all we know. We just need to push them a bit harder...'

Massey watched the expression on Portas' face change. She glared at Flowers, pinning him to a spot on the floor like a butterfly to a display board. Massey had never seen cool green eyes turn to fire so quickly.

'Push them harder? Really? Are the horrors these women have already gone through not traumatising enough? You think we should treat them as suspects now. As criminals. You want us to strip them of what little dignity they have left now, do you?'

Flowers closed his eyes. 'I didn't mean that the way it came out.'

'I sincerely hope not, DCI Flowers. And besides, as I understand it, the levels of the substances found in the women's systems following the attacks do not indicate a causal link. They weren't drugged and immediately raped. It wasn't the same drug found in all of them, and certainly not any of the date-rape drugs. In fact, it's more than possible that the drugs had nothing whatsoever to do with the attacks. Isn't that correct?'

Flowers cast his eyes anywhere but towards his boss. Could the love affair be over? Massey ducked his head and coughed to hide a smile.

'However,' Portas continued, 'We mustn't rule a drugs angle out completely. I believe it is still worth taking a closer look, but not at the further expense of the victims, and not by cutting out the Serious and Organised Crime team. Are we clear on that?'

'Ma'am,' Flowers said.

Since the exchange so far had excluded him, Massey didn't feel the need to respond, until the fiery green eyes turned on him with an enquiring hook of one eyebrow.

'Ma'am,' he said, as he watched Flowers swallow his dream.

He agreed with Portas that Serious and Organised Crime should be brought in. It would be insane to go after someone like Stevie Grant, or even just to sniff around his fence without all the intelligence and authority they could muster.

They had nothing to go after him with anyway until they could prove a link between the drugs taken by Musk Man's victims and Grant's organisation.

And that would not be easy. It may well be impossible.

'Alright then,' Portas said. 'I'll have a word with DSU Elsom over there and get the ball rolling. I understand that DI Poole has recovered from the flu and will be back at work on Monday...' She paused, waiting for a nod from Flowers. 'So I want him to liaise with them.'

'What about the DNA link, ma'am?' Massey asked.

'I hadn't forgotten, DI Massey.'

Portas appraised him and, not for the first time since she'd entered Flowers' office, she wrinkled her nose.

'Since you now have a solid grasp of Operation Bryony, I want you to liaise with DI Keegan on the Julie Probert cold case. Spend however much time you need over there. DCI Flowers, I'd like to give Massey a small team to work with. I think we may end up having to help solve Julie's murder before we can identify Musk Man. Now, it's late and it's

Friday, so I say we all go home, have a good weekend, and come at this afresh on Monday morning.'

***

Massey sniffed his sleeve as he crossed the car park and remembered what Keegan had said about his wife's threats of divorce if he didn't wash off the stench of the old flood-damaged files before returning home. Hardly five minutes in the swamp, an hour or so in Keegan's company over lunch, and several intervening hours since, but his own clothes still bore a faint but distinctive trace of rancidness.

Although overall pleased with Lou Portas' decision, he intended to spend as little time as he could over there. He'd managed to score the two officers he'd have chosen himself though, had he been given the option. From Monday he'd have DS Kirsty Brooks and DC Robyn Moodie to work with. He suspected that Flowers had picked those two specifically because they'd made it clear they did not agree with his plan to use Abigail to get to her father.

His phone buzzed in his pocket. He pulled it out and saw Sparks' name on the screen.

'That you on your way home now?' she asked.

He turned back towards the building and saw her exiting the main door.

'Time for a drink?'

He didn't need to think about it for long. 'Okay, where?'

CHAPTER 19

Not far off seven o'clock on the first Friday evening after New Year, with pay day still weeks away and a grey drizzle outside washing away the last traces of icy slush, the Jolly Bowman was devoid of customers, and the bartender looked more than a little reluctant to leave the heat of the radiator over which she hovered, or to take her eyes from the TV screen. The pub advertised itself as a sports bar, but it was *A Place in the Sun* that absorbed her attention on the screen this evening.

Once served, Massey and Sparks picked the table in the corner furthest from the bar and sat at right angles to each other with their backs to the wall.

'Has Lou Portas spoken to you yet?' Sparks asked.

'What about?' It was hardly an hour since he'd wished Portas a good weekend as she strode out of Flowers' office, but he didn't imagine that conversation could be what Sparks was referring to.

'About you and me. I mean, not you and me as in... you know what I mean. She asked about the mentoring arrangement. She collared me the other day about it. Asked me if I thought I still needed it.'

'No, she hasn't said a word. What did you tell her?'

'I said no, I don't think I do.'

'Oh, right. So this drink is you letting me down gently, is it? Thanks but no thanks. Bugger off Massey, I don't need you anymore?'

'Don't be daft. That's not... Look, what I mean is—'

'It's alright, Christine. I understand.'

'I don't think you do. It's just... Portas put me on the spot. What was I going to say when she pretty much asked me outright if I was still a liability? Of course I wasn't about to admit that.'

'And are you? A liability, I mean.'

'You tell me. Am I? I don't feel like it.'

He couldn't believe how hurt he felt. Already cut off from his team by Portas, now she wanted to cut his remaining ties to Sparks. 'You never have been a liability, Christine. Not to me. You'd just lost your way a little for a while, that's all. But I understand. Really I do. If you don't want to—'

Sparks clenched her fists and thumped them on the table, making their drinks jump. 'Look, shut up will you, please? This is difficult for me. You know I don't like talking about this sort of stuff.'

Massey held up both hands then mimed zipping his mouth closed.

'By the way,' she said, 'have you been moved over there to Flowers' team permanently?'

Massey clamped his lips together and shook his head. She'd told him to shut up.

Sparks sighed. 'Well, whatever. However it ends up. Can we still be friends? Please?'

That's what she was so concerned about? 'Christ's sake Christine, of course we can be bloody friends.'

He smiled at the look of relief on her face, amazed at the swell of emotion he felt in his own chest. 'What did you think?' he said. 'That as soon as the mentoring arrangement stopped, we'd never speak to each other again?'

She laughed, unable to keep the grin from her face. 'It's just that everyone else thinks I'm weird, and I thought that you might be happy to—'

'Earth to Christine. You *are* weird.'

They laughed together this time, as if they'd just heard the funniest joke. After that, it felt as if a huge weight had been removed – one Massey hadn't even known he was carrying – and they lapsed into comfortable chat.

They were about to release Sonia's body to the family, Sparks told him. They'd found no evidence that the incident had been anything more than what it appeared on the surface, a driver fleeing the scene of a fatal accident, probably because they'd been drinking. It had been New Year's night after all. The file would remain open in the hope the driver would eventually be caught, but they had nothing left to chase up.

Massey told her about going to see Dimeter and hearing about the DNA link between Abigail and a forty year old rape and murder.

'How did Abigail take that?' she asked.

'She doesn't know about it yet. I only found out about it this morning. But that's not the only issue she's faced with, because you'll not believe who her father is.'

'Who?'

'Stevie Grant.'

Just about to take a drink, Sparks' eyes opened wide. 'No wonder it took three years to report it. I'm surprised she came in at all.'

'And just the other day, she thought she'd been followed home from work. She called Kirsty Brooks. I went out there with her. Abigail was convinced someone had followed her home. I had a look around, talked to the neighbours. Nothing. But Kirsty managed to persuade her to stay with a friend, for a while at least.'

'A touch of paranoia, do you think? Worrying about her father finding out now that she's finally reported it? It's not like he doesn't have contacts.'

'Maybe. That's what some of the team believe anyway, but I think there *was* someone there. Having said that, if we're to believe it was the rapist come back to haunt her for coming to us, then that must mean he's been keeping track of her for the past three years, otherwise how could he possibly know she'd finally reported it?'

'Unlikely, unless it was someone she knows after all.'

'She swears it wasn't. And I don't know how much of an eye I'm going to be able to keep on what's happening from now on. Portas wants me to liaise with Keegan on the cold case while Flowers follows the drugs angle. Flowers has been clever in the way he's split the team though. He's given me Kirsty and a DC called Robyn Moodie, because he knows they disagree with him about using Abigail to get to her father.'

'Robyn Moodie? Isn't that who Phil Jackson is seeing?'

'Is it? I've no idea.' Although it would make sense of how she knew about his family bereavement. Phil Jackson. Class clown on the MIT. The team he should still be a part of.

'Using Abigail to get to her father, how?'

'Flowers has got it into his head that he could be the one to finally bring Grant down if he can use Abigail as bait. The fact that four of the other six Musk Man victims had drugs in their systems following the attacks has only fanned his flames. Not that drugs were used in the attacks, just that the victims had used an illegal substance recreationally sometime prior. And now two of the four have admitted to using the same dealer, and we know who controls all the dealers around here.'

'But that's Serious and Organised territory. And surely he can't intend to use a rape victim as bait. Whose idea was it to put such a prat in charge of Bryony?'

'One guess,' Massey said.

'Hitchins,' they said in unison.

CHAPTER 20

Saturday 6th January 2024

Helen woke first on Saturday morning but as soon as she sat up Massey awoke too. 'Go back to sleep,' she told him as she slid her legs out of bed and stood up.

'Come back to bed.'

He reached out for her, but she pulled away, moved towards the window and slanted the blinds open. He got a view of the darkness outside, the clouds bruised and pendulous with unshed rain. Just the sort of day to stay indoors and snuggle.

He lay on his back and patted her side of the mattress. 'Come back to bed. Please.'

'I'll make coffee,' she said. 'What do you want to do today?'

'I want to stay in and make love to my wife.' He slid out of bed and moved up close behind her, putting his hands on her shoulders and nuzzling her neck, but she ducked her head.

'I'm awake now,' she said. 'I need coffee.'

'I'm awake too.' He moved his hands to her breasts and nudged his erection against her back, feeling the fabric of his pyjama pants and her nightdress between them. 'You know you want to. Come on. Then I'll go down and make the coffee.'

She turned and made as if to push him away, but he pulled her in close and claimed her mouth, feeling her resistance flicker and die. Her hands still pushed against his shoulders, but her hips moved against his. Loosening the button of his pants he carried her back to bed.

But whatever ideas he'd had, she took charge. In one smooth movement, she pulled her nightdress over her head and threw it onto the floor. With both hands on his chest now, she pushed him onto his back and mounted him, setting the rhythm. Hot and urgent. Taking what she wanted.

Not at all like their usual lovemaking. But he wasn't about to complain.

'Wow,' he said afterwards, his eyes drinking in her naked, breathless body as she lay spent across the bed. 'Where did that come from?'

'Coffee,' she demanded. 'Now.'

***

By the time he came back upstairs, a coffee mug in each hand, he found the bedroom empty. Helen had the shower running and the door of the bathroom shut tight. When she emerged, with all traces of their passion scrubbed away and her wet hair piled high in a towel, she accepted the coffee and repeated the question she'd asked earlier.

'What do you want to do today?'

He knew there'd be no chance of more sex, and if that was the case then the last thing in the world he fancied doing was the very thing he knew Helen would prefer – going January sales shopping at the Metrocentre or some other retail hell.

'We could go out for lunch,' he suggested. 'But I need to call in at my mother's at some point.' Then he had another thought. 'She might like to come for lunch too.'

Helen sighed and dropped her comb on the dressing table. She stared at him through the mirror. 'If we must,' she said.

CHAPTER 21

When her phone rang at half nine on such a miserable Saturday morning, Ellie felt extraordinarily pleased to hear from her eldest son. He'd call in at around eleven to see her, he said. With Helen. And would she like to go out for lunch? Lovely, she replied, she'd love to see them, but no thank you to the lunch.

And it would have been lovely. If it had been just him. She'd never tell James this, but there'd always been something about Helen that didn't ring true, and given her own low emotional state right now, she wasn't sure she'd be able to conceal her irritation for long today. Certainly not over a protracted lunch, at which Helen would no doubt be slugging down wine and James wouldn't have a drink at all because he was driving.

Ellie wished he'd found himself someone else. Someone better? No, that was the wrong word. Someone less spiteful then. Helen was certainly that, although James could never see it. Something had happened early on in their marriage that Helen continued to hold against him. James had never told her what it was, but she'd gathered that he must have been the one in the wrong, or at least he thought so.

Whatever it was, he'd never been able to say enough Hail bloody Mary's to satisfy Saint Helen. Yet aren't Catholics supposed to believe that there's no sin, no matter how serious, that cannot be forgiven? And surely the church says something about if a person can't forgive others then their God can't forgive them.

So Helen's good little Catholic act was just that. An act. And if the situation hadn't involved James and Helen, or anyone else in her close family for that matter, Ellie would have been able to laugh at the absurdity of it all.

While her eldest son's marriage may be less than ideal, at least it was nowhere near as bad as her own first marriage to Des Massey, which had been a nightmare she and James had been lucky to escape, so who was she to preach? The fact James had grown into such a good and loving man rather than an abusive bully like Des was down to David's unstinting beneficial influence.

There weren't many couples who'd managed to find the level of love and commitment she'd had herself with her second husband. That was just so rare.

She missed David so much.

She sighed and looked at the clock. An hour and three quarters to sort herself out and put on her serene face. She so wanted to see James, and for him to see that she was alright, that she was coping, and that she wasn't the frail old biddy he'd begun treating her as. She might be a widow, but she wasn't ready for a rocker yet.

***

When they arrived, Ellie was in her studio, attempting to render the mercurial form and colours of the dark skies outside to a moody abstraction on canvas. She wiped her hands on a rag as she ran downstairs to answer the door. Painting had taken her out of herself for a while, calmed her down, as she knew it would. She could cope with Helen for an hour or so now.

James swept her up in a gentler hug than usual. Perhaps he thought she looked too fragile these days for his usual bear hug. Helen eyed her painting shirt and delivered a distant kiss to the cheek before handing her a large bouquet of gaudy out of season flowers that she'd obviously chosen herself. At this time of year, James would have gone for something like hellebore and narcissus and eucalyptus, something he knew would be far more to her taste. If he'd had the choice.

She raised the flowers to her nose and breathed in their barely-there fragrance. 'Mmm, they're beautiful, Helen. Thank you. Come in out of the cold, both of you. It's lovely and warm in the kitchen.

While she made coffee and put the flowers in water, determined to ward off the inevitable questions about how she was coping on her own, Ellie asked Helen how her new job was going. Was she still pleased she'd made the change? Helen responded with enthusiasm, although still tinged with that edge of spite.

'I adore it,' she said. 'I get far more job satisfaction than in my last job. If you know what I mean, Ellie. With you never having had a career yourself.'

Ellie wondered what Helen would say if she had any idea of just how much some of her paintings sold for. And that, despite what she'd said to Megan the other day, her art was all the career she'd ever needed. But she said nothing, and neither did James.

'And how are you doing, James? Have they put you back with your usual team yet? I'm so sorry about all that, by the way. I know it's because of me.'

'Don't be daft, Mam. It's hardly your fault. Just a coincidence really that you'd only recently run into Sonia again after so many years and happened to be talking to her on the phone at the time.'

Ellie sighed. 'I don't trust coincidences.'

'Anyway, they've got me working on something else for the moment. I can't talk much about it, you understand, but do you remember JoJo's nightclub? I'm sure you've told me in the past that you used to go there when you were young.'

'Mmm.'

Noncommittal. Keep it noncommittal. Why on earth was he asking her about JoJo's now?

'Something's just come up,' James said. 'Linked to a forty year old inquiry that involved the nightclub. Something that also happened at New Year.'

Ellie turned her back to pour the coffee, and so that James couldn't see her face. Forty years ago on New Year's Eve at JoJo's. The night Julie was murdered. Exactly what she'd been talking to Sonia about right before she was killed.

Another coincidence?

The teaspoons rattled on the saucers.

She felt James' eyes on her.

She replaced the shock on her face with a smile before turning round, then picked up the tray and sat down beside them.

If anyone had asked her later, she could not have told them how she managed to hold herself together, but she did. And for the next hour the conversation didn't falter, so she must have held up her own side of it, although by the time they left she could hardly recall any of what they'd talked about, except for the couple of noncommittal snippets about JoJo's she'd felt obliged to recite for James' benefit.

He gave her another solicitous hug on the doorstep, and she felt a frailty in her own bones when she hugged him back. She really needed to start eating properly again.

'Call me if you need anything,' James said from the gate, just as the cloud burst above them and Helen ran for the car. 'Any time. It doesn't matter when. Just give me a call.'

CHAPTER 22

Sunday 7th January 2024

Sitting cross-legged on the settee with her laptop open and her backpack ready by the door, Sparks scrolled through information on behavioural changes in Frontotemporal Dementia, which she'd just discovered was also known as Pick's Disease. Twice her mother had got up through the night last night, fully dressed and convinced it was time for her to go out and pick up her children from school. The second time, Sparks hadn't heard her until the chain on the front door started rattling. Just as well she'd begun double locking the door and taking the key out. After both incidents, it had taken a while to get her mother settled again. And now this morning, when she needed her to be up and at her worst so that her brother could actually experience what she was up against, the poor woman was still off in the peaceful land of Nod, and it wouldn't be right to wake her and put her through all that unnecessary confusion.

At least not until Ian and Sara were here, and she'd escaped.

She looked at the clock on her Fitbit. Five to nine. They'd better not be late. Not that it mattered for any reason other than that it would be wrong of them to do that to her. Especially when they were under the impression she was off on some work thing. Because that had been the only way she could persuade them to take a turn at caring.

She didn't like lying. It annoyed her that she'd had to do it.

As it happened, she had no idea what she was going to do for the day, but she planned to start with a drive up to Druridge Bay and a nice bracing walk, so long as the weather stayed dry enough. Then maybe she'd find somewhere for Sunday lunch. Somewhere with a fire. And then? She hadn't decided yet.

She heard a car outside and leapt to her feet, stowing her laptop into its bag. By the time they opened the gate she was already at the door.

'Are you allowed to go to work dressed like that?' Sara asked as she eyed Sparks' leggings and trainers. 'Where's your uniform?'

'I haven't been in uniform for years now, Sara. I'm a detective. I wear what's necessary for the job in hand.'

'Which is what, running round a race track?'

Jesus wept. Didn't the woman know the difference between running gear and walking gear? Sparks gritted her teeth into a thin smile. 'Not at liberty to say.'

'Where's Mam?' Ian asked. 'Isn't she ready to go?'

'Go? You're kidding, Ian. She's still asleep in bed. She's been up and dressed twice through the night and wanting to be out and about, so she's having a bit of a lie in this morning.'

'But we're taking her out for the day,' Sara wailed.

'Then you'd better get in there and get her sorted. I've put everything out that you'll need for her breakfast, and I've told you already about her medication. Make sure she actually takes it, won't you. She likes to hide it under the cushions. Oh, and you might want to make sure she's dressed herself properly before you leave the house.'

She couldn't swear to it, but did Ian just take a step back towards the car?

'Right' that's it. I'm off.' She clicked her car fob and opened the gate. 'Have a good day. Not sure what time I'll be back. But I'll let you know if I'm not going to be able to make it home tonight.'

The look on their faces as she climbed into the car was priceless. Of course she'd be back tonight, but it wouldn't hurt the pair of them to be worried for once about whether they'd be able to make it into work tomorrow morning. After all, that's what she went through every day.

CHAPTER 23

Monday 8th January 2024

Monday morning. Most of the Operation Bryony team were in and chatting among themselves while waiting for the meeting to begin at eight o'clock. Even Flowers had deigned to come out of his office early and get involved in a conversation about Iain Johnson's engagement party that most of the team had attended over the weekend. Massey thought he recognised the name of Johnson's betrothed as that of a civilian worker at Etal Lane station. He'd contributed to the collection for a wedding present last week and had received a last minute invitation to the party from Johnson on Friday, but he didn't go. And apparently Flowers hadn't gone either.

'Sorry we couldn't make it, Iain.' Flowers pulled the sleeves of his navy checked jacket over the cuffs of his sky blue shirt and straightened his cufflinks. 'Already booked. Parents' golden wedding party on Saturday so we had family staying all weekend. Thought we'd never get rid of them yesterday.'

'Golden wedding,' Lieb said. 'What's that, fifty years? Think you and what's-her-name will last that long Iain?'

'What's-her-name?' Natalie Clark shot Lieb a look of disgust. 'You mean poor Holly, who you were nearly sick over when you tried to give her a goodnight smacker?'

'Yeah well, I was fine until that last pint. It must have been off.'

'Nothing to do with the half a dozen shots you necked before that then?'

Massey laughed along with the rest of the team. It sounded like a good time had been had by all. Despite the invitation, it wouldn't have felt right to go, which was no reflection on the Bryony team at all, but more that he was missing his actual MIT team. Anyway, it wasn't often he and Helen had a whole day together, and this weekend they'd managed two. With Helen having been happy to go and see his mother with him on Saturday, he could hardly have refused going to see her parents on

Sunday. And it hadn't been a bad day at all, especially when they got home, and Helen had been in the mood for an early night.

Eight thirty and Flowers drew everyone to attention. 'Sounds like you all had a good time on Saturday, but I hope you've all recovered now, because we have developments and there's no room for slackers this morning.'

This would be the first the team as a whole knew about the DNA hit, although he and Flowers had already had a few words earlier with Kirsty Brooks and Robyn Moodie, so they knew what was coming. They'd seemed excited about it then, and looking across at them now, they still did, but he'd see how long that lasted once he'd introduced them to the horrors of the swamp and the task they had before them.

Flowers had also spent ten minutes sequestered in his office with DI Adam Poole freshly returned from sick leave, presumably about him liaising with Serious and Organised.

A stocky and fit-looking Scotsman, dressed in a sharp suit and silk tie, Poole looked like emulating the sartorial elegance of his boss had been his life's work to date. Massey had seen him around but knew very little about him. The man, looking anything but overjoyed that another DI had join the team in his absence, oozed aggression.

Had he acted the same way with Ange Roberts? Massey couldn't see Ange being willing to take any shit from him. Not the Ange he remembered anyway.

***

As soon as the briefing ended, Massey gathered together Brooks and Moodie and they set out to the swamp in his car. He'd need to sort out some other means of travel if he was going to be doing this regularly, or else the local car valet service would be seeing a substantial uplift in trade.

'Should we be worried they call it the swamp, sir?' Moodie asked.

'Put it this way,' he replied. 'The name is apt.'

Once again, it was Lonnie Burke who opened the door to them, his blue surgical face mask hanging from one ear. 'You two pulled the short straws then,' he said, smiling at each of the women in turn.

Brooks and Moodie glanced at one another, their noses wrinkling in disgust as they stepped through the door and followed Burke along the echoing corridors of the old Victorian brick building.

'We keep the boxes in the old cells down below,' Burke said. 'But we've got ourselves set up nicely just along here on the sunny side of the building.'

The way he said it made it sound almost idyllic, but the smell worsened the closer they got to the nucleus of the salvage operation. To the actual swamp.

'Bloody hell!' Moodie said, hand to her nose. As they turned the last corner, she gave a dry heave and pulled out a small tin of menthol rub from her bag. She dabbed some under her nose and offered it around.

'You know that stuff actually opens up the nasal passages,' Brooks said. 'It'll make it worse after a while.'

'Hopefully, we won't be here long enough for that to become a problem.' Moodie replied.

Massey didn't like to disillusion her just yet, but they'd be working as much out of here as Area Command for however long it took to chase this thing down. All three of them. The job not so much about liaising as bloody hard graft.

Brooks puffed out her cheeks and accepted a dab of menthol. 'This is what we get for disagreeing with the boss.'

***

Today, Keegan sat next to an electric heater, his back to the wall, with several sheets of wrinkled and yellowed A4 paper spread out on the desk before him.

He took in the presence of the two newcomers.

'Who the hell have you two upset?' His beard bristled around the edges of his face mask as he spoke.

'Beg your pardon, sir?'

Brooks shuffled to one side as Lonnie Burke edged past her to sit at his own desk behind the door, the one most protected from the cold draught that all but whistled along the corridor.

Massey noticed another electric heater tucked behind his desk.

'You must have upset someone,' Keegan said. 'Why else would you be sent to the swamp?'

Brooks gave a short, embarrassed laugh and peered around the room. 'I can see why you might think that, sir.'

'DS Kirsty Brooks and DC Robyn Moodie,' Massey said, 'meet DI Guy Keegan and DS Lonnie Burke.'

Massey looked around the large room and took in the strange set up he'd missed before.

Three translucent plastic storage boxes stood on one table; two of them part-filled with liquid, the other lined with what looked like an old grey army blanket. Another two tables had been covered in towels, upon which lay more sheets of paper, in the process of drying, and a thin plastic washing line had been strung across the room and anchored to hooks screwed into the woodwork at shoulder height. Curled photos hung from it on pegs like laundry.

'The task isn't quite as awful as the smell might suggest.' Keegan's eyes crinkled at the corners and Massey could picture the wolfish grin beneath the mask. 'Honest. You see, when the storage facility flooded, some bright spark discovered the damage relatively quicky and had a brainwave, or else they had the nous to google what to do. Bloody YouTube, eh? Conserving flood damaged paper records and photos. Who knew you could find that kind of information on there?

'Anyway, they managed to get most of the records transferred to new boxes. They begged, borrowed, stole or bought all the big chest freezers they could lay their hands on, set them up in decommissioned stations like this one, and froze the lot, until us poor sods could get round to defrosting a few boxes at a time and dealing with the contents as best we can. So what you're smelling is the original floodwater from the defrosted boxes. The battle we have is to get it all processed, dried, copied, whatever, before any mould can set in.'

Eyebrows raised, Massey, Brooks and Moodie all stared at the objects around the room.

'Here.' Lonnie Burke passed round a box of face masks and another of nitrile gloves. 'You'll need these if you want to have a closer look.'

He pointed to the blanket-lined box, which they could now see contained a soaking wet manila folder. 'You see here, this file is from that defrosted archive box over there and this plastic box here with the blanket acts as a support and helps by absorbing some of the floodwater until I'm ready for the next step. There's quite a bit of muck just lying on the surface of it, can you see? So I need to rinse that off first.'

He picked up two pairs of wide kitchen tongs – the sort you'd use for battered fish – and used them to grip the folder and gingerly transfer it to the tub with the cleanest water, moving it back and forth a couple of times under the surface. Then he lifted it out, held it vertically for a few beats to let it drip, before placing it like a precious relic onto the next table on top of a towel.

'Now then. This is the tricky part. It might not look too bad on the outside, but whatever's inside could already have disintegrated, and we won't know...' This time, he picked up a long plastic spatula and eased open the front cover. '...until we have a look inside. And there you see, this one's not too bad by the looks of it. It's salvageable. We'll be able to separate these pages quite easily once I remove these... metal fixings.'

When he was ready, Keegan handed him an A4 sheet of acetate, probably originally intended as a transparency sheet for a now obsolete overhead projector.

Burke laid the acetate carefully over the first sheet of paper in the file and eased the spatula between the first sheet and the second. 'You see, the first sheet clings to the acetate and that makes it easier to lift it, so I can ease the sheets apart with the spatula. Gently though. It's not something that can be rushed.'

He lifted the first sheet over to the next table and placed it down on top of the towels in a new row below other sheets.

'And then it's just a case of air drying them. But of course it's a different process entirely for the more damaged files.'

'Patience of a saint has our Lonnie,' Keegan said. 'Because the longer this all takes, the longer he'll be able to put off the day when he's got nothing better to do but sit at home and watch sport on the telly.'

'I'll have you know,' Burke said, 'that I've got a lot more than that planned for when I retire.'

'Yeah, like dying of boredom. So instead he's happy to plough through this lot every day. And why not, when he's immune to the smell. A piss easy job like this?'

There was that grin again behind the mask.

Moodie, who'd been examining the sheets of paper on the drying table, turned back to Keegan. 'None of this looks like it refers to the Probert inquiry.'

Keegan guffawed. 'And therein lies the catch, people. Because when they piled everything into new boxes and froze them, no-one had time to put files into their original order. The priority was just to rescue them. And they didn't mark on the new boxes what they contained either. So it's all jumbled up and we have no idea what's in each box until it's defrosted, and then we have to make sure it's *all* conserved as far as possible, because there's a lot more than just one unsolved murder case among this lot. All of these victims deserve their cases to be looked at again.

'That's what Operation Casper is about. Salvaging what we can, putting the files back together, digitising them, and giving them all another chance. It's not *only* about Julie Probert. She's just the first we've got a hit on. And even then we've gone and got it all arse about front because we sent the clothes off for forensic testing before we'd found the case files.'

'You mean we've got to go through the whole lot to find the stuff on the Probert case?' Moodie's horrified expression said it all.

'Maybe not all of it,' Keegan said with a twinkle in his eyes. 'Think of it as a massive frozen lucky dip. But how unlucky if you found nothing until the last box? On the other hand, even if you found something in the first couple, or even halfway through, how would you know you had it all unless you go through the lot? Anyway, now there's more of us we can get through it much quicker, and then Lonnie can cash in his chips and sail off into the blue yonder.'

Massey shook his head at the mixed metaphors.

'How many boxes are there left?' Brooks asked.

'Oh, around another hundred or so.'

Brooks' jaw dropped. 'Seriously?'

'That's what you get for upsetting people.'

Still horrified, Moodie shook her head and glared at Massey. 'This is a joke.'

'It is what it is,' Massey said. 'Think about Julie Probert's family who've waited forty years already for justice, and about Abigail and all the other victims of Musk Man.'

'I'm going to have to buy a job lot of Vicks Vapour Rub.'

'Where are all the freezers?' Brooks asked.

'We've got nine big chest freezers in the basement here,' Keegan said, 'each one holding between ten and twelve boxes, depending on the model size. We've concentrated on clearing out all the other locations first so the electricity can be turned back off there.'

'So then, nine freezers here. Say an average of eleven boxes each. That's ninety-nine boxes. You must have just about finished bringing the rest over here by now then if you're saying around a hundred boxes total.'

Keegan looked towards Massey and cocked his head in Brooks' direction.

'Not just a pretty face, that one. In fact there are ninety-eight boxes left in the chest freezers here. We brought the last of the rest over on Friday. Half a dozen of those are in a couple of upright freezers in the kitchen and four have had the weekend to defrost. That's what we're working on this morning.'

'And what about more towels or blankets, and those big plastic tub things, do you have more of them?'

'This is what I like to hear,' Keegan said, rubbing his hands together. 'Someone wanting to get stuck in straight away. As it happens, we can oblige with towels and blankets because you might remember we put a shout out when we started, asking staff to donate any old stuff they wanted shot of, and I can sort you out with some plastic tubs later today. You'll have to have a look around and see what desks or tables and chairs you can find and set yourself up in one of the other rooms. And we've got plenty of PPE: masks, gloves, even some plastic aprons if you want them. We pinched the fish tongs from the kitchen, and we picked up our spatula from the art shop on Front Street, so you'll have to source your own.'

'Which rooms have heat in them?' Moodie asked.

'None. The last time the central heating was on in this place was eight years back. You're braver than I am if you want to try to get it started now. And you're not getting one of our electric heaters either. They're like gold dust.'

Moodie turned a mutinous look on Massey.

'Don't fret, Robyn,' he said. 'We'll sort something out. We can use the rest of today to get things together, and then we can start properly tomorrow.'

She didn't look mollified. 'Heaters too. Sir?'

'I'll buy some myself if I have to.'

Burke, whose head had been moving from side to side like a centre court spectator at Wimbledon, cleared his throat. 'If you want to get started straight away tomorrow, that means we're going to get through what's already defrosted much quicker, so we'll need to take out another couple of boxes from the freezer. Walk this way and I'll show you what's what.'

They visited the kitchen first. This was probably the last building still owned by the force that had such facilities, and still equipped with all its old stainless steel units and big range cooker that, even sold as scrap, would bring a fair bit. While he and Brooks helped Lonnie Burke carry frozen archive boxes encased in black bin bags from the upright freezers through to the men's old shower room, where any leaking liquid could drain easily during the defrosting process, Moodie raided every drawer she could find in the kitchen in a search for any remotely useful utensils that hadn't already been requisitioned by Keegan and Burke.

'You might as well see the rest while you're here,' Burke said once they'd finished.

They heard the hum before he'd even opened the door onto the stairs. Kirsty Brooks reached the bottom of the short flight first. Hands on hips, she gazed around the ancient custody suite – which could never qualify as such these days – at the nine huge commercial chest freezers lining every inch of spare wall. The din reverberating around the stone-walled space sounded like ten thousand angry bumble bees trapped in an echo chamber.

'Flippin' heck,' she said.

CHAPTER 24

The hit and run case had gone nowhere and the team now had a fresh homicide to investigate, just in this morning. A fourteen-year-old boy who'd never returned home from his paper round yesterday, his body found in undergrowth in the early hours. So the hit and run would be shelved, and Sonia's body would be released immediately to the family for cremation. It occurred to Sparks that someone should maybe let Ellie know, and with her own presence not immediately required at the murder scene, Portas had agreed and allowed her a couple of hours to go and deliver the news to Ellie.

And at least it was a break from all the comments in the office on where the cut on her cheek had come from.

She'd stayed out as long as she could yesterday. Her walk around Druridge Bay had taken a couple of hours. Then she'd gone to the Fishing Boat Inn at Boulmer for Sunday lunch and had drawn it out for as long as she could. Afterwards, she'd sat in the car for a while, looking out at the sea, trying and failing to read the book she'd brought with her. But it was pitch dark by then and the cold had become biting. Unwilling to risk running the car battery down in order to keep warm, it didn't feel worth the effort to stay away any longer. So by the time four o'clock came, she'd given up and driven home.

When she'd let herself in the front door, she followed the sound of voices and found a cosy little tableau awaiting her. Her mother, who'd obviously decided that Ian was her long absent brother, had got out all the photo albums and spread them across the dining table. From the hall, she listened for a while to her mother regaling Ian and Sara with tales of her little boy's prowess at school and about Eddie's promotion prospects at work. Nothing about a daughter. Nothing at all.

And when her mother became aware of her presence, she'd begun screaming like a banshee and demanding Ian throw her out. 'She's Eddie's floozy,' she'd screamed. 'Get her out, get her out.' And, while Ian and

Sara had sat with their mouths flapping like fish, her mother – bloody invalid that she'd claimed for years to be – had launched herself across the room at her face.

Automatically, she'd taken evasive action by stepping sideways, but Ian had stood up at the same time and tried to grab his mother's arms, which had knocked Sparks off balance, so she'd fallen against the corner of the wall unit and split her cheek.

'She was perfectly fine until you came in,' Sara had whispered as she helped her staunch the blood in the kitchen and put a dressing on the cut. As if it was Sparks' own fault her mother had attacked her. 'Off her trolley, but totally fine. She has been all day.'

'I bloody live here too,' she'd hissed, batting Sara's hands away from her face and pressing down the edges of the dressing herself. 'I should be able to walk into my own home without being attacked. And if she's been so good all day, how about you having her for a while. Just give me five minutes to pack a case and you can sodding take her with you.'

Ian's head had appeared round the door then.

'She's quietened down now. Bloody hell Christine, I never saw that coming. She was fine until—'

'I know,' she'd growled. 'Until I came in. Yadda yadda—'

'Yes well, I've got her under control again now—'

'She's not a sodding dog.'

'We'd best get out of your hair then,' Sara had said. 'If that's all the thanks we get.'

'Thanks? That's rich. She's Ian's mother too, you stupid cow. He has as much responsibility for her as I have. And this isn't anything unusual, you know. It's a regular thing, her lashing out at me. It's a common symptom of fucking dementia, you useless dimwit.'

'Sara.' Ian had huffed. 'Get your coat. We're obviously not welcome here.'

'Don't you dare use this as an excuse to slide out of doing your bit, Ian. It's not like you do much anyway. What's this, the first time this year you've been to see her? And then I had to beg. You didn't even show your face at Christmas. Some precious son you fucking are.'

Lips pursed, fists clenched, he'd jutted his face towards hers.

'That's it, Christine. I've had enough of your griping and your demands. It's a terrible thing to have to come in here and see my mother in such a state.'

'Tell me about it. This is what I live with.'

'And this...' He'd waved his hand towards her face. 'If you hadn't been so clumsy—'

'Get out!' she'd shouted. 'Get the fuck out.'

And they had. And when she'd gone back into the dining room to check on her mother, she'd found her in a terrified, quivering heap, hiding behind the door, with tears streaming down her face and a couple of old photos crumpled in her hand.

***

She hadn't pre-warned Ellie she was coming. She hadn't even thought about it. She'd just assumed she'd be home, which was a stupid thing to do, and she put the oversight down to her rush to get out of the office and away from the enquiring looks. For all she knew, Ellie could be out shopping, or with her daughter somewhere, or she could have returned to work by now. If she worked.

She realised she had no idea what Ellie did for a living. She assumed she'd be around the same age as Sonia since they'd known each other at school. So around fifty nine, sixty. Nowhere near old enough for State Pension yet, although perhaps the death of her husband had left her comfortably enough off to retire anyway and she wouldn't ever have to work again.

As it happened, Ellie was at home, and she came to the door wearing an old well-worn men's shirt daubed with paint.

'Detective Sergeant Sparks. Good heavens, what have you done to your face? Come in. It's lovely to see you.'

Sparks put her hand up to the dressing on her cheek. The wound had developed quite a bruise around it now too, although thankfully it hadn't resulted in a black eye.

'I'm sorry, Ellie. If you're decorating I can come back another time.'

Ellie looked down at the paint splodges and laughed.

'This is my work attire. I'm an artist. Come in and I'll make some coffee, or tea if you prefer, and we can take it up to the studio.'

While Ellie prepared coffee, Sparks stood at the huge plate glass doors and stared out at the garden, where there were still a few small heaps of icy snow lying in the shadiest spots. She could tell the garden would look lovely in summer. Nothing like her own father's regimented plot, with angular well-hoed borders filled with equally spaced annuals. Lobelia, alyssum, petunia, lobelia, alyssum, petunia, each individual plant surrounded by bare weed free soil, all the way around a scalped lawn with an over-pruned dwarf weeping willow in the centre. As if he revelled in stamping control on his own small patch of earth in a way he'd never been able to do on his marriage. Ellie's summer garden would be the polar opposite. Lush and informal and bursting with flowers to feed the birds and the insects. There'd be lots of little nooks and crannies where she could hide herself away—

'Sugar?' Ellie asked.

'Um, no thanks. Just milk.'

'Are you a gardener, Sergeant? I'm afraid it's rather got away from me this past year or so, but hopefully the weather will improve, and I'll be able to get out there and start to sort it all out again myself soon.'

'Please, call me Christine. No, I'm not a gardener.'

Since her father had died, she'd taken up the offer of a neighbour who'd volunteered to keep their front garden in order. He came cheap, only accepting the odd case of beer every now and then in payment.

'One day.' she said. 'I'd love a garden like yours. When I have my own place. But I'd have no idea where to start.'

Ellie laughed. 'The secret is to put the right plant in the right place and then let it do its own thing as much as possible. Then all it takes is a little clipping and dead heading here and there and mulching everywhere. Of course, James has tried his best to keep on top of things for us over the past couple of years. Since David became too ill—'

'I'm sure it's nowhere near that easy.'

Somehow, Sparks had never imagined Massey as a gardener.

***

Sparks carried the coffees and followed Ellie upstairs. At the top, on the landing wall, hung a huge family photo of a younger and very elegant Ellie with an attractive man she assumed to be her recently deceased husband, and three children. The girl with the mop of curls had to be Megan, and the older boy with the short back and sides and the serious expression could only be Massey. So the baby in Ellie's arms must be the younger son, Alex. There'd been another child too, she'd heard. Massey's full sister, who'd died when just a toddler.

'It feels odd seeing him as a child,' she commented.

'We were all children once,' Ellie said as she threw open the door of her studio. 'Here we are.'

'Oh wow!'

Sparks breathed in the scent of oil paint and turpentine. Her boots sounded loud on the stripped and polished oak floor as she turned around in wonder.

Directly above the huge room downstairs, the studio took up the whole width of the house. Three windows: two on the back overlooking the garden, the other on the side of the house. Canvasses of all shapes and sizes, most depicting landscapes and seascapes with huge skies, stood stacked against the white-painted walls, with one or two portraits here and there.

For the first time Sparks realised that Ellie herself had painted the two enormous aqueous abstracts downstairs.

Clamped to a wheeled contraption much larger and more complicated than any artist's easel Sparks had seen before, Ellie's work in progress faced away from her towards the windows, so she couldn't see straight away what it depicted. Another huge canvas. At least as big as those downstairs.

'Just put my cup down on the trolley there please,' Ellie told her. 'And you can sit over on one of the window seats if you like.'

Sparks got settled and then stared for a moment at the unfinished canvas. Dark hills and a sky full of ominous brooding clouds that reminded her of when she and Massey had been stuck on the Western Bypass last year in the middle of Storm Casper. She wondered if Ellie's art reflected her moods and whether painting gave her an emotional outlet. This canvas certainly appeared to reflect the deep sorrow of a soul in grief.

She shook herself and wondered why she was here. She knew why she'd come of course. To tell Ellie about the inquiry being shelved and Sonia's body being released to the family. But she could have done that just as easily on the doorstep. She didn't have to have accepted the offer of coffee and interrupted Ellie's work for any longer than necessary. But whether it was the feeling that this house wanted to embrace her if only she'd step inside, or Ellie's wonderfully welcoming nature at a time she could be forgiven for preferring her own company, Sparks had found herself saying yes, but she couldn't stay long. She glanced at the clock on her Fitbit. Portas had only given her a couple of hours.

Ellie squeezed a blob of emerald paint from a tube onto her palette. 'So tell me what on earth happened to your face, if it's not one of those things you police officers can't talk about?'

Sparks found she couldn't help herself. Briefly, she told Ellie about her mother's worsening dementia that had begun to manifest itself in bouts of physical violence. She made a joke of tripping over her brother's feet last night and falling against a wall unit in an effort to dodge her mother's claws. But she sensed that Ellie could see behind the jest to the pain beneath.

She took a last sip of her coffee and got to her feet. 'I need to go now. I'm sorry for laying that on you, Ellie. You have enough problems. You don't need to be concerned about mine.'

'Dementia is a terrible disease. But, you know, any time you need someone to talk to. Any time. I'd be happy to listen.' She selected a broad paintbrush from a jar full of them and ran her finger over the bristles. 'And you can't go yet. Finish your coffee. You haven't told me why you came. I assume it's about Sonia.'

So Sparks explained about the lack of forward motion on the inquiry and the need to shelve it. The file would remain open, she said, although it was entirely possible they might never discover who was responsible. But anyway, Sonia's body would now be released to the family so that a funeral could be arranged.

'Will you go?' she asked.

Ellie turned towards her canvas. 'I'm not sure. It's not like I knew her anymore. We were close when we were young, but we hadn't seen each other for decades. It was just a coincidence we ran into each other again recently. And her family probably blame me for her death anyway. If she hadn't gone outside to call me, that car would never have hit her.'

***

Driving back to HQ, Sparks thought about what Ellie had said. She'd never thought of it like that. If Ronnie Wragg had thought about it at all, he'd never given any sign he blamed Ellie for what happened to Sonia, at least not to the police. But there was a son too. Nicholas Wragg. She wondered what his thoughts were on the subject. Would he be feeling bitter towards Ellie?

And what on earth had made her open up to Ellie about her mother's violent episodes? It wasn't something she talked about. Not to anyone. Not unless she was forced to. Like when Portas put her under the microscope the other day.

For the rest of the journey back to base, she tried to think of a half-convincing lie to tell her colleagues next time they quizzed her about the cut on her face. Maybe she could tell them she slipped on rocks on her walk at Druridge Bay yesterday. Yeah, like they were going to believe that. Just like when Massey tried to tell her he'd smashed his nose last summer because he'd slipped in the garden, when all along she and everyone else knew that Helen must have hit him. No-one in their right minds believed it had gone down the way he'd claimed.

CHAPTER 25

Feeling guilty as soon as she entered the frenetic incident room atmosphere, Sparks forced back her shoulders and ordered the cogs in her head to switch up a couple of gears. A young boy's body had been found. Presumed, but not yet confirmed to be the missing paperboy, Leon Robinson, who hadn't returned from his round yesterday. The rest of the team had been full at it all morning while she'd been drinking coffee and licking her wounds in Ellie's studio. She needed to shove what happened yesterday to the back of her mind and put all her concentration front and centre on the case. Now.

She looked towards her desk, expecting to see Massey at the one opposite, but his seat was empty. Surely he'd be coming back now though. With the hit and run shelved, there was no reason to keep him away anymore.

'Sparks. With me.' Superintendent Portas had entered the room behind her.

They used what used to be Keegan's office, now free of the detritus he'd surrounded himself with.

'Where's DI Massey,' Sparks asked, before Portas could get a word in, attempting to keep an accusatory tone out of her voice.

'I need him where he is for the moment.' Portas scrutinised the injured side of her face. 'And I need to know that you're alright to be at work.'

Something thudded in the pit of Sparks' stomach. 'Of course I am, ma'am. I told you that.'

'You didn't look it first thing this morning. So, now you've had a couple of hours to pull yourself together I need to know if you have your head in the game or not. For starters, you need to tell me what happened to your face. And I'm warning you. I will know if you're lying.'

Sparks raised her eyes to the ceiling and sighed. 'It was just a little accident at home. My brother and his wife came over yesterday. My mother got up out of her chair suddenly and we both stood up at the same time to help her. I tripped over his feet and fell against the edge of a wall unit, which resulted in a cut and bruise on my face. That's it.'

Essentially, it was the truth, just not the whole truth. And she hadn't so much been trying to help her mother as dodging out of her way. But still.

'What happens when you have to come to work?' Portas asked. 'With your mother, I mean.'

'There are carers who go in on weekdays to help her with medication and a bit of personal care stuff. I've had one of those key safe things fitted, so they can let themselves in and out. And she belongs to a local dementia group, so they come and pick her up in a minibus three days a week. No idea what they get up to though.' Sparks sighed heavily and stared out of the window at the rain. 'It's not ideal, but … well, it is what it is.'

Portas sucked her teeth and regarded her for a moment.

'Alright then. This is how it's going to work until we see what it is we're dealing with here. I've asked DS Brown to step up. She'll be acting DI in Massey's absence and DC Scott will be an acting DS. They're both ready for it anyway. And you, DS Sparks, are going to be my bag man, for now.'

Sparks clenched her fists, then forced herself to unclench them. Portas intended to keep her under bloody scrutiny. For every minute of her sodding working day.

Portas raised an eyebrow, waiting for her response.

She gritted her teeth. 'Ma'am.'

'Good. Now, I want you to get out there and familiarise yourself with where we're up to.' She looked at the Fitbit on her wrist. The same model as Sparks' own. The same colour strap even. 'You have half an hour and then we're going out to see Leon's parents. I've already sorted a pool car. You'll be driving.'

'Ma'am.'

***

The main office was deserted now save for DC Ana Horvat, who, in her usual efficient manner, had updated the screen with everything they knew to this point. Leon Robinson. Turned fourteen last month. Lived in Ashington with his parents, John and Nicola Robinson, and two siblings: an older brother and a younger sister. Delivered papers for the Routledge Newsagent shop on Station Road and had not returned from his Sunday round, although he had delivered all the papers on his list. Found strangled this morning on waste ground between garages on the Filcher estate, not far from the location of his last delivery. No sexual interference, as far as anyone could see so far, but of course that couldn't be ruled out yet.

Madge Brown had taken Donaldson with her to interview the newsagent staff, while Paul Scott and Phil Jackson, who looked so alike they were often referred to as Tweedledum and Tweedledee, had taken a list of Leon's classmates and had arranged with the local school to see them one at a time.

As she studied the screen, DC Rob Laidler wandered into the office, slumped down at his desk and began pecking on his keypad between coughing and sniffing and blowing his nose. When he turned to look at her, she could see how heavy-eyed he looked.

'Do you think you should really be here?' she asked.

'Probably not. I haven't started spewing yet though, so I'm fine.'

'Yeah, right.'

Even if he hadn't caught the flu bug that raged through the ranks, it was still something she didn't want to catch herself and carry home to her mother. No way was she going anywhere near him. She wondered if she had time to go to her locker and collect the extra little bottle of sanitiser gel she kept there before—

'Ready? Portas asked from the doorway.

CHAPTER 26

On the drive to Ashington, Portas said very little, which made Sparks, who would usually prefer silence, fret a lot more than she should. She felt as if she were being marked out of ten on her driving ability with every manoeuvre she made, when really Portas must have far more important things rattling around her head right now. Hers couldn't be an easy job; parachuted in to take over from her predecessor, who'd been charged with murder and several other heinous crimes related to the historic grooming and abuse of a child. And then, already short-handed because of the fallout from all of that, and having to cover the vacant post of DCI herself, in her second week on the job she'd had to move her best detective to another team because of a stupid conflict of interest thing. And on top of all that, the staff she did have had all begun to fall like flies with flu. And now she had the murder of a teenager to contend with.

Sparks thought about it for a moment while she negotiated the North Seaton roundabout on the A189. Falling like flies might be a bit of an exaggeration, but it must be on its way if the state of Rob Laidler was anything to go by. And the virus had already decimated Northumbria Police ranks at other stations across the commands. She turned left at the next roundabout, negotiated two more, then drove up onto Rotary Parkway and through to the other side of town. The Robinsons lived in one of the old miners' terraced houses, where the fronts of the terraces had long narrow gardens and a footpath in between the rows, and vehicle access was only via the back lanes.

***

A Family Liaison Officer responded to their knock on the rear door, which clearly operated as the property's main access, with a letter box set in it at hip height. 'Sergeant Marie MacEvoy, ma'am. The family are in the front room waiting for you.'

Sparks followed Portas and MacEvoy through a kitchen diner and into a small lounge. Mr and Mrs Robinson sat well apart on a worn settee. He wore a grubby Newcastle United strip top and she a baggy sweater dress and leggings.

Between them sat a teenage boy, aged about fifteen or sixteen, and a younger girl, somewhere around nine or ten. By the looks of it no tears had yet been shed. The family all looked too shell-shocked, but it would hit them soon.

'John, Nicola, this is Detective Superintendent Lou Portas and um …' The FLO looked at Sparks and raised her eyebrows.

'Sparks,' she said. 'Detective Sergeant Christine Sparks.

MacEvoy gave a thin-lipped smile of thanks before turning back to the Robinsons. 'They've come to talk to you about Leon.'

'Thank you, sergeant,' Portas sat down in an armchair facing the family. 'Can I call you John and Nicola?'

John Robinson responded first with a faint nod, echoed by his wife.

'And you are?' Keeping her voice soft and non-threatening, Portas directed her question to the boy, but still he became flustered and looked at his lap.

This is Joey Robinson, ma'am,' MacEvoy moved around to sit on the arm of the settee next to Nicola Robinson and held her hand out towards the little girl. 'And this is Elsa.'

'Hi Joey. Hello Elsa. Do you think it would be okay if DS Sparks and I talk with your mam and dad just on their own first for a bit?' Portas drew a twenty pound note from her pocket. 'Sergeant MacEvoy, I'm sure I saw a shop round the corner that could sell something Joey and Elsa might like.'

It took a while to prise the girl from her father, but Joey looked relieved to be excused.

As soon as the back door had closed behind them, Nicola Robinson wrapped her arms around her body and released a howl of anguish. It came out as a series of soundless jerking coughs that used up all the breath inside her and forced her to take in a huge noisy gasp of air.

With a horrified expression on his face, her husband backed further away. It fell to Portas to grab hold of Nicola's wrists and talk to her gently until she calmed down. Only then did John Robinson shuffle along the settee and put his arm around his wife's shoulders. Sparks saw little husbandly concern in the gesture, only awkwardness and embarrassment. She asked herself how she might have reacted in the same situation and decided it was entirely possible John simply felt painfully uncomfortable with public displays of emotion. Or else he wasn't as affected by Leon's disappearance and probable murder as much as he should be.

'Now, Nicola,' Portas said. 'I'm so sorry we have to go through all this again, but we do need to find out what happened to Leon as soon as we can. Are you alright to continue?'

At the sound of her son's name Nicola almost lost it again, but Portas' soothing words calmed her down enough to allow her to utter the first words she'd spoken since they'd arrived. 'I thought he'd come in,' she wailed. 'I heard the door slam and someone running up the stairs, and I thought it was Leon, but it can't have been, because... because, his bed, he hadn't... It must have been... Joey.'

Both boys had keys to the front door rather than the back door, John told them, which led straight onto the stairs up to their shared room. With a door between the front living room and the stairs, often John and Nicola wouldn't see the boys coming and going so much as hear them. Yesterday morning, they'd heard Leon go out around 8 am to do his paper round.

'And where were you when he went out?' Portas asked.

'I was still in bed,' Nicola said. 'But John had got up earlier.'

'I was in the front room watching the telly,' John said.

'Do you not enjoy a lie in on a Sunday too?'

'I would. If it wasn't for my bowels. That's what always gets me up.'

Sparks shuffled her feet. *Lovely. Thanks for sharing.*

'So did you see Leon before he went out?' Portas asked. 'Didn't he come through to the kitchen for some breakfast?'

'No, straight out the door, as per usual.'

'And he'd go directly to the newsagent's and pick up the papers?'

'I suppose,' John said.

'And do you know where he went after that, which streets his round covered?'

John shook his head.

'I know it's a big round though,' Nicola said. 'There's not as many people have papers delivered anymore, you see, so there's lots of walking. Between the deliveries, you know?'

***

By the time MacEvoy returned, with Joey and Elsa clutching sweets and magazines, Portas had managed to chivvy at least the bones of the story out of the couple. As well as having an apprenticeship at a local garage, sixteen-year-old Joey had a part time job at a local café and was supposed to be working there on Sunday morning, but when he'd got to work he'd been told his services weren't required after all, so he'd come back home and gone straight upstairs to his room. So it had been his footsteps John and Nicola had heard, not Leon's.

'Would you not expect Leon to have come downstairs for something to eat at some point,' Sparks had asked. 'Or even just pop his head around the door to say hello?'

'He was in a strop,' John said, 'because we couldn't afford to pay for a school trip. So we were getting the silent treatment.'

'And he usually ate upstairs anyway,' Nicola added. 'Joey would bring food home, you see. Sandwiches and sausage rolls and things. Stuff that hadn't been sold by the end of the shift at the café, so his boss would let the staff take it rather than have it go to waste.'

As they were leaving, MacEvoy followed them out to the car. 'I don't imagine they've told you this ma'am, but John is not the biological dad of Joey and Leon. Elsa, yes, but not the boys. Just thought you should know. In case it should become relevant at some point.'

'Thank you, sergeant,' Portas said. 'We'll need the father's details. And you can do something for me. Find out, if you can, how long John was downstairs on his own yesterday morning after Leon went out.'

'I will, ma'am.'

***

At six o'clock, Lou Portas called the team together for an update. She'd sent Rob Laidler home earlier when she'd seen the state of him, yet they were still two up from the start of the day since they'd gained three civilian investigators – two of whom Sparks had previously worked with.

Portas opened the meeting by relating the information she and Sparks had gleaned from their visit to the Robinson's home. Then Madge Brown informed them that the owner of the newsagent's shop, a Mr Trevor Routledge, had called all the customers on Leon's round to confirm the time they'd received their papers. One of the houses, he'd said, was only thirty metres or so from where he'd heard Leon's body had been discovered and was a natural last drop for someone living where Leon did. So Brown and Donaldson had made that address their next stop and they'd discovered that Leon pushed the paper through that letterbox at a little before 10.30 am. No-one in the house at the time had seen or heard any disturbance, which they'd already explained to the officers conducting door to door enquiries, but it looked likely that Leon had met his death moments after having delivered that last paper.

Scott and Jackson had spent a fruitless day interviewing Leon's classmates, who all said they knew little about the lad out of school. No-one claimed to be or to know anyone who was a particularly close friend of his, and as far as anyone was willing to admit, he had no girlfriend either. They'd spoken to his form teacher, who'd said that Leon was a hard worker determined to do well in his exams, but that he was disappointed not to be able to go on his class geography trip at Easter. Especially since he'd have been the only one in the class not going.

At just after seven they called it a day. Sparks climbed into her car and sat for a moment staring out across the almost deserted car park. She touched the dressing on her cheek and wondered what she'd be faced with at home tonight.

CHAPTER 27

Thursday 11th January 2024

It took until Thursday to find anything at all relating to the Julie Probert inquiry. By then the team at the swamp had settled into a pretty efficient routine.

They had three rooms all next door to each other now, the second replicating the production line nature of the original. Blanket tub, rinse tubs, processing table, drying table and washing line, with Moodie in the third room – with an electric heater turned to high on the floor next to her – sorting out the dried material into specific inquiries and recording the information in a manner that could then be uploaded to HOLMES 2, the Home Office Large Major Enquiry System.

Keegan and Burke continued to work together, but at a faster speed now that they didn't have to worry about all the sorting and recording, while Massey and Brooks had quickly established a good working rhythm. As soon as they had a table of dry material, they stacked it and took it through to room three for Moodie to do her bit.

The process was still slow going, but much faster than previously.

'Eureka!' Brooks cried.

Within seconds, the others crowded round to see what she'd found. On the processing table, she'd eased open the cover of a manila folder and there, just legible at the top of the first page, was the reference number they'd been looking for, along with the name of the victim, Julie Elizabeth Probert.

'Is that the only folder?' Burke asked?

'It's the first one I've found so far. But look, I'm almost at the bottom of this box, so this can't be all of it.'

Burke gently lifted out the last folder from the box Brooks had been working on, laid it inside the blanket box to blot some of the flood water, then swilled it gently in the fresh water a couple of times. 'This has to be another,' he said as he waited for the water to drip.

And it was.

'Why the hell didn't they at least number the boxes as they repacked them before sticking them in the freezer?' Moodie demanded. 'How thick were they that they didn't think to do even that little thing? Anyone with any sense would have, surely.'

'The original boxes might not have been in the correct order in the storage facility,' Massey pointed out.

'Rubbish. If they'd been numbered, we'd know that the rest of the Probert stuff would most likely be in the following boxes.'

'But surely,' Burke pointed out, 'If these files were at the bottom of this box and there were no Probert files above, then it would be the previously numbered boxes that held the rest.'

Moodie clenched her fists and stamped her foot. 'You know what I sodding mean.'

'And it makes no difference,' Brooks said in a calming voice, 'since the boxes weren't numbered anyway.

Keegan picked up the discarded box lid from the floor. 'Here, lay it on this. We'll take this one next door and work on it straight away.'

***

Once Brooks had got down past the top couple of sheets that had suffered the most, the first folder looked to be mostly witness statements. Several handwritten statements attached by paperclip to typed transcripts of the same. The ink on both versions had faded but they all agreed it would likely be legible enough to read once dried.

'Well, will you look at this,' Burke called from the other room. 'These are all transcripts of detectives' notes. Look at this signature. I remember this bloke. Ken Parks. Detective Sergeant Ken Parks as he was then. I went to his funeral a couple of years ago.'

'And that's what we're stuck with,' Keegan said. 'How many of the detectives who worked this case all those years ago, are still going to be around today for us to talk to? Not one I bet. Not the ones who knew all the ins and outs of the case anyway. No offence Lonnie, but you were just a pup back then, one of the foot soldiers. The senior detectives would probably have had twenty years on you.'

'None taken,' Burke said. 'And you're right. The SIO in charge of Julie's case, DSU Stan Jobson, had a heart attack at the wheel of his car in the early nineties. Veered into the path of a big articulated wagon. Stood no chance. If he wasn't already brown bread from the heart attack, he was strawberry jam once the lorry finished with him.'

'Thanks for that, Lonnie, 'Keegan said. 'Lovely image to take home. But seriously, this is forty years ago. They'd already have been in their forties and fifties. Just like us now.'

Moodie put her hands on her hips and glared at him. 'Speak for yourself. *Sir.*'

Massey took in a breath. This wasn't the first time he'd noticed a touch of hostility in Moodie's attitude towards his ex-boss. Perhaps she believed demotion hadn't been a harsh enough punishment for Keegan's misdemeanours last summer.

Keegan laughed, looked at Massey and nodded his head towards Moodie. 'I'm not sensing a great deal of respect from this one.'

Moodie pressed her lips into an insincere smile. 'Some people deserve respect more than others,' she said.

'So how about we crack open another box or two,' Massey said, in an effort to change the subject before Moodie let her mouth go too far. He'd only reached his thirty-ninth birthday himself three months ago, so he hadn't been born either when Julie was murdered. 'You never know, we might get lucky.'

The discovery had given them an impetus. They carried two unopened boxes into each drying room, leaving six in the old shower room at various stages of defrosting. They'd have enough work to see them over the weekend. They set up more drying tables in another room too, and with Massey and Keegan running back and forth refreshing the water tubs, they all continued working long after their shift ended, clearing all four boxes. But with no sign of any further material from the Probert inquiry in any of them, Keegan decided enough was enough for the day and the rest agreed. But before they left, they took the time to haul more boxes up from the cellar to begin defrosting.

'Your turn for the launderette, Lonnie,' Keegan said, pointing to the pile of dirty and soaked towels and blankets.

'I did the last lot,' the older detective grumbled.

Massey, Brooks and Moodie escaped before they could be roped into taking a turn.

***

Switching on his car ignition, Massey held up a hand in acknowledgement as Keegan locked up, climbed into his own car and exited the car park, leaving Massey's the last one there, its LED beams like twin floodlights on the brick wall of the old station.

About to put the car into reverse, he paused when his phone rang. He clicked a button on the dash and Sparks' voice filled the car.

'Thought you should know,' she said. 'The garages next to where Leon Robinson's body was found, they're pretty much directly opposite Abigail Grant's front door.'

Shit.

There were coincidences, and then there were coincidences.

He rattled off a text to Brooks, who he considered to have formed more of a personal connection with Abigail than he had himself. By the time she replied, he'd got home, stripped off and had a shower, and then dressed again in clean jeans and an old rugby shirt in case he needed to go back out. But Brooks had spoken to Abigail by phone. She was still staying with her friend and Brooks had advised her to continue staying there for as long as possible while they investigated the murder of Leon Robinson.

CHAPTER 28

Monday 15th January 2024

Ellie crept into the crematorium behind the main procession and sat at the back, with a whole row to herself. She wore a dark coat, not black, with a mulberry dress underneath. She hadn't been able to bring herself to wear black today since it would have meant wearing the same outfit she'd worn for David. Her widow's weeds. And that wouldn't have felt right somehow, certainly not just two and a half weeks since she'd watched his coffin disappear behind those same curtains to be devoured unseen by flames. In fact, she couldn't see herself wearing that outfit ever again, And besides, black made her look so old and haggard.

Before she'd left the house this morning the funeral director had called to tell her David's ashes were ready to be picked up, and she absolutely couldn't cope with that yet either. Her David, the love of her life, reduced to a pile of grey dust in a wooden box. Where would she put him, for starters. It wouldn't feel right to hide him away in a cupboard, but equally she didn't want to have that box staring at her every time she walked past. David but not David.

But today was for Sonia. The day she too would be turned into a pile of dust. Two weeks to the day since their middle-of-the-night telephone conversation had culminated in the tragic incident that had ended her old friend's life.

She'd only come back here to this depressing place for Sonia. When it came down to it, it was also the place that had brought them back together after so many years. Sonia's red coat approaching the funeral car. Her hand print on the window of the limousine. 'Ells', she'd shouted. And although it had taken a little while for the information to work its way up through the fog of her grief, Ellie had known it was Sonia because no-one else had ever called her Ells; only Sonic. And Jools, of course. But Jools too was dead. Forty years dead.

Three friends who'd gone out to celebrate New Year all that time ago, and now only she was left.

Her insides heaved. She felt trapped. She shouldn't have come here today. It was too soon. But the service was about to start. She couldn't walk out now. She took a deep breath, put a hand on her chest and told her racing heart to calm down.

She only knew about the funeral from the Journal's death notices page. Ever since David's death she'd developed a morbid fascination for checking up on how many other people had lost loved ones before their time, like David. She'd reasoned it was a way of reassuring herself that the grief she waded through every day wasn't unique, that dying was a part of life, something that came to us all eventually; at least she hoped that's all it was, and that the compulsion to check would fade in time. She didn't want to end up as one of those ghoulish old biddies whose social life consisted entirely of attending the funerals of people she never knew.

At the front, in the seats reserved for closest family, where she herself had sat so recently, she saw the backs of three male heads. Sonia's husband Ronnie and son Nicky, she assumed, and someone else. The brother-in-law named in the funeral announcement perhaps, although she couldn't remember his name. There was a female head there too, the top of which barely came up to the shoulders of the three men. Perhaps that was Nicky's new fiancée.

Nina, was it?

Nicky and Nina.

Ellie had to put her hand to her face to stifle a snort of laughter at the sudden recollection of Sonia's opinion on that subject.

The service was short and to the point, with only one reading, delivered by the celebrant rather than a family member or friend, in which Ellie could find nothing close to a personal tribute for the woman whose remains lay in the ornate coffin disappearing from view as the curtains closed around it. Even the music – Michael Bublé singing about rain turning into tears on your face – smacked of a suggestion the undertaker might have made rather than something Sonia would have wanted. Although perhaps she might have. It wasn't like she'd really known Sonia anymore when she died.

***

Outside the crematorium, Sonia's son and the diminutive woman had already moved away from the entrance to conduct a heated discussion, but Sonia's husband and brother-in-law stood where Ellie herself had stood so very recently to thank those who'd attended and accept their condolences.

Not that she could remember much about it; she'd been too numb at the time.

She considered not going over, but then noticed the brother-in-law gazing at her – the man looked so like Sonia's husband, he could be no other. So she really had no option but to go and pay her respects.

'I'm so sorry for your loss,' she said as she reluctantly accepted his hand to shake.

'You're the old friend Sonia was on the phone to when she was killed.'

Oh God, here it comes. Exactly what she'd been afraid of.

But the man's startling blue eyes had a smile lingering somewhere near the back. At least he didn't look as if he blamed her for his sister-in-law's death.

'Yes, that's me.' She shook his hand more firmly this time in the hope he'd take the hint and release hers. 'I'm Ellie, and I'm so sorry for your loss.'

The man turned his head towards his brother. 'Ronnie, this is Sonia's old friend. You remember. The one she was on about running into after thirty odd years.'

Ronnie gave the woman he was talking to a final pat on the arm before responding. 'Sorry Billy. What did you say?'

'I'm so sorry for your loss,' Ellie said, feeling like a stuck record.

Ronnie Wragg stared at her for a moment. 'Huh, you're the one she went outside to call, aren't you? The reason she's dead.'

Ellie felt the blood drain from her face. Even though she'd expected his antagonism, she understood now what people meant when they wished the ground could have opened up and swallowed them. She should never have come, or at least she should have walked away as soon as the service had ended. She didn't know these people. She didn't even know Sonia as she was now. Or as she had been before—

'Don't mind him,' Billy said. 'If you're up for it, we're having a bit of a wake at the Brockwell Seam up in Cramlington once we're done here. You should come.'

Ellie claimed back her hand and said she'd think about it, yet all the way back to her car she had no intention of going to the wake, and every intention of driving straight home. How could she sit in the same room as the family of a woman who would still be alive if it wasn't for her?

But then she turned left onto the road from the crematorium car park rather than right and found herself driving towards Cramlington.

It was the smile she'd seen in Billy's startling blue eyes that had decided it in the end.

***

The Brockwell Seam, the name of which she'd heard had something to do with coal mining, felt warm and inviting as soon as she stepped inside. She hesitated just inside the door and gave serious consideration to whether she should turn tail before Sonia's family arrived and drive straight home, like she should have done in the first place. But she needed to at least visit the ladies before going. Then, just as she emerged back outside again, a long black limousine pulled up to deliver the funeral party to their wake.

There was nowhere she could hide.

Ronnie glared at her as he pushed past to enter the lounge bar. Nicky gave her a twitchy look, as if trying to decide whether to say something or not, so she knew his father must have told him who she was. Instead, he grabbed the shoulder of the tiny young woman at his side and bundled her through the lounge door ahead of him.

Billy climbed out of the limousine last. 'Ellie, I'm so pleased you could come,'

She stepped further away from the door. 'I'm sorry, I shouldn't have. I have to go.'

'Wait, you're not disappearing before we've even been able to get to know each other a little, are you? Come on, have a drink with me. Please Ellie.'

Ellie looked down at the ground. 'Really I can't. I've got my car with me and—'

'Just one. You could have a soft drink or a coffee if you really don't want to drink alcohol.' He fixed her with a raised eyebrows look and batted his lashes a couple of times, his eyes shining with an electric blue sparkle in the light of the winter sun they'd seen so little of lately. 'Please Ellie. I know you're recently bereaved too, so this must be difficult for you. I get that. My mother died just last month, and now Sonia. So can't we just have one drink together to toast absent loved ones?'

'I don't think your brother wants me here. Or your nephew. And I can't say I blame them.

'Sod them, first chance they get they'll be busy playing pool. They probably already are.'

In two minds, she looked up at him and felt the pull of his charisma. Perhaps two or three years older than her. Tall and broad. Still with a full head of coppery fair hair that glinted in the low sun and betrayed only the odd strand of grey. And possessing a cocky roguery so very different from David's dark and gentle studiousness. She knew she should say goodbye, walk away and get back into her car. And yet the magnetic attraction of his personality and those blue eyes felt so irresistible.

She sighed and shook her head at her own foolishness. How could she say no? She could have just one drink with the man, surely. Of course she could. It didn't have to mean anything beyond simply toasting Sonia's life.

Slipping her hand through the elbow Billy offered, feeling the solid muscle beneath the funeral black, they walked into the pub lounge together.

CHAPTER 29
Tuesday 16th January 2024

It was Tuesday afternoon before they found any more documents relating to Julie Probert's murder. Almost three full boxes of it, among the last batch of defrosted boxes. They'd worked late on Friday and had come in on Saturday too, the worst part being the forced inaction on the production lines while waiting for the boxes to defrost, which they eased by all jumping in to assist Moodie with the sorting, copying and uploading. By mutual agreement, they'd collected all of their electric heaters into one room, stood them up on crates around the still frozen boxes to keep them away from any potential water leakage, and kept the heaters switched on for every moment they were in the building. Health and Safety would have had a fit, but what they didn't know wouldn't hurt. And it had the desired effect, for as soon as they began pulling folder after folder of material relating to Probert out of one of the boxes, they hardly noticed the cold. In the first few folders they found more witness statements, what looked like hundreds of them.

'Mostly young people who were at the club that night, I'll bet.' Lonnie said. 'And witnesses to the brawl outside. Or participants. But the majority of them were off their faces at the time. Drink, drugs, you know the drill. So most of those we did manage to trace straight away could hardly remember their own name when we interviewed them, let alone a tiny scrap of a lass who may or may not have stood next to them at the bar or in the queue at the door, or walked past them at some point in the evening.'

'Brawl?' Massey asked.

'That's right. A huge fight broke out at the end of the night. A couple of lads having an argument. The bouncers ejected them not long before the lights went up. They were still arguing outside as the club started emptying. People took sides, one thing led to another, you know how these things happen. It ended up with fifty or so blokes scrapping in the street.'

'And in the middle of it all,' Keegan said, 'with everyone's attention on the fight, Julie Probert vanished without a word to her friends. And the next time anyone saw her was when a couple of blokes taking a short cut through a back lane on their way to the taxi rank tripped over her body. And then of course, when our mob finally turned up, the assumption initially was that she was a prostitute. Back lane, no knickers and all that. You know?'

'You were there too, sir?' Moodie asked, with a flash of her eyes and a wicked grin she directed squarely at Keegan.

'Bloody cheek. No I sodding wasn't. I was still a little kid in short pants, riding around on my Raleigh Burner BMX. But I remember seeing it on the news and hearing my parents talking about it. They refused to let my older sister out on her own for months on end. The mass hysteria the press whipped up went on for months too, partly because she was such a pretty scrap of a girl who looked so young and innocent in the photo they had of her, but mostly to have a go at our lot for not doing their jobs properly.'

'I remember, ' Lonnie said, 'they did a push for the tenth anniversary over the 1993/94 New Year. But nothing must have come from it, otherwise this lot would already have been digitised.'

'HOLMES – the original programme that is,' Keegan said, 'was up and running by then. Had been since just a couple of years after Julie's murder. But it was crap and so it wasn't used properly. She'd been dead for almost twenty years by the time we got HOLMES 2.'

They fell silent for a moment, until Keegan clapped his hands together and gave them a rub. 'Anyway children. That's story time over for the day. We've got work to do.'

'She was strangled, wasn't she?' Brooks said.

'Strangled and raped, yes.'

***

Another late one. By 8 pm they had all the boxes emptied and every document at various stages of drying and being recorded or set aside for further processing to make it more legible. That included what they hoped was the entire Probert inquiry file, made up of dozens of individual files and folders, some that had held up to a hundred pages each. Witness statements, investigators' notes, photos, maps and diagrams, postmortem report and more. Tomorrow Massey, Brooks and Moodie would concentrate on getting all the copying and uploading finished while Keegan and Burke devoted themselves to all the other non-Probert files. At least that was the plan, although Burke especially had a vested interest in helping towards finding the killer of Julie Probert after all these years. He wouldn't be letting it go easily.

Of course, if – when – they found Julie's murderer, they should also be able to identify a serial rapist and take him off the street through the familial DNA link. And if they managed that, then DCI Ray Flowers could no longer justify involving his team in anything to do with investigating Stevie Grant.

CHAPTER 30

Wednesday 17th January 2024

Wednesday morning first thing, the whole Operation Bryony team had gathered around a conference table at Area Control HQ. Massey still felt uncomfortable about counting himself as a member of Bryony. Not so much because of the people around the table here – except Flowers, and possibly Poole – but because the injustice of having been turfed out of the MIT still rankled.

Lou Portas and two extra bodies were also present. He'd already briefed Portas on Probert, and Flowers would no doubt have kept her up to date with the rest, so she must either be here to watch her boyfriend in action, or because of the extra bodies, one of whom was her counterpart over at Serious and Organised.

Detective Superintendent Don Elsom, a bruiser of a man with a pockmarked face, hadn't yet taken a seat at the table. Instead, he leaned against the wall and talked in a low tone to his DCI, Marion Baker of the Drug Squad, who Massey remembered from their mutual days in uniform. Baker leaned her head in close to Elsom and acknowledged everything he said with a series of economical nods and eye flicks but said nothing in return.

For a regular team briefing these were heavy guns in attendance. Something must be up.

Looking nervous, Flowers yanked on the cuffs of his shirt, jerked his chin and straightened his shoulders, before clapping his hands to draw everyone's attention. First he introduced Elsom and Baker, who both nodded and took seats at the table near the door. For their benefit, he did a swift round of introductions – so swift that Massey doubted the two could possibly have even registered most people's names, let alone commit them to memory.

Flowers then surrendered the stage to Portas, who looked around the faces at the table, her eyes alighting on each person in turn, before taking a deep yoga-like breath.

'It seems we've been upsetting someone's cornflakes.' She gave a grim smile and raised her eyebrows towards Elsom, who gave an equally grim smile in return. 'Our discreet enquiries about a certain dealer, who supplied drugs to at least two of our rape victims, have jangled someone's tin cans. DSU Elsom and DCI Baker are here today to talk to you about it. That is not the only new development we have to discuss today, but it's the first one up since our guests have somewhere else to be. I've already briefed them on everything they need to know, so without further ado...' She pinned her counterpart with a hunter's gaze. 'Detective Superintendent Elsom?'

Elsom leant forward and spread his elbows on the table. 'This won't take long folks. We really do need to be elsewhere. As said, we have already been briefed. And we in turn have already briefed DSUPortas and DCI Flowers. Now, plain speaking, that's me, so here it is in a nutshell. And do not mistake my meaning. Any roads that might lead anywhere close to any of Steven Grant's operations – and I mean any, no matter how small the connection to the man himself may be – are off limits to anyone but my team. Barring your rape investigation of course. That's still yours. Even Grant's daughter. So long as you stay away from Grant himself and his operations. So now, here's how it's going to go. You get anything relating to the work of my team, anything at all, and you bring it to us. DCI Flowers will funnel info to us via your DI Poole.' He nodded towards Poole, who sat next to Flowers at the top of the table like his Mini-Me. Then he patted the tabletop in front of Baker, who still hadn't uttered a word since she'd entered the room. 'Right. That's us done. We're off. Thank you for your hospitality.'

As the door closed behind them, Poole's expression turned mutinous. 'Excuse me ma'am, but what the hell was that?'

'Exactly what it sounded like, DI Poole. On this occasion, Serious and Organised are happy to take, but reluctant to give or to share. Take from that what you will.'

After a glance from Flowers, Poole stayed silent.

To Massey, and no doubt to everyone else in the room, it sounded very much like Elsom had an operation either in progress or imminent and was keen to plug any holes through which even the slightest snippet of highly sensitive information might escape. And he couldn't blame the man for that. There'd been plenty of rumours of Stevie Grant having multiple paid informers among serving officers on the Northumbria force.

***

'Now,' Portas said. 'DI Massey, could you please update the team on how far you've got in tracing the Julie Probert inquiry files?'

Massey nodded and then addressed the room. 'As you all know, DS Brooks, DC Moodie and I have been working with Operation Casper to locate the case files from the forty year old Julie Probert inquiry. That's the case that scored a partial DNA match to the semen found on the clothes Abigail says she was wearing on the night she was raped three years ago. We now believe we have all the files, or at least all that have survived almost forty years in storage and being flood damaged during Storm Casper. They are now all at various stages of being dried out and recorded.

'How come they were still wet?' Poole asked. 'The flood was six months ago.'

'Because someone had the sense to freeze them as soon as they'd been rescued. The files were stacked in fresh boxes, wrapped in bin bags and frozen. If they hadn't been, mould would have set in within days, which wouldn't only have destroyed the files, but would also have posed a serious health risk. So the boxes have been stored frozen in chest freezers in a number of decommissioned stations since then.'

'So surely you could just have collected the Probert files, and we could have dealt with them here,' Poole said.

Massey smiled. 'You'd think so. But as great an idea as freezing them was, it led to a huge headache in that it all had to be done in double quick time. Case files ended up being separated and mixed up with those from other inquiries, and none of the new boxes were labelled. Eventually, Operation Casper was set up to get it all digitised and to look at the cases afresh, but it's been an incredibly slow process. The boxes could only be defrosted a few at a time, with the smell from the original flood water horrendous and possibly a health hazard in itself. And the Casper team had only two members, so to defrost any more all at once and have them standing around would have risked the same problem with mould spores. And then folders of documents needed to be separated into their individual sheets so they could be read, and you can imagine how slow-going that would be when they're all sopping wet. They've had to be spread out to dry individually, then scanned, copied and uploaded under their individual case reference numbers. And of course drying hundreds of sheets of paper individually takes masses of space – another reason they could only do so many boxes at a time – although it did speed up a bit with us three there helping.'

Poole held up his hand. 'Alright, I get it. But how come there's been a DNA match before the Probert files were found?'

'Because evidence bags containing Julie's clothes were found early on. They'd become separated from the rest of the files and, rather than risk them deteriorating further once defrosted, the Operation Casper team sent them direct to the lab. It was pure coincidence that Abigail had brought her own frozen clothes in on New Year's Eve and that this team had sent them off to the lab too. And here we are now. A familial match.'

'And now you have all the files?' Portas asked.

'We believe so, ma'am. Everything that has survived anyway. There are a few papers that are still very hard to read,' he said. 'But we think we'll be able to improve that if we can create high quality digital images from them and use photo editing software to enhance them. Another couple of days and we should have it all sorted and ready to go.'

Flowers opened his mouth to speak just as Superintendent Portas did.

'Thank you, DI Massey,' she said. 'Please don't rush off when we're finished here. I need a word.'

***

While Massey wondered what he'd done wrong, Portas waited a moment for people to settle again. 'Now' she said. 'I need to talk to you about another new development. Another potential link has come up. But this time a link to a current homicide. To that of fourteen year-old Leon Robinson on Sunday last.'

A loud murmur went up around the room. Portas held up her hands for quiet.

'You may already be aware that Leon's body was found on the same estate in Ashington where Abigail Grant lives. That in itself is quite a coincidence, but now we have another, which makes the likelihood of either of them actually being coincidental negligible.'

She waited a moment for the murmurs to die down again.

'You'll all know – or if you don't, you shouldn't be here – that the only foreign fibres found on any of the rape victims bar Abigail and Jessica Elliot, have been of a variety so common they are virtually useless to us. Some sort of smooth surfaced sports gear. That's all we can say for sure. But now, here's the kicker. That's exactly what the lab has found on Leon. And that surely cannot be a coincidence.'

'You're saying Leon was killed by Musk Man?' Moodie's eyebrows were in danger of disappearing into her hairline.

'I'm saying I don't like co-incidences, and this is one too many for me.'

And it was way too many for Massey. Now they had a murder linked to a series of rapes that had already been linked to a forty year old rape and murder cold case. Thank Christ Abigail had been staying away from home with a friend for the past couple of weeks. Or at least he assumed that's where she still was.

'But Leon wasn't interfered with, was he?' Lieb said. 'Sexually, I mean.'

'That's correct. So what was the motive for his killing?'

Massey could think of only one thing. After all, Abigail lived there. 'What if he saw something he wasn't supposed to?'

'They were my thoughts too,' Portas said.

'He came back,' Brooks said.

Portas looked at her sharply. 'I'm sorry?'

'Two weeks ago. Abigail thought she'd been followed home. DI Massey and I went out to see her. There was no sign of anything untoward and we weren't one hundred percent sure whether there really had been someone or if she'd imagined it, which would have been perfectly reasonable given all the stress of coming forward and the fear of her dad finding out. But, just to be safe, we persuaded her to stay with a friend and we dropped her off there that night. As far as we know, she hasn't been home.'

Portas clicked her tongue against her teeth a few times. 'Any thoughts anyone?'

'I don't get how he could know she'd come to us,' Johnson said. 'unless he's been keeping an eye on her for all this time?'

'Or she does know him after all.' Lieb held up his hands to ward off any attack from Moodie. 'I'm not saying she knows she knows him. We've already discussed that the musk smell could be something he reserves especially for his attacks. After all, if that's the only way any of the victims could identify him, he's going to have the sense not to be covered in it the rest of the time. But that means he could be anyone. A boyfriend, a work colleague. Anyone.'

'So if he killed Leon because the lad saw him outside Abigail's house,' Massey said, 'what could he have been doing there? She wasn't home. Had he been in the house? We need to find out.'

'All of this,' Poole said, 'is on the assumption that Leon's death is linked to Musk Man, but what if it's totally unrelated. The fibres are as common as you can get. They could have come from anyone. It doesn't have to have been the rapist.'

'Too much of a coincidence, DI Poole,' Portas said. 'And on that note, we're finished here. Or at least I am. DCI Flowers, I'm sure you have fresh actions to dish out. DI Massey, my office as soon as.'

CHAPTER 31

Massey knocked on the door and heard Portas bidding him to enter. Previously her predecessor's office, the room looked familiar but unfamiliar. Gone was the clinical sparsity of the Hitchins era, and in its place not so much an informal feel as a possibility of informality should the occasion warrant it. He had no idea if this one did.

The room smelt of coffee and held more furniture than before, which wouldn't have been difficult. Hitchins' huge desk still remained. It was probably too big to get out of the door anyway. In fact, the beast would need to have been put together in here. But where the previous occupant had preferred the desk to present an intimidating expanse of bare polished wood to those on the other side of it, Portas had arranged personal items on the surface besides her police issue laptop. A pottery pen holder, which looked like something a child would have made, sat near her left hand and for the first time he wondered about her family. There was a lush green plant on the desk too, and a photograph that faced away from the eyes of visitors, so he couldn't see if it featured a child – a son or a daughter maybe – who might have made the pen holder, or perhaps a husband who'd be devastated if her dalliance with Ray Flowers ever came to light.

'You wanted to see me, ma'am.'

'I did. I do. Just give me a moment and I'll be with you.' She gestured him over towards a small table by the window.

He wouldn't like to swear either way if it was a new addition or Hitchins' survivor. After all, he'd only ever been in the room in the past to receive bollockings, which Hitchins preferred to deliver from behind his desk, under the impression that the sheer size of it had lent him a certain gravitas. It hadn't. He'd been a short man for a copper, and the enormous desk had simply made him look ridiculous.

On the way across the room, he took a long glance at the contents of a tall bookcase that definitely hadn't been there before. Policing manuals, an operational handbook, several books on the criminal justice system and domestic violence, a whole shelf devoted to psychology, and another healthy looking plant.

To one side of the bookcase, a vintage coffee percolator with an elegant French turn to it sat on the top of a filing cabinet. It looked vintage, so would likely have needed a rewire to pass a PAT test.

Portas finished whatever she was doing on her laptop, then joined him and got straight to the point. 'Two things DI Massey, one of them a little sensitive, hence bringing you in here.'

Immediately, Massey knew what was coming, although not why. She was going to ask him about Sparks. He wasn't wrong.

'I understand there's been an arrangement in place for some time now for you to act as a mentor to DS Sparks. She has some anger issues relating to the death of her father that overspilled into her work, I believe.'

'She *had* some anger issues. She's fine now.'

Although Sparks had told him of her own conversation with Portas in this very room about the arrangement being ended, no-one else had told him that, and he didn't believe Portas had the authority to end it anyway without at least the input of HR. And if that had happened he'd have had an email from them surely. But either way, he wasn't about to drop Sparks in it with Portas. She was his friend, whether or not he was still her mentor.

'When was the last time you spoke to her?'

'On Friday ma'am. A swift catch-up call.'

'And when did you last see her.'

'To speak to? A week gone Friday. Why? Is something wrong?'

'You haven't seen the state of her face then.'

What?

'Like I said. No. Why? What's happened?'

'She claims it was an accident, that she tripped over her brother's feet when her mother got up suddenly.'

'Since we're having this conversation,' he said, 'I take it you don't believe her.'

'I don't know her well enough yet to know. That's why I'm talking to you. She has anger issues. She's the sole carer for her mother who has dementia. When she comes into work injured, I try not to make unwarranted assumptions, but I have a duty of care here.'

'I repeat. She *had* anger issues, which were perfectly understandable at the time.' He shook his head. 'You can't possibly think... No, definitely not. She couldn't do that.'

'Are you one hundred percent sure about that, DI Massey?'

'Yes, of course I am.' But was he? She hadn't volunteered information about any injury during their phone conversation. But on the other hand he hadn't gone round shouting about his own facial injury when Helen knocked him out last year. 'Didn't you say it's her who's injured, not her mother.'

'How can I be sure it's only her? Dementia patients can be a handful. If her mother went for her, would she be able to control her own temper?' Portas ran a hand through her hair and sucked her teeth. 'Look, I don't want to take this to HR unless it's absolutely necessary. She's had a tough time of it over the past couple of years from what I can gather, and I don't want to do something that might end her career unless I'm one hundred percent certain.'

'So what are you saying, ma'am? What do you want from me?'

'I want you to stay close to her. Like you were before.'

He sighed and looked at the ceiling. 'How can I do that if I'm off the MIT?'

'And now we come to the second reason I wanted to talk to you. I want to see what you're made of DI Massey.'

Massey knitted his brows. 'Ma'am?'

'I'm told you've completed the Inspector to Chief Inspector promotion process in the last few weeks and have all the SIO training modules under your belt. You're being considered for the vacant DCI post on the MIT – along with several other applicants, I might add. However, what with me filling in there in the meantime because we're so short staffed, and you moved over to DCI Flowers' team because of a little conflict matter, I've had no opportunity to see you in action. And now we have this three-way link, and I need to take a step back to take in the wider view. In short, I need to concentrate on being a Superintendent now. We're in the midst of an active homicide investigation, we have a serial rapist who could strike again at any moment, and we have a fresh chance to solve a forty year old rape and murder case that could also identify the rapist. But I'm still missing that key role on your MIT.'

Massey felt a little leap in his chest. Where was this going? He wanted back on his team, and he'd jump at the chance if that was what she was offering. And yet the rapes and the cold case had got to him. He wanted to follow them through too.

'So what are you saying, ma'am?'

'Here's what I'm thinking, Massey. And I've already discussed this with Chief Superintendent Crowder. You're in a unique position. You have extensive experience of working homicides and all the underpinning knowledge you need for promotion, and you also now have first-hand knowledge of Operations Bryony and Casper. In short, you have more than just an overview of every link in this three way chain, and I want you to be working across them all.'

Whoa.

'In what capacity, ma'am? And what about DS Sparks?'

'As acting DCI, until the vacant post is filled. With Sparks as your bagman. If you do well – and I wouldn't be offering this if I didn't think you were capable – then it couldn't help but make your application sparkle in front of the appointments panel.'

'What about DCI Flowers, ma'am? How will he feel about it?'

'DCI Flowers has DI Poole back in the fold now, so I'm sure he won't be too upset.'

'I didn't mean about losing a DI, I meant about the role you want me to take on.'

Portas shrugged. 'A little diplomacy goes a long way Massey, and I'm told you have that in spades. DCI Flowers will continue as before. Having you working across the board as an acting DCI should help, not hinder. I will however insist that DS Brooks and DC Moodie continue working on both Bryony and Casper for now.'

He didn't feel quite as sure as Portas about how Flowers was going to take it.

'Look Massey, I already have Madge Brown acting up as DI and Paul Scott as DS, when ideally they'd have been required to take a promotion on other teams. None of this is standard practice from the NPPF official promotion process point of view, but the team is already down a DCI and this bloody flu epidemic is playing havoc with staffing across the entire force. I need to play the best game I can with the players I already have available, not shuffle the good ones off to another board, and Chief Superintendent Crowder agrees with me. So, what do you think?'

What did he think? He had nothing to lose. If he hadn't thought he was up to the role of DCI, he wouldn't have put in for promotion and applied for the vacant post. And Portas' proposal would not only get him back with his own team, with Sparks at his side, but would also allow him continued access to both the serial rape investigation and the cold case.

'When would you want this to start, ma'am?'

Portas looked at the clock on the wall and checked the time on her Fitbit. 'How about first thing tomorrow morning?'

CHAPTER 32

Driving back to the swamp after the briefing, with Robyn Moodie lost in her own little world in the passenger seat and happily singing along to the radio, Kirsty Brooks felt her phone vibrate in her pocket. But it wasn't until they pulled up outside the old police station that she had a chance to look at it.

Abigail Grant. She'd left a text message too, begging Kirsty to call her as soon as possible.

'You go in,' she told Moodie as she raised her phone to her ear. 'I just need to make a call first.'

Abigail picked up on the second ring.

'Hi Abigail, it's DS Kirsty Brooks.'

She heard sobs on the other end of the line.

'Abigail, what's wrong? Where are you?'

It took a while to calm the girl down enough to find out what was wrong, and even then just the bare minimum. Abigail had gone home that morning to pick up some clean clothes. On the doormat, she'd found an envelope full of photos.

'Photos of what, Abigail.'

'Of … of me,' she replied, before descending into a paroxysm of fresh sobs.

Brooks could hear another female voice in the background. 'Are you still at home Abigail? Is that your friend with you?'

But Abigail must have handed the phone over, or had it taken out of her hand, for the person in the background now spoke directly into the phone.

'Are you the police?'

'Yes, I'm DS Kirsty Brooks of Northumbria Police. Who are you?'

'I'm her mother, that's who. She's just turned up at my door like the hounds of hell are after her, with some tale I don't understand about photographs. I want—'

'Can I take your name please?'

The woman tutted. 'Patti. Patti Rose. Are you coming over then?'

'What's your address.'

Brooks wrote down Patti's address, not far from Abigail's in Ashington, then contacted control to see if there was a patrol car in the area that could get there before her. Next, she rattled off texts to Moodie for abandoning her and to Massey to bring him up to date, then backed out of the space and headed towards Ashington.

***

As soon as he left Portas' office, Massey pulled his phone out of his pocket and found a text from Brooks. He called her on the way to his car, then instead of going direct to the swamp as he'd intended, he took the A19 northbound and headed towards Ashington and the address she'd given him. When he arrived, Brooks must have spotted his car pulling up outside for she came to the door to meet him.

'Abigail went home to collect some fresh clothes. No college today, so she could wait until it was fully light before going. Anyway, there were a few envelopes on the doormat. She picked them all up, put them to one side while the kettle boiled and she'd packed the stuff she needed, then she made a cuppa and went into the lounge to go through the post.

'There was a large envelope there with no stamp or postmark. When she opened it, she found a load of photographs. Of her. Taken in all sorts of places. Walking along the street, standing at a bus stop, through the window of her own house. She says there's even one taken at her friend's house where she's been staying – which to me is much more worrying.'

'Where are the photographs now?'

'She just dropped them on the floor, ran out of the house and came straight here to her mother's.'

'We need to secure them. Do you think she's in any fit state to go back there?'

Brooks screwed up her face. 'Not sure, sir. Her mother's not exactly helpful. More like she's getting Abigail even more worked up.'

Hysterical mothers were not Massey's forte. 'I'll wait here,' he said. 'You go and ask Abigail if we can borrow her key so we can go and let ourselves in.'

'Didn't Abigail say previously that she didn't want her mother to know about the rape?' Brooks asked when she returned with the key. 'She said she couldn't trust her mother not to tell her dad about it. So I can't understand what made her come here today.'

'Instinct probably,' he said. 'She is her mother after all. Or proximity. Maybe she's the only person Abigail knows within running distance. We need to be vigilant though. An angry father is bad enough at the best of times, but Stevie Grant?'

***

The place felt eerie as they let themselves in, but the staleness they might have expected of a house that had lain empty for almost two weeks, especially one that was usually home to two cats, had been overlaid with a strong smell of coffee. They discovered why as soon as they entered the lounge and spotted the large dark stain on the carpet and a fallen mug in the middle of it.

Scattered around the stain and spilling down from the arm of the sofa was a collection of full colour photographs, A5-sized, all of Abigail in various locations as she moved through her days, just as she'd described them.

'Don't touch,' Massey warned. 'We need to get forensics in. I think it's very likely whoever put these through Abigial's letter box is her rapist. And, if this is the first time she's been back here since we took her to her friend's house—'

'I know, they could have lain here for as long as two weeks now.'

'Or since the day Leon Robinson was killed.'

CHAPTER 33

Sitting at a small table in Café Des Amis, a bijou little coffee shop in Morpeth, Ellie opened her phone and tried to look nonchalant, as if every nerve in her body weren't already jangling like a fire alarm. She'd arrived early, which felt ridiculous now because she'd almost never arrived at all. Terrified of going, but eager to get there. How ridiculous was that? Even the fact she'd said yes in the first place had caused her nightmares ever since.

But not enough to cancel. Because why shouldn't she have said yes? This wasn't a date for goodness sake. Just lunch with a friend who happened to be a man.

A man who wasn't David. So soon after David's death.

This morning though, once the day was upon her and not just some theoretical event she could push to the back of her mind, she'd woken up paralysed with horror at the thought of what she'd agreed to. With Megan's face at the forefront of her mind.

Disapproving. Disgusted.

Because if Ellie was sure of one thing, it was that Megan would not think of this as just lunch with a friend. Especially not if she knew it was lunch with a handsome man she'd never met. With her father's ashes barely cooled in their little wooden box.

Ellie gathered up her handbag and gloves, preparing to leave. Billy would understand why she couldn't do this so soon after—

'Ellie, I'm so glad you came.'

Billy bent down and gave her a peck on the cheek, one cold hand briefly touching her face, and her belly gave the sort of flip she hadn't felt in years.

He must have come in the back door. She'd been so preoccupied she hadn't heard him approach, and now here he was, and it was way too late to change her mind.

'Billy. Um, hi.'

The frigid air outside had nipped his cheeks and the tips of his ears, and yet the sense of warmth from him as he sat down opposite her at the table for two, which now felt way too small, was intoxicating. He really was a big solid man. And an attractive man. Like his brother in terms of physical construction, and yet so very unalike too when it came down to the personality that radiated from within. How on earth had Sonia fallen for Ronnie instead of Billy?

Stop it, Ellie.

'You haven't ordered yet I hope.' He picked up the menu and cast his eyes over the café's regular offerings.

'Um, no, not yet.' She couldn't exactly tell him that until the moment he arrived she'd still been in two minds as to whether she should be here at all. 'I didn't...'

He smiled an impish grin. 'You thought I might not come, didn't you?'

Looking directly into his eyes, she saw that the electric blue sparkle she'd noticed the other day hadn't been a trick of the light after all; his eyes really were that vivid a blue. She looked away. Perhaps she should make a joke by saying she might have felt safer if he hadn't turned up at all, but she couldn't. He'd think she was flirting with him.

Embarrassed, she ducked her head. 'No, of course not.'

'Because you can be sure Ellie, that when I say I'll do something, I mean what I say. Always.'

She put on her brightest smile and nodded towards a chalkboard on the wall. 'They do lovely flatbreads here.'

***

Once Ellie had got over her initial reservations, she found herself enjoying Billy's company. Partly because he went out of his way to make her feel comfortable but mostly because their conversation never faltered. Not even for so much as a beat. They had so many things in common, so much shared history, especially back when they were young. They'd both loved the New Romantics movement and had haunted the same pubs and nightclubs during the same time frame. The Delby on Low Friar Street, Balmbra's in the Bigg Market. And JoJo's of course. They'd even seen the same bands live at the City Hall and the Mayfair. Siouxsie and the Banshees, Spandau Ballet, Human League. She and Billy could have been within touching distance of each other so many times in those days, they discovered, with no idea that death would bring them together all these years later.

'I'm trying to imagine what you'd have looked like then,' Billy said. 'I'm thinking a cross between Clare Grogan and Madonna. Am I right?'

Ellie laughed. 'A bit more extreme than that, I'm afraid. Head shaved on one side, beaded plaits and feathers on the other, and a huge platinum blonde bird's nest in between. I either set it so hard with gel and hairspray before going out that a hurricane couldn't have shifted it, or I wrapped it all up in twisted scarfs.'

Billy's blue eyes widened. 'Really?'

'Oh yes, no joke. And always a full face of make-up too for going out. Multi-coloured eyeshadow, masses of eye liner and painted lips like a Japanese doll. Do you remember what it was like?'

'I do. I'm trying to imagine you like that again now. What did you wear?'

'It depended where we were off to. Tatty denim dungarees most of the time for just knocking around, but I had a couple of go-to looks for special nights. Striped harem pants with a bolero jacket and little embroidered slippers. Or a black leather mini skirt, with an antique lace blouse I got from Tynemouth market, that had all these huge ruffles... I loved that blouse. All my friends were jealous. And I had this battered old leather waistcoat I'd wear over the top that I'd customised with chains and things...'

She noticed the expression in his eyes and had to turn her head away. 'You're laughing.'

'No I'm not. I'm picturing you in them.'

'Anyway, enough about me. What about you?'

'Oh you know. Somewhere between Adam Ant and Nick Rhodes.'

Ellie's eyes widened.

'You wore all the make up too?'

'Mostly just eye liner and face contouring, but I did the full whack too, for gigs, you know.'

'You were in a band?'

He laughed at the look on her face. 'For a little while, yes. The Blue Dragoons. We thought we should all be wearing those Hussar jackets, like the one Adam Ant wore – so we were hardly original. That didn't last long. Not once we realised how difficult the real jackets were to come by. But we were crap anyway. No great loss to the local music scene when we disbanded.'

'Where did you play?'

'The Barley Mow, the Broken Doll, upstairs at the Redhouse, that sort of place.'

The waitress came to collect their empty plates and take their order for coffees. Busy lunchtime sounds intruded into their bubble of memories for a moment; the clatter and scrape of cutlery, the throaty roar of the coffee machine and the voices of other customers wrapped up in their own conversations at neighbouring tables.

'Do you remember that awful free food they served there?' Billy continued. 'In the upstairs room at the Redhouse I mean. Well, not free exactly, since it was included in the entrance price.'

'Oh God yes. Sonia told me once that they used to buy in the buffet leftovers from some hotel nearby, because if they could claim they provided food then the licensing laws allowed them to keep the bar open until midnight. Otherwise they'd have had to close at half ten.'

Billy laughed. 'It was shit, wasn't it? The food I mean, wherever it came from. And it did actually look like leftovers.'

'A bit dark and dingy in there for me. We only went there a couple of times I think. And it hadn't been in existence for very long anyway before... Well, I stopped going out so much not long after it opened.'

'You mean after your friend died.'

Ellie jerked her head back. When Julie was murdered, he'd meant.

Yes, that was exactly what had been in her mind, but she hadn't wanted to give voice to the thought. And now he had, and his words hadn't just brought Jools back, but Sonic too.

'I'm sorry, Ellie. I didn't mean to upset you.'

He tried to take hold of her hand, but she snatched it back, then felt bad about it.

'No, I'm sorry. It's just... It's what we were talking about you see, when... Sonia and me, when... I mean, we weren't talking about the awful food upstairs at the Red House, that's not what I meant. But about... our friend, Julie. It was forty years you see. Since the night she died. On New Year's Eve. Sonia died on the fortieth anniversary of Julie's death. So it's a bit raw right now.' She squeezed back tears and clamped her lips together.

He tried to take hold of her hand again, and this time she let him. 'It's okay, Ellie,' he said. 'I didn't realise. I'm sorry.'

The waitress arriving with their coffees gave Ellie the opportunity to take her hand back without a fuss, but she still felt the imprint of his hands on hers, so big they'd swallowed her own hand whole. And they'd felt so warm now and... not rough exactly, but definitely not soft. The sort of hands that were accustomed to manual labour but didn't have to do it every day.

She sighed. 'You keep apologising, but you don't need to. I shouldn't have reacted like that, I'm sorry for being a wuss.'

'You've been going through an awful lot of grief recently. It's perfectly understandable. And, by the way, you've done a fair bit of apologising yourself since we met.'

'I'm sorry.'

And there I go again.

'Let's make a pact,' he said. 'No. Let's make two. First one, no more saying sorry.'

He waited until she gave a little nod.

'Second.' He shrugged. 'Not so much a pact, this. More an assurance if you like. Because... well, I love being in your company Ellie, and I think you're enjoying yourself too. Am I right? But I also appreciate how things are for you just now. So I want to assure you that this – whatever this is, between us – can be whatever, however you want it to be for as long as you want it. We can be just friends, if that's what you want, and maybe in time we can see where it goes. Or you can take me home now and shag my brains out if you prefer. I won't put up a fight. Honest.'

His eyelashes batted again over those brilliant blue eyes.

How many times through his life had that look got him anything he wanted?

Ellie couldn't control the bubble of laughter that pushed itself up from her belly.

Billy smiled and gave the eyelashes another bat. 'You're a beautiful woman, Ellie. I can feel myself being drawn to you. You're like a siren pulling me towards the rocks.'

Heavens.

She felt something writhe in her stomach. Something that took her breath away, that she hadn't felt for a very long time. She looked at her lap, so she didn't have to lose herself any further in those deep and dangerous pools of blue.

'Look at me Ellie, please.'

He held out his hand for hers.

'What I'm trying to say here is that I don't want you to feel under any pressure. I don't want anything from you at all unless it's something you absolutely want to give. So can we simply be friends? Please. For as long as you want us to be. And then one day, maybe. When, or if you want it just as much as me, we can see where it takes us.'

She looked up then and found his eyes waiting to claim hers. She searched for the sincerity in them and saw the beginnings of a twinkle emerge from the depths of seriousness.

He cocked his head to one side, grinned and waggled his eyebrows. 'And of course, you could still shag my brains out. If you like. If you ever fancy taking a wander with me down the friends with benefits path.'

CHAPTER 34

All the way home Ellie's hands shook on the steering wheel while guilt sat in her belly like a lead weight. The feeling had hit her as soon as she'd fished her car fob from her handbag and felt its familiar carved acorn keyring attachment that she and David had bought at the National Trust shop the last time they'd visited Wallington Hall together. Guilt, because she'd spent the last two and a half hours giggling and flirting with a man she hardly knew, less than three weeks after David's funeral.

David. The man she'd always thought of as the love of her life. As her saviour. Because at her lowest ebb all those years ago he'd picked her up from the ground – literally – and given her a future she could never have dreamed of without him. And yet the first time she'd ever set eyes on him he'd almost run her over and killed her, which was uncomfortable to think about now, after what had happened to Sonia.

She'd been a broken mess at the time. Abandoned by an abusive husband. Grieving the loss of Louise, her infant daughter. Her reactions dulled by alcohol and prescription drugs. No surprise really that she hadn't looked properly to check the road was clear. She'd stepped out, dragging a protesting four-year-old James with her, right into the path of David's brand new sports car that he'd only driven off the garage forecourt less than an hour before.

Her family had all believed she'd tried to commit suicide. After all, she'd tried once before and failed – hence the prescription drugs. But that hadn't been the case, at least not on that occasion, because whatever damage she might have chosen to inflict upon herself, she would never have knowingly put James in danger. But looking back years later from the safety and security of the life David had given her, she could see why they'd all thought that. If she'd never met David, she would more than likely have gone on to try to kill herself some other way. And she would probably have succeeded. So when it came right down to it, it was only because of David she was still here now.

But without him...

Could she continue living the way he'd have wished her to?

Look at what she'd done today. Already she was getting herself into a fix. Not even a month after David's death, and she'd all but thrown herself at another man. And she couldn't deny that she'd wanted so much to push it that little bit further and take up Billy's offer of commitment-free sex.

On only the second time she'd ever met the man.

How could she have even thought such a thing?

She had no idea what had stopped her from saying yes to him, but she thanked her lucky stars it had.

She glanced at the speedometer. God, she'd hit ninety miles an hour on the spine road without realising. She eased up on the pedal and wiped away tears with the sleeve of her coat, then wondered if perhaps she should put her foot down harder instead. Smash up the car and kill herself.

Or get herself arrested.

James would love that.

Oh good God, the kids. All of them: James, Megan and Alex. How would they feel if they found out what their mother had been up to today? And about what she'd wanted to do, for heaven's sake.

Megan especially. She'd developed a habit of dropping by the house unannounced at different times of the day, just to check she was alright, when it should be the other way around.

Ellie sucked in a deep breath and took her foot off the accelerator again, trying to banish the image of Megan walking in on her fifty-nine year old mother, naked on her marital bed astride a big hunky stranger and, as Billy had put it, shagging his brains out. Crikey. Megan would go into labour there and then. Ellie's new grandchild would be born on the bedroom floor aided by its mortified naked grandmother, while Billy hopped around in a panic trying to put on his socks and pants.

Ellie let go of a snort of gallows laughter, sniffed hard and blinked away her tears.

CHAPTER 35

'How you doing, Flash?'

Massey jumped. He hadn't noticed Keegan still sitting in his car as he'd pulled into the pub car park alongside it. He'd driven to the Snowy Owl in response to a text from Keegan about something found in the old files today, which had intrigued him enough that he'd agreed to meet up.

'Got an email from Lou Portas today,' Keegan said as they sat at a table in the far corner with their pints, well away from any other early evening punters. 'She wants us all at Area Command first thing tomorrow. But I'm sure you already know about that.'

Massey inclined his head. 'Things are getting interesting. She wants the different teams working together. Linked but still separate.'

Keegan nodded his head but then, in a classic Keegan move, went off on a tangent. 'Moody Moodie must have got her leg over last night. She's been like Little Miss Sunshine today. It's been a nice change from the usual snapping Nile Crocodile act anyway. Any idea what's going on there?'

'I heard she's been seeing Phil Jackson recently.'

'Ha, the class clown. That makes sense. Long may it last then. It might keep her from trying to rip me a new one whenever I open my mouth.'

Massey laughed. 'You ask for it most of the time.'

'I get enough of that sort of shit from the girls back home. I'm not a complete Neanderthal, am I?'

'You want me to answer that honestly?'

Keegan shook his head, then looked at him for a couple of beats before speaking. 'So then, are you going to enlighten me?'

'About what?'

'About why you and Brooks ducked out this morning and haven't been seen since.'

'Ah. We've been a bit tied up.'

Keegan raised his eyebrows. 'Come on then, give.'

Massey took a swig of his shandy. 'Okay then, fine. You'll hear about it in the morning anyway. Brooks got a call this morning from Abigail Grant. Someone's been taking photos of her in all sorts of places and has posted a load of them in an envelope through her letter box.'

'Jesus. You're thinking the rapist?'

'That's the consensus.'

'When?'

'The photos cover a huge time frame. From way before she came to us at New Year, she says. She's been staying with a friend for a couple of weeks, but she went home this morning to pick up some clean clothes and found them there on the door mat. We don't know when they were put through her letterbox, but—'

'You're thinking Leon's murderer,' Keegan said.

'Same fibres on Leon as on the rape victims.'

'Thin, given how common they are, from what I hear, but still.'

'So the MIT has spent the day gathering CCTV and home security camera footage from around the area, and revisiting the door to door, while Brooks has been dealing with Abigail and I've been trying to persuade her mother that it wouldn't be in anyone's interest for her to go running to her ex.'

'Which one of Stevie's bimbos is the mother? I might know her of old.'

Massey raised his eyebrows and gave Keegan a long look.

'Not in that way, you dick. I'm a one woman man, always have been, despite the rubbish that comes out of my mouth at times.'

'Patti Rose.'

'Thought so. I remember Patti. She held on in there with Stevie for far longer than most. She was a croupier when he first met her. And I knew her back then too. A right stunner, she was. They made quite the couple around town for a year or more, until he got her up the duff. He replaced her with a newer model while she had the kid and then he pimped her out. She went with the flow because it kept her and the kid in his orbit, for a few years anyway, until he got more heavily involved in running drugs and lost interest in keeping a stable of girls. Then I imagine he put her out to grass in a property he owned so he'd still be able to keep an eye on her, or on the kid anyway.'

'Abigail wants nothing to do with him, but Patti probably still has him on speed dial. And I have no idea if we've convinced her enough that it wouldn't be in her daughter's best interests for her to go running to him.'

'She'll tell him. She won't be able to help herself.'

'I hope for all our sakes that you're wrong.'

Keegan finished his drink and waggled his glass. 'Another one?'

'Go on then, one more. Just a shandy though.'

'Then you can tell me the rest of it.'

'The rest of what?'

'There's a bigger reason we're all expected at HQ in the morning. What is it?'

***

Massey didn't want to be drawn into a conversation about his new role until after Portas had announced it, not even with Keegan. His text said he'd found something, and Massey would far rather talk about that, whatever it was.

But by the time Keegan returned with the drinks, he'd decided it wasn't worth keeping anything from him that he would find out about anyway first thing tomorrow, even though the telling of it felt uncomfortable before he'd even started. Keegan's demotion to DI last year must still rankle, so he had no idea how the man would react to the news of his own promotion, as temporary as it was. Best just spit it out.

'Well?' Keegan said, as soon as he sat down.

'Portas wants me acting up as DCI and having oversight of all three inquiries from tomorrow. That's why she wants everyone there. Or part of it anyway.'

Keegan closed his eyes and said nothing for what felt like a long time.

'Is that going to be a problem for you?' Massey asked.

Keegan's eyes snapped open.

'What? God no. Not in the way you're thinking. Good on you. You've worked hard for it and Lou Portas will go down in my estimation if she doesn't recommend you to the panel for the DCI position permanently. It's just that I might have found something in the Probert papers – the main reason I asked you to meet me here. I thought it was just a weird little coincidence, but in my head now it's taking on the proportions of a hand grenade that could just put the mockers on your acting DCI gig.'

'How is that possible?'

'Remind me why you were moved over to Flowers' team.'

'I told you. Because I had a personal connection in a hit and run case. My mother was a witness, and the victim was her friend, who I'd recently met for the first time.'

'Okay, so remind me, what was the victim's name?'

'Sonia Wragg. Why?'

'And her husband's name?'

'Ronald Wragg. Ronnie. What is this?'

'A Ronald Wragg was interviewed in connection to the rape and murder of Julie Probert in 1984. He was there that night. Your mother's dead friend's husband was there.'

Shit!

***

They talked for another half an hour but eventually, once Keegan had driven away, he could put off the inevitable no longer. He had no choice but to inform Portas before she made any announcement about his new role in the morning.

He clicked her number on his phone and listened to it ring for so long he thought she wasn't going to answer.

'DI Massey. Not finished for the night yet? What's up?'

She sounded a little out of breath and he imagined what might be going on at her end of the connection. With Ray Flowers?

'Something's come up that I thought you needed to know about straight away, ma'am.'

'Sounds ominous,' she puffed. 'One moment while I get off this machine.'

He heard a beep. He must have caught her on a running machine rather than in the middle of a steamy session with her lover.

'Sorry to interrupt your night, ma'am,' he said.

'Not a problem. I'd done my five miles for the day anyway and I have some time before I go back out. Fire away.'

He told her about what Keegan had found today in the old files.

'You can't be serious.'

'I'm afraid so, ma'am. Now we have a four-way link. This time between Julie Probert's murder and Sonia Wragg's hit and run.'

'Which I had to remove you from because of your personal connection. For goodness sake, why is nothing ever simple over on this side of the Pennines?' He heard her clicking her tongue against her teeth. 'You realise what this could mean, don't you, DI Massey?'

He let out a big sigh, seeing his chances of making DCI disappear. 'I do, ma'am.'

'But hopefully it won't come to that. I need to speak to Chief Superintendent Crowder. I'll get back to you tonight.'

CHAPTER 36

'What's wrong with you?' Helen demanded. 'Stop pacing around, for heaven's sake. You're making me miss my programme.'

Massey looked at the TV. *The Great British Sewing Bee?* She'd never sewn a seam in her life. And she was watching from the hard drive anyway, so she was hardly missing it.

'Sorry. I'm waiting for a call.'

'Wearing a path across the carpet is not going to make it come any sooner. Haven't you got something... policey you can do? Preferably somewhere else.'

He sighed and strode through to the kitchen, just as the phone in his hand rang. 'Massey,' he said.

'Lou Portas here.' He heard the hubbub in the background. Multiple voices talking and laughing. A clatter of crockery. She must be out somewhere for a meal. 'Look, I can't talk here, so can I come round to yours for a quick chat? And it will be very quick. I'm in company.'

'Yes, of course.'

He gave her his address and she ended the call. Surely she didn't have to come all the way over here to deliver the verdict he knew was coming. She could have let him down just as easily on the phone.

***

Portas arrived in less than twenty minutes and parked at the kerb. The car's interior light revealed three other occupants as she stepped out from the driver's door, at least one of whom was male. As she walked towards him down the drive, Massey had time to notice how much younger she looked with her hair down and her face made up, and how the femininity of the outfit she wore made a stark contrast to the more masculine cut of the suits she usually wore for work.

'Ma'am. Come in out of the cold.'

'Thanks. This will only take five minutes.'

As Portas stepped across the threshold, the lounge door opened, and Helen's face appeared, instantly reminding Massey of a previous occasion when a woman had called on him unexpectedly at night, when Helen had jumped to all the wrong conclusions. He rubbed the bump on his nose and regretted not having interrupted her viewing again to let her know Portas was on her way.

'Helen, this is my new boss, Detective Superintendent Lou Portas. Ma'am, my wife, Helen.'

'Mrs Massey, I hope I'm not spoiling your evening. If I can steal your husband for just a few minutes, I'll be on my way.'

Through the still open front door, Helen must have caught sight of Portas' car with its internal light still illuminating the other occupants and seemed reassured by it. She held out her hand. 'No problem, although it looks more like James is disturbing your evening.'

'Not at all. This was on our way home anyway.'

'Are your friends alright out there? They're welcome to come in too, aren't they James?'

Maybe not so reassured then.

Portas gave a polite smile. 'Thank you for your hospitality, but no, this really will only take a minute and then I'll be out of your way.'

'Well, good to meet you anyway. I'll leave you to it.'

Massey took Portas into the kitchen and offered her a seat at the oak table.

'You have a beautiful wife DI Massey.'

He nodded. 'Thank you, ma'am.'

It was the truth. Helen was very beautiful. Throughout all the years of their marriage, he'd never failed to appreciate just how far above his weight he continued to punch. Even through the bad times, and there'd been a lot of those.

His fault.

'Right then,' Portas said. 'Enough of the niceties. I've spoken to Chief Superintendent Crowder. He made a comment about things always being complicated when you're involved. Care to expand on that?'

Massey grimaced and shook his head.

She looked him in the eyes and smiled. 'No? Thought not. But beware, I'm sure to find out what he meant, given time. Anyway, it's not something I need to worry about too much now, since the chief is happy for the arrangement we discussed earlier to stand. Apart from the fact we're so short-handed with this flu bug doing the rounds and there literally is no-one else available with the knowledge you have across these inquiries, he feels as I do. The likelihood of this latest discovery in a case that's been dormant for almost forty years impacting your work now is negligible. Guy Keegan tells me Ronald Wragg was ruled out of the Julie Probert killing back then, and he was in his house with more than a dozen witnesses when his wife was hit by that vehicle.'

Massey breathed a sigh of relief and felt a weight lift from his shoulders.

'So,' Portas continued. 'I'll see you at seven in the morning. My office. Full team briefing at eight.'

As he showed her to the door, Massey felt the adrenalin tingle of a new challenge reassert itself, already fraught with complications, any one of which could trip him up and put paid to his chances of landing Keegan's old job. The latest development in particular niggled.

He checked the time, picked up his phone and found his mother's number. She'd still be up. And perhaps she could tell him a bit more about Ronnie Wragg.

CHAPTER 47

'James. This is a surprise.'

'How are you, Mam?'

'I'm fine James, thank you for asking, but I know you wouldn't be calling me at this time of night to simply ask about my welfare. Anyway, I'm just on my way to bed, so perhaps tomorrow...'

In fact, Ellie sat curled up on one of the big settees in the kitchen, with a huge glass of pinot grigio in her hand – her second of the evening so far and, the way she was feeling, unlikely to be her last.

She'd shocked herself today with her instinctive but unwanted reaction to Billy's masculinity. And the fact she'd almost said yes to his suggestion... Heavens, just thinking about having sex with the man made her tingle all over. Nothing at all like the warm and gentle feelings David had always inspired. And it had taken her until just quarter of an hour ago – around the time she got up to refill her glass – to realise the difference.

Raw animal attraction versus deep abiding love.

But it hadn't made her feel any better to have identified the distinction. Because the fact that she could have fallen so easily for that animal attraction so soon after the abiding love had been lost had shocked her to her core.

She still loved David. She would always love him, for as long as she lived. And she had no wish to paper over that depth of love with cheap thrills, to sully David's memory with a quick... shag. Or more than one. What if she enjoyed the first time so much she couldn't help but go back for more?

So, as much as she loved her eldest son, with all this going on in her head, she really couldn't face a long drawn out conversation with him tonight about how she was faring in her widowhood. And anyway, James' talent for perceptive deduction would surely kick in at any moment. He'd pick up on some inflection in her voice and know something was up.

Just tell him you're too tired to talk to him.

But then, cutting him off like that would be sure to alert him anyway. He'd immediately assume something was wrong, and then she'd have him at the door instead.

'What's on your mind, James? Why such a late call?'

'Ronnie Wragg. Sonia's husband. I wondered what you know about him.'

Oh God. Billy's brother.

Ellie's hands started to shake. She put her glass down on the side table, almost toppling it on the edge of a tile coaster.

'Why are you asking about him? I thought the case was closed. I went to the funeral.'

'Calm down, Mam. It's alright. Nothing to worry about. Actually, it's nothing to do with Sonia's death at all. Ronnie's name has come up in connection to something else. Remember that cold case I told you about. Forty years ago. A murder outside that nightclub you used to go to. I just wondered if you remembered Ronnie from way back then. Maybe Sonia was already going out with him in 1983?'

***

Ellie had no idea how she managed to get through the rest of the conversation. She'd ended up telling James she had no memory of Ronnie Wragg from so long ago, when she had. She'd never actually met him back then though, and she was convinced that, at that point in time, Sonia hadn't either. But they'd all heard about him. They knew his reputation as a bad boy, and she remembered spotting him across the room a few times in various places, surrounded by all his unpleasant acolytes, always the most brash, and always looking for trouble.

So yes, she did remember him from back then. She'd lied to her son. And now she felt awful about it.

But she knew she hadn't seen Ronnie Wragg on the night Jools was murdered. Not in JoJo's, nor in anywhere else. Although that didn't mean he wasn't there. They'd done their usual round of pubs, everywhere packed out because it was New Year's Eve. Really packed out, not like nowadays. So many people, all jammed in so tight that even if you were too drunk to stand, you'd still remain upright. Ronnie could have been in any one of those pubs and she wouldn't have seen him. She probably wouldn't have even heard him.

Around ten that night they'd walked up to JoJo's from Balmbra's. No queueing. Straight in the door. They could bypass most queues in those days because they'd made it their business to get to know the bouncers, to stroke their egos with the odd accidental/on purpose too-close brush past, and the occasional suggestive whisper in the ear. Just enough to keep them dangling. No chance of them ever actually scoring. Their tactics even got them past the pay booth sometimes. And that's exactly what had happened that night at JoJo's. Then, once inside they'd taken up their usual position. Halfway between the sunken dance floor and the main door. Always in the DJ's eye-line. Posing and making eyes, because the DJ was hot, and they'd made a bet on which one of them would get off with him first.

If Ronnie and his cronies had been in JoJo's that night, they'd have had to pass where she stood with Sonic and Jools. She'd have noticed. Because normal people tended to give Ronnie a wide berth. Like a shoal of mackerel parting when a shark swims into their midst.

Yet now James was saying that Ronnie *had* been there that night. His name was in the old police files. He'd been interviewed about Jools' death. Sonia's husband, Billy's brother, could have been involved in Julie's murder?

But how could that be? If they'd never charged him, then he must have had an alibi.

Ellie went to take another drink of wine and realised she'd emptied her glass. She moved to the fridge to fill it up, then stood staring out into the pitch black of the winter night. Remembering.

***

It had been a long and eventful day, and tomorrow promised to be even longer. By rights Massey shouldn't have any problem sleeping – he never usually did – but tonight he couldn't settle. A bout of nervous dread over what the morning would bring had hit him from nowhere, despite the fact that both Lou Portas and the chief had expressed their confidence in him. Keegan had given his blessing too. And when he'd called Sparks earlier she'd sounded overjoyed to be getting him back.

He needed to make sure he justified their faith in him.

Flowers could be an issue. As an actual DCI, whatever Lou Portas thought to the contrary, her beau was hardly likely to take kindly to having someone merely acting up as DCI overseeing his work. And whatever stance Flowers took, his Mini-Me Poole was sure to follow.

He'd have to watch his back.

But there was something else causing his mind to work overtime tonight too. The conversation he'd had with his mother. He could swear he'd heard a note of defensiveness in her voice, but he had no idea why, except that it had something to do with his question about Wragg.

Had his mother lied to him? Did she know something about Ronnie Wragg from back then after all?

CHAPTER 38

Thursday 18th January 2024

It felt good to be back with the MIT. Like coming home after a spell abroad, even though he'd only been down the hall. There'd been handshakes and back pats as the core team arrived, which had heartened him. Sparks in particular had looked glad to see him, even when she realised he'd clocked the still evident damage to her face.

Now, a few minutes before eight, the kettle over at the coffee station spat out steam as it came to the boil for what must be the fourth or fifth time, and two stacks of extra chairs had been pressed into service.

Ana Horvat had achieved a miracle of organisation in next to no time, and the big screen displayed both the Leon Robinson investigation and the most salient points of Operation Bryony. A smaller screen had been wheeled in next to it and uploaded with the information Keegan, Burke and co. had gathered so far from the flood damaged files on the Julie Probert case, including the link to the Sonia Wragg hit and run inquiry.

As people arrived, Ana doled out the information folders she'd also prepared, which contained all the information on the screens but in greater detail, along with photos, maps and diagrams; victim lists and profiles; forensics results, and a mind map Massey had created during his sleepless hours that showed how and where the inquiries linked up.

Julie Probert's rape and murder forty years ago, now linked by DNA to the rape three years ago of Abigail Grant, who looked to be the first victim of the serial rapist the press had dubbed Musk Man.

The link between Julie's murder and the death of Sonia Wragg by virtue of the fact that Sonia's husband had been interviewed all that time ago in connection with the murder.

Then there were the similarities between fibres found on Musk Man's more recent victims and those found on Leon Robinson's body, as well as the fact that Leon had been killed on the same street where Abigail lived when an unknown stalker may have been posting photos

Yes, a couple of the links might be described as tenuous at best. More odd coincidences than solid links. But they were too numerous to dismiss out of hand.

As Massey had predicted, DCI Flowers hardly looked overjoyed after having been briefed on the new arrangement by Lou Portas following Massey's own seven o'clock meeting with her. On second glance though, the man looked a little pukey. Maybe the olive green of the latest suit just wasn't his colour, although his forehead bore a faint sheen of sweat too.

And there, right next to him, stood his Mini-Me, who must have received a fashion memo this morning for he wore a suit only a very slightly paler shade of green. Perhaps Poole had passed on his flu virus to Flowers in exchange for tips on sartorial elegance.

One thing though, if Flowers ended up on the sick with it, he'd hardly be a miss given the amount of time he spent away from the office in the normal course of events.

***

At a couple of minutes past eight, Lou Portas still seemed to be waiting for something to happen before calling everyone to order. Massey realised what it was when the door opened, and Chief Superintendent Crowder slid in to stand against the back wall.

Portas nodded towards him and clapped her hands to gain everyone's attention.

No-one so much as batted an eyelid in surprise when she announced Massey's temporary promotion to DCI and his new remit of oversight across all three inquiries, by which he gathered that the jungle drums had been busy.

He scored a few congratulatory nods and comments, and Keegan even gave him a proud wink, as if Massey could not have achieved such heights were it not for him.

Only DCI Flowers and DI Poole looked less than pleased.

For the record, given there were more than just the MIT in the room, Portas also announced the temporary acting promotions of Madge Brown as Detective Inspector and Paul Scott as Detective Sergeant.

'Right then,' Massey said, once Portas handed over to him. 'Let's get started. You should all have a folder containing material pertinent to everything we're going to cover this morning.'

His eyes roamed the room. 'Good. Looks like everyone has one. We'll start with Leon. Madge?'

Madge Brown moved to the front of the room. For the benefit of the other teams, she gave a precis of the investigation so far into the murder by strangulation of the young paper lad: the door to door, the POLSA team search of the area, and then onto persons of interest.

'We believe Leon to have been murdered around 10.30 am on the morning of Sunday the 7th of January just after he'd delivered the last paper on his round. We've ruled out the family. We don't believe the mother or the little sister to be viable suspects given the strength needed to kill in that manner, and at that time the stepfather, John Robinson, was in the back lane outside his home offering unsolicited advice to a neighbour on how to get his car started, while the older lad, Joey, was just arriving at the café he works at on a casual basis. Granted, when he got there, the manager told him he wasn't needed that day, but it would have taken him too long to get from there to the locus in time to catch Leon just as he'd delivered that last paper, so he's ruled out now too.

'We've found no-one Leon might have had a beef with, or who could have had a reason to kill him. We've spoken to friends, classmates, fellow paper lads and lasses. But by all accounts he was a quiet unassuming lad who kept to himself most of the time and stayed out of trouble.

'Now then, on to forensics. As you'll see from the report, we believe Leon was strangled with the strap of his own paper sack. But apart from the fibres from the sack, there is also a concentration of black fibres across the back of his coat and on his face that suggest his assailant grabbed him from behind and held a gloved hand over his mouth while dragging him behind the garages to finish him off. And, although those fibres are very common, they are identical to fibres found on recent victims of the serial rapist being hunted by Operation Bryony, which on its own is suggestive, but nothing more.

'As I said, the fibres are as common as they come. But when you consider the proximity of the locus to the home of one of Operation

Bryony's rape victims, Abigail Grant...' Madge pointed towards Abigail's photo on the screen. '...and that Abigail discovered an envelope of photos on her doormat that indicate she has also been the victim of a stalker over a protracted period of time, then it becomes more than just suggestive, although granted there's a two week window in which that envelope could have been pushed through her door.

'So we need to ask ourselves, are Abigail's stalker and the killer of young Leon one and the same, and is the killer also the rapist dubbed Musk Man?'

CHAPTER 39

Massey thanked Madge and looked for Flowers to take over, only to see him rushing out of the door at the back with his hand over his mouth.

'It seems DCI Flowers is indisposed for the moment,' Portas said in the midst of a couple of good natured jeers and sounds of mock regurgitation. 'DCI Massey, perhaps you could give the run down on Operation Bryony yourself.'

DI Poole shot a glower towards Massey. No doubt he thought he should be the one to stand in for Flowers.'

'No problem,' Massey said. 'I'll take it from where Madge left off, in that fibres identical to those found on Leon's coat and face have been found on five of the six confirmed victims of our serial rapist over a fourteen month period. The other one of the six did not report her ordeal until three months after the event, and by then she'd binned the clothes she'd been wearing at the time of the attack, so we had nothing to test. Abigail Grant is not among those six women.

While it's possible – likely even - that she was the rapist's first victim, this is not set in stone. The man who raped Abigail was not forensically aware. The man who raped the other six victims absolutely was. Abigail was raped out in the open. The others were all attacked in their own homes. He left Abigail covered in his DNA, and yet he left virtually nothing on the others.

Given those differences, we are keeping our minds open on whether or not we're dealing with one rapist or two.

'Now, the gap between the attack on Abigail and that on Sophie Robson, the first of the confirmed serial rapist victims, was almost two years. So we've been exploring the possibility that the rapist, realising he'd cocked up big style – in a manner of speaking – with Abigail...'

He paused to allow a collective groan to die down.

'... then spent the next two years perfecting his art by learning how to leave nothing behind that could identify him. He uses condoms now.

Probably goes double-gloved, just to be sure. Whereas with Abigail he rode bareback and even wiped himself on her dress when he'd finished.'

Several of the audience, particularly the women, grimaced.

'Of the six confirmed victims, every one of them has described the flimsy plastic sheet he lays out and rapes them on, and how he forces them to clean themselves afterwards with wet wipes. He brings the sheet and the wet wipes with him and then takes them away again when he leaves. But you'd still imagine that with so many victims we might have found he'd missed a hair or two here and there. But no. And I had a thought earlier that he could be a member of the back, sack and crack waxing brigade. Maybe he waxes before an attack to make sure he's baby smooth when he strikes so he's even less likely to leave any hairs behind.'

Looking around, Massey saw several men in the room wincing and felt a bit of a twinge downstairs himself. A couple of the younger officers, including Dan Lieb, cast their eyes to the floor.

'A wax could even be a part of his ritual. A little pain before the pleasure you might say.'

A ripple of uncomfortable laughter ran through the ranks.

'Some people call it a Bro-zilian, I believe,' Lonnie Burke said. 'Get it? As opposed to a Brazilian that women have. They're a lot more common than you might think.'

All heads turned towards the oldest detective in the room. 'Trying to tell us something there, are you Lonnie?' Keegan said.

'Don't be daft. Not me. I read about it, that's all. A lot more men go in for it than I would have guessed. Male intimate waxing is what it's actually called. Or MIW if you want the acronym. Actually, that bit I didn't read. MIW doesn't sound quite right somehow, does it? Not if you say it as a word rather than just letters. As if it's something nasty you're turning your nose up at. "Just off for my regular miw, love." See what I mean? It doesn't sound right.'

'None of this sounds right,' Keegan said.

'MOW would have been more appropriate,' Phil Jackson quipped. 'As in mowing the lawn. Going for a mow, you know?'

'Plucking hell.' Keegan said.

The room erupted in laughter.

Massey waited until everyone calmed down. 'Thanks for that insight Lonnie. Now back to business. As said, whether this is one and the same rapist we can't yet be certain, but we do know that Abigail was convinced recently she was being watched because she came to us on the 4th of January, just three days after finally reporting the rape that happened three years earlier, saying she was sure she was being followed. We found nothing, and we speculated that it could have been her imagination playing tricks, as a result of finally having reported what happened to her. But now these photographs prove she was right. And not only on that one time, when she sensed someone there, because even without Abigail's confirmation we can see by the different lengths of her hair and the clothes she was wearing that the photos were taken over a number of months. Years even. They could possibly even cover the whole three year period since she was raped.

'But, and it's a big but, we still need to keep an open mind because what if this is someone else? What if Abigail's stalker is not the man who raped her, or the serial rapist?

'On the other hand, think about it. If it was Musk Man who raped her, then she's his weak point. She's the one where he made all his rookie mistakes. His attack on her has all the hallmarks of a spur of the moment thing. A lot more personal than the others. It could be someone she knows. It was New Year's night. Maybe she'd spurned him, and he wasn't about to let her get away with that. Or maybe he's someone she doesn't even know exists and he just got sick of only looking at her from a distance.

'My point is that, with Abigail, he probably didn't go out with the intention of committing rape. Whereas now he goes equipped.'

'And if it isn't Musk Man?' The question came from Lonnie Burke.

'Then ditto. He must still see Abigail as a liability. If he's her stalker too, he probably knows she's finally come to us, although I doubt he could ever have imagined she'd have had the foresight to preserve the clothes she'd worn that night in her freezer. And she swears she's told no-one about that until she brought them to us. Not even a best friend. So now we have his DNA, and I'm ninety-nine percent certain he doesn't know we have it.'

'But sir,' Brooks said. 'If Abigail's rapist and her stalker are one and the same – and you can see how obsessed the stalker is by the sheer number of photos he's taken of her – then New Year's Eve must be a very special night for him. He'll probably see it as an anniversary. So isn't he far more likely to have been watching her then? He'll have seen her come to us. He'll know about the cool box. What other interpretation is he going to put on that.'

'That's a very fine point, Kirsty.'

How had he not seen for himself the importance the anniversary would hold for him. It made perfect sense.

'Have you had any success in tracing the source of the musk smell?' Lonnie Burke asked.

'Kirsty, would you like to take that one?'

Brooks explained the testing of toiletries they'd carried out with the victims in the hope that one of them would recognise a specific fragrance as the one worn by the rapist. All without success. 'We think it could be something he wears only when he attacks,' she said. 'Another part of his ritual.'

'Or the smell of the body wax,' Phil Jackson suggested.

Keegan laughed and Jackson's face flushed, but he continued with the subject.

'Seriously though, there can't be that many local salons doing that sort of thing. And I'd have thought any that do would be by appointment only. Maybe a bloke who is a regular would stick out more in people's memories, and there could still be appointment records.'

'Another excellent point. Thanks Phil.'

'Unless he goes in for the DIY approach,' Sparks said, with a wicked grin that widened as an involuntary hiss of imagined pain whispered through the audience.

'Back to the musky smell,' Donaldson piped up. 'What if it's something vintage? We've got a link to a cold case here, and a familial connection between the offenders, so what if it's something from back then that isn't manufactured anymore? Something Julie's murderer has kept at the back of the cupboard for all these years and passed on to a young pretender.'

Every member of the Bryony team turned to look at him.

Massey nodded. 'You could have something there. Could it be that the rapist is deliberately trying to emulate Julie's murderer? Creating a ritual out of what he knows of his relative's crime, like a special tool passed on to an apprentice? That could also explain why the victims have described the smell as being a bit rank. A forty year old bottle of aftershave is bound to have gone off. Good one, Andrew. Well done.'

'He's not killing them now though, is he?' John Land said. 'At least not his rape victims.'

'Don't forget Leon,' Sparks said.

That sobering thought silenced everyone, for a moment at least.

'Okay then,' Massey cut in. 'So now we've come to the Probert inquiry, DI Keegan, can you bring us up to speed on what's happening at your end?'

***

This time last year, the man had been a DCI, and Massey wouldn't have been given this opportunity if Keegan had not faced disciplinary action just a few months ago. If he'd continued as Senior Investigating Officer on the Murder Investigation Team, he would have been asked to oversee these inquiries, not Massey. But if the thought bothered him at all, Keegan didn't show it. Standing, he bared his teeth at the assembled teams and gave his beard a scratch.

'I'm not going to bore you rigid again with all the details on how a load of cold case files got damaged in last year's flood, then got frozen and gradually defrosted until all the information was preserved and uploaded to HOLMES 2. You don't need to know about all that. What you do need to know is that the first items we recovered relating to the Julie Probert murder were the evidence bags containing the clothes she'd been wearing on the night she was killed. A small amount of flood water had got into the bags, although the items themselves were relatively unscathed. But having been defrosted, we didn't want them hanging around any longer than necessary, because that would have run the risk that any evidence they carried would deteriorate further while we tried to locate the rest of the case files. So in December we sent them off to forensics. Then on New Year's night Abigail Grant brought in her own frozen party clothes.

'To say I was gobsmacked when informed our cold case had scored a familial DNA match with trace evidence found on Abigail's party clothes is an understatement. I mean, you hear of that sort of thing happening, don't you, but come on, not here.

'So anyway, there you have it. Julie's murderer and Abigail's rapist – who may or may not be the serial rapist known as Musk Man – share around twenty five percent of their DNA. That means they could be grandparent and grandson, uncle and nephew, or half-brothers. Personally, I'm not holding out much hope of them being half-brothers. That would likely make them anywhere from their late fifties up over today. Way too old to be enjoying ripping hair from around their arsehole. That's a young man's crack, don't you think?'

He bared his teeth in a grin again at all the groans and shaking of heads.

'Back to the point. Once the DNA results were in, and we'd established that neither already had form, the race was on to locate the rest of the case file, and for various reasons that aren't worth going into, that's been a pain in the arse to achieve. But we have them now.

'Granted, some of the more damaged papers aren't so legible anymore, but we have a plan for that. And in the meantime, we've found another little coincidence in that one of the men treated as a person of interest in the Probert inquiry forty years ago, just happens to have been the husband of a woman killed in a hit and run incident on New Year's night just gone – at the very same time that Abigail Grant was finally telling us of her ordeal at the hands of her rapist, who shares DNA with the killer of Julie Probert.'

DI Adam Poole raised his hand. 'Can I just clarify a point?'

'Fire away,' Keegan said.

'Wasn't the main witness in that hit and run the mother of DCI Massey?'

What the hell?

Murmurs rippled around the room.

Massey looked for Flowers, wanting to see the expression on his face, but he hadn't yet returned. Poole had stuck his own knife in.

Portas got to her feet, but Keegan held up his hand and jutted his chin. 'That is my understanding too, DI Poole, but that hit and run incident has been investigated and shelved. The peripheral involvement of the husband of that victim in another case forty years earlier is another matter entirely.'

'I have a point to mention too,' Lieb said before Massey could jump in. 'We know that Abigail's father is the drug runner, Stevie Grant, and I believe we could use Abigail—'

'I'll stop you right there.' Portas' voice betrayed her annoyance. 'We've already been through this with Superintendent Elsom. Beyond what was discussed and agreed at that meeting, I reiterate what I have said before. Abigail Grant is the victim of a horrendous crime, not some asset to exploit, and she will be treated as such. In fact we need to be thinking about how better we can protect her, not use her.'

'Ma'am,' DI Poole stuck up his hand like a child in class. 'DCI Flowers and I have been discussing the possibility of offering her a deal. Quid pro quo. Information on her father's operations in exchange for protection, and I—'

'Have you indeed.' Icicles hung from every word. 'I shall discuss that scenario with DCI Flowers when he is less indisposed.'

CHAPTER 40

'Well this is nice.' Sparks stroked the centre console of Massey's car, as if she'd missed the vehicle as much as him. And perhaps she had, if she'd been using pool cars for the past couple of weeks. 'Back where we belong.'

He put the car in drive and made for the exit onto Middle Engine Lane. Although still annoyed by Poole's malicious comment, he smiled. It did feel right to have Sparks by his side again, only this time as his bagman rather than his mentee.

Once he'd turned the car north on the A19, Sparks looked at him.

'What's Poole's beef?' she asked.

He shrugged. 'I expected some flak from Flowers over my new role. Seems, in his absence, his sidekick must have decided he had no choice but to take a swipe himself.'

'While his boss was chucking his ring in the bogs. Bad curry, do you think, or this flu bug?'

'Whatever. He's no good at work in that state.'

'And why might Flowers have it in for you?'

'Perhaps he thinks he would fit these shoes better than me.'

'He doesn't have any murder investigation experience, does he?'

'Not that I'm aware of, but he transferred from another force I think, so he could have worked on a murder squad there.' As soon as he said the words, it struck Massey that Lou Portas had also transferred from another force. From Cumbria. It would be quite the coincidence if that's where Flowers had come from too. 'What happened to your face?'

She put her hand to her cheekbone, the damage bare now of any dressing, revealing a straight vertical wound an inch long, surrounded by bruising on the turn from purple to yellow. 'Nothing.'

'It can't have been nothing, Christine. That cut looks deep. You should probably have had it stitched. Looks like you'll be left with a scar.'

'It's nothing. Really.'

He couldn't force her to talk to him about it, and he didn't want to betray that Portas had already told him what had happened, or at least what Sparks had chosen to tell Portas. She needed to want to tell him about it herself.

At the Moor Farm roundabout, they took the A189 spine road north towards Ashington. He wanted to see for himself where Leon Robinson's body had been found in relation to Abigail's house. He already had a pretty decent picture in his head from when he'd walked around looking for signs of Abigail's stalker. He'd even taken a walk around the garages on that occasion, but it had been too dark to see much. And then when he and Brooks had returned for the photographs, he'd been too focused on those to do much more than glance towards where Leon had been found, and it might just as well have been night-time then too since the clouds had been so black. That's why he'd wanted to come back now. He needed to see the place in daylight, with his mind focused on both Abigail *and* Leon.

He took the long way around the curving network of roads on the Filcher Estate, driving slowly around the u-bend of Avalon Place. At the top of the bend on the left, they passed a junction opposite a pair of detached houses on the inside of the bend, one of which he knew to be the last drop on Leon's paper round. Then the first of two pairs of semis on the left, each with a garage on its unattached side. Abigail lived in the third house along. So garage, house, house, garage, then a pointless narrow gap through which a fence ran, before Abigail's garage and house, and then another house attached to Abigail's and its garage. Next on the left, once the right hand curve straightened out, came two three-storey blocks of flats, opposite which ran a small access road that led to twin side-by-side terraced rows of six garages that probably belonged to, or were rented separately by the six flats in each block.

Massey pulled in, parked the car and they both climbed out.

Sparks pointed as they walked towards the back of the gap between the two rows of garages. 'That's where Leon was found. Looking from this angle, he'd have been partially concealed by the last in this row here, although his legs must still have been visible from either the parking area or from the flats should anyone have happened to glance along there.'

'And yet it was Monday morning before he was found.'

'Shitty weather,' Sparks said. 'It didn't rain, but it was icy cold and miserable, and dark. And his family hadn't yet missed him.'

They walked along the gap between the backs of this row and another row of garages on the other straight leg of the u-bend until they came to a pizza slice segment of grass and shrubbery, bounded by a detached house on one straight side and the last garage in the row on the other, with the curved pizza crust side facing directly towards Abigail's house. The u-shaped curve of the road meant that the garages ran offset and at right angles to the rear fence of the detached houses at the top of the curve, with a gap between the corner of each that would have been ideal as a shortcut for kids, but not so much for adults because of the branches that had been allowed to grow unhindered through the fence from the garden beyond.

'The stalker would have had a clear view into her front room from here,' Sparks said. 'Pretty much concealed too. He could have watched her anytime she had the curtains open, confident no-one was likely to see him unless he wanted to be seen.'

'But what if Leon did spot him. We should check that the POLSA team's parameters covered this end of the row. Can you sort that please?' He paused while Sparks made a note to follow it up. 'Maybe Leon did use this as a shortcut that day, despite these branches.'

'He'd have run right into the stalker.'

'Who likely knew Abigail wasn't home anyway, so he can't have been here to spy on her, which means he was here for another reason. We know he's aware she's been staying with her friend. He took photos of her there.'

'He *was* here to deliver the photos. Leon might have seen him putting them through her door rather than hiding back here. Maybe he even saw him coming out of her house.'

'No, they had to have been posted through the letterbox. The envelope containing the photos was on the doormat with the rest of her mail.'

'Stalker, rapist, burglar,' Sparks said, jamming her hands into the pockets of her jacket. 'Whichever way you cut it he'd have been hyper-vigilant. He'd have noticed if Leon was watching him. And he'd have known that even if the boy wasn't actively looking his way, he'd probably still have been able to say he'd caught sight of someone.'

'And this was around half ten on a Sunday morning, don't forget. The stalker couldn't assume there'd be no-one out and about. So walking around the streets with a black balaclava covering his whole face would have been a no-no. Even a covid face mask. Very few people walk around in the open with those on now, so even that would have drawn attention. Which means Leon would probably have seen his face, or at least a good portion of it, and that's why he had to die.'

'Poor kid,' Sparks said.

They both stood and considered the possibilities.

'We're making an assumption here,' Massey said, 'that the photos were delivered that Sunday morning, when it could have happened anytime. We could have it all wrong.'

And yet it felt right.

CHAPTER 41

Back in the car, Massey drove back onto the A189 and headed towards Newcastle.

Lorraine French, who'd carried out the postmortem on Leon, had agreed to give them half an hour of her time at eleven thirty. They'd be pushing it to get into town, parked up and to the mortuary on time though.

This would be the first time he'd seen Lorraine in a couple of months. Just last summer she'd stayed with him and Helen for a while during a time when she herself had been the victim of a stalker, who'd murdered her sister years before. Lorraine had gained a great niece then, who she'd never previously known existed. It had been a traumatic time for them, but he understood from what Helen had told him that they and Lorraine's parents had made great strides towards forming a tight family unit with the child since then.

He'd been surprised that the intense friendship forged between Helen and Lorraine during that harrowing time had survived. He'd never known Helen to embrace the whole best friends forever thing before, and especially not with a female who'd been his own friend for so many years previously. But the pair had bonded in crisis, and they continued to keep in touch. They'd even shared a few nights out together, although maybe not for a month or so now he came to think about it. But that was probably down to Christmas and New Year getting in the way.

The doors of the mortuary whispered closed behind them. They signed in, and since they weren't there to observe a postmortem and so didn't need to cover up, were allowed to make directly for Lorraine's office.

'Come in,' Lorraine called, her voice muffled by the handful of crisps she'd just shovelled into her mouth. Rubbing her hands together to dislodge crumbs, she told them to sit. 'Sorry. Starving. Missed breakfast and there's still a way to go before I'll get any lunch. Coffee?'

'No thanks,' he said, answering for both of them. 'Sorry we're a bit later than intended. Merry Christmas, by the way, and Happy New Year. How was yours?'

Lorraine's face lit up. 'It was wonderful. At home with my parents for the first time in years. Rachel there too. It was just …' She couldn't find the words, but that didn't matter for her expression said it all.

'How's the court case coming on?'

Lorraine shrugged. 'Oh, you know. There's still a way to go with the whole legal identity thing, but the DNA results have done a lot of the work. They showed the familial relationship. They proved that Rachel is my parents' great granddaughter, and my great niece. We're a proper family again now. Little Rachel has brought us all together.'

'I'm glad,' he said.

'What about you? Back in harness with the MIT, I assume, or you wouldn't be here. Christine's been missing you, haven't you Christine?'

Sparks raised her eyes to the ceiling. 'Oh, you know. Like a fart in a spacesuit.'

Massey gave Lorraine a brief explanation of his new remit.

'Wow, I'm impressed. There'll be no holding you back now. So then, you're here about Leon Robinson. Let me just get the information up.' She rattled her fingers over her keyboard for a moment, clicked enter a couple of times, then a double click. 'Yes, here he is. What do you need from me that isn't in my report.'

'Just a bit of insight. Like who did it. That would be useful.'

Lorraine laughed. 'As if. Right then, let's have a look. Fibres found on the boy's neck show that the strap of his own paper sack was used as a ligature, you know that already. Compression of the cervical blood vessels and tracheal occlusion, combined with suffocation – in this case a gloved hand over his nose and mouth – would have caused a complete and immediate lack of oxygen to the brain. In an adult male, brain death would have occurred in anything from four to seven minutes. But Leon was a teenager. Still just a child really. He didn't have the well-developed neck musculature of a man. In his case, death would have occurred in three minutes or less. However, he'd have been unconscious in probably less than a minute.'

'Can you tell us anything about his assailant?'

'Hmm. Well, judging by the angle of the abrasions on Leon's neck, I'd say he's tall. A good bit taller than Leon anyway. Not your sort of tall though James, but still over six foot probably. And he's strong. We can tell that by tracking the external force applied.'

'What sort of strong?' Sparks asked. 'Are we talking Incredible Hulk strong, gym bunny strong, or just the sort of strength an average male in a physical job, maybe a brickie, would have?'

'I think the Hulk would have taken his head off his shoulders, so either of the latter two. And another thing I'd say about him is that he has some nerve. I went out there when Leon was found. It's a big housing estate, and he was killed in the middle of a Sunday morning when anyone could have been about. Kids playing, residents using the garages, anyone. Three minutes is a long time to be prepared to stick around to make sure his victim was dead when someone else could appear at any time. Particularly if this was his first kill. He took a huge risk. So he's cool under pressure too.'

Massey caught Lorraine steal a glance at the clock on the wall. They'd taken up as much time as she had available and had interrupted her snack in the process. He nodded to Sparks. 'Thanks for your time Lorraine. We appreciate it.'

'My pleasure. Hope you catch the bastard soon. Oh and Christine, that cut looks nasty. You should maybe have had a couple of stitches in that.'

***

Sparks stomped up the stairs to the very top of the multi-storey, where they'd had to leave the car, and flung herself into the passenger seat. She waved her fingers towards the cut on her cheek. 'You want to know how this happened, do you? Alright, I'll tell you. You know my mother's going doolally. Well now she's living in the past. Like she's regressing. And half the time she doesn't even recognise me as her daughter anymore.'

In the tense jaw and clenched fists Massey saw the anger building inside her. He could see her grief too, as if she'd already lost her mother.

And in a way she had.

'All I am to her most of the time now is just this strange woman who keeps coming into her house. Which is my home too, by the way. But every time I walk in the door, she thinks I must be my father's flaming fancy woman. Eddie's floozy, that's what she calls me now. And really, you could not have met a more faithful husband than my dad was to her.'

She clenched her fists in front of her and gave an exasperated growl.

'And then the other Sunday. The same day Leon was killed, as it happens. She went for me. Claws and all. I dodged her and fell over my stupid brother's big feet. Ended up crashing into a wall cabinet. That's how I got this.'

Jesus. And he thought he had problems when Helen went into one of her strops.

'Is there nothing the doctors can do? What about—'

His mobile rang. He looked at the screen. Keegan.

'Take it,' she said.

He accepted the call and Keegan's voice filled the car.

'Flash. Wherever you are, whatever you've got going on, you need to get over to the swamp now.'

'I'm—'

'This can't wait.' Keegan hung up.

Massey looked at Sparks.

'Drive,' she said. 'And no more talking about me today.'

CHAPTER 42

Seeing signs of ice forming across the pitted car park, Massey made sure to park as close to the door of the old station as he could get. He didn't want either of them to break their necks skidding across icy tarmac.

Other than his own, the car park held four others. He recognised Keegan's and Burke's cars, and Brooks and Moodie must have arrived together in the pool car parked in between them. The other car, he couldn't identify. Someone else must be here. Massey wondered if that was the reason Keegan had called.

This was Sparks' first visit to the swamp, and she'd asked him to describe it to her on their way over, which took him the majority of the journey.

'All the paperwork is dry now,' he reassured her. 'And I'm told the wet boxes and bin bags are gone now too, so it's not going to be as bad as it was when I first walked in there.' But when Kirsty Brooks responded to their knock and they made their way through the labyrinth to the centre of operations at the back of the building, he took back what he'd said and apologised to Sparks for having misled her. The smell seemed to have permeated the very fabric of the building.

'The windows are all painted shut,' Brooks explained. 'And it's way too nippy to have them open anyway. Looks like we're stuck with the smell for the duration.'

'I'm sure DS Sparks will get used to it soon enough,' he said.

Sparks' expression told him she had no intention of staying long enough for that to happen. 'You should be wearing hazmat suits in here,' she said. 'With breathing hoods.'

'What brings you here today, sir?' Brooks asked. 'We didn't expect to see you. Not now that you're... you know.'

'We just need a word with DI Keegan.'

They passed one of the rooms that, last time he'd seen it, had still been set up with tubs of water and towel-covered tables. He noticed

Moodie and Burke in there with another man, who he assumed to be the driver of the fourth car. All the tubs and towels had been cleared away now to make way for some sort of apparatus on a table with a camera suspended from it, which he assumed must be for taking UV photos of all the papers too faded to read with the naked eye. The threesome, engrossed in their task, were oblivious to their arrival, even though they couldn't have failed to hear his banging on the door.

In the end room, sitting at a desk with a freshly printed A4 photo and a single sheet of discoloured and distorted paper in front of him, Keegan awaited his arrival.

'Thought I heard two sets of footsteps,' he said. 'But this is for your eyes and ears only Flash, so DS Sparks, you might want to go and familiarise yourself with the rest of the operation and leave us boys to talk. Close the door on your way out.'

Eyebrows raised; Sparks looked to Massey for confirmation.

He shrugged and nodded.

She turned on her heel and left the room, banging the door closed behind her.

'Was that necessary?' Massey asked, uncomfortable with the terse dismissal.

'You can let me know once you've seen what I've got. Sit.'

With gloved hands, Keegan shoved the discoloured sheet towards him first.

The document could only be one of the dried sheets from the Probert case, too far gone to still be legible. Sure enough, once he'd snapped on his own gloves and picked it up, he could barely read a word, although he could still see from the page layout, given he'd seen so many of them over the past couple of weeks, that this was an ancient witness statement.'

'We only have this first page of the statement photographed and enhanced so far. They're still working on the others. But when I saw the name of the witness, which is much clearer in the photo version, I thought you'd better see it before it goes any further. Not that we can stop it going any further mind. Moody Moodie wants this back to upload as soon as the other pages are done.'

He placed his fingers on the edge of the photo that Massey had been attempting to read upside down.

'Are you ready for this, Flash? Because, if I'm right, this is going to blow your mind.'

'Just get on with it.'

'Your funeral.' Keegan turned the photo and slid it across the desk, then sat back and folded his arms.

At first it didn't register. Despite the fact Keegan had pointed out that this was something to do with the name of the witness, he'd started by reading the handwritten statement itself, which was still far from a hundred percent clear, but a lot more legible than it had been before. Finally, when he could bear to look at the top of the page, he saw immediately why Keegan had called him.

Under 'Name of witness:' had been written 'Eleanor Carolyn Crewe.'

His mother's full maiden name.

'Bloody hell!'

'My sentiments entirely,' Keegan said. 'Or they would be, if she were *my* mother and I'd just been promoted and tasked with re-investigating a case she was involved in.'

***

'How did you figure out this is my mother when it's her maiden name?'

'I've no idea why, but when your stepfather died, and then again when Sonia Wragg was killed, the papers published your mother's full name. Eleanor Carolyn Morgan. Can't be many women with that combination of first and middle names.'

Massey bit his lip and shook his head. 'I just spoke to her last night. I called her and asked if she'd known Ronnie Wragg back then or had Sonia met him later. She said that no, she didn't know him at all then. And now this. She knew perfectly well I was talking about the night Julie was murdered. If she was there on the night, her most natural response, her only response, whether or not she knew Wragg back then, should have been, "I was there. The police interviewed me." That's not something anyone would forget. Even after forty years.'

'Maybe she didn't lie exactly. She might have genuinely not known Wragg. But do you see what it says in the first couple of lines of her statement? Not only was she there that night, but she was there with Sonia and with—'

'What? Julie? She was actually there at JoJo's with Julie Probert on the night Julie was killed. Good God, why didn't she say? She can't have failed to know what I was talking about.'

'Fucked if I know Flash. But – and I take no pleasure in saying this – it looks to me like she has something to hide. Something happened that night that she didn't tell us about back then. Something relating to Julie's murder, or else why the hell didn't she say?'

Massey clasped his hands above his head and blew out a long breath.

'And now here's you,' Keegan continued. 'Her darling little boy, with his shiny new promotion, tasked with re-investigating a case she could be up to her neck in. So you know what you're going to have to do, don't you, Flash? And you know what will have to happen then?'

'They'll crucify her, and there'll be nothing I can do about it because I'll be off the case.'

***

'What do you mean you need to drop me off?' Sparks demanded. 'What's going on? What did Keegan say?'

'Nothing to worry about. I just need to go and see Lou Portas.'

He'd called Portas while he was still in Keegan's office and asked for an urgent meeting. She'd told him to get himself there straight away.

He knew Sparks wasn't convinced. And in fact he did have lots to worry about. Mainly, why the hell was his mother being so evasive? He'd talked to her on two separate occasions about that night at JoJo's, and while she might not have outright lied to him, she'd certainly avoided telling the whole truth.

The first time, when he and Helen had called to see her on the first weekend after New Year, he'd said he was working on a forty-year-old case involving something that happened at JoJo's on a New Year's night. He'd noticed she'd refused to be drawn on specifics and had just rattled off a couple of stories from the time she used to go there. He'd assumed at the time it was the grief; that she didn't want to reminisce about a time before she'd met David. She hadn't lied exactly, but at the same time she hadn't told him she'd been there on a New Year all those years ago when something dreadful had happened and that she'd been interviewed by the police because of it.

And then last night, when he'd asked a direct question about Ronnie Wragg, in effect he'd gifted her a second opportunity to tell him about being interviewed by the police. It would have been natural for her to tell him about it, and the fact that she hadn't...

Jesus, if this were anyone else but his mother, he'd be demanding to know why.

Even though she *was* his mother, he sodding wanted to know why.

Could she simply believe she was saving him from something? Like from finding out about what she got up to as a young girl?

But no, that couldn't be it surely. He'd already gathered from some of the tales she'd told in the past that she'd been a bit of a wild child, and while he wouldn't care to know the gory details, he doubted it could be any worse than some of the things girls of his own generation got up to when they were young.

So why hadn't she told him? Was it possible she knew who'd murdered her friend?

Sparks persisted. 'What's so important you need to see Portas straight away, but you can't tell me about it?'

'It's not that I can't tell you. I just need to inform Portas first.'

'I'm coming back to HQ with you then. I'll wait for you.'

He parked the car up and they entered HQ together. Sparks peeled off towards the incident room while he carried on to Portas' office. He stood outside the door for a moment or two while he rehearsed in his head how he was going to explain this latest development. Then he squared his shoulders and knocked.

CHAPTER 43

'James.' Portas put Massey off his stride by her first ever use of his given name. 'To what do I owe this pleasure? Whatever it is, it sounds important.'

'It is ma'am. I think I'm about to throw a big bloody spanner in the works.'

She raised her eyebrows and sucked her teeth. 'I was going to suggest you call me Lou when there's no-one else about, but I think I'll reserve that privilege until I know exactly how big a spanner you're talking about.'

When he said nothing, she gestured to the table by the window. 'Right. That big. Sit, I'll pour the coffees. I assume by the look on your face you could do with one.'

He took a seat and closed his eyes, all the possible scenarios of why his mother had kept quiet about being at JoJo's with Julie on the night of the murder still pulsing through his brain. When he opened them again, a mug of coffee stood on the table in front of him and Lou Portas sat facing him.

'You're beginning to worry me,' she said.

He closed his eyes and took a deep breath. 'Okay, so you know how you took me off the hit and run because my mother was a witness?'

'I remember.'

'Well we've now discovered she was a witness in the Julie Probert cold case too.'

He couldn't bring himself to tell Portas his mother had also lied to him about being there, because he didn't think he could speak the words out loud yet. And it could still have been more innocent evasion than outright lie. Hopefully.

'And you've just found this out now, how?'

'DI Keegan's team have found her statement among the papers that had initially been too damaged to read. They're photographing the pages under UV light and playing with the contrast to enhance their content.

When I left the swamp half an hour ago, they had only the front page of my mother's statement done so far, which gave her name. DI Keegan recognised it and gave me a call, so I went up there to see it for myself. Obviously I... we thought you should know immediately.'

'The swamp?'

'The smell. It's very apt.'

Portas massaged her temples with the tips of the fingers. 'Why is nothing over here ever simple?'

'Ma'am?'

'Not five minutes before you arrived, I had a call from DCI Flowers' wife. As you'll have gathered, he became violently ill during the briefing this morning and had to go home. And it appears he won't be back anytime soon. He has the flu, and now he's probably also infected anyone else he came close to in the briefing.'

'Ma'am.' He sincerely hoped Flowers had spewed all down the front of his olive green suit and his William Morris tie. But how long would it be before Portas herself succumbed to her lover's lurgy?

'And it's not as if DI Poole has it in him to step up,' One hand on her hip, Portas pushed the other through her hair, and clicked her tongue repeatedly. She paced back and forward a few times. 'And there's literally no-one else we can call on. What a sodding mess.'

'I'm sorry, ma'am.'

'You realise we're going to have to reinterview your mother.'

'Yes, ma'am.'

'Oh for God's sake, stop calling me ma'am. It's Lou. At least when there's no-one else around.

'Thank you, ma'am ... I mean Lou.'

She stopped pacing and breathed in a couple of bracing breaths.

'I'm going to have to take this to Crowder but I'm pretty sure the only alternative that makes any sense, given all the circumstances, is to leave you where you are. After all, it's not as if your mother was ever implicated in the Probert murder.' She pinned him with a glare. 'Was she?'

'Not to my knowledge, no.'

'Good. Well then. That's the way it needs to go.'

She clicked her tongue a couple of times, thinking.

'Although you know you won't be able to have anything to do with any part of the inquiry that concerns your mother, don't you. We're clear on that, aren't we, James?'

'We are ma... Lou.'

'You say Guy is already on top of this.'

A statement, not a question. It sounded strange to hear Keegan referred to so informally in his presence by her. He nodded.

'That's good because instead of having all the strands under one umbrella, as planned, he's going to have to maintain the separation of the Probert strand for now. We'll need to keep it apart from everything else. He and Lonnie Burke can interview your mother. Hopefully, she'll have nothing new to tell us anyway and we can push on in a different direction.'

The way things were going, he didn't like the chances of that.

'Alright then,' Portas said. 'I'll take what we've discussed to Crowder. Hopefully he'll agree, and we can get on with the job without further delay before the whole squad ends up on the sick.'

As the door closed behind him, he heard Portas' voice on the phone requesting an urgent meeting with Chief Superintendent Crowder.

**

It was pushing four thirty when Massey entered the incident room. Sparks had spent the time he'd been with Portas writing up all the intelligence and suppositions they'd gathered from their visits to the murder scene and mortuary. Earlier in the day, he'd claimed Keegan's old office as his own. A glance through the door told him he needed to spend some time ploughing through the gathering pile of admin paperwork that goes with the role of DCI. With hopefully a permanent promotion riding on how he performed, he couldn't allow the pile to get out of hand. He'd give it an hour or so. It was way too early to knock off for the night anyway.

Sparks' head appeared around the door. 'Am I allowed to know now what that was all about?'

'It's nothing.'

'Bollocks. It's something.'

'It's nothing important.'

'Bog off, James. You don't jump like that to Keegan's tune and then high tail it to see Portas for nothing.'

No point in denying it, and zero chance of pulling the wool over her eyes. And when it came down to it, he didn't want to leave her out of the loop anyway. The whole team would have to know there's been another change. He wanted her to know first.

He sighed. 'Give me an hour while I try to make a dent in all this paperwork, then we'll get out of here.'

***

Sparks' car pulled up next to his just half a minute after he'd parked up. Thursday evening, pitch black outside, a tang of brine in the air, an icy wind pushing huge waves against the shore, and clanking the moorings of small boats in the tiny dogleg harbour. But the welcoming interior of the King's Arms enveloped them as they walked through the tiny lobby and into the pub. This was the first time Massey had been through the door since his stepfather's funeral, which was also the day he'd met Sonia Wragg for the first time. The only time he'd met her, as far as he knew, since he was too young to remember.

The place was almost empty, but he kept his voice down while he laid out what he'd learnt about his mother from Keegan.

'She won't have deliberately not told you though.' Sparks said. 'You can't have said specifically you were investigating Julie's murder.'

'I didn't. I couldn't. The first time I mentioned it, I simply asked her if she remembered JoJo's because I can remember her reminiscing years ago about having gone there when she was young. Just a casual question really, after she'd asked if I'd been moved back to the MIT. I said I hadn't but that I was working on a cold case that involved JoJo's. Something that had also happened on a New Year.'

'But you didn't ask her if she knew anything about the case?'

'Of course not. Why would I?'

'Well then. She'll have had enough death on her mind lately without having to discuss that of another friend so long ago.'

He'd had the same thoughts earlier, but it was good to hear someone else echo them. The fact his mother had neglected to tell him was perfectly reasonable from that point of view. 'But then when I asked her whether Sonia already knew her husband Ronnie forty years ago, she'd said no, that neither of them did.'

'What makes you think that was a lie?'

'It wasn't necessarily. But it gave her a second chance to tell me that Julie was also her friend, that they'd all been there that night, and that she'd been interviewed by the police. Why would she not tell me about that?'

'Maybe because it's painful still, especially at the moment. And, since you didn't ask a direct question about it, why should she tell you?'

'Why should she not?'

'Because she's still devastated about the deaths of her husband and an old friend. Have some bloody sensitivity, for God's sake.'

He laughed out loud. For the person most accused of insensitivity to be labelling him as such sounded ridiculous. 'You've met my mother a couple of times now. What do you think of her?'

'I think she's a normally strong woman who's going through a completely understandable period of frailty.'

'How do you think she'll cope with having it all dredged up again. With being reinterviewed about Julie's death.'

'That's a difficult one. It's bound to be traumatic, but maybe it'll depend on who interviews her.'

'Portas wants Keegan and Lonnie Burke to do it.'

'Good grief. To Keegan I mean. I know next to nothing about Lonnie.'

'He worked on the case the first time round, as a young PC.'

His phone buzzed and he opened the text message. Lou Portas. 'Call me,' she'd written. He swigged his pint off and stood. 'I need to call Portas and get home. See you first thing.'

Sparks looked to be mesmerised by the flames of the log fire, mulling something over. He thought maybe she hadn't heard what he'd said until she lifted her hand.

'Yep. See you,' she said.

CHAPTER 44

With his heated seat turned to the max, and the blowers going to clear the windscreen, he rang Portas from the car. Chief Superintendent Crowder hadn't been happy, she told him, but he'd endorsed all her suggestions, given the circumstances. Everything would go exactly as she'd laid out earlier in her office. Massey would continue as SIO of the Leon Robinson case and of the Musk Man rape cases, including Abigail, while Guy Keegan led the cold case investigation.

'I've already spoken to Guy about it,' she said. 'And just to make sure we have this clear James; I'll spell it out once again. You will have nothing whatsoever to do with the Julie Probert cold case inquiry until such time as your mother is cleared of any involvement whatsoever. Tell me you understand and agree to those terms.'

The way she said it, he wondered if she was taping the conversation. 'Yes, ma'am. I understand and I agree.'

'I'm sorry, James. It has to be this way. And it's not as if I'm saying you have to stay away from your mother. That wouldn't be fair on either of you, given your recent bereavement.'

That scenario hadn't even occurred to him yet, being too ridiculous to even contemplate. But he appreciated the fact Portas had thought it needed stating.

***

He was surprised to see no lights on downstairs as he pulled onto the drive, and just one solitary light in the front bedroom. Helen must have gone to bed already. He crept upstairs and found her propped up on a pile of pillows and looking as pale as he'd ever seen her.

'Are you alright?' he asked. She'd looked fine this morning when he'd left for work. Complaining of a headache, yes, but otherwise okay.

'Do I look alright?'

'Not really, no.'

The whites of her eyes had turned yellow. Sweat glistened on her brow in the blue light from the television that screened another rerun of *The Great British Sewing Bee*.

'I feel like shit. I was sent home from work this afternoon. Probably best if you sleep in the spare room tonight.'

Fine by him. He didn't want to catch whatever bug she had, although he probably had it already, given they lived together and shared the same bed.

'You *look* like shit. Can I get you anything?' He spotted the whisky glass on the bedside table. 'How many of those have you had?'

A couple of trebles probably.

She gave him a weak sarcastic smile. 'Thanks for the concern. Only a couple actually, warmed up with honey and lemon. You could make me a cup of weak tea though please. And can you bring up that other box of paracetamol from the drawer downstairs? I've already used the ones from the bathroom.'

'You need to be careful with the tablets. Don't take too many, especially on top of whisky.' He'd seen two or three fatal paracetamol overdoses in his time on the force, at least one of which had been accidental. Alcohol and paracetamol should only be consumed together in extreme moderation. But moderation was a word missing from Helen's vocabulary when it came to booze.

'Yes, doctor.'

Knowing she had no intention of heeding his warning, he shook his head and went to put the kettle on. It wasn't until he'd delivered Helen's cuppa to her and got settled downstairs with some music playing that he noticed he had a WhatsApp message from Keegan waiting. It must have come through while he was upstairs.

He opened the message and found a zipped folder containing a collection of high resolution PNG images waiting to be downloaded, each one – he assumed – a page of the full enhanced version of his mother's forty year old statement.

There was a caption too. 'Read at your peril,' Keegan had sent. 'You can't put a genie back into its bottle.'

And from that cryptic message, he gathered that his mother's statement contained details of her past a son had no business knowing. So why the hell had Keegan sent it to him? He knew he shouldn't have it, and if what it contained were that bad, and Keegan was any sort of a friend, he should have wanted to save him the agony of reading it.

Massey looked at the time the message had been sent. Four twelve. While he was still with Lou Portas in her office, before she'd got confirmation of her proposals from the chief and contacted Keegan. But, given the promise he'd just made to Portas, he absolutely should not have the document in his possession, let alone read it.

Full of indecision, his finger hovered over the screen of his phone.

Open or delete.

CHAPTER 45

Today had been a good day. For most of it Ellie had managed to take her mind away from all her worries by losing herself in her painting. Not the grief. She didn't think of that as a worry. She accepted it as a process she had to go through. She wore it as a mantle that had settled on her shoulders even before David's death, when he'd been so very ill before the end. She'd come to accept the weight of it and hold it close. She knew it would lift of its own accord, given time. But the lie she'd told James, her unwanted feelings for Billy, and whatever it was that Sonia had been trying to tell her when that car had mown her down; for the most part today she'd managed to leave all those niggling concerns at the door of her studio and lose herself in her work.

And then at around three, her daughter Megan and her little granddaughter Livvy had arrived. And if there was one thing guaranteed to drive selfish concerns from one's head, it was the wonder a two-year-old sees in everything she encounters. And the worry that a heavily pregnant woman might announce at any moment her waters had broken, of course. But they hadn't. Megan might look fit to burst, but she still had another couple of weeks to go before her due date. And anyway, Livvy had not been born on time, and nor had any of Ellie's own four babies. They'd all arrived late. So maybe Megan still had another three or four weeks.

Megan's husband Mark had arrived around five and they'd all enjoyed dinner together. Something from the freezer, granted, but that didn't matter. At least she'd remembered to take it out to thaw last night.

As soon as dinner was over, Mark had stacked the plates in the dishwasher, helped his wife to her feet and gathered up his sleeping daughter.

And now Ellie sat in her usual place on the settee with a glass of wine in her hand, waiting for the worries to emerge from their hiding place again. And with them would creep that sense of foreboding that had been gathering in strength from the moment Sonia had placed her hand on the window of the hearse, and called out to her by her old nickname, Ells.

Her phone jangled on the side table. A message. Oh God, from Billy.

Fancy dinner tomorrow night?

Ellie felt a warm twist deep in her gut.

CHAPTER 46

Friday 19th January 2024

Friday morning. Ellie's mobile tinkled and the Ring Video Doorbell that James had installed for her a couple of years ago sounded simultaneously. She sighed and balanced her paintbrush on the edge of her palette. On her phone screen she tapped the Ring app and saw two strange men staring into the camera lens, looking as if they were making a concerted effort to appear non-threatening. She tapped the two-way talk button.

'Yes?' she said, her tone brusque.

She didn't like interruptions from strangers while she painted. In fact she'd usually ignore the doorbell, but these too looked a bit dodgy. Best to let them know the house was occupied and they were being watched.

It was the bigger, shaggy-haired one with the full beard who spoke first. 'Mrs Morgan, I'm Detective Inspector Guy Keegan and this here is Detective Sergeant Laurence Burke.'

Ellie felt her whole body go cold as they each held their warrant cards up towards the camera for inspection.

'What do you want? I'm busy.'

'We'd very much like to speak to you.'

'I'm sorry, now isn't convenient.'

'We can wait until you've finished whatever it is you're doing.'

'What's this about? I thought everything to do with Sonia's death was over and done with now. I went to her funeral.' Given the questions James had asked her recently, she knew this was going to be about Julie, not Sonia. In seconds, she was proven right.

'I'm sorry Mrs Morgan,' the big man said. 'We're here on a different matter. Your maiden name has come up in connection with a cold case we're working on. We'd like to speak to you about that. Now, if you don't mind.'

'No. Sorry. I don't feel up to it right now. Not today.'

She could see the shorter, slimmer man, who looked older than the other by a decade or so, saying something in a subdued tone to his colleague. She could hear the low murmur of his voice but couldn't make out the words until he turned back towards the camera. 'Mrs Morgan,' he said eventually. 'We appreciate you've been having a difficult time of things lately...'

Difficult bloody time? Fuck you. Ellie could feel her temper rising. What right did he have... And what did they know anyway? Had James told them she was a fragile old widow who needed careful handling? And why wasn't he here instead of them? For God's sake, Jools was dead. It had all happened so long ago. Let her rest in peace.

Except that someone who'd been raped and strangled to death probably never could rest in peace, especially when the man who'd killed her still walked free.

An angry sob rose in her throat. She tried to force herself under control. She hated getting angry. Such a pointless emotion.

'... but this is not going away, Mrs Morgan. We need to speak to you. Today preferably. We can do that here, in the comfort of your own home, or you can present yourself at a police station. But one way or another, we do need to have a conversation with you.'

The paintbrush began to roll from the palette. She tried to catch it, but it fell, smearing aquamarine paint across the wooden floor she'd just scrubbed clean before she started work this morning.

'Oh for fuck's sake,' she cried, then clamped a hand over her mouth.

She heard the shaggy-haired man chuckle and could have sworn he said something about James. She stomped down the stairs and flung open the door, glaring up at the two men, who looked much bigger in reality than they had through the camera lens.

'Here I am. Ask me whatever it is you want to know and then bugger off.'

The shaggy bear looked at the ground, but not before she'd seen the twitch of his lips and the laughter in his eyes.

'Something funny?'

'Not at all, Mrs Morgan,' the older man said. 'But perhaps we could talk to you inside.'

Ellie thought about it while she tried to relax the tension in her jaw and her fists. 'I didn't catch your names. Show me your ID again.'

'I'm DS Laurence Burke,' he said, holding out his warrant card for her to inspect.

The shaggy bear held out his own warrant card. 'Detective Inspector Guy Keegan. Can we start this whole conversation off again inside, please Mrs Morgan?'

'I've heard of you.'

'I'm sure you have. Your son will have been calling me all the names under the sun at the time, no doubt.'

She took them into the lounge, a room she barely used, because she didn't want the memory of them in the kitchen when she relaxed in there later. If she were ever able to relax again after this.

She didn't offer any refreshments. If they were here to ruin her day, her life even, then they wouldn't be doing it with a belly full of her hospitality.

She told them to sit on the settee but remained standing herself.

'Wouldn't you be more comfortable sitting down while we discuss this?' DS Burke asked, indicating the armchair.

'No. Get on with it.'

DI Keegan's lips twitched again but he disguised what might have been the beginnings of a laugh by catching the end of his moustache in his mouth and giving it a suck. His eyes twinkled a dark grey green.

He'd be an interesting subject to paint.

'Fair enough,' he said, pulling some sheets of paper from a courier bag she'd only just noticed. He laid them on top of the bag on his lap and then tapped them with the end of a pen that had miraculously appeared in his hand. 'Can you confirm for me please that your name is Eleanor Carolyn Morgan and that your maiden name was Crewe?'

'I can.'

'And that on the 2nd of January 1984, in the name of Eleanor Carolyn Crewe, you gave a statement to the police concerning the rape and murder of Julie Elizabeth Probert that happened in the early hours of the morning on the 1st of January of that same year in Newcastle upon Tyne.'

'Yes.'

Why couldn't she control the tightness in her voice?

'Now, I have here a copy of the statement you made to the police at that time. You know of course that this all happened forty years ago and I'm sure you can appreciate that a lot can happen to paper files in that length of time. So, because of damage caused to these particular files, this is an enhanced photographic copy of your statement. The quality is still not the best, but it is mostly legible. See here at the end. That's your signature, is it not?'

Tears prickled Ellie's eyes. She wrapped her arms around herself and gave a stiff nod.

James should have warned her this would happen.

'Please, Mrs Morgan,' DS Burke said, reaching out a hand towards her elbow. 'Won't you sit?'

'You must have read my statement. So you'll know how embarrassing this is for me.' At least they both had the decency to cast their eyes down when they nodded. 'You must appreciate that this is not a subject I want to discuss with two strange men. Policemen or not.'

'Believe me,' DI Keegan said, with the sort of concerned expression plastered across his face that policemen must need to practice in the mirror. 'We've both seen and heard a lot worse than this in our time.'

Ellie couldn't keep a lid on it anymore. She felt the anger rising up in her chest like a kettle coming to the boil. 'I don't care how *fucking* worldly wise you *think* you are, Detective Inspector Keegan. You're not much older than my son, for fuck's sake. I am not going to talk to you...' She pointed a shaking finger towards DS Burke '... or you, about anything to do with my *fucking* sex life forty *fucking* years ago.'

Shoulders heaving, tears streaming down her face, Ellie clamped a hand over her mouth.

Both police officers stared at her with their eyes wide and their mouths open, probably wondering where the hell the frail widow had disappeared to. And no wonder. She couldn't believe what she'd just said. Oh God, the sentiment, yes, she'd meant every single word. But the language she'd used...

She'd seen something on social media a while ago. Some tongue-in-cheek mental health support thing. It said that if you don't give a fuck for too long, you end up carrying around too many fucks, and you have to get rid of them by giving a fuck now and then. Today must be her day for disposing of fucks. And she had a feeling it wouldn't be her last.

'I have a request,' she said, her voice shaky but under control now. 'Actually, it's not a request at all, it's a demand. It's the *only* way this is going to happen in fact. Because despite what you must think; what James must obviously think, I want to see Julie's murderer finally caught just as much as you do. I always have done. And if I have to go through all this *shit* again, I will. But not with you. Not with James. And not with any other man. In fact the only police officer I will speak to about any of this – the *only* one – is Detective Sergeant Christine Sparks. Is that clear?'

CHAPTER 47

'She said what?' Lou Portas exclaimed.

'You heard. She'll only speak to Sparks.' Leaning back in the visitor's chair, long legs stretched out in front of him and crossed at the ankle, Keegan glanced around her office, taking in the coffee percolator, the bookcase and the table by the window. 'I like what you've done with the place, by the way. Any chance of a coffee?'

'No there bloody isn't,' she snapped. Then she relented. 'Next time. I have to be somewhere soon.'

Keegan grinned. 'I'll hold you to that.' He'd much rather they shared a brew when they both had time to chat and enjoy it anyway. He'd always enjoyed their chats.

'What's she like then, Ellie Morgan.'

He smiled. 'She's magnificent. Strong, dignified, very well preserved for her age, with a little smear of paint just on her jawline...' He pointed towards his own hairy jaw. '... right here.

Portas glared at him. 'Oh for goodness sake, Guy. I meant...' But then she noticed the laugh he was trying to hold in. 'Clown. I meant do you think she might not have told us everything she knew back then?'

Keegan shrugged. 'Everyone changes over time. She was just a kid then. Nineteen. Shouldn't even have been allowed in JoJo's. They had a twenty-one age limit, yet she and her mates were in there regularly. And she admitted to me and Lonnie today that she still feels embarrassed about what she said in her witness statement.' He blew out a long breath and scratched his beard. 'You know what the job would have been like back then, Lou. Christ, look what it was like when we started out. Sexism was rife. Female officers had a really hard time.'

Portas looked at him over the top of her reading glasses. 'And you feel you need to point that out to me, why? Female officers still have a hard time today. And you're one of the worst offenders when it comes to the sexist language that comes out of that big fat mouth of yours, Guy.'

He winced. 'But not in my head I'm not. My girls won't allow me to be. You're right, it's the stuff that comes out of my gob that gets me into trouble. But I'm trying to change. At least since all that crap last year.'

'Hmm. You're lucky I know you so well.'

'Speaking of which, the word is you've been getting to know another colleague a lot better than you've ever known me. A married colleague.'

'What do you mean? Who are you talking about?'

'That ponce, Flowers. Everyone's talking about you shagging him.'

Portas' face drained of colour. 'What? You can't be serious.'

'Hand on heart. That's the word going round.'

'Oh for Pete's sake.'

'Not true then?'

'No it's not bloody true. Quite apart from the fact he's a junior officer, under my direct command. And married. You can't possibly think...' She shivered. 'Oh God no. No way is he my type. You know that Guy. And besides, I just wouldn't.'

'I didn't say it's what I think, but it's what others are saying. I've thrown in my two penn'orth in your defence, which may not have been the wisest move if they start looking at me as a candidate rather than Flowers.'

She closed her eyes and sucked her bottom lip for a moment. 'So what should I do about it?'

'My advice? Do nothing. It would only add fuel to the flames if you denied it. You're not the first to be the subject of a bit of unwarranted gossip, and you won't be the last.'

'It's a fine example of that still rife sexist attitude we've just been talking about though, because they wouldn't even think of talking about a male superintendent in that way, would they? And that brings us back to Ellie Morgan. You're right. The attitudes of the investigating officers back then would have left a lot to be desired.'

'No female officers on the team at all from what I can gather, just men. Really, it's a wonder a young nineteen-year-old lass had the courage to tell us as much as she did, because as soon as she opened her mouth – if not as soon as they clapped eyes on her – they'd have treated her as a scrubber, as if she were begging for it, simply for being in a nightclub.

She'd have been treated like the shit on their shoes. And if what she actually got up to that night was even wilder than she'd already told us, then she'd have bitten off her tongue rather than utter another word.' He chuckled. 'The Ellie I met today would have bitten off their heads, chewed them to a pulp and spat them out.'

Portas laughed too. 'I want to meet her myself now.'

They were quiet for a few moments while she closed down her laptop and transferred it to her bag, and he contemplated his fingernails.

'What do you think then?' he asked eventually. 'About Sparks.'

'I have some concerns, frankly.'

'We're not talking about an interview in custody here, but she is a tier three interviewer. She's proven herself to be an astute—'

'Yes, I know that, but I still have concerns.'

Portas gave a heavy sigh and then sucked her teeth.

'Alright then. Looks like I need another conversation with James. If she's to do this, then he's going to have to lose her again for a while. He still needs someone though, and if you're getting an extra person on your team, you're going to be over-resourced. What do you think of a swap? Christine Sparks for Kirsty Brooks.'

That was exactly the solution he'd already come to, but Portas still looked troubled.

She slammed her hands on the desk. 'Sodding hell. This whole bloody mess is like musical chairs. Why couldn't you have just sat Ellie down and insisted she talk to you.'

He held up his hands. 'We tried.'

She closed her eyes for a moment. 'I know. Sorry. No point shooting the messenger. Alright, I'll give James a call and he can tell Sparks. I gather she's already established a good connection with Ellie anyway, which has to be the one good thing about this. You speak to Brooks and tell her she's back with James from tomorrow morning.'

***

'My mother said that? I know she liked Christine when she met her, but—'

'That's who she's asked for,' Portas replied. 'And that's who she's getting. Starting tomorrow morning, Sparks will move over to DI Keegan's team for however long it takes. You'll have DS Brooks working with you in the meantime. Hopefully, your mother will have nothing of consequence to add to her old statement and we can all get back to the original plan.'

But if there was nothing of consequence, why the hell had she made such a fuss about not speaking to Keegan and Burke? Massey had a bad feeling about this.

CHAPTER 48

Ellie wore a fitted jersey dress in midnight blue that fell almost to the ankles of her knee-length tan suede boots. At least when she'd bought it the dress had been fitted. Now it didn't so much skim her curves as drape her bones, but it was good enough. She'd bought it from Fenwick's on a day out with a friend and had never worn it, so of all the clothes she owned that might be suitable for tonight it held the least association with David.

She'd decided to give a beautiful 1920s beaded handbag a rare outing too, having kept it wrapped in tissue paper at the back of her wardrobe for decades. Something she'd bought from a market stall in the early eighties. It belonged to a time before David, a time even before her previous marriage and the births of her children. A time when she might easily, had she just turned her head at the right moment, have spotted Billy playing with his band, talking to friends, or even looking right at her.

Stop it, Ellie.

He hadn't even arrived to pick her up yet and already she could feel his magnetism.

When she got the text from him last night, she'd thought about it for half an hour and then replied to say thank you but no, she couldn't go out with him. But then those two detectives had turned up this morning and ruined her day. So as soon as the door had closed behind them, before her brain had returned to rationality, she'd texted Billy to tell him she'd changed her mind and would love to go out with him tonight. After all, he remembered what it had been like back then.

She sprayed perfume on her wrists and dabbed a little behind her ears, then she squared her shoulders and gave herself her most confident smile in the mirror.

Fuck you, DI Keegan and DS bloody Burke.

And now she'd wasted another one. Did she have enough left to see her through everything she was going to have to face?

Billy arrived spot on time, a quality she'd always liked in a man, even when she herself had been at her most erratic. He lifted her chin and she thought he was going for her lips, but he kissed her cheek, letting her know with those vivid blue eyes how much he approved of the way she looked.

'I've already told you this Ellie, but I'll say it again. You are a beautiful woman.'

She didn't feel like it most of the time. Generally, she felt haggard and old these days. But it was like a shot of pure unadulterated nectar from the fountain of youth to hear him say it, and it robbed her of breath for a moment. So she simply smiled and allowed him to escort her out to the taxi he had waiting at the kerb.

'Where are we going?' she asked as the driver pulled out onto the main road.

'It's a surprise,' he replied.

So she sat back and tried to enjoy the ride, gathering from their direction of travel that they were headed into the centre of Newcastle. It wasn't until they turned towards the bottom of Westgate Hill that she began to be concerned. And when they pulled up outside the huge old, repurposed cinema building that used to house JoJo's, she felt her pulse pounding in her ears.

'Why... why have you brought me here?' she demanded, shaking her head in panic, pushing his hand away as he bent to help her out of the taxi. 'Of all places, why here?'

'Because it's a restaurant now and I thought you'd like to see what it's become. I thought... Oh, shit. Your friend.' His face morphed into a picture of abject horror. 'Oh Christ, I'm so sorry Ellie, I didn't think at all, did I?'

Ellie saw herself standing in the doorway of JoJo's. The bouncers holding her back. Protecting her, she'd thought at first, from the fight raging outside. But Sonic and Jools were already out there. She needed to find them. To make sure they were alright. And right in front of her, against a free-for-all of vicious writhing bodies, she saw a man, a boy really who she'd been speaking to earlier, flipping backwards into the air and landing on his back on the pavement. Felled by a single punch to his chin from a much bigger man, his head bouncing off the edge of the steps. She heard the sickening crunch of bone... And then she'd felt herself being dragged back inside JoJo's and heard the doors slamming shut to stop the fight spreading inside.

Or so she'd thought. At the time.

Billy climbed back into the taxi and directed the driver to Three Mile, a pub and restaurant on the Great North Road. He put his arm around her and drew her shivering body in close to his. She could feel the beat of his heart against her shoulder, strong and regular, her own heart fluttering like a trapped bird.

'I am so, so sorry, Ellie. I thought it would be nice to go to one of the places we both knew back then. I checked them out. Everywhere we talked about. The Delby is a block of flats now and Balmbra's is closed for renovations. I knew the Redhouse was still operating, but the menu was all pies and mash and, well, you deserve far better than that Ellie. But the Parisi Palace, JoJo's as was. It only opened last year, and it has rave reviews. I thought... But I didn't think at all, did I? Can you ever forgive me? Please, Ellie?'

He sounded so ashamed, so stricken. She grasped his free hand in hers and held it close to her heart.

CHAPTER 49

For the most part, by the time they pulled up outside Three Mile, Ellie had got herself under control and felt ashamed of the fuss she'd made. After all, Billy had no way of knowing what had happened to her that night, the same night Jools had been raped and murdered. He'd have assumed she'd panicked because seeing the restaurant that used to be JoJo's had brought back distressing memories of Julie's death.

It *had* brought back memories. How could it not. Particularly when she'd had detectives at her door just this morning wanting to rake the whole business up again. But Julie's murder wasn't what had sent her spinning into a panic attack.

'Double G & T coming up.' Billy let go of her hand with a reluctance that made her feel embarrassed all over again at her outburst, as if he thought she'd panic as soon as he let go.

While he got the drinks in, Ellie stared around her. She had no idea how old the place was, but it had originally been called The Three Mile Inn, not just Three Mile, because it stood at a point on the Great North Road that was three miles from Newcastle city centre, although where in the city the centre had been measured from she had no idea.

She'd been in here a couple of times many years ago with David in their early days together. But now she hardly recognised it as the same place. For a start, it was way more than just a drinking hole now. They might have shortened the name, but the building itself must occupy a footprint twice the size of the original. More a complex than a pub. With a pizza restaurant, and a coffee shop. And a three-story hotel extension.

God, she hoped Billy didn't suggest staying the night here together.

He returned to the table quickly and placed a drink in front of her that looked more like a treble than the double he'd said he was getting. He probably thought she needed it for the shock, and perhaps he was right. For all she'd thought she had her emotions under control, her hand still shook as she poured in the tonic and lifted the glass to her lips.

Billy took her hand again and gave her a look that conveyed both anxiety and contrition. 'Ellie, I am so sorry I put you through that. I can't believe what a prat I was to think you'd be happy going back to that place after what happened to your friend.'

'No Billy, I'm sorry. Truly sorry for ruining the evening. You weren't to know that I'd become a quivering wreck as soon as I saw the place again. I had no idea myself that would happen. And besides, what was that pact we made just the other day?'

They said it together. 'No more saying sorry.'

'So, if you can find it within yourself to forget the jibbering wreck I turned into back there, can we please restart the evening from this point and never, ever refer to that embarrassing episode again?'

'What episode?' Billy said, with a grin and a slow bat of the eyelashes.

Mesmerised, Ellie felt her insides twist. 'Just so you know,' she said, her voice husky all of a sudden. 'Getting me pissed will not get you into my knickers.'

Gazing across the table at her, Billy lifted her fingers and pressed his lips to them. 'We made another pact too that day Ellie, as I recall,' he said, 'and I fully intend to stick to it. This thing between us can be anything you want it to be. Just say the word. You're in the driving seat.' He kissed her fingers again. 'Only please be careful of that gear stick.'

Ellie giggled. She couldn't help it. The gin must already be going to her head.

***

After a second drink, smaller this time but still potent, Ellie asked for food. She needed a lining on her stomach if she wanted to avoid making a fool of herself for a second time tonight.

They ordered two sharing platters: a mezze board and a seafood board. But as soon as she watched Billy pick up a fish goujon, trail it through tartare sauce, raise it suggestively to his mouth and then lick batter crumbs from his fingers, she knew she should have opted for burgers instead. With those amused blue eyes fixed on her, every little mouthful now felt awkward. So she ended up having very little to eat. It was just as well his own appetite was healthy and so he didn't seem to notice.

It occurred to her that, other than the fact Billy was the brother-in-law of her deceased friend and that they'd frequented the same haunts in their youth, she knew nothing about him. In every conversation so far, they'd always got lost in reminiscing or ended up discussing the mutual attraction between them, to the point that she couldn't believe they'd never even mentioned their respective lives in the present. She knew nothing about his current life, and he knew nothing about hers.

She asked him what he did for a living.

'I work with Ronnie,' he said. 'In a way. We're builders.'

That accounted for the solid muscles.

'Nothing big, you understand. A bit of a family thing. Wragg and Sons. It was our dad who started the business off, although he's gone now. We each concentrate on different aspects. Ronnie buys up small parcels of land and builds from scratch while I do renovations, extensions, that sort of thing. It works well. A lot better anyway than it did when we used to work side by side all day.'

'Don't you get on?'

He laughed. 'We do. As long as we're not living in each other's pockets. Anyway, he's not so involved anymore in the actual building work. Getting a bit long in the tooth for it now.' He laughed. 'Don't look at me like that Ellie. I know. I'm no spring chicken myself. But he's three years older and he's had a few health problems from old injuries. I'm alright to carry on for a few years yet. I have a good team, so it's not like I have to do all the heavy work myself.'

'You look very alike, you and Ronnie.'

'We are very alike. That's the problem.'

'Does your nephew work in the business too? Will he take over from his father eventually?'

'Nicky? Not likely. Ronnie wants him to, but Nicky's not ready to settle down to doing hard work any time soon. He's enjoying being free and single too much. And I don't have any kids of my own, so the business will likely end up being sold once we're both too long in the tooth.'

'Maybe Nicky will come round to the idea eventually. When Sonia and I talked on the phone at New Year. You know, before... Anyway, she told me he'd just got engaged.'

'I thought you said you talked about the anniversary of your friend's death?'

'Oh, we did. We talked about both. In fact she rang me twice that night.'

He looked thoughtful for a moment. 'Earlier, you know, after what happened in the taxi tonight...'

Ellie shook her head. 'You promised to forget about that.'

He grinned and mimed pulling a zip across his lips. 'That subject is closed. But it got me thinking about Sonia. That must have been an emotional conversation for the two of you. You know, talking about your friend having been murdered on that same night forty years ago. And I wondered—'

Ellie stopped him. 'You think the upset of talking about it might have made her so careless that she fell into the road?'

For a while, she'd wondered the same.

'It did occur to me, yes. That and the fact she was so rat-arsed.'

'That's not what happened.' She didn't feel at all sure she wanted the conversation to go down this route, but it would be good to tell someone besides the police, who'd failed to find the person responsible.

'How can you be sure?'

'Because I could hear the car. And the more I think about it, the surer I am that it accelerated before it hit her. Now, you need to excuse me. Do you know where the ladies are in here?'

'You can't just leave the story there, Ellie.'

***

By the time she came back to the table, she found that Billy had got the drinks in again. She already felt unsteady on her feet, just like Billy had said Sonia was.

'You think someone ran over her deliberately?' Billy asked, as if she hadn't been gone for the past few minutes.

'Either that or whoever did it was drunk and playing racing drivers, and they didn't realize how icy the road was.'

'Did you tell the police about this? They interviewed you, didn't they?'

She took a gulp of her drink. Way too late now to worry about getting pissed. She was already there. 'Yes, and of course I told them what I could. But I wasn't there. I didn't see the car so I couldn't describe it. Hearing the tone of an engine change is no help to anyone.'

'But why the hell would anyone do that? Yes, Sonia could be bloody annoying at times... sorry, I know she was your friend but...'

Ellie smiled. 'I hadn't seen her for more than thirty years until my husband's funeral. She could be annoying back then too. But a good friend. The best.'

'What could she have done to upset someone that much?'

'No idea. I know nothing of her life before she died. And, as I said, it could have just been some drunken idiot using the road as a race track.'

Billy shrugged. 'Don't suppose we'll ever know now that the police have closed the case.'

'Oh, they won't have closed it yet. Just shelved it for now.'

Billy gave her a quizzical look.

'My eldest son is in the police.' She couldn't keep a smile from her face. 'He's just been promoted in fact, well temporarily anyway. He's acting Detective Chief Inspector now.'

Billy smiled too. 'I can see how proud you are of him.'

'Of all of them. I have two sons and a daughter. I had another daughter too, but she died when she was just a toddler. I was a mess for a while after that, especially after—'

Good grief, had someone flipped a switch that operated her tongue? Why on earth would he want to know all that?

He stroked his thumb over the back of her hand. 'I had no idea. You've had quite a tragic life, haven't you?'

She snatched her hand away, the drink making the action sharper than she'd intended. That wasn't the way she saw her life. She didn't want him – or anyone else for that matter, but especially him – thinking of her as tragic little Ellie.

'I have a granddaughter too, and another grandchild on the way.'

She threw the information down like a gauntlet. He needed to know what he was getting himself into, should this relationship become any more than it already was. But that was ridiculous. She'd just been widowed for heaven's sake. She had no intention of embarking on a new relationship.

Not that sort of relationship anyway.

Absolutely not.

But then she recalled how all her senses responded to having him near and she blushed like a schoolgirl.

Change the subject. Anything but herself and her family.

But all she could come up with was the visit she'd had this morning from DI Keegan and DS Burke.

'The police have reopened their investigation into Julie's murder.'

'Sorry?'

'My other old friend. Mine and Sonia's. Julie Probert. They've reopened the murder investigation.'

Billy blinked. 'After forty years? Why?'

'I had two detectives at my door just this morning wanting to go over the statement I gave then.'

'What did you tell them?'

She smiled as she remembered her indignation this morning. 'I refused to talk to them.'

His eyebrows shot up and he laughed. 'Even though your son is one of them? Go Ellie.'

She giggled. She couldn't help it. She'd had way too much gin. 'I'm so sorry I ruined tonight Billy. Especially after all the thought you put into making it perfect. And if I'm not to make a fool of myself again, I really need to go home now. Can you order a taxi for me please?'

CHAPTER 50

Saturday 20th January 2024

In her dark bedroom, Sparks' eyes shot open. Something had woken her, but she didn't know what. And then she heard it again. A scratch and a rattle.

Her mother trying to get out of the front door. In the middle of the night. Again.

She knew exactly what she'd find if she got out of bed and went downstairs. Her mother would be lost in a world where the middle of the night in the present had become the middle of the day in the past, at a point somewhere in Spark's childhood. She'd be desperate to get out of the door, convinced she needed to get to the school on time to pick up her children, so they could all come home for tea.

Sparks looked at the clock. Twenty something past three.

Fists clenched, growling in frustration, she slammed her head back on the pillow. She had no choice. She had to get up. But still she lay there, listening to the scratch and the rattle, wondering if she'd secured the door well enough.

The last time this had happened, she'd found her mother at the door with her coat on over a nightdress covered in butter and eggs. The kitchen had looked like a bomb had dropped. The bloody woman must have been in there for ages trying to prep the eggy dippy bread sandwiches that had been Ian's childhood favourite. Luckily, she'd stopped short of attempting to cook the sodding things, so hadn't managed to burn the house down in the process. But what was there to say she hadn't set something alight this time?

She couldn't smell burning, but that didn't mean...

Bollocks. Just get up and check.

Swings and roundabouts though. Because going down there to make sure her mother was safe and hadn't done something stupid risked setting her off with the screaming heebie-jeebies again, convinced that her husband's piece of strumpet had found her way into her home.

What if her mother attacked her again, and this time left her with more than just a cut cheek. There were sharp knives in that kitchen.

No choice. She had to get up and go down. She sighed and swung her legs out from under the duvet, scattering the care home brochures Ian had dropped off through the week, that she'd fallen asleep reading.

***

She was going to be late for work. She didn't dare leave the house until the carer arrived. Not with the state her mother was in. And, since neither of them had got another wink of sleep following their nocturnal disturbance her eyes felt tired and gritty already.

The cold was mind-numbing, and she thought for a horrified moment she wasn't going to be able to get the car started but eventually, on the fifth try, the engine turned over.

On the way to the swamp, a news report on the radio mentioned a snowstorm on its way. A slow moving storm that had hit the east coast of the US last week and caused a four-day blackout, and which now crouched halfway across the Atlantic, eying up the UK.

She liked snow. In moderation. When she didn't have to go to work. But she did not want a snowstorm taking up a lengthy residence across her patch. The few days they'd had snow on the ground at the beginning of the month had been quite enough for one winter. But today felt too cold to snow anyway, and the only good thing about that was that it might make the godawful smell at the swamp a little more bearable.

Expecting the building to feel even colder inside than it did outside, she'd wrapped herself up well. Layered, so she could remove garments if she needed to. But she had no intention of spending the whole day in the old station if she could help it. The sooner she could get out of there to see Ellie and walk her through her old statement the better. But Keegan had insisted they go through the process of forming a full interview strategy first, and she had no idea why. Maybe he was just miffed that Ellie had refused point blank to talk to him and Lonnie Burke yesterday and wanted Sparks to put her through the wringer on his behalf. And that wasn't happening any time soon.

Keegan's was the only other car in the skating rink car park at the old station when she turned in through the brick pillars, and he'd parked on the only ice-free patch of tarmac. If she ended up having to work here for more than just today, she'd be putting a fresh bag of rock salt in the boot of her car.

She had to knock twice before he answered, and that riled her up even more. They'd been working here for months now, so why hadn't they had the electronic door release reactivated? Although maybe that was as obsolete as the rest of the old place.

'Sorry,' Keegan said when the door finally swung open. 'I was in the shitter.'

'Why would you tell me that? I don't need to know about your bowel habits.'

Keegan bared his teeth in a grin. 'Get out of the wrong side of the bed this morning, did you?'

'Whatever.' She stomped along the corridors behind him to the room at the end that he'd now claimed as his own, where he had three electric heaters blasting now, making her want to strip off her top layer of clothes straight away.

'Where are the others?' she asked.

'We've got most of the Probert papers sorted, including witness statements from some of the lads involved in the fight outside JoJo's that night. So Lonnie has taken moody Moodie with him to have a chat with a couple of them. And I imagine Kirsty Brooks will be warming your seat in Massey's car about now, or maybe they're still sat in HQ with their heads together over coffee. Shooting the breeze. Just the two of them. You know, like he used to do with you.'

'Fuck off, Keegan.'

'You mean fuck off DI Keegan, sir.'

'Do I?'

He laughed. 'Definitely the wrong side of the bed. Flick the switch on that kettle, will you, and I'll make the coffees while you read Ellie Morgan's original statement. Superintendent Portas tells me you know her quite well already. Well, I warn you, once you've read this you may decide you don't know her at all.'

CHAPTER 51

As well as Ellie's witness statement, Keegan had laid out a copy of notes made by one of the original investigating officers following Ellie's interview, in which the writer had included his own impressions of Ellie, her family, friends and social life. Keegan had also written copious notes himself, which amounted to three A4 sheets of his clear and distinctive handwriting.

Sparks read the documents in order. Ellie's statement first, then the notes made in 1984 and lastly Keegan's notes. Then she read them all through again to make sure she'd got all the salient points in consecutive order, so she could see the events in her head as they happened. Or as Ellie had claimed they happened at the time.

Given his cryptic remark, none of it turned out to be quite what she'd expected. Had she missed something? She read it all through for a third time. No, she didn't think so.

Ellie had been nineteen. Taking a foundation course in art and design at college, with the intention of going on to study the subject further at Newcastle Poly, now Northumbria University. She still lived at home with her parents, who did not approve of her chosen career path, or her clothes, hair, friends, social life, or any of her other life choices. The 1984 notes described her as a 'punk rocker', with an 'extreme hairdo', 'outlandish makeup' and ripped clothes.

Sparks tried to imagine the woman she knew today, Massey's mother for heaven's sake, as a young punk rocker. She wondered if Ellie had sometimes deliberately set out to shock her parents just for the hell of it. She'd done the same to her own parents when she was that age.

But while Mr and Mrs Crewe would probably much rather their only child had dressed conservatively and got a job as a bank teller, as a secretary in a solicitor's office, or even as a librarian, there'd been nothing at the time to suggest the parent/child relationship had been dysfunctional beyond the usual day to day spats.

In fact, it was clear at the start that they loved their daughter dearly, platinum blonde bird's nest and all.

Ellie had gone out with her friends, Julie Probert and Sonia Chambers. To the city centre her parents had assumed, although they had no idea of where to exactly. They'd probably learned not to ask.

They hadn't seen Ellie leave the house because they were themselves out at a New Year's Eve party. Believing her to have crept in late and to still be sleeping off her celebrations in bed, it wasn't until the turkey dinner was almost ready to be served on New Year's Day and they had two police officers knocking at their door that they realised their daughter had not returned home.

By 6 pm on New Year's Day, they'd reported Ellie missing. It was then more than twelve hours since Julie's body had been discovered, and Sparks imagined Ellie's parents would have been beside themselves with worry, terrified a similar fate had befallen their own daughter. The team investigating Julie's murder had initially taken Ellie's disappearance seriously and a full search had been launched, probably in the expectation they'd find another dead body.

And then, at around ten o'clock the following evening, on the 2nd of January, Ellie had wandered into the house, dishevelled but seemingly unhurt, and had refused to tell her parents or the police where she'd been, or who with. She'd also claimed that until she'd walked in the door and her parents had told her about it, she'd known nothing about her friend's murder.

The investigating officers hadn't bought it. The 1984 notes, full of prejudice and sexist preconceptions, made it clear Ellie had been put under pressure. Investigating officers had assumed by her alternative fashion choices, and the fact she and her friends had gone out clubbing at a venue the police already had on their radar as a drugs den, that Ellie had to be hiding something. Something that could help them find the murderer.

Eventually, blood tests carried out on Julie's body and on Ellie when she returned home, although not for some reason on Sonia, showed the girls to be free of drugs. But by that time the relief of Ellie's parents at having their daughter returned to them would have turned to anger at the hell she'd put them through. And no doubt repeated visits by the police, and Ellie's continuing refusal to say where she'd been for so long and who with, would have created a toxic atmosphere at home.

With so much pressure on her young shoulders, Ellie had eventually cracked and told detectives what they wanted to know. She said she'd left JoJo's with Sonia and Julie after the bar had closed and the music had finished, while a fight was raging in the street outside. They'd seen a man punched unconscious right in front of them at the bottom of the nightclub's broad steps, his head hitting the bottom step, and had edged around to a safe distance where, along with many others leaving the club at that time, they'd stayed for a while to watch the entertainment. At some point she'd noticed her friends were no longer close by. She'd looked around but couldn't see them, and with the fight by that point becoming more vicious and bloody and sucking in more and more of the bystanders, she'd felt relieved when she'd bumped into a man more than ten years her senior, who also happened to be her college lecturer, later identified as Garry Paver.

Garry was someone she knew relatively well and trusted. He'd volunteered to 'keep her safe', and so, after a joint but unsuccessful renewed effort to spot her friends, she'd assumed they must have left without her and had happily gone off with her lecturer. She'd said he claimed to have had a bottle of vodka at his flat, which he'd offered to share with her to 'see in the New Year'. It turned out he had plenty of other booze at home too and so she'd ended up staying there with him until he'd paid for a taxi to take her home on the 2nd of January. The pair of them had been too pissed and too busy, she'd said, to watch the news and so she really had known nothing about Julie's murder until she returned home.

After interviewing Paver and checking his whereabouts before the two had bumped into each other, the team had no choice but to accept Ellie's story as true. However, it appeared the attitudes of the murder team, reflected in the 1984 notes, had altered as a result of her admission. For if Ellie had been 'gagging for it' to the point she'd seduce an older man in the street and put her parents through such hell by staying away from home for two whole days, then by extension maybe Julie's morals had been equally lax. Perhaps she too had behaved no better than a prostitute, with the result that she'd brought rape and murder upon herself.

Keegan's notes indicated that he'd come to the same conclusion about the attitudes of the original team. From the point Ellie had given her statement, he'd written, the investigation would likely have taken a turn.

***

'Finished?' Keegan asked, making Sparks jump.

'He should have lost his sodding job for seducing a student and keeping her locked in his flat for two days. But I bet he got off with no consequences at all. Bastard.'

'Save it for someone who deserves it, because I don't think he does.'

'He corroborated her statement.'

Keegan brandished another sheaf of papers; six or seven sheets stapled together. 'This one is Sonia's statement. Read it and tell me what jumps out.'

Sparks sighed and pushed her empty coffee mug towards him. She unzipped her body warmer and hung it on top of her jacket on the back of her chair, then settled down again to read. By the time he placed the refilled mug in front of her she'd read through to the end, then flipped back to the beginning to check the bit she'd snagged on.

'See it?' he asked.

'They both claimed that all three of them left JoJo's together, but they can't have.'

'Gold star. Tell me why.'

'This bit here. Sonia stated that they'd left the club as the fight was starting on the opposite side of the road. Whereas Ellie described a fight already raging and a man being punched in the face at the bottom of the steps when they left, right outside the club doors.'

'Which means one of them lied.'

'Not necessarily,' she said. 'Maybe Ellie was straggling behind a little. Together but not side by side. So they could have each simply described what they saw from a different perspective. Scuffles can move quickly. It's possible the action moved from one side of the road to the other in the time it took for all three girls to descend the steps. Especially if they were a little the worse for wear.'

'If what Ellie said is true, and she did see a man knocked unconscious at the bottom of the steps right outside of JoJo's door, then why didn't Sonia say the same thing? If Ellie was still at the top of the steps looking down when Sonia was already at the bottom, then surely that would have been a lot more in Sonia's face than Ellie's, and yet she didn't mention it. So I don't think Sonia saw it. Not right in front of her. She'd already moved well away from the entrance, so it would have been a huge stretch to say they all left together.'

'Perhaps Sonia didn't want to get involved. If the team were being hard on her too, and no doubt they were, then no way would she want to be grilled as a witness a second time if the guy who'd been punched had died. Ellie described his head bouncing off the step. We've seen it before. Death by a single punch. And if he survived, maimed or not, he might have wanted to sue. If she had her head screwed on, no surprise she didn't mention it.'

Keegan considered it, then shrugged. 'Don't buy it. This modern claim culture crap is all very American. It didn't exist in the UK back then. Not the way it does now. So the possibility of him suing wouldn't have entered the head of a daft young girl. And he can't have died. If he had, we'd have found something in the case notes about another death in the same area on the same night. No, by my reckoning, both girls lied. They didn't leave JoJo's together and so we have no idea from these statements which one of them, if either, left with Julie.'

'But what makes you think that the lecturer is any better than a pervert? Are you saying Ellie's whole statement is a lie, that she didn't go off with the bastard on the promise of some free booze? What would she have gained by making herself look so bad?'

'With Sonia gone, and until we trace this Garry bloody Paver, there's only one person we can ask. She's expecting you at one o'clock. In the meantime, get yourself over to Newcastle and have a look at the building where JoJo's used to be. It's an Italian restaurant now. The Parisi Palace.

They've jazzed the exterior up a bit, but the steps are still the same, so you should be able to visualise the events better when you talk to Ellie. And, if you've a mind to, you can even go and see the back lane where Julie's body was found, although the buildings on both sides are different now. Modern apartments mostly.'

CHAPTER 52

While ice had formed a skin over puddles in the gutters, the constant stream of traffic in the deep ravines of city centre streets in the west end of Newcastle had kept frost from forming on the tarmac. Sparks stepped from her car just along the road from the Parisi Palace, off the main street, her breath pluming around her head. She shivered and zipped up her jacket over the body warmer.

She'd carried out a little online research on the building before leaving the swamp. The current licensee for the property was listed as a Romeo Conti Parisi, which explained the first part of the restaurant's name, while the cinema that had originally occupied the building before the advent of JoJo's, had been called the Westgate Palace, which explained the second part.

The Palace had closed down as a cinema in 1972 and had reopened within two years as JoJo's nightclub, with membership – according to an old flyer she'd found attached to a ten-year-old nostalgia piece on the Chronicle website – restricted to persons of twenty-one years of age and over. The flyer proclaimed JoJo's to be 'the ultimate in late night disco', although by 1982 – according to a blog on Newcastle nightlife through the decades – it had become *the* late night place to go on the city's alternative club scene as Punk morphed into Goth and New Romantic, with music until 2 am.

At this time of day, the street was quiet. She could see lights on inside the restaurant. Cleaners, kitchen and waiting staff prepping for service. According to images on the website, the interior had been renovated to 'celebrate the building's origins as part of the golden age of cinema'. Anything relating to the building's nightclub era would have been stripped out and scrapped, so she had no reason to go inside.

She climbed the flight of ten shallow tiled steps in a broad curve. Tall billboards on either side, which would originally have featured full length movie posters, now gave a taste of the restaurant's glittering interior and the dishes on offer. At the top, she turned and faced the street, trying to picture what the girls would have seen in the early hours of that New Year's morning all those years ago.

The street was wide. Still contraflow, as it had been then, with generous lanes and room for metered parking on both sides. Probably the meters hadn't existed in 1983/84, and the buildings on the opposite side had been old disused warehouse buildings back then, which were demolished in the nineties and replaced with modern apartments.

She glared at an inquisitive passer-by, then half-closed her eyes and tried to focus her mind on a New Year's night forty years ago. No traffic. Sparse street-lighting. A drunken argument on the other side of the road descending into a vicious brawl; Sonia's version. Then she pictured the ongoing fight Ellie had described. The punch. A head bouncing off the bottom step in front of her.

It didn't make sense. Not if, as they'd claimed, they'd all come out of the door together. Not even allowing for a few seconds between them.

Sonia or Ellie, or both, had lied.

Or perhaps Sonia had only been mistaken. If she led the group out of the building, and her attention was on what was happening in front of her, she might not have been aware that Ellie and possibly Julie had lagged behind.

She could have assumed they were all still together.

But Ellie must have lied. No two ways about it.

So, had her whole account been a lie?

***

Sparks arrived at Ellie's house way earlier than arranged. Before leaving the city centre, she'd walked the short distance from the Parisi Palace to the back lane where Julie Probert's body had been found. Keegan had been right about all the new apartment buildings. The place bore no resemblance now to the old photos that had managed to survive their dunking in flood water, so she didn't linger.

As she turned into Ellie's street, she saw a Land Rover Discovery at the kerb. Ellie must have a visitor.

She parked up across the road and was about to get out when she realised Ellie's door stood open and Ellie was there on the step, talking to a man, a big bloke who looked oddly familiar. Powerfully built, gingery fair hair, dressed in jeans and a battered leather jacket. Maybe Massey's brother? Although she'd have expected him to be dark, like Massey and Megan. Megan's husband then? But no. This man looked older. Maybe Ellie's own age. A family friend perhaps.

As she watched, the man cupped Ellie's face in his hands and gave her a lingering kiss on the cheek. Not just a family friend then. Ellie wasn't letting any grass grow beneath her feet.

Did Massey know?

She kept very still so as not to draw the man's attention as he walked to the Discovery and drove off. Then she drove around the block and returned to park in the spot he'd just vacated so that Ellie would think she'd only just arrived.

The woman who answered the door to Sparks this time looked nothing like the warm, confident Ellie she'd met last time. This Ellie looked flushed and awkward, her hair in disarray, as if she'd only just got out of bed. Sparks wondered if that were true and if the man at the door was already her lover. And then she couldn't decide if the thought made her feel admiration for the woman or disappointment, since it would mean she was as human as everyone else.

'Are you okay, Ellie?' she asked.

She must have looked concerned for Ellie straightened her shoulders and lifted her chin.

'A bit hungover, I'm afraid. Your boss's fault. I'd said no to going out last night, but his visit yesterday annoyed me so much that I changed my mind. I'm paying for it now.'

Good grief. What the hell did Keegan say?

'Would you prefer to do this another time?'

She hoped not. Keegan would not be pleased if Ellie said yes.

'No, no. Come in. Let's just get it over and done with.'

Ellie led her into a lounge to the left of the front door, where she spotted some indentations on the carpet. Furniture had been moved recently in here. She realised that Ellie must have prepared the room for this interview so that two armchairs faced each other, with a huge square coffee table in between. Erecting barriers before the interview had even started. That wasn't good.

She sat on the settee instead.

CHAPTER 53

When the detective sat on the sofa instead of the armchair she'd been offered, Ellie groaned inwardly. 'On second thoughts, Christine,' she said. 'Let's go into the kitchen. It's much cosier in there and we can sit at the table, so you can have somewhere to put your papers.'

And at least there'd still be the table between them.

Sparks smiled and followed her through to the back of the house.

Ellie crossed straight to the kettle and flicked the switch. 'I only have instant coffee, I'm afraid, until I get to the shops.'

'None for me thanks. I've just had two cups at the station.' She blew out her cheeks. 'Do you mind if I take off this body warmer while we talk?'

'Not at all.' Ellie turned the kettle back off and sat down at the table. She'd had her own fill of coffee this morning. Strong and black. Lots of it. But it hadn't made a dent yet in the gin-induced headache and had only made the nausea worse.

Of course, Billy turning up so unexpectedly on the doorstep looking so chipper and cheerful, when she felt, and no doubt looked like such a mess hadn't helped. And just as she was expecting Christine to turn up too.

And then he'd completely thrown her for six, and she still had no idea what she felt about his proposition. But there was no point thinking about it now. Not until all this was over and done with.

She really must cut down on the alcohol. Before it got too much of a hold again.

Sparks patted the file in front of her and took a moment to gather her thoughts. 'I appreciate that this is going to be difficult for you Ellie, particularly with everything you've been going through recently, and I'm so sorry for having to take you back to such dark times. All I can say is that anything you tell me now could be vital to finally catching the killer of your friend Julie, which I'm sure is something you want too. Oh, and also that we do things a little differently now compared to how they were in 1984, so please try not to worry.'

Ellie bit her lips to stop them from quivering. She couldn't imagine that making such an apology was listed in the police manuals as a recognised method of buttering up a witness in a murder inquiry, and she appreciated it. She smiled, but found herself unable to respond verbally, which didn't bode well for what was coming.

'Are you alright to go ahead?' Sparks asked.

Ellie nodded.

'I'm afraid I'm going to need to record this interview.' Sparks pulled her phone from her pocket, brought up the voice recorder and set it on the table between them. 'Are you okay with that?'

Again, Ellie nodded.

Sparks stated Ellie's address as the location of the interview and gave the date, time and her own name and rank. Then she asked Ellie to state her own full name.

'Eleanor Carolyn Morgan.'

'And please also state your maiden name.'

'Crewe. Eleanor Carolyn Crewe.'

For the tape, Sparks then explained the context of the interview within the cold case investigation and read out the original crime reference number from the file in front of her. She explained that the purpose of the interview was to take Ellie through the events of New Year's night 1983/84 with the objective of gaining as full a picture as possible of what happened on the night of Julie's murder and in the immediate aftermath. She then told Ellie that she could take as much time as she needed and as many breaks as were necessary to get the interview done.

'Alright then Ellie, I'd like to take you back to that night on New Year's Eve on 1983. The night your friend Julie Probert was killed. So then, as soon as you're ready, please tell me what you remember of that night from the time you met up with Julie Probert and Sonia Chambers.'

Ellie let out a huge shaky breath, her hands feeling just as shaky in her lap. She'd expected this to begin with Christine reading out her original statement and asking her to confirm the truth of it. That's what she'd been preparing herself for ever since those two detectives had turned up yesterday, not to be asked to recall the whole godawful night from start to finish in detail, without that statement in front of her as an aide memoire of all the lies she'd told. Christine's approach was diametrically different to the original interviews she'd been put through.

Interviews plural, because she's been forced to go over and over her story time and time again, as if she were a suspect rather than a witness. Looked upon by those contemptuous sniggering arsehole detectives as something disgusting and worthless when she already thought of herself as much worse.

This morning she'd promised herself that this time she'd put the record straight. She'd tell the truth about what happened to her that night. The reason for all the lies. But sitting here now, looking through that wormhole into her past, she wasn't sure if she could say it all out loud. Seeing her friends waiting for her at the bus stop, with the whole evening still yawning ahead of them and all those little decisions they'd made through the evening, each one seemingly inconsequential at the time: which place to go next, whose turn it was to go to the bar, who to talk to, who went first out of the door; any one of which could have had the power to change the whole course of that night, if only they'd done even one tiny thing differently. Then Julie might still be alive, married now with children and grandchildren of her own. And what happened at the door of JoJo's that night might not have happened.

'I'm sorry,' she mumbled. 'I can't do this.' Hand over her mouth, she clattered her chair back and ran.

'Ellie has left the room,' she heard Sparks say as she slammed the toilet door behind her. 'Interview paused at thirteen twenty-three.'

***

Not quite how Sparks had imagined the interview would go. Should she take Ellie a glass of water or something? Was the nausea a result of the hangover? Or of being forced to relive that New Year's night so long ago?

Or, like DCI Flowers, maybe this was a sign Ellie had succumbed to the dreaded flu bug?

Sparks pulled the little bottle of sanitiser she carried everywhere with her from her pocket, squirted a good dollop onto her hands and treated them to the full NHS-approved hand-washing technique. Then she squirted more onto a clean paper hanky and wiped down the table in front of her. And the back of her phone where it had been lying on the table.

While she had the opportunity, she wandered around the room checking for signs the big man at the front door earlier had recently been making himself comfortable here, but she saw only one dirty cup in the sink and no signs of any shared breakfast or lunch.

Ellie's phone sprung to life on the other side of the room and danced across a side table next to one of the big sofas. Sparks listened for any signs of Ellie's return but when she heard only a retching sound she couldn't resist a quick peek at the screen.

She caught the name of the caller just before the call cut out. Billy Wragg. Not Sonia's husband. He was called Ronnie. So was this the son? No, he would be too young. Sonia's brother-in-law then. No wonder he'd seemed familiar. He certainly looked like Ronnie.

She was still looking at the screen when a text message popped up from the same caller.

'Say yes.'

Say yes to what? Sparks stared at the door to the bathroom. And what the hell should she do with this information? Because if Ronnie Wragg had been a person of interest in the 1984 case, perhaps Billy had been too.

***

When Ellie emerged from the bathroom she felt frail, and a lot older than her fifty-nine years. Way too old to be swanning off to some lodge in the wilds with a man she'd only recently met, while her husband's ashes were still warm in their oak box.

She was a grandmother, for fuck's sake.

Another one squandered.

But at least she hadn't said the word out aloud this time, so perhaps it could still be retained in her arsenal of fucks. Because by the time this interview was over, she might have needed to give every single one she could muster.

She drew in a lungful of air and blew it back out in a haze of minty fresh mouthwash. Bull by the horns, she told herself as she walked back into the kitchen.

Admit the worst and get it over with.

'I lied back then,' she said as she sat back down at the table. 'A lot of that witness statement is bollocks.'

Sparks pulled her head back in surprise. 'Well then, this is your opportunity to set the record straight. Let's get it on tape.'

Once she'd started, the words just fell out. Everything she'd said originally up to the point they were leaving JoJo's had been true, but now she shocked herself with how much clearer it all was. She could see details she hadn't mentioned back then, as if a phantasmagorical stage show had imprinted itself on her brain. All the black-clad, white-faced eeriness of the Goths; Sonic's preferred style. The spiky Brutalist edginess of the Punk Rockers, which they'd all emulated a couple of years earlier. And, the delicious height of fashion that both she and Jools aspired to, the fabulous peacock strutting of the New Romantics with their flamboyant make-up and bouffant hair. All of these voguish modes melding together in an intricate renaissance dance.

Until Auld Lang Syne had played.

And then the music stopped, and the lights had come on, exposing the seediness. Broken glass and cigarette ends trodden into the sticky carpet. The mirror ball just that; a dreary ball with tiny dusty mirrors stuck to it, hanging from a motor on the ceiling, no longer the glittering cosmos of light it had been moments before.

The bouncers had started from the back. Rounding up the stragglers. Herding everyone towards the doors and out into the night...

Ellie stopped talking.

Her breathing quickened. She licked her lips and twisted her fingers together.

'Take your time,' Sparks said. 'We can take a break if you want to.'

'No, I need...' She blew out a couple of shallow breaths. 'I need to get this done.'

'Sure?'

'We were at the door. But then I decided I needed to go to the ladies. I knew we'd have to wait for ages in the taxi queue. I couldn't wait until I got home. So I went back in, and... Sonic and Jools, they said they'd... that they'd wait for me inside the door. But when I came back, they'd been made to wait outside. So I opened the door, and... and I looked around for them. And then I saw that poor boy... We'd only been talking to him and his mates earlier and I saw him get hit. Punched. He fell. His head... it... it bounced off the bottom step. Oh God...'

'Ellie. Ellie. Take some deep breaths. Calm down. Let's take a break.'

'... and one of the bouncers was right behind me at the door, and he pulled me back inside. And I thought he was protecting me...' Ellie could feel her face twisting in disgust. 'But he put his hand over my mouth, and they dragged... they... they dragged me into the ticket booth. And...'

'Jesus Christ! Ellie, breathe.'

A noise like a dentist's drill whined in Ellie's head. She panted through her fingers, her vision narrowing to a pin prick.

'Ellie. Look at me, Ellie.' Sparks reached for her phone. 'Interview paused at... fuck's sake... at fourteen fifty-seven. Ellie.'

CHAPTER 54

'Sir.' Hunched over his desk, peering at his screen as if he couldn't quite believe what he was seeing, DC Iain Johnson waved his hand in the air.

'What have you got?' Poole demanded.

But Johnson's eyes were on Massey, who'd just entered the incident room with Kirsty Brooks in tow.

'What is it, Iain?' Massey asked, as he and Poole reached Johnson's desk together.

'Been working on that pattern analysis that Kirsty and Robyn set up sir.' He nodded to Brooks and gave her a quick smile. 'Just seeing what else I can add, you know?'

'Come on man,' Poole said. 'Spit it out.'

Johnson ignored the DI and addressed Massey. 'I've found a new link sir. Between two of our victims. Abigail Grant and Nicole Selby. They're first cousins.'

Poole raked his fingers through his hair. 'How the hell did we not already know this?'

Johnson continued to ignore him and to look directly at Massey. 'Stevie Grant and Nicole's mother are brother and sister.'

'Good work, Iain.' Although Massey wasn't at all sure how the connection might help them.

'It was something Nicole's father said, sir. He's still calling every day, but now that DCI Flowers is off ill, his calls have been coming through to here, and I had the misfortune to speak to him myself this morning.' Johnson's eyes rolled to the ceiling. 'First time. Hopefully the last.'

Massey remembered his first morning on the Bryony team, when Kirsty had been giving him a run down on each of Musk Man's victims. 'This is the guy who collared Robyn out on the street, isn't it?'

'That's right, sir,' Brooks said. 'The one who's over the top protective. Nicole is terrified of him. Does exactly what he tells her to do, including refusing to provide a blood sample after the rape.'

'He said something strange to me today,' Johnson said. 'It got me thinking. He said he wasn't having either of his daughters turn out like the rest of them. When I asked what he meant, he backtracked. Then he ended the call.'

Odd.

Massey looked at the faces around the room. 'And he's never said anything like that before to anyone?'

Everyone shook their heads. 'No, sir.'

'He sounded frustrated that he couldn't speak to DCI Flowers again,' Johnson said. 'Feels he's being fobbed off with junior officers and he lost the plot a bit. Anyway, it made me think about what he might have meant. The rest of who? We've already been through Nicole's friends, or at least all the ones she's told us about. And he's always been very clear that there's no extended family. Too clear in fact. So I thought I'd check, and the first thing I came across was his wife's maiden name. Grant. Marie Grant, younger sister of Stevie Grant. Which makes Abigail the cousin of Nicole and her older sister, Nina.'

'Good call,' Massey said. 'Well done, Iain. Keep on it.'

Nina.

Not a common name, yet he'd come across it somewhere else recently. But where?

He walked across to the big screen and scanned the information there. Nope, not there. His brain clicked through all the other intelligence that had come his way over the last few days. The Probert cold case, Musk Man, Leon's murder, Abigail's stalker. Still nothing.

But for some reason Keegan popped into his head.

Something the man had said.

He sighed and closed his eyes. Keegan walking back from the bar with two pints in his hands. They'd talked about Abigail's mother and her relationship with Stevie Grant, then about his temporary promotion to DCI, and then Keegan had told him he'd found something he reckoned could throw it all up in the air again. Something to do with the hit and run. His mother's friend—

'We're going to the van for sarnies, sir,' Brooks said. 'Want anything?'

Bugger. He'd almost had it.

He turned around and looked at the clock. After twelve. 'Too late for a full breakfast butty, do you think?'

'They do those all day, sir.'

'Great.' He handed Brooks a tenner. 'Brown sauce please.'

Brooks disappeared with Natalie Clark and Dan Lieb in tow. Massey turned back to the big screen, but with his eyes closed again. Whatever it was, it wasn't up there. What the hell else had Keegan told him that evening? The hit and run victim's husband. He said they'd found Ronnie Wragg's name in the Julie Probert files. So, something to do with Ronnie Wragg then. Or with Sonia. Or... shit, with both.

It hadn't been something Keegan had actually said, after all. But after their conversation that night at the Snowy Owl, and with the conflict of interest over the hit and run no longer an issue, he'd taken a look at the file on Sonia's death to gain a better understanding of Ronnie Wragg. Because if Ronnie had been involved in the 1984 case too, even if it looked so far as if he'd been cleared at the time, then Massey had wanted to know all there was to know about the man whose wife, an old friend of his mother, had recently died a violent death. He cast his mind back to everything he'd read, picturing it on the screen of his laptop. They had a son together. He'd been there at the New Year party. Sparks had taken a statement from him, and from his fiancée, whose name was Nina.

That was it.

Nina Selby, if his memory served him right.

Another coincidence?

Too many bloody coincidences.

Nina Selby – the sister of one of their rape victims, Nicole Selby, and cousin of Abigail Grant, another rape victim, who was also the victim of a stalker who may or may not have murdered Leon Robinson – was engaged to be married to Nicky Wragg, both of whose parents had been interviewed forty years ago in connection to a rape and murder, and whose mother had recently been killed in a hit and run incident.

Bloody hell. Try saying all that out loud without three Weetabix for breakfast.

He needed to speak to Keegan ASAP. He needed to know if they'd found any more paperwork in the Probert files relating to Ronnie Wragg.

He was also supposed to stay well out of the way of the Probert case. He called Keegan's number. No reply.

'DI Poole, I'd like you to keep Iain on with this please, and to organise someone else to work with him. We've already had the familial link with the DNA and now this. Maybe family is the key to this whole thing.'

He'd expected an objection from Poole, just for the sake of it, but he didn't get it. For the first time, the man looked to be on board with something he'd said.

***

He'd tried Keegan's number three more times and left a couple of messages before finally receiving a response in the form of a text message.

Can't talk now. Half six. Same place.

So here he was, sitting in the Snowy Owl, waiting for Keegan to arrive. Saturday evening, the place was busy, but he'd managed to bag a table he'd sat at once before. On a Sunday lunchtime last summer. Sparks had come along on that occasion to help him ward off the amorous attentions of the ex-fiancée of an old friend of his. The woman had asked him to look into some weird goings-on at the Lady of the North landform sculpture behind the pub. Long story, for another day.

The table was secluded enough that he and Keegan could have the conversation he wanted without anyone earwigging. It was reserved for diners usually, but maybe Keegan would want to order something. He quite fancied one of the burgers himself. He knew Helen still wouldn't be feeling like having much to eat when he got home. The virus had hit her hard.

Keegan arrived through the back entrance with a clatter of doors. As soon as he sat down, he took a long drink of the beer that Massey had got in for him, then he picked up a menu and they each ordered the pub's signature burger.

After first taking them down a couple of obligatory small talk alleys, Keegan sat back and crossed his arms. 'You first then. Has to be a reason for all those calls.'

'Ronnie Wragg. You said he'd been interviewed by the Probert team in 1984.'

'I did. What's your interest now? Aren't you supposed to be keeping your bucket and spade well away from my sand pit?'

'His son is engaged to Nina Selby. She's the sister of Nicole Selby, who is one of Musk Man's victims. They're both first cousins of Abigail Grant, also a rape victim and daughter of Stevie Grant. Could simply be yet another coincidence, but I'm developing a serious allergy to that word.'

Keegan took another swig of his beer and then sucked foam from the ends of his moustache while he considered the information. 'Interesting,' he said at last.

'Have you found anything else about Ronnie in the Probert files, or not?'

'No.'

Massey would have felt a crushing disappointment if he hadn't known Keegan so well, for that one syllable answer had been loaded.

There was a lot more to know.

But, typically, Keegan wasn't about to give it away without going off on a tangent first.

'Sparks is doing good. You should be proud. I knew that mentoring crap would see her right in the end. You've done a good job there.'

Massey gave a short laugh. He knew Sparks' need for support had not yet come to an end.

'You fought against it, if I remember rightly.'

'Only to stiff Hitchins. It was his idea see, not HR's, but he didn't suggest it for Sparks' own good. He did it to hobble you. You were too smart by half for that arsehole. And you proved it by bringing the bastard down.'

'You were there too. We did it together.'

'Yeah well, you could have made things a lot worse for me than they turned out, but you didn't. So hats off.'

That wasn't quite the way Massey remembered it. 'Careful. This halo is heavy enough already. That's... how many? Two compliments you've just paid me in what... five minutes. Something's up.'

At that moment, the waiter returned with their food.

'Later,' Keegan said. 'Eat.'

***

They waited until the waiter had returned, taken away their empty plates and delivered coffee. Neither fancied another pint.

'Need to collect my girls from a friend's party later,' Keegan said. 'Don't want to turn up stinking too much of booze.'

Massey laughed. 'Best not.' There'd been a time, years ago, when he'd almost become the father of a daughter himself, but Helen had lost the baby because of something stupid he'd done. They'd got back on track and kept trying, but it had never happened, and now he thought it never would.

He pinned Keegan to his seat with a stare. 'Are you going to answer my question properly now?'

Keegan sighed. 'I've just spent the last couple of hours with Lou Portas again.'

Massey thought his friend was about to go off on another tangent and started to say something to rein him in, but Keegan held up his hand.

'All because of you and that mother of yours.'

Massey jerked his head back. 'What?'

'Sparks has been to interview your mother today. Spent hours with her. Traumatic, by all accounts.'

Massey thought about everything his mother had gone through lately. That was bad enough but being asked to go back in time and relive another distressing event from forty years into her past on top of all that, must have felt like scraping out her soul with a teaspoon. 'Is she alright?'

'Sparks? A bit shell-shocked, but okay.'

'No, you tit. My mother.'

Keegan grinned but there was little amusement in it. 'You'll be pleased to know that, while she was able to give us a much clearer picture of what went on that night before they all got separated, we do not consider her to have been in any way connected to what happened to Julie Probert later.'

'I knew that. But how did they become separated? Did she say?'

Keegan leant forward, elbows on the table. 'Look Massey, there are things I can't tell you and you'd be best not asking about them—'

'But—'

'No, wait. If you want to argue that point, you need to go and have it out with Lou Portas. Her decision, not mine. But, for what it's worth, I agree with her one hundred percent. Now, getting back to Ronnie Wragg, who is the reason behind this little tête-à-tête, is he not?'

He raised his eyebrows and waited until Massey gave a reluctant nod.

'We have not as yet found any further information on Ronnie Wragg in the Probert files. We do still have some of the old papers to wade our way through, but it looks very much as if they were correct in discounting him at the time.'

Massey didn't know whether to feel relieved or disappointed.

'There is something I need to tell you though,' Keegan said. 'And I haven't told Lou Portas this bit yet. I'm telling you because I think you ought to know.'

Massey froze with his coffee cup halfway to his mouth. 'Go on.'

'I'm talking present day now, not the distant past, so nothing to do with anything you're supposed to stay away from. Not in my mind anyway.' Keegan sighed and looked down, as if trying to decide if he was doing the right thing, but then he looked Massey in the eye. 'It appears your mother has something going on with Ronnie's brother, Billy Wragg. Looks like he's her new fancy man.'

Massey blinked. 'What?'

CHAPTER 55

Helen was fast asleep when Massey got home, and he couldn't settle to anything. He put *Sky News* on the TV and fretted through a report about ongoing efforts to deal with the damage wrought by storm Arlo along the eastern coast of the US. The storm was now fast approaching this side of the Atlantic and predicted to loop around the north of the UK and regroup before hitting the entire country from the east with a ferocious arctic blast. He'd believe it when he saw it. He couldn't remember the last time a weather forecast had been accurate.

He should ring his mother.

But what could he say? That he had it on good authority she'd found herself a new boyfriend so soon after his stepfather had died?

He couldn't say that.

He'd always had a close relationship with his mother. A different type of closeness to that she shared with his half-siblings, Megan and Alex. Forged in his early childhood, before the abusive bastard who was his natural father had buggered off in the middle of the night, telling him he was the man of the house now and that it was his turn to keep his mother in check.

Billy Wragg? What the hell was she thinking, so soon after having been widowed? She shouldn't be getting mixed up with *anyone* yet, and *especially* not with a man whose name had come up in connection to two police investigations she was mixed up in, for Christ's sake.

Yes, alright, a bit of an exaggeration. It was his surname that had come up. And in connection to his brother, not him.

But still.

Sodding bastarding buggeration.

Massey got to his feet and paced the room. He pulled out his phone and stared at the screen before swearing again and stuffing it back into his pocket. He shouldn't even try to have a conversation with her about it while he was so bloody angry.

He sat down again and flicked through the channels on TV. Fuck all to watch. He got up again and looked through the blinds into the frozen night. Only the neighbour's calico cat to see out there as it sauntered along the middle of the road beneath a street lamp.

He took out his phone again and tapped on his mother's number.

She answered almost immediately. 'James, this is a surprise.'

'What the hell are you doing with that man?' he seethed.

'What man?'

'Billy bloody Wragg, that's who.'

CHAPTER 56

With her mother asleep on the settee, deep breaths rattling from a mouth wide open, Sparks laid her head back in the armchair and tried to calm the nightmare thoughts going round on a loop in her brain. Ellie being dragged away from her friends all those years ago and raped by three men, two bouncers and the DJ, one after the other. Then thrown out into the night, alone, with a horde of angry blokes still out there, all still souped up on the testosterone-fuelled aggressive remnants of the fight.

With no sign anywhere of her friends, Ellie had run as fast and as far as she could. She'd ended up on the quayside, staring down into the river. And that's where her college lecturer had found her. By chance, he'd been weaving his way home after leaving another New Year's party in another nightclub.

'Why didn't he call the police?' Sparks had asked. 'Or an ambulance? He could have got help.'

Ellie had tutted impatiently. 'People didn't have mobile phones in those days. He'd have had to find a phone box that worked for a start, and there weren't many of those around. And anyway, I wouldn't let him. I told him to take me to his place. I needed somewhere safe.'

'He could have taken you home.'

'I didn't want to go home. I couldn't face my parents. Not after... Don't you see?'

And Sparks *had* seen.

'But surely, in the morning. He could have made sure you got home then.'

'I wanted to stay there, and he didn't dare say no. I had something on him, you see, because he *had* been screwing a student, just not me. It was someone else in my year. And I threatened to tell if he didn't let me stay.'

'For two days?'

'The vodka. That was real. He had a cupboard full of booze and I was determined to kill myself by drinking the lot. Luckily, I fell asleep before I could do that. But the hangover was a doozy. It took me almost that long to be able to stand again.'

'And he didn't touch you? He didn't take advantage? If he was that way inclined—'

'He was a good man; he still is a good man. He wouldn't have done that. He was appalled by what had happened to me. It was true love he had with the girl he was seeing back then. He ended up marrying her. As far as I know, they're still together now with half a dozen kids and a tribe of grandchildren.'

'So why did he lie to the police?'

'Because he was terrified of losing his job if I told the college what he'd been up to.'

'Why didn't you tell the police yourself what had happened to you? Surely—'

Ellie had swatted away her words. 'Because when I walked into my parents' house and I saw those two detectives sitting there on the settee sucking up to my parents, drinking tea from my mother's best china cups, with their fucking little pinky fingers stuck in the air, they took one look at the state I was in, and they judged me. As far as they were concerned, I was no better than a whore. A trollop. A prick-tease. If I'd told them what had really happened, they'd have thought I deserved it anyway just by the way I was dressed. So why should I have said anything to further their opinion? And do you know the worst thing about it all, Christine?'

She'd raked her hands through her hair at that point, battling to keep a sob from her voice, and that had made Sparks' heart break.

'It's that all their unjust impressions of me coloured what they thought of Jools too. She became less deserving as a victim because of the way they judged me. They hardly even bothered trying to catch the bastard who killed her after that.'

***

Propped up on the settee, Sparks' mother snorted and muttered for a moment before sinking back into sleep. Sparks, sitting in her father's old armchair, sniffed and wiped a tear from the corner of her eye, wondering how the hell Ellie had coped for all these years with what had happened to her.

She should have asked her for their names. The bouncers and the DJ. She could have checked them out to see if they'd ever got their comeuppance.

Sparks thought about the old JoJo's flyer she'd found online and picked up her mobile to search for it again. The device vibrated in her hand. She shot out of the armchair and hurried into the kitchen as she heard the first notes of the ringtone. She didn't want her mother to wake up yet if she could help it.

'Ian. What do you want?'

'Thanks for the birthday greetings, sister dear.'

'I didn't forget your birthday. I just don't give a toss about it. I have more pressing things to worry about.'

'Have you read them?'

'What? No. I haven't read the bloody brochures you sent yet. What did you expect?'

She *had* read them. From cover to cover. She'd investigated the care homes online too, but she wasn't about to tell her brother that.

She missed his next words, but she could tell by his tone that she wouldn't have wanted to know anyway. 'Sod off Ian. The only thing I need is for you and that insipid wife of yours to give *our* mother some of your precious time, not just some fucking information about the best places to hide her away until she does you a sodding favour and dies—

'What? Yes, even if she sticks me with a bloody knife next time. She's my mother, and she's yours too.'

She ended the call and threw her phone on the kitchen table. She'd meant what she'd said. That demented old lady snoring in the next room was her mother. Not a good one, but her mother, nonetheless. She had an obligation to do the best she possibly could for her. But she couldn't help but draw a parallel between her mother, who'd never suffered a day of hardship in her life until she became too ill to realise it anyway, and Ellie, who'd suffered so much pain and loss in her life, and yet was still full of grace and compassion.

And marbles.

And then a thought smacked Sparks between the eyes. Birthdays. Massey had his birthday at the beginning of October. And hadn't he said something about the next one being the big four oh? That meant he must have been conceived...

Bloody hell!

She squeezed a dollop of sanitiser onto her hands and gave them a thorough scrub. No way did she want to open that can of worms.

CHAPTER 57

Sunday 21st January 2024

It was after one in the morning and Ellie still couldn't stop her hands from shaking. How did James even know about Billy? She hadn't told Christine about him. She'd unburdened herself of everything else. Not that anything she'd said would help the police in finding Jools' killer now, although it might at least stop them wasting time on the lies she'd told forty years ago. But she hadn't mentioned Billy.

She'd heard that getting things off your chest, even after so long, could be cathartic, but she wasn't so sure about that. Yes, she'd felt physically purged after laying it all out there, but that was hardly surprising given she'd thrown up so violently she'd almost turned herself inside out. Of course the gin last night hadn't helped, and she probably shouldn't be drinking wine now on an empty stomach. But a psychological catharsis? No sign of that yet.

How could James have even spoken to her like that?

The trembling in her hand made the foot of the glass rattle against the tile coaster. She needed two hands to get the wine to her lips. But it wasn't James' angry words, nor drinking on an empty stomach that had given her such a bad case of the jitters. It was what she'd done *after* James' call. Something she would never have done if he hadn't made her so *fucking* angry.

And look, another one wasted.

But Billy had been so very sweet when he'd come round this morning. Yesterday morning now.

She'd said no then. Oh God, why the hell couldn't she have stuck to it?

But instead, as soon as she'd hung up on James, still seething with anger, she'd texted Billy and asked if his offer still stood. He'd called her straight away and said great, of course it did, and could she be ready for nine in the morning?

'Tomorrow?' she'd cried.

'Come on, Ellie,' he'd said. 'Time to live a little.'

So, against her better judgement, with her lips working completely independently from her brain or her heart, and operated instead like a puppet by the anger that still swirled in her gut, she'd said yes. Nine o'clock would be fine. She'd even gone straight upstairs and packed a bloody bag.

But now she felt mortified. How could she even consider going away with a man while the love of her life had hardly been gone a month?

And what if Billy took her acquiescence as a sign she was ready to sleep with him? Because she wasn't.

But could she even trust herself *not* to jump into bed with him when all her emotions were rubbed so bloody raw, and she wanted so much to be made to feel whole again?

Oh God, she was too old for all this nonsense.

And what if James came knocking on the door to have another go at her while Billy was here?

She picked up her phone to call Billy back, then remembered what time it was. She'd call him first thing in the morning to tell him she'd changed her mind. Again.

God, this was all James' fault.

CHAPTER 58

The first thing that registered in Abigail's mind that Sunday morning, before she'd fully opened her eyes, was that the cats weren't on the bed with their stereo rumbling purr, patting her face with their paws or kneading her shoulder to wake her up. She stuck one bare arm out from under the covers and raised her head to check they weren't asleep at the bottom of the bed.

No cats.

She checked the time on her phone. Almost quarter past seven. Still pitch black outside but usually they'd have woken her by now. Had she accidentally locked them downstairs last night?

No, they wouldn't have let her get away with that, not while they were only just getting settled back into their own home again. She'd have heard them crying straight away.

Two days she'd been back here. There hadn't been much point in staying away once she knew her stalker could find her no matter where she went. It still felt scary being home alone again, apart from the cats, but the thought that her friend could be in danger if he came for her there was equally terrifying. She'd lived with fear for more than three years now. Her friend hadn't. And she shouldn't have to. So she'd come home. With her cats.

Where on earth are they?

In one fluid movement, she swung herself out of bed and into her fluffy hooded robe, slipping her feet into faux sheepskin bootie slippers. Like Uggs. Almost. If you didn't look too closely.

She shivered and put a hand on the radiator on the landing. Barely warm. The timer had turned the heating off again ages ago. She'd turn it back on as soon as she'd located the cats and fed them. Then tea. She'd left the pot with the tea bags already in on the bench next to her favourite mug and the kettle she'd pre-filled last night.

She'd missed that mug while she'd been away.

At the top of the stairs something made her pause. Something on the air. A faint whiff her brain at first refused to acknowledge. Hardly there. Just a faint trace, but her gut must have recognised it on some level, for one knee began to tremble.

She took the first step down, then another. With every step she descended, the smell got stronger, and her legs trembled harder.

Where were the cats? The lounge door stood open, so she couldn't have locked them downstairs. Had she left it like that?

She heard a distant yowl and a frantic scrabbling sound.

The back door. At least one of her cats trying to get inside. Yet they'd both been indoors when she went to bed. She wouldn't have locked them outside on so cold a night.

She took a deep breath and stepped through the lounge door.

Onto thin plastic sheeting.

Oh God! Oh God!

A whisper of movement from behind her. A gloved hand covered her mouth and nose, yanking her head back. She struggled to breathe and then regretted the breath he allowed her when that disgusting never forgotten stench made her retch in terror.

His voice hissed into her ear. 'Remember me?'

Something clicked in her brain. She did. And not only from the last time he attacked her. Because now she knew exactly who he was.

How could she not have realised?

He shifted his grip, she felt the rustle of the plastic sheeting under their feet, and her knees gave way.

CHAPTER 59

Massey felt out of sorts. It was Sunday. Leon Robinson had been dead two weeks now and the investigation had gone nowhere. So this morning, the whole MIT was at work, and a couple of the Bryony team had come in too. Insulated coffee mug in hand, he stalked between the two incident rooms, brooding about his mother and where she could be. He'd called at her house just before nine on his way into work. He'd wanted to apologise. To explain calmly why it was necessary for her to avoid the Wragg family for the time being. Even if officially he shouldn't be telling her anything of the sort. But she wasn't at home, she didn't answer her mobile, and when he checked, he found she wasn't at Megan's either.

He'd definitely told her he'd call this morning. But perhaps she'd gone for a long walk precisely because that's what he'd said. To avoid him. Or maybe she *was* at home and just ignoring his calls, imagining he'd launch straight in where they'd left off last night. And he couldn't blame her if she had. Hopefully, if he called in on his way home she'd have calmed down enough by then to forgive him.

'Sir,' Iain Johnson called as Massey was about to walk out of the room. 'Got something here.'

'What is it, Iain?'

'You know what we talked about yesterday, about Nicole Selby and Abigail Grant being cousins because Nicole's mother is the sister of Stevie Grant?'

'I do. And Nicole's sister, Nina is engaged to the son of Ronnie Wragg, whose name appears in the Probert files.'

'It goes further back than that. Look at this. Nat's put it all together.'

DC Natalie Clark, the officer Poole must have tasked with supporting Johnson's work, handed over a lined A4 sheet with a family tree roughly drawn out by hand. 'I only wrote it down, sir. Iain did all the work.'

Massey couldn't care less who took the credit if it took them a little further towards solving all these interlocking puzzles.

'See here,' Johnson said, 'Stevie Grant and his sister Marie Selby – Nina and Nicole's mother – are both the children of Donald Grant and Margaret Dawson. And Margaret's sister, Elizabeth Dawson married Thomas Wragg and had two sons, Ronnie and Billy Wragg.'

Jesus Christ. Even more reason for his mother to stay away from the man.

'So they're related as well as engaged. Ronnie Wragg's son Nicholas and Nina Selby have a set of great grandparents in common. So what does that make them? Not sure how all this stuff works. Third cousins maybe, or second cousins?'

Massey wasn't a hundred percent sure himself, and how the hell could knowing this take them any further?

'But that's not all sir,' Clark said. 'We found this too.'

She handed him another A4 sheet. Printed this time. A copy of a newspaper article; an old Evening Chronicle front page.

'It's about a trawler that sank back in 1950,' Clark said. 'Three blokes from North Shields lost at sea. Bodies never recovered.'

'What's that got to do with this?'

'No idea yet,' Johnson said. 'But it's the same three surnames. I did a search for them, looking for more connections, and this is what came up. Best mates, sir. Alan Dawson, Arthur Grant and Robert Wragg. Skipper, Mate and Bosun respectively. All of them lost at sea when the Missy Rose-James went down.'

'And?' How the hell could something from 1950 be relevant to what was happening now, or to what happened back in the 1980s for that matter?

'And that's all we've got, sir.'

'Okay. This is good.' And it was. He just wasn't quite sure how yet. But maybe it did all come down to family. He raised his insulated mug in a salute. 'Thank you both. Excellent work. Keep going with it, please. Who knows what else you could dredge up?'

'Ha, good one sir,' Clark said. 'Like what you did there.'

CHAPTER 60

Ellie stared out at the frosted rolling fields as they zipped past. After her argument with James last night and her stupid reaction to it, she'd hardly slept a wink. In fact, she hadn't even gone to bed, and had instead spent the night propped up on the settee in the kitchen. Consequently, this morning she had niggling aches everywhere to go with the rising sense of panic.

But at least she'd had the sense to stop drinking. After having agreed to this jaunt with Billy under the influence of alcohol and then immediately regretted it, she'd poured more than half a bottle of wine down the sink to prevent herself from making any more rash decisions. But that hadn't helped much, because she'd then neglected to call him this morning – as she'd promised herself she would – until it was too late. And when she did get round to it, he hadn't answered. Because he must have been driving, she'd discovered when he arrived at just after eight, almost an hour earlier than they'd arranged.

She'd only just stepped out of the shower when the doorbell rang. She was still in the middle of drying her hair, so she'd had to leave him to his own devices for a while downstairs while she finished the task. Then, when she did come back downstairs, she'd found that the bag she'd packed in anger last night and had neglected to take back upstairs had already been stowed away in his car.

Why had she even let him over the doorstep for heaven's sake? She should have told him as soon as he'd arrived that she'd changed her mind. It would have been so much easier to give him the brush off out there, like she'd had to do yesterday.

And then, somehow, she'd allowed herself to be chivvied along by him.

He'd chatted constantly. He'd made her laugh. He'd told her how beautiful she looked when she was flustered. But not once had he paused long enough to give her an opportunity to back out; to actually tell him that she couldn't go away with him. Oh, she'd brought up a few objections, but he'd knocked them all out of court.

'My daughter could go into labour at any moment,' she'd told him.

'It's not like we're going to the back of beyond, Ellie. We'll just be an hour's drive away.'

'I haven't told anyone I'll be away.'

'You can text or call whoever you need to tell from the car,' Billy had said. 'It's not like you've got a cat that needs feeding or anything, is it? You haven't, have you?'

'Haven't what?'

'Got a cat.'

'No, but what if the police need to talk to me again?'

'They haven't managed to solve the case in forty years. What difference will a few days make?'

He took hold of her by the shoulders then and subjected her to the full wattage of that electric blue gaze. 'And anyway Ellie, what could you possibly tell them now that you haven't already told them?'

Not a bloody thing.

She'd bared her soul to DS Christine Sparks yesterday. Told her things she'd never told another living being. And no doubt Christine had gone straight back and uploaded everything she'd said onto that bloody huge computer system the police use. So from now on, every policeman she ever met would be giving her pitying looks.

James might even know already. He and Christine were close, she could have gone straight round to his and told him?

Oh God. She didn't want to be forced to have *that* conversation with her son. Not ever.

And certainly not in front of Billy.

Although if James *had* arrived in time, it might have given her the excuse she needed to back out. But he hadn't.

'What about supplies?' she'd said. The very last objection she could come up with. 'I don't have any food I could bring. I haven't had the chance to go shopping. I can't let you pay for everything.'

'The lodge is stocked up to the rafters with tinned and frozen food. We can stop at a supermarket on the way for fresh stuff – bread and milk and anything else you'd like. There's a shop in the village that has a fantastic selection of wine and spirits, you'll love it.'

Good God, he had her down as a raving alcoholic?

'And,' he'd continued, 'the local pub serves good food too if we don't fancy cooking. Stop worrying, Ellie.'

He'd managed to prise her away from the house at around ten to nine and now they were in the car, miles away from home – more than an hour away already – and Billy had given no sign yet that they were getting close to their destination.

And when it came down to it, despite the missed calls she'd found on her phone from James, she'd put off calling him back. She knew she wouldn't be able to find the words to explain why she was going away with the man he'd got himself so worked up about last night.

But at least she'd spoken to Megan to let her know she'd be away for a few days, although she avoided saying who with, just that she was with a friend.

And she still had no idea where they were going.

'I want it to be a surprise,' Billy had told her when they'd first set off.

When it had finally occurred to her to ask him.

She'd tried to make a joke about being carried off by a strange man, with no-one knowing where she was, but it fell on deaf ears.

She should have got back out of the car there and then and refused to go anywhere until he told her exactly where they were headed. After all, she'd already had a negative experience of one of Billy's surprises. And yet, here she was, somewhere in the wilds of Northumberland. Still with no idea.

How the hell had she got herself into this situation?

***

When they finally pulled up outside Billy's place, miles away from any village shop or local pub, Ellie couldn't believe what she was seeing.

When he'd told her it was a lodge, she'd expected one of those modern wooden cabin things on a park filled with others, all looking identical and not much bigger than a static caravan. But this was a solid old building of grey stone that stood in the middle of a field miles from civilisation.

'It's an old hunting lodge,' he said. 'Used generations ago by the lord of the manor and his friends when they all went out grouse shooting on the moors.'

They'd certainly come across plenty of frosty moorland to get to it. Three or four miles of it she reckoned, along the narrowest, most badly maintained single track road she'd ever encountered, with passing places and cattle grids, bordered in places by pine forest.

At one point, they'd gone down a dip and across a little bridge over a narrow stream, where a small herd of highland cattle had congregated.

In Northumberland?

She'd always thought the shaggy beasts were confined to Scotland, which was a bit of a daft assumption when she thought about it since half the fields in England now seemed to be full of alpacas, which hailed from South America.

And anyway they'd travelled west mostly, not north. So far west they could easily have crossed into the next county, into Cumbria, according to the place names she'd seen. In fact, she was pretty sure they had.

Maybe Billy would be happy to tell her exactly where they were now that they'd arrived, so she could at least let the kids know.

'It's beautiful,' she said.

He smiled proudly. 'I knew you'd love it. Just wait until you see inside. I warn you though, it's nowhere near being finished, but it has all the basics. You'll be more than comfortable here.'

She pointed to a collection of ruined buildings they'd driven past on their way in. 'What's over there?'

'Just an old derelict bothy and barns. I'm thinking of doing them up too and renting them out as holiday lets, eventually, to help fund my retirement. But I need to get the lodge finished first before I can think of starting over there.'

'You're doing all the work yourself?'

'It's my trade. That's what I do. Come and see inside.'

But she lingered a moment, taking in the stark grace of the old windswept ruins.

'I don't want you going over there. Most of those old walls are unsafe. Can't have you getting hurt on my property can I?' Billy gave her a cheeky grin. 'Not on your first day, anyway.'

***

'Oh wow.'

Much of the lodge's ground floor had been converted to open plan and what struck her first from the front door was the view she could see through a big window in the back wall, a sweeping vista that stretched all the way down to what she assumed to be the narrow river they'd crossed on the way here and then up again on the other side of the valley.

That view was eye-catching enough, but the interior of the lodge itself, with a wood burner at one end and an open fire at the other – both visible from the front door between exposed upright timbers – was amazing. She wandered into a huge kitchen diner on the right of the door, from where she could see right through to an equally huge lounge area on the left.

'This is fabulous, Billy.'

'I bought it from the Forestry Commission years ago, but for a long time I just camped out here at weekends and the odd full week now and then. The lodge was almost as much a ruin as those old buildings you saw outside. I had good intentions. Every time I came, I ferried loads of building material up, fully intending to make a start, but I never actually got round to it until Covid hit. In fact I spent a lot of the time during the lockdowns up here. At least it gave me the opportunity to dry the place out and get all the basics done then. And I've been coming up most weekends ever since to do bits here and there.' His hand trailed along a bench top and grasped hold of a polished timber post. 'But anyway, enough of that for now. Come upstairs and I'll show you the bedrooms. Don't worry. I'm a man of my word. You have an en suite room all to yourself. But if you do fancy a bit of... you know...' He waggled his eyebrows '... hanky panky, please don't hesitate.'

The room he showed her to was one of only two upstairs he said he'd finished work on. All the walls and all the soft furnishings were white. Apart from the black wrought iron framed bed, the room contained only what looked like a genuine Lloyd Loom bedside table and a battered old chest of oak drawers. No wardrobe. Instead, Billy had installed a row of shaker-inspired hooks on the wall to the left of a door that led to a small shower room that was tiled from floor to ceiling in stark white.

'It's very basic,' he said.

'It's also very beautiful.'

Other than a big shaggy sheepskin rug by the bed, the floor was bare. She ran a foot over stripped and polished boards that she knew were going to be cold to walk on and congratulated herself on having remembered to pack a pair of thick slipper socks. She crossed to a window that looked out over the back of the property, giving her a higher perspective of the sweeping view she'd seen from downstairs. It also gave her a view of the land directly below the window at the back of the lodge.

'Is that an actual garden I can see down there, out here in the wilds?'

He moved up close behind her to look out of the window. 'It's the remnants of a garden, I suppose. Can't have been cultivated in years.'

Ellie traced the broken line of what might have been a substantial mixed hedgerow around the plot, the skeletons of a few gnarled and bent shrubs still surviving to give a clue to its makeup. She could make out the oblong shapes of a couple of raised beds, overgrown and the wood no doubt rotten now. 'I can still see the bones of it. Someone must have loved it once.'

'You like gardening?'

'Mm, I do.'

'I'll have to bring you back up here in the spring then and you can help me put it to rights.'

She felt his breath on her neck. Although they weren't touching, her whole body was alert to his closeness, and she shivered.

'You're cold,' he said. 'I'll get your bag out of the car for you now, then I'll get the fire started and the boiler going while you get settled in. We'll have heat and hot water in no time.'

'What's the name of this place? Just so I can let my daughter know.'

'Sorry Ellie, you won't be able to get a phone signal out here.'

CHAPTER 61

Abigail jumped when she heard the doorbell ring, but remained where she sat on the edge of the settee, her arms wrapped tightly around her.

As soon as he'd gone and she knew the cats were inside and safe, she'd locked the doors, front and back, and wedged dining chairs under the handles. Then she'd run upstairs and changed into old jeans and a jumper and consigned her nightdress and fluffy robe to a bin bag in an effort to rid herself of the foul pervading stench. But it still hung around her like a vile cloud, in her hair from where her head had been pressed against his ski mask.

She didn't dare have a shower because she wouldn't be able to hear if he came back and she couldn't bear to be naked and defenceless if he did. Instead, she tied her hair back as tightly as she could, so no stray strands could fall loose across her face to make her retch in terror.

She couldn't believe she hadn't even attempted to defend herself when she'd had the chance. She'd known something wasn't quite right before she'd come downstairs, yet the thought of grabbing something heavy she could use as a weapon hadn't even entered her head. Even after everything she'd already gone through at the hands of the same monster three years ago.

But this time, she knew who the bastard was. She'd recognised the stance and the shape of him. And even though he'd tried to disguise his voice, she'd recognised that too.

How could she not have known sooner?

She'd been careful not to let him know she knew.

At least she hoped he hadn't noticed.

He'd left after doing nothing worse than calling her disgusting names and telling her what he intended to do next time if she failed to listen and heed his advice. Every time he caught so much as an inkling she'd talked to the police, he told her, he'd 'do' one of her friends, and then another, and another, saving her mother for last. And he'd be watching. She knew he'd already been watching, didn't she? He'd sent her the evidence of how he'd watched her for years, ever since their 'first date'. Had she liked his little gift?

When he'd gone, she'd felt a crushing relief he hadn't raped her again, but also an overwhelming terror. She had no doubt he'd keep his word, because now she knew exactly who he was.

The sound of the doorbell made her jump again, but still she ignored it, until it rang a third time.

Creeping to the window, she peered through the blinds and saw her mother on the doorstep. Patti spotted her before she could duck back out of sight and gesticulated wildly towards the front door. Abigail knew she wouldn't be put off.

'What the hell are you doing back home?' Patti ranted once the door opened. 'And why haven't you been answering your phone? I had to call that daft friend of yours, and she told me you'd come back here? You could have come to me you know. But oh no, I'm not sodding good enough for you again now, am I? I was alright the other day when you got those bloody photos through the door wasn't I? When none of your friends were around to run to instead.'

Only when she paused to take a breath did Patti notice the dining chair and the tears streaming down her daughter's face.

'What's happened?' she demanded. 'Tell me what's happened.'

***

Patti managed to stay silent until Abigail finished telling her all of it. The lack of cats on her bed. Coming downstairs. Becoming conscious of the smell. The plastic sheeting that he'd made her roll up before taking it away with him. His hand over her mouth and nose. Everything except the fact she'd recognised him this time.

'Did he—'

'Did he rape me? Not this time Mother, no. But he told me in graphic detail what he would do to me and my friends, and even to you next time, if I went to the police again. The bastard took great pleasure in that.'

'You're going to have to tell him, you know. Your dad.'

'No.' Abigail shook her head in horror. That was the last thing she needed, her father on a rampage. He had no off switch.

'Because if you don't, I will.'

'You can't do that. I don't—'

'I don't give a toss what you want now. Your dad will swing for me if he gets to know later what some pervert has done to his precious daughter, and that I knew already and didn't tell him. You know what he's capable of. Do you want the police at your door again, only this time to tell you my body has been found floating in the River Wansbeck? Well, do you? Because I sodding don't.'

CHAPTER 62

His mother hadn't been home when he'd called in again on his way home from work, and now another call had gone straight to voicemail. Massey didn't want to call Megan again to check whether she'd heard anything. The last thing his sister needed right now, so close to her due date, was extra worry. She'd already told him as much as she knew; that she'd had a call from their mother this morning saying she was going to stay with a friend for a few days.

'Which friend?' he'd asked. 'When is she coming back?'

'No idea. I never had a chance to ask. Does it matter? As long as she gets back in time for the arrival of this little one.'

He sighed and glanced at the screen of his phone, then looked towards Helen, who was staring at him from the bed. She looked a good bit better today. The flu virus must be abating.

'I don't know why you keep trying to call her,' she said.

He'd noticed that her own phone hadn't stopped buzzing with a new text message every five minutes, and made a point of looking at it.

'What?' she demanded. 'It's about work. Obviously they couldn't cope without me on Friday.'

'Are you going back tomorrow?'

'See how I feel in the morning. Probably.'

He tapped his mother's number again and heard the call go straight to voicemail.

'Your mother is perfectly capable of looking after herself you know, without you chasing after her every five minutes.'

He glared at her. 'It's who she could be with I'm concerned about.'

She gave a derisive snort. 'So she's found herself another bloke. At her age. Good for her. Big deal. She's enjoying putting it about again. With any luck, it might keep her from looking down her nose at me like she usually does. She's not the bloody angel you make her out to be, you know.'

'What the hell do you mean by that?' His voice sounded ice cold even to his own ears.

Helen sneered. 'It wouldn't be the first time. From what I've heard, she'd have spread her legs for anyone before Saint bloody David came along. And she frequently did, so I've been told. That's probably why daddy Massey did a bunk.'

Fists clenched, blood pounding in his ears, he rounded on her. 'What did you say?'

He saw Helen's alarm, the way she pulled up her arms to protect her head and shrank back into the pillows. He dropped his hands to his side in shame. Head low, he turned away from her.

'That apple hasn't fallen so far from the bloody tree after all then,' she screamed, her voice shaky with relief despite the bravado.

CHAPTER 63

Monday 22nd January 2024

Monday morning. The start of another week in the hunt for a serial rapist and a murderer, and still they couldn't be sure whether they were looking for one, two, or even three offenders. And that wasn't counting the man who'd raped and murdered Julie Probert forty years ago, which technically was not his case, although it was linked by DNA to Abigail's rape, which *was* within his remit.

In fact, all they could say for sure was that Julie's murderer was not the same person who raped Abigail, because the DNA had come back as a familial rather than an exact match.

Having been in the office since six thirty, by seven he was already onto his second cup of coffee.

He'd slept in the spare room – sleep being the wrong word to describe the anguished twisting and turning he'd endured – and he still felt twitchy.

He had no idea how he'd managed to stop himself from hitting Helen last night, but thank God he had.

Never in his life had he felt such anger towards a woman. But the fact that Helen could even have been thinking those awful things about his mother, who'd never been anything other than loving towards her...

He didn't know if he could ever forgive her for what she'd said. Or if she could ever forgive him for what he'd almost done.

How could he even forgive himself?

When he'd arrived at work this morning, he'd found a note on his desk. Clark and Johnson had continued working yesterday after he'd left, and they'd managed to add more details to the family tree they'd started. They asked to see him first thing.

Their first thing obviously, not his. He looked at the clock to find it still just 7.09 am.

Having no idea yet whether Ray Flowers would be back at work today, he rattled off an email to Adam Poole asking him to organise a short briefing with the whole Bryony team as soon as everyone was in the office. They all needed to hear whatever it was that Clark and Johnson had found.

***

Ten minutes before the briefing started, Massey had received a text from Lou Portas telling him that Flowers had called in sick again. It made him think of Helen and whether she'd decided to go back to work. And in turn that made him think again about the terrible things she'd said last night. He thrust the thoughts aside and forced himself to concentrate on listening to what the two DCs had discovered that was so important.

Standing before a whiteboard, with Iain Johnson next to her, Natalie Clark opened an A4 notepad and laid it on the desk in front of her at a diagram she'd scrawled over with notes.

'This is a complicated tale,' she began, pulling the top from a dry wipe pen. 'And we'll be going through it all again at this afternoon's briefing, only I should have a slide presentation ready by then. In the meantime, shout out if you struggle to read my writing or need us to go over anything again.

'Okay, so we've been looking for a familial relationship among the names we've come across to match the DNA link we have between the rape of Abigail Grant three years ago and the rape and murder of Julie Probert forty years ago. And now Iain and I have found DNA links that will blow your minds.' She paused and looked around at her audience, which looked back as if waiting for a movie to start. 'Iain?'

'All this goes back to three trawlermen who were presumed drowned in 1950,' Johnson said, as Clark began scrawling on the whiteboard. 'Their trawler – the Missy Rose-James – sank during a storm. Actually, the whole crew perished bar one, but the fact these three had been best mates and inseparable since infants school inspired a front page news story in the Evening Chronicle a few days after the tragedy, which we found online yesterday.'

He pointed to the top of the board, where Clark had written three names.

'These three men all grew up together: the trawler's skipper, Alan Dawson, the first mate, Arthur Grant, and the bosun, Robert Wragg, known as Bobby. They all had young families when they perished, and their children ended up intermarrying when they grew up.'

Clark elbowed Johnson to the side and began drawing connecting lines and scribbling names with the squeaky dry wipe pen.

'Alan Dawson had two daughters, Bobby Wragg had just one son, while Arthur Grant had both a son and a daughter, and all these five kids were aged between ten and three years of age when the Missy Rose-James sank. Roll on through the years – and pay attention here because this is where it all starts getting complicated –we find that Bobby's son, Thomas Wragg, married Alan Dawson's eldest daughter, Elizabeth, and they had two sons, Ronald and William Wragg – better known now as Ronnie and Billy Wragg.'

Massey gritted his teeth as he thought about the argument he'd had with his mother over Billy Wragg.

'Ronnie Wragg,' Clark continued, 'who we now know was interviewed in 1984 in connection to the Julie Probert murder, eventually married Sonia Chambers, who was one of the friends Julie had gone out with on the night she was killed. You might remember that Sonia was herself killed in a hit and run incident in Morpeth on New Year's night three weeks ago.' She paused for a moment to let the murmurs die down. 'Ronnie and Sonia had one son, Nicholas, known as Nicky, while Ronnie's brother Billy, as far as we know, has never been married and has no kids.'

Clark blew out a big breath and tapped her pen at the top of the board again.

'Now then, back to Alan Dawson, the skipper. His younger daughter, Margaret, married Donald, the son of Arthur Grant, and they had a son and a daughter. The son's name you'll all be familiar with. He's the infamous Stevie Grant – father of Abigail, our rape victim who preserved the clothes she'd been wearing at the time in her freezer for three years. Stevie's sister is Marie, who married a Robert Selby and had two daughters. They are Nina Selby, who is currently engaged to Nicky Wragg, and Nicole Selby, another of our rape victims. This means that

Nina and Nicole are first cousins to Abigail, while Nina and Nicky are second cousins.'

'She did say this was complicated,' Johnson chipped in.

'And you both said you had something new.' Massey said, unable to prevent a testy note creeping in.

'We do,' Johnson said. 'We have two new bits of intelligence, and the second one will blow your socks off.'

'Spit it out then,' Poole said.

'The first thing we found,' Clark said as she drew another line on the board, 'is that Abigail has two half-brothers. Different mothers. Not sure if she even knows about them herself, or if they know about each other. My opinion, she has to know. Both of them are a good bit older than Abigail, but Stevie Grant has acknowledged them both as his sons. Only in recent years though, so I suppose it's possible that neither he nor Abigail knew they existed before that.'

Massey wasn't convinced that Abigail knew. Hadn't she said, on the day he'd first met her, when she'd told him whose daughter she was, that she was her father's only child? 'And the other thing?' he said.

Johnson and Clark looked at each other, then Johnson grinned and performed a drum roll with his fingers on the desk in front of him.

'Arthur Grant's daughter,' Clark announced, rapping her pen on the top of the board again. 'Sheila Grant. The sister of Stevie Grant's dad, Donald. She married the son of the only survivor from the Missy Rose-James. His name was John Probert, and they had a daughter called Julie. Julie Probert. That means that Julie – whose murderer shares twenty something percent of his DNA with the man who raped Abigail – was a first cousin of Stevie Grant and first cousin once removed of Abigail.' She scratched beneath her pony tail with the end of the dry wipe pen and frowned. 'I think that's how it works. Whatever, this gives Stevie Grant two reasons to get upset about all of this.'

Massey stared at the board. Beware of what you wish for. They'd been looking for a familial DNA connection, and now they had a melting pot of intrafamilial relationships to rival any soap on telly. There were bound to be other family members still to trace within this sprawling hotchpotch, with potentially dozens more intricate DNA connections between them all. But surely only a handful at most could possibly match what they were looking for.

Grandfather and grandson, uncle and nephew, or half-brothers. They were the most likely options. And one of them would need to be old enough to have been Julie's murderer, while the other had to be young enough and fit enough to be Abigail's rapist and, more likely than not, Musk Man. And as unlikely as it might seem, they couldn't rule out the possibility of half-brothers. He'd known a woman once whose half-brother was forty years her senior. So it could happen.

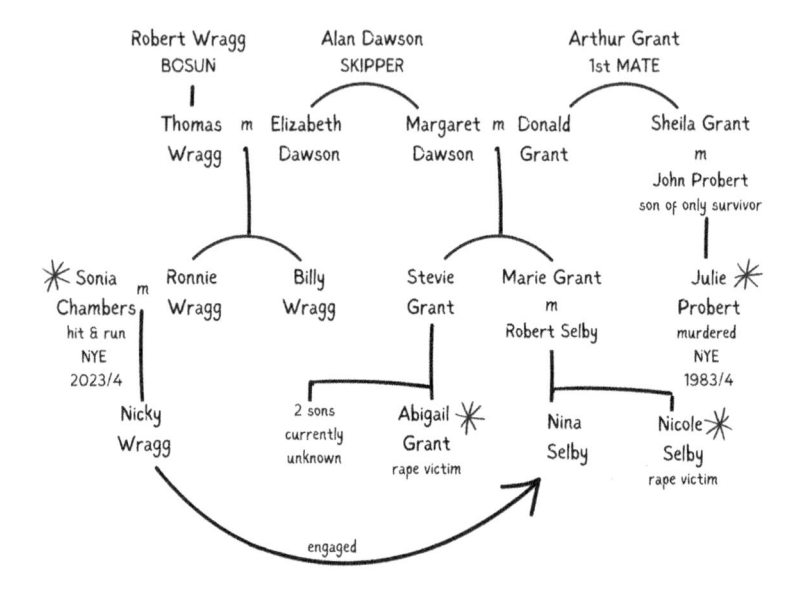

```
Robert Wragg          Alan Dawson              Arthur Grant
   BOSUN                SKIPPER                  1st MATE
     |                  ⌒⌒⌒                     ⌒⌒⌒
  Thomas  m  Elizabeth     Margaret  m  Donald       Sheila Grant
  Wragg      Dawson        Dawson       Grant             m
                                                      John Probert
                                                   son of only survivor
                                                          |
*Sonia  m  Ronnie    Billy      Stevie      Marie Grant      Julie *
Chambers   Wragg     Wragg      Grant           m            Probert
hit & run                                   Robert Selby    murdered
NYE                                                           NYE
2023/4                                                       1983/4
   |                                          |
  Nicky         2 sons      Abigail *       Nina      Nicole *
  Wragg        currently    Grant           Selby     Selby
               unknown      rape victim               rape victim

                        engaged
```

They needed an expert's opinion.

He assigned the action of finding one to Brooks.

And he should also speak to both Portas and Keegan ASAP. Certainly before springing this on them at the big briefing this afternoon.

He wondered if he should also contact Sparks and ask if his mother had said anything about her plans over the next few days. He had a horrible feeling she'd only decided to go away because he'd been such a pig on the phone to her on Saturday. But surely, even if she had, she'd have forgiven him enough to take his calls by now.

CHAPTER 64

Ellie awoke on Monday morning to the smell of bacon cooking – in her opinion, the most heavenly smell in the world besides oil paint and guaranteed to get her out of bed in double quick time to investigate. When she stood up, her head ached and felt as if it didn't quite belong to her body, but she was growing used to hangovers lately. She dressed quickly and made her way downstairs. Some fluids and a good breakfast inside her and she'd feel fine.

Before she left her room, she stood for a moment by the window. Much of the frost had disappeared and the clouds in the half-light of the morning had a strange yellowish cast. Snow on the way.

She wouldn't like to get snowed in all the way out here.

Her feet, in slipper socks, made no sound on the still untreated treads. When she reached the bottom, she saw Billy facing the cooker with his back to her, humming a tune she thought she recognised from years back. But he must have caught sight of her reflection in the black glass splashback for he turned round and gave a rueful grin.

'You caught me. I wanted to bring you breakfast in bed.'

'I'm sorry,' she said, laughing at the slogan written in red on the black apron he wore. 'Hot stuff coming through', it said.

When he realised the object of her amusement, he pulled the apron out at the sides and performed a mock curtsy.

'The delicious smell of bacon woke me up,' she said. 'I couldn't resist.'

'That's a relief. I forgot to ask last night if you like bacon. Thought I'd take a chance. I mean, who wouldn't? Food of the gods if you ask me.'

'Absolutely.'

'It'll be two minutes. How do you want it? In a butty, or on a plate with fried eggs? Or scrambled eggs even?

'Just in a butty please.'

'Do you want to make coffee while I do this, or do you prefer tea in the morning? That's another thing I should have thought to ask last night. Sorry.'

'Didn't we agree no more saying sorry? And here we are apologising to each other again first thing in the morning.'

'We did. But at least that's the only thing I have to apologise for, because I was sorely tempted to creep into your bed and ravish you last night. I managed to keep my cool though, and my promise.' His eyes twinkled and he gave her a cheeky grin. 'With great difficulty,.'

Ellie could feel her cheeks flush. She turned to examine a framed picture – a replica of an old British Railways poster featuring Hadrian's Wall – examining the smaller details, sheep grazing in the foreground, a couple of hikers appearing over a rise. Anything but think about what might have happened if she'd woken in the night to find such a strong and sensuous male body snuggling into her. In the fog of half-sleep, could she have resisted? And then it struck her. She'd slept. For the first time in what felt like months, she'd actually slept the night through.

She'd eaten well last night too – another miracle. She'd gone to bed with a belly full of breaded cod fillet, chips and peas from Billy's enormous freezer, followed by microwaved sticky toffee pudding and custard from the packed larder cupboard. He hadn't been exaggerating about all the provisions he'd stocked the lodge with. She had little recollection of the going to bed bit. Probably due to the huge measure of single malt whisky Billy had poured for her. But it must have been relatively early. The whisky had probably been a step too far after the wine she'd drunk with dinner, but maybe at home she should switch to that before bed if it knocked her out so easily.

'Earth to Ellie,' Billy snapped her out of her thoughts. 'Tea or coffee? We have both. There's even a collection of herbal tea bags somewhere. Not my sort of thing. Leftovers from a phase Nicky went through a couple of years ago.'

'Has he spent much time with you up here?'

'Yeah, of course. Uncle and nephew bonding stuff, you know. Not for a year or so though. And he won't have much time for all that anyway now he's engaged to Nina. Looks like he's cast his old uncle aside.'

'Sonia told me about the engagement. They announced it that night, didn't they? New Year.' She wrinkled her brow, trying to think back. 'Sorry, we might have already had this conversation when I'd had a few too many gins the other night.'

'They did, yes. Big surprise to Sonia. She was gobsmacked. A young whippersnapper like Nina stealing away her darling boy. Shock horror.' He busied himself for a moment preparing the bread. 'Maybe that's what made Sonia so careless. You know. That night.'

'No, that wasn't it. It was something she'd heard someone say.' Ellie sighed, remembering her old friend. The loss of her so soon after David's death, just as they'd found each other again. 'Anyway, let's not go over all that again now. It's depressing. And it's pointless. I'm never going to be able to figure out now what she meant, and she's not around anymore to enlighten us.'

The coffee machine clicked. She busied herself pouring the steaming brew into two mugs and carrying them over to the table just as Billy served up the bacon sandwiches.

'Eat up,' he said, 'and no more gloomy thoughts. There's enough gloom outside this morning.'

'It looks like it's going to snow.'

'Possibly, but my 4x4 will cope, whatever comes. So, what do you fancy doing today? There's not much happens around here at this time of the year – or any time of year, come to that. We could take a drive through the forest.' He nodded his head towards the front wall of the lodge and the field beyond it that was bordered on the far side by tall pine trees. 'If you like trees, that is. Or we could go over to Greenhead. There's the Roman Army Museum there, if you're interested, although it might not be open today come to think of it. Or there's Brampton. There'll be more going on there.'

'Civilisation of some sort would be good. I should be able to get a signal then, so I can give Megan a call, just to make sure everything is still okay. I'd hate to be away from home when the baby's born.'

'And your policeman son? You can call him too.'

'He'll be way too busy to talk to me,' she said, blushing all over again as she thought about the last uncomfortable conversation she'd had with

James, which had been all about the man now sitting directly across the breakfast table from her. 'I might just send him a text though. Let him know where I am, so he can stop worrying.'

Billy laughed. 'Why should he worry? You're a grown woman Ellie, and a beautiful one at that. You don't have to answer to your son.'

The way he said it made it sound as if he'd been privy to her telephone argument with James and the things he'd said about her getting involved with another man so soon after David's death.

Not that she *was* involved with Billy.

Not in that way.

Not yet.

'Stop,' she said. 'You're embarrassing me.'

He stroked the back of her hand and looked into her eyes. 'Nothing to be embarrassed about when it's the truth.'

He held her gaze, mesmerising her. She felt unable to pull her hand or her eyes away from his. The man should have a safety warning stuck to his forehead. Dangerous waters: look into these eyes at your peril.

He smiled. 'Finish your breakfast Ellie, and we can make a day of it.'

CHAPTER 65

'Come on, Ellie. Time to go.'

Billy already stood outside the open door, arms outstretched, taking in big breaths of the clean, pine-scented air. After they'd finished a leisurely breakfast she'd insisted on doing the washing up. Now it was after half ten and he wanted to get going.

She pulled on her boots, fastened her coat and grabbed her shoulder bag from the settee where she'd left it. The bag was open. She must have left it unzipped. Thank goodness none of the contents had spilled out onto the settee. No man should have to be subjected to the contents of a woman's handbag.

Billy had the car running already by the time she closed the front door, its engine smooth and steady in the cold morning air, like the purr of a big cat; the only sound other than the sough of the wind in the pine trees to disturb the quietude of the landscape.

Once out of the lodge gateway, the barren blacks and browns of the winter moorland looked bleak without the sparkling frost of yesterday. Over to the left of her vision – to the east, she believed, now she was developing a better idea of roughly where they were – the sombre colours melded into the bruised mass of clouds hunched on the horizon, making it difficult to discern where the land ended, and the sky began.

Descending into the dip where she'd seen the highland cattle yesterday and up the other side, a silver pickup truck loomed unexpectedly down the dip towards them on the narrow, single-lane road. Billy yanked the car over, its passenger side wheel skidding off the road. Ellie lurched to one side and felt the car fishtail before it ground to a halt with less than an inch between the vehicles. Billy stormed out of the car and wrenched open the driver's door of the truck.

The female driver shrank back as his clawed hand shot towards her face. But then sanity must have prevailed, for he pulled back his hand and flexed his fingers.

From where Ellie sat in the Discovery's passenger seat, she couldn't hear their exchange, but the wide-eyed look the truck's driver gave her as Billy threw himself back behind the wheel of the Land Rover and lurched the car back onto the road imprinted itself onto her brain.

'Stupid bitch,' he seethed as car righted itself and catapulted up the road.

They sat in silence then, with Billy taking the bends far too quickly for Ellie's liking. She could feel tension emanating from him like a forcefield.

For a while the moorland gave way to drystone-walled fields, and they skirted a farmyard. But soon they had the desolate moorland on both sides of the road again, and Ellie caught sight of a warning sign on the right as they whizzed past. A red circle with a line through it and a yellow triangle edged with black. 'Military Firing Range', the sign said.

'What's that?' she asked. She'd noticed them on the way to the lodge yesterday, set at regular intervals along the road, and already had a good idea what they must be, but anything to break the tension.

'What?'

'That warning sign. A firing range?'

'Used to be a rocket research centre or something during the Cold War. It's RAF Spadeadam now. NATO aircrews use it to learn electronic warfare tactics, so you'd better make sure you don't wander across that side of the road if you ever get stuck out here alone.'

Ellie shivered. She had no intension of ever ending up out on these bleak, desolate moors alone. But at least the ice between them had been broken, although not yet melted. She'd seen a different side of Billy during their encounter with the truck. She couldn't believe he'd actually been about to grab that poor woman driver by the throat.

She'd got a glimpse of a monster lurking behind those disarming blue eyes and the charming smile?

What if he lost it with her like that back at the lodge?

She was stuck out in the back of beyond, with a man who'd barely managed to stop himself from throttling a woman. With no phone signal to call for help.

Maybe she could try to talk him into cutting their time away short, and then when they got back home she'd distance herself from him. No way would she allow herself to get wrapped up in a relationship with another abuser. She'd had enough of that with her first husband.

***

They'd have reached Brampton sooner if Billy had taken the road through Gilsland and then turned west on the A69, but instead he took a roundabout route across country, as if he were deliberately trying to confuse her. But now she was wise to him. The incident with the woman in the van had unnerved her. At least now she had a much better idea of where they were, and where the lodge was situated. He'd given the game away when he'd confirmed they were close to RAF Spadeadam. Because, while she'd never been anywhere near the place before, she knew where it was on a map because David had been stationed there for a couple of years when he was still in the Royal Air Force during the early days of their courtship.

They parked in the centre of Brampton, facing the Howard Arms Hotel, and wandered the streets looking in shop windows, with Billy keen to re-ingratiate himself with her, while she struggled to concentrate on where they were going and what she was supposed to be looking at.

He suggested stopping for a coffee and she agreed. It would give her an opportunity to make some calls. She'd happily ring Megan in Billy's presence since she had no intention of saying anything to cause her heavily pregnant daughter worry, but she'd need to find a moment or two away from him if she wanted to try calling James. And she should call him, or at least send a text. Just so that someone knew where she was.

In the end, it was Billy who excused himself first when his own phone rang, as soon as they'd sat down in the only café they could find open. He'd take it outside, he told her.

When the door had closed behind him, with the people on the next table chatting about a snow storm hitting the north east coast and working its way west, she pulled her own phone out of her bag and tried calling James, only for the device to tell her she had no internet connection, and sure enough she had no bars showing at the top of the screen.

How can that be?

She could see Billy outside now, or at least his outline through the steamed up window. He faced away from her with his mobile to his ear, so she assumed his was working.

With her senses still on high alert, she remembered how she'd found her bag open on the settee, when she'd been sure she'd zipped it closed.

Had Billy done something to her phone?

But why?

She was about to check the settings when the waitress brought their coffees and bent down close to her ear. 'There's someone over there would like a word.' She spoke from the corner of her mouth, rolling her eyes and inclining her head slowly towards the back of the shop, where Ellie caught sight of a tall woman standing at the door to the kitchen and beckoning her over. The woman from the pickup truck. Perhaps ten years younger than herself, with wild black hair and weather beaten cheeks.

Was this about the incident on the road? Was she about to complain to her about Billy's behaviour?

Ellie checked Billy was still busy with his call outside before stepping over to talk to the woman. 'I'm so sorry about earlier,' she began.

'Don't worry about that,' the woman said. 'How well do you know that man? Are you staying with him at the lodge?'

'What? How? Why do you want to know?'

The woman gripped her hand. 'Because he's bad news. You need to be very careful. Are you stuck out there with him?'

'Yes. But look. About the incident this morning, I know he—'

'A friend of mine knew him. He ruined her life. You need to be careful. Please, be *very* careful.'

Billy turned to come back into the café. Ellie had no time to ask what the woman meant but, making an instant decision to trust her, she fished her own business card and one of James' cards from her purse with the intention of asking her to contact James to tell him where she was. But the woman had gone. She'd disappeared already through the kitchen door, leaving Ellie to push the cards into her pocket and make it look as if she were just returning to the table from the ladies as Billy came back through the front door.

'Made your calls?' he asked, a distracted look on his face.

'No. I still have no reception. How is yours working when mine isn't.'

'It's only just working. The connection kept dropping out. Reception is shit around here anyway, and maybe my network has better service out here than yours if we're with different providers.'

Ellie looked away from him and out of the window. She knew Northumberland and Cumbria still had dead zones for mobile reception, but nowhere near as many as there used to be. If he really had messed with her phone, it would probably be better to let him believe she'd accepted his explanation.

She looked at her watch. Not yet two o'clock but the sky looked so dark it might just as well be dusk out there now. And she could see from the way passers-by were walking that the wind had risen considerably since they'd arrived.

Billy reached for her hand. She tried not to flinch as he took hold and stroked the back of it with his thumb. He looked into her face, attempting to engage his devastating eyes with hers so he could charm her again, but she looked away.

'Let's buy something nice for dinner,' he said. 'And a bottle of good wine. Then we can go straight back to the lodge, sit by the fire and block out the world. By the time the morning comes, this bad weather will have passed, and you might have forgiven me by then for my atrocious behaviour towards that woman in the pickup truck this morning.'

Ellie frowned at him, wondering if he'd spotted her exchange with the woman at the kitchen door.

'I'm concerned about the weather,' she said. 'There's supposed to be heavy snow coming. Perhaps we should just collect our bags and go back home now, today.'

'The snow's not forecasted to get this far west. At least not the heavy snow they're getting back home. If we go now, we'll be driving straight into it. Better to leave it until the morning when the snowploughs and gritters will have been out in force to clear the roads.'

She sighed. For all she wanted to draw their little holiday to an end now and get back home, she couldn't fault his logic.

It wasn't until they were pulling back up outside the lodge that she remembered what he'd said that morning about his 4x4 being able to cope with snow however bad it got. And that made her feel vindicated for having slid the two business cards onto the table behind his back as they left the café. She hoped the waitress would make sure they found their way to the woman from the pickup, and that she would know what to do with them.

CHAPTER 66

While Massey had been in the Operation Bryony briefing, Operation Casper had begun the process of moving into the MIT suite – the lap of luxury compared to the swamp.

Now that all the cold case files had been digitised, the dried but still smelly original papers had been incinerated. And with the threat of a severe snow storm on its way – almost upon them in fact, judging by the sky – it didn't make sense for them to remain out of the fold in a cold draughty old station with no facilities.

It didn't take Keegan long to turn up at Massey's desk, having received a text message from him already.

'Portas is expecting us, as soon as you arrive,' Massey said.

'Best let her know I'm here then so she can get that coffee pot brewing. She knows exactly how I like mine.' Keegan tapped out a text message and sent it.

Massey would pay to know how the pair of them knew each other so well.

They took along Iain Johnson, armed with a photocopy of Clark's handwritten family tree, while Clark herself concentrated on creating an electronic version for this afternoon's briefing.

***

Once Johnson had explained the information on the tree and answered a couple of questions, Portas dismissed him with some words of encouragement. 'This is brilliant work, Iain,' she said. 'Thank you, and please pass on our thanks to Natalie too.'

As soon as the door closed behind him, Portas and Keegan looked at Massey with disbelieving expressions.

'This is huge, James.' Portas said.

'But let's not get ahead of ourselves.'

He felt obliged to bring their feet back to the ground.

'This had me going for a while too, but it could be a false lead. There's nothing here to say that the DNA evidence we have belongs to anyone on this tree. Julie's murderer and Abigail's rapist are related in some way to each other, we know that, but they may not be related to any of these people here. They could be from a different family altogether and this could all be just a huge coincidence.'

'Another one,' Portas said.

'And without something against one or more of them, we don't have anything that could help us check whether or not we're on the right track,' Massey said.

Keegan held up a finger. 'What about DNA from the rape victim? Not Abigail, the other one, her cousin. Didn't we take a sample from her as part of a rape kit for comparison?'

'Nicole Selby. Sadly no, her father was obstructive. Wouldn't allow her to submit to any blood or swab tests.'

Portas sighed. 'Stupid bloody man.'

'Probably didn't want us linking his family to Stevie Grant,' Keegan said.

'Don't we have Grant's DNA?' Portas asked. 'Surely that should have lit up in the system.

Both Massey and Keegan shook their heads.

'Believe it or not,' Keegan said. 'While we know pretty much what he gets up to, we've never had enough on him to even bring him in, let alone charge him with anything. Whenever he thinks we're getting close, he sets up one of his crew to take the fall instead, and they're always too scared to finger him. Somehow he always manages to stay one step ahead of us. Make no mistake, he has more than one crooked copper on his payroll.'

'So we have two routes we can go,' Portas said. 'We ask the families nicely for saliva samples, in which case we'd need to explain why we want it, which would risk possibly alerting a murderer and a rapist if they *are* part of this family.

'Or we put every single one of them under a microscope until we find something, anything, that will allow us to bring them in and get a sample without consent.'

'We could ask Abigail,' Massey said. 'She could be up for giving us a sample. She's desperate to find some sort of resolution to what she's been through. I'll get Kirsty onto it. She has the best relationship with her.'

'Good,' Portas replied. 'If she's willing. If she shares any of her DNA with her attacker and with Julie's murderer, then we'll know it's her extended family we need to be concentrating on.

'And that could take weeks,' Keegan said. 'So we'd better hope for another break in the meantime. Do we have any idea what's happening with the operation Serious and Organised are so keen to keep under wraps?

'Not yet, but DSU Elsom and DCI Baker will be with us this afternoon. It appears they have something they'd like to share.'

Keegan snorted. 'That must be a first.'

***

Massey hadn't had the chance to ask Sparks anything about her discussion with his mother yet. He didn't want to. It wouldn't be fair to put her on the spot like that, but she'd understand, surely.

If he could just manage to snatch a few moments alone with her.

He'd expected to see her just across the room, back where she belonged, but she wasn't here yet. Where the hell was she?

Keegan noticed him looking over, so Massey tapped his watch and mouthed her name. Keegan shrugged.

Wherever she was, he didn't have time to worry about it now. The room was filling up and the noise level rising. He couldn't hear himself think.

And then DSU Elsom arrived with DCI Baker of the Drug Squad, followed closely not only by Portas but by Chief Superintendent Crowder too.

CHAPTER 67

With a muscle jumping in her jaw, Lou Portas opened the briefing with a quick update on the investigation into the murder of Leon Robinson, delivered in a clipped voice, and the team's continued belief that the boy had been an unfortunate witness to an event taking place at Abigail's house on Sunday 7th January, while Abigail herself was away, since she'd been staying with a friend since Thursday 4th January.

'What event would that be?' Elsom asked.

Portas glared.

The tension between the two DSUs thrummed like a forcefield. Something must be up, but Massey had no idea what.

'When Abigail returned home for the first time on the 17th to pick up a few things, she found a package of photos on her doormat. They all featured her, taken covertly by someone who has been tracking her movements over a long period of time. We believe it's likely Leon saw that package being delivered. He might even have seen the face of the person who delivered it, and he was killed to keep him quiet.'

Marion Baker ducked her head to scribble a note, then edged her pad towards Elsom.

Portas made a silent point of having noticed, before asking DC Clark and DC Johnson to lay out the family connections they'd discovered.

Clark flicked slowly through the slides of her new presentation, which made the family connections much clearer, while Johnson provided commentary all the way from the sinking of the Missy Rose-James, through the intermarriages of the trawlermen's children and the children they had, down to the youngest generation, the great grandchildren of the trawler's lost crew.

Elsom nodded his bull mastiff head and rubbed his pockmarked jaw. 'Hmm,' he said.

'Something in there tugged another string, Elsom?' Keegan demanded.

He too must have felt the tension, for his shrewd gaze darted between the two senior officers.

Portas made a gesture inviting Elsom to take the floor.

'I can talk just as well from here, thank you very much.'

'Then please do,' Portas said.

'Alright then.' Elsom lifted his chin, ran a finger around the neck of his shirt and harrumphed. 'You'll all appreciate, I'm sure, that for operational reasons, I can't share a great deal. Only as much as it impacts your own investigations. Most of you here already know that we've been looking at Stevie Grant. No great secret. Sadly much of our work is impacted one way or another by the man's activities.'

He paused and glanced at the notes Baker had pushed his way.

'As you'd expect, we have eyes on several members of Grant's outfit, and not just the big boys. Lately, we've been watching one of the lads lower down the ladder who, from what we've observed, has ideas above his station. He's making like he wants to climb all the way to the top. Sees himself as Grant's future right hand man. And those already at the top, even the current second in command, Nigs Bowen, appear to be humouring him. So far.'

Elsom drummed his fingers on the desk in front of him, as if working out how much he could and couldn't say. Then he waved one hand towards the big screen with the last slide of Clark's presentation still showing. 'And now we know why. Because he's bloody family.'

'Who?' Massey demanded.

'Nicky Wragg. If what I've just seen is correct, young Nicholas' father is Stevie Grant's cousin.'

'And something else you need to know,' DCI Baker said – the first words she'd spoken since she entered the room. 'It's looking as if Nicky Wragg could have something going on with Grant's daughter.'

'What?' Massey said.

Brooks knitted her brows. 'But he's engaged to Nina Selby.'

Baker gave a snort of derision. 'Since when has a little thing like that ever stopped a bloke?'

Keegan sat back in his chair and stretched his long legs out in front of him. 'Are you going to enlighten the rest of us?'

Baker gave Elsom a sideways glance before speaking. 'Wragg was spotted entering the home of Abigail Grant at four thirty two yesterday morning and leaving again at ten thirteen.'

'Abigail answered the door to him?'

'No need. Wragg let himself in.'

'He did what?' Portas demanded.

Massey looked at Brooks. He couldn't believe what he was hearing.

'As far as I know,' Brooks said, her expression worried, 'Abigail's still at her friend's house. I've tried contacting her a couple of times today but she's not picking up.'

'Someone was at home.' Baker said. 'The heating was on. There were a couple of cats sitting on the sill between the glass and the blinds at the front window.'

'Jesus wept.' Massey's brain ran through the possible scenarios and landed on only one. 'What was he wearing?'

'Sportswear. Dark.'

'Was it black? Did he have anything covering his head?'

Baker faced Massey, but her eyes swivelled towards Elsom. 'It was the middle of the night.'

'Answer the questions,' Massey snapped.

She raised her eyes to the ceiling and let out a patient breath, as if talking to a child. 'Yes, the dark clothing might have been black. Might, not was. And yes, he wore a hat. A beanie.'

'Could it have been a ski mask folded up?'

Massey saw the realisation dawn on Marion Baker's face. 'Shit!'

'But you're telling us now that they're related ...' Elsom blustered. 'It could have been just a family visit.'

'At half four in the morning? Dressed all in black with a ski mask on? And you didn't try to stop him?'

'Fucking hell, Elsom!' Keegan butted in 'You think it's normal behaviour for a bloke to drop in on a girlfriend for a shag or on family for a cosy chat, at stupid o'clock in the morning?

'These aren't normal people.'

Baker's face had turned puce. 'I never said it was definitely a ski mask.'

Massey tried to slow his breathing. 'Kirsty, give Abigail another call now.'

Brooks paused and looked at Portas, seeking permission.

Portas nodded and Brooks tapped her phone. The whole room waited expectantly.

'No answer.'

'Try the friend she's been staying with, and then her mother. If you still can't get hold of her I want you to go around there as soon as we're finished here.'

'Go now, Kirsty,' Portas said. 'This briefing is over.'

'Something else you might like to know first,' Elsom said, before Brooks could make her escape. 'We've also had eyes on the big man himself, and Stevie Grant turned up at his daughter's address yesterday afternoon with his minders. They stayed for a little over an hour and a woman we assume to be his daughter left with them. They didn't drop her off anywhere and so as far as we know, she's still with him.'

Chief Superintendent Crowder made his way around the edges of the room towards the door. 'Superintendent Portas, Superintendent Elsom. My office.'

CHAPTER 68

Massey stalked the room. Other than Kirsty Brooks and John Land, who'd both gone looking for Abigail, and Superintendent Lou Portas, who was still with the chief, the entire on duty complement of officers from the MIT, the whole of Operation Bryony and the Probert cold case had stayed in the office after the briefing.

Baker hadn't hung around to chat while she waited for her boss. No surprise there.

His phone buzzed. Brooks. He put the call on speaker so everyone could hear.

'Abigail's not home. Apart from her two cats, which look frantic pacing the internal window sills, as if they've missed a couple of meal times, her house looks deserted. Hopefully she'll be back before it becomes necessary to do something about the animals, because neither her best friend nor her mother have a key to get into the house to feed them.'

'What did the friend have to say?'

'That she'd normally expect to have a couple of text conversations per day at least with Abigail, but she hasn't heard from her at all since Saturday night and all her attempts to start a conversation online have gone unanswered. She says she can see that Abigail hasn't even opened her messages, and apparently that's so unheard of between them that she'd begun to think she'd said something to upset her.'

'It didn't occur to her that Abigail could have been in trouble?'

'Don't think it entered her head, sir,' Brooks said. 'But to be fair, I don't think there's much going on up there beyond gel nails, boob lifts and the Kardashians, and maybe whoever's the hottest male celeb.'

'What about Patti?'

'She says she saw Abigail on Sunday morning and that she was perfectly alright then. She claims she has no idea where she is now because Abigail never tells her anything unless she wants something in return. She's lying though. She knows more but that's as much as we can get out of her.'

'Do you think she knows Abigail left with Stevie Grant?'

'I'm sure she does sir. Which means there's no point at all in trying to push her. She'd chew off her own arm rather than talk to us about him.'

'It was probably Patti who got Grant round there.'

Keegan nodded his head in agreement.

'Look sir, I know what Superintendent Elsom and DCI Baker said, but can we be sure Abigail didn't return home later? I'd like to go back to the house and have a look inside. Make sure she's not in there and in trouble.'

'We could easily argue just cause,' he said. 'You and Land get yourselves back there and I'll send round uniform with the big red key. Better feed the cats while you're there.'

***

When Portas returned, it was only to summon Massey and Keegan to her office.

She didn't speak until they'd got themselves settled at her little table by the window, where they could see the first flurries of snow starting to fall, although the tension in her was clear when she spoke. 'We lay off Stevie Grant and his operation.'

'We what?' Massey glared at her. 'Even if one of his men is a serial rapist and murderer?'

'I agree with you, the whole situation stinks. But we have our orders. We do nothing that could alert Grant to Elsom's operation. We need some other way.'

'We look at the familial DNA match again,' Keegan said. 'Because if Nicholas Wragg really is Musk Man, or at least if he's the bastard who raped Abigail, then that narrows the pool of potential familial matches considerably.'

'Indeed,' Portas said. 'So let's see who we have?' She returned to her desk to collect her laptop, tapped a few keys and turned the screen so they could all see. 'Here's the full family tree from Natalie's presentation.'

Massey barely heard her. Grandfather and grandson, uncle and nephew, or half-brothers. His subconscious had already got there before his rational mind caught up.

Uncle and nephew. He flung back his chair and surged to his feet. If Nicky Wragg was the rapist, then Billy Wragg – his father's brother – had to be the murderer of Julie Probert.

Keegan had seen it too. He shook his head. 'Not necessarily, Flash. There's the grandfather to consider too. Thomas Wragg. And this isn't the full tree anyway. We haven't got Sonia's side on here. There's another grandfather. There could be other uncles.'

Portas looked from one to the other. 'What am I missing?' she demanded.

Keegan gave a big sigh. 'It's his mother. She's having it off with Ronnie Wragg's brother Billy. The paternal uncle of Nicky Wragg—'

'She is not... Oh for fuck's sake...' Massey pushed both hands through his hair.

Keegan carried on speaking over him. '—and therefore, quite possibly the flip side of our familial DNA match.'

'Good God!' Portas gave a humourless laugh. 'That woman gets everywhere.

'Seriously Flash, if we're right about Nicky Wragg for Abigail and possibly – probably – for the other women, then we need to investigate Sonia's side of the family too before going off half cocked.'

'No we don't,' Portas said. 'Sonia Wragg had no siblings, and her father died when she was just a kid. I remember that from the hit and run case. And any half-brother of Nicky Wragg could never have been old enough to be Julie's murderer. James, you need to speak to your mother urgently. She needs to stay away from the Wragg family.'

Still standing, Massey stared out of the window, where the snow was falling heavy now. 'I've been trying to get in touch with her since first thing yesterday morning. We had an argument on Saturday night. I thought she'd just been ignoring me since then until she calmed down. But now—'

'You need to make sure she's alright,' Portas said, 'but Abigail has to be our first priority.'

'Speak to Sparks,' Keegan told him. 'Maybe your mother mentioned something to her apart from the interview. Something Sparks didn't think she needed to report to me on.'

Portas shook her head. 'I don't think that's appropriate.'

'Fuck's sake Lou. This is his mother we're talking about.'

'Which is precisely the reason he shouldn't be involved. You know that. I'll talk to Christine myself, but it'll need to wait until she's back at work. She has her hands full right now.'

What? 'Is she alright? What's happened?'

'She's fine, James. Just a problem at home.'

CHAPTER 69

It took a little less than fifteen minutes to get to Megan's house, and Massey was out of the car and charging towards the front door before the sensible part of his brain made itself heard. Calm down, it said. You don't want to alarm her. Not in her present condition.

But Mam is Megan's mother too.

Yes, but Megan could drop that baby at any moment. Calm down.

By the time his ring on the bell got a response, he'd managed to rearrange his face into a less frantic expression.

It was little Livvy who pulled the door open, with help from her mother.

'Well, look who's out here in the snow Livvy. Hello Uncle James? To what do we owe this pleasure?'

'Have you heard from Mam?'

'What, no cuddle for your favourite niece? Naughty Uncle James.'

'Sorry.' Massey closed his eyes and gave a grimace of suppressed impatience before stepping inside out of the cold. The child held her arms out to be picked up and he swung her in the air. 'Hello Livvy. Can I have a cuddle please?'

Feet apart and fists in the small of her back, Megan stretched. 'What's got your knickers in a twist?'

'I'm looking for Mam.'

Megan laughed. 'I gathered that already.'

'She's not at home and I haven't been able to reach her by phone.'

'I've already told you, she's away for a few days with a friend.'

'Which friend?'

'She didn't say. It was first thing in the morning. I had my hands full with this little menace.' She gave Livvy a tickle. 'I didn't think to ask.'

Massey disentangled himself from Livvy's clinging limbs and set her down on the floor. 'I need a list of her friends. Names and addresses too if you have them.'

'What? Why?'

'Because nothing is getting through to her phone. All I'm getting is a message saying her number is not available. So I'm concerned.'

Megan snorted. 'Oh right. So the rest of us have to jump because you're a little worried. For God's sake James, she'll be fine. She's always fine.'

'And what if she's not? What if everything is not alright?' So much for trying not to worry a pregnant woman. He raked his fingers through his hair, puffed out his cheeks and remembered that Megan had never experienced the dark days he'd shared with their mother. She'd never had to witness the horrors an abusive man could inflict. 'Please Megan, just tell me which friends you think she could be with. Names and addresses. I'll take it from there. Oh, Megan... No, please don't cry... I'm sorry.'

'Bastard.' She sniffed away the sudden tears and picked up her daughter, settling her to one side of her distended belly. 'Making a pregnant woman cry. Nasty policeman. Isn't that right, Livvy? Uncle James is a nasty policeman.'

'God, Megan, I'm so sorry. I shouldn't have... I'm just—'

She punched him on the shoulder. 'Concerned? Yeah, I got that. And you'd never have made me cry if I hadn't been full of raging pregnancy hormones.' Moving back into the hall, she hooked a small book from the window sill. 'Any addresses I've got are in here. You'll recognise most of the names. Try Rita or Anne first. Even if it's not one of them, they might know where she's gone.'

Massey jotted down addresses and phone numbers for five people whose names he did indeed recognise because his mother had known them for decades, and another couple Megan said were more recently acquired friends. Then he gave his sister a hug, trying his best not to crush Livvy between them.

'And you should speak to the nosy cow next door,' Megan said. 'She'll know if Mam was picked up from the house rather than drove herself. And if so, she'll probably have seen who it was.'

'Thanks. I'll let you know what happens. Try not to worry.'

'I wasn't bloody worried at all until you showed up, and now I'm going to be beside myself.' She gave him a tremulous smile and whacked him again on the shoulder. 'You'd better find her. And she'd better be alright.'

***

He tried Rita first.

'To tell the truth James, I've been a bit worried about your mother lately. We all have actually. It's only natural of course, with everything she's been going through since your dad died. And she'll come out of it eventually. You just have to be patient and support her.'

'Yes Rita, but do you have any idea of where she might have gone, or who with? She told Megan she was on her way off for a few days with a friend, but not where to or who with, and now we can't contact her.'

'Oh goodness. Well I know she's not with Anne, because I saw Anne in the Co-op this morning and she just got back yesterday from Spain. She goes every winter you know, for the heat. Her arthritis you see. But then she always comes home in time for her daughter's birthday, which is today. I just said to her—'

'What about any other friends she might go to visit or go away with?' He'd known Rita since he was a child and knew exactly what was coming next; a monologue that would go precisely nowhere. Better to cut her off or they'd be here all day.

'There's no-one springs to mind, I'm afraid. And I'm sure she'd have told me if she was going to be away for a while because she usually asks me to go in and check on things. You know, to open and close the curtains every day, that sort of thing, so the house doesn't look empty. And she hasn't asked me to do that this time.' Rita looked lost for a moment before putting both hands on her cheeks. 'Oh goodness James, do you think something could have happened to her?'

'I hope not.'

***

Back in the car, Massey was about to enter the next postcode on his list into the car's satnav when his phone rang, and Sparks' name popped up.

'Where are you?' he asked.

'Stuck at home waiting for Ian and Sara to arrive. A problem with my mother. Tell you about it later.'

'I've got a problem with my own mother right now Christine. So if this is a social call—'

'That's why I'm ringing. I just logged on and saw all the stuff about the family tree and about Sonia's son entering Abigail's house yesterday morning. So when I put them together, I saw... Shit, James, that means that Billy Wragg—'

'Could have murdered Julie Probert. Yes, I know this already. Look, I'm sorry but I have to go. I'm trying to find my mother. She's gone missing.'

'Then I think she'll be with Billy.'

'What?' Although on some deep subconscious level he'd already known. He'd recognised the signs of something corrupt slithering below the surface from the moment Sonia appeared like a ghost from the past at the crematorium to lay her hand on the window of the hearse. Like a djinn, marking his mother out for the devil to find. All the things that had happened since: Sonia's brutal death, Julie's unsolved murder rising up from the flood after forty years, Abigail's frozen party clothes that provided the umbilical link between a malevolence of the past and its present day counterpart. They were all part of it. Even the murder of young Leon Robinson.

But the analytical side of his brain still had the urge to rationalise. 'She can't be,' he said. 'She told Megan she was going away for a few days with a friend.'

'What the hell else is she going to refer to him as to you and Megan?'

'What do you know, Christine?'

'I saw him on your mother's doorstep on Saturday, and then later, when she was in the bathroom, I saw a text from him to her phone. "Say yes", it said. I didn't think—'

'Yes to what? Fuck's sake, Christine, why haven't you told me this before now?'

'I couldn't, could I? I'd have had to—'

'I need to go. I have to find his address.'

'Here's Ian's car just pulling up now. Come and pick me up. I'm coming with you. I'll have Wragg's address by the time you get here. I already have his vehicle reg. I'll call it in.'

CHAPTER 70

'He lives on Carlow Drive in Choppington,' Sparks said as she threw herself into the passenger seat, scattering still frozen snowflakes from her hair. 'The newish estate near the Foresters Arms.'

With swirling snow making visibility poor, Massey performed a careful three point turn, giving parked cars a wide berth. The wind had risen in the last hour and snow had begun to drift against the kerb and garden walls.

'I called Lou Portas on the way here,' he said, when they finally hit the A189. 'Brought her up to date.'

'Didn't she try to stand you down again?'

'She knew that would be pointless. She's going with it for now. With provisos. That we don't go off half-cocked and we coordinate with Keegan. She wants a chat with him about it first though.'

'What is it with those two?'

'No idea. Nothing romantic, as far as I know. She'll have her hands full with Flowers anyway. But I gather she and Keegan have known each other for years.'

Billy Wragg's home was at the far end of the estate and backed onto the steep slope that led to the south bank of the River Wansbeck. He'd have a good view from his back windows of the railway bridge that spanned the river, known locally as the black bridge.

Massey couldn't help but think about last summer when, a little upstream from here and on the north side of the river, the body of a young girl had been pulled out of the water in the middle of the night by a group of young campers. One young lad had decided in the dark to try giving the kiss of life to the girl, not realising until he locked lips with her that she was past any hope of resuscitation by two or three days at least. Had the boy's nightmares faded yet?

The house looked to be in darkness. No vehicle stood on the drive, and the Land Rover Discovery Sparks had seen outside his mother's house on Saturday would be way too big to fit into this garage, so he felt pretty sure Wragg was not inside the house. But to be on the safe side he pounded on the front door a couple of times, while Sparks took a walk around the back to see if any sign of life showed there.

Nothing.

They took a neighbour each, and Massey got confirmation from his that Wragg had driven off at around half seven on Sunday morning and hadn't been seen at the house since.

They shook off the snow and climbed back in the car. 'Maybe Ronnie knows where he is,' he said.

***

'This takes us right back to when we entered this sorry mess,' Sparks said, as Massey made the turn from Pottery Bank in Morpeth onto the unnamed road. 'We've come full circle.'

It may be the same place they'd come to in the early hours of New Year's morning, and the snow may be falling again, but this time they were able to drive up the hill instead of having to trudge up it on foot.

They had to pull onto Ronnie Wragg's driveway, so as not to block the narrow road. The curtains were drawn, but lights seeped between them from the room behind the big bay window on the left of the front door.

'Full circle implies that we're at the end of whatever this is,' Massey said eventually. 'But I think we're nowhere near yet. No sign of a Land Rover Discovery for a start.'

Sparks pressed the doorbell hard, and they heard it ring inside the house. The door opened after just two beats.

Massey held out his warrant card. 'Mr Wragg. Good evening. I'm DCI Massey of Northumbria Police. This is DS Sparks.'

Ronnie Wragg peered at them both, his sandy brows tented over his nose. 'But I haven't called yet.' A look of horror dawned on his face. 'Oh God, no, has something happened to Nicky?'

'Mr Wragg,' Sparks said. 'Could we come in please sir? Better if we talk to you inside.'

The man looked to be in shock, and it took no effort to guide him backwards so they could move inside out of the snow. They steered him into the lit room on the left, where a waif-like young girl stood, nervously twisting a tissue between her fingers.

Massey stopped, momentarily taken aback. He'd stared regularly at this face, or one very like it, up on the screen in the Operation Bryony incident room. Then his brain caught up. This must be Nina Selby, fiancée of Nicholas Wragg, not Nicole Selby, victim of Musk Man. The girls could be twins. Perhaps they were.

'Is there anyone else in the house, Mr Wragg?'

Wragg looked confused.

'Your brother, or your son. Are they here?'

'What? Are you not here about Nicky?'

'Please answer the question. Is there anyone else in the house?'

'No-one's here but us,' Nina said. 'Is this about Nicky? Tell me. Has something happened to him?'

'Or Sonia?' Wragg said. 'Have you finally caught the bastard who killed her? Is that why you're here?'

Massey glanced over at Sparks, who gave an infinitesimal shrug. 'Look, Mr Wragg, Miss Selby, can you both try to stay calm and sit down please? Then we can tell you why we're here.'

It took a while to get them settled, during which time Massey asked Sparks to fetch two glasses of water from the kitchen. As distracted as they were, neither Wragg nor Selby objected, and he knew Sparks would take the opportunity to check they'd told the truth about there being no-one else in the house.

'Mr Wragg,' he said eventually. 'We came here to ask if you have any idea where your brother Billy might be, but I gather you're upset about something else. Can you tell us what that is?'

It was Nina who spoke, her fingers now shredding the tissue into tiny pieces.

'It's Nicky. He's gone missing. We can't find him anywhere.'

'When did either of you see him last?'

'He took me home on Saturday night,' Nina said. 'That would have been somewhere between half eleven and midnight. We were supposed to be going to my parents' for dinner on Sunday, but he never showed up to collect me and he's not answering his phone.'

'Mr Wragg, when did you see him last?'

'He came home after dropping Nina off. Got back just as I was going to bed, but then I heard him get up and go out again in the early hours. He hasn't been back since...' Tears sprang to his eyes, and he put a big hand over his mouth. '... and no... no-one has seen him.'

'Have you checked with all his friends?'

'Yes,' Nina said. 'I called everyone I could think of, but no-one knows anything.' She sobbed and pulled a handful of fresh tissues from a box on the coffee table. 'Where is he?'

Massey turned to Ronnie Wragg. 'Do you think he could be with your brother Billy?'

'What? Why on earth would he be with Billy and not tell us?' Massey could see the moment that Wragg's mind clicked, but it took a second or two more before the man spoke. 'Wait. You said you were here looking for Billy. Why? What's he done?'

'Why would you think he's done anything, Mr Wragg?'

Wragg exploded off his seat. 'Because I've got two bloody detectives in my house looking for him. That's why!'

'Calm down Mr Wragg,' Sparks said.

'Calm down? Calm bloody down? How can I calm down with my wife dead, my son missing, and police searching for my brother?'

'Please. Come and sit back down.'

With tears streaming down her face now, her lips quivering, Nina moved over to her future father-in-law and stroked his arm. 'Please Ronnie. Come and sit back down. Please?'

He patted her hand. 'I'm sorry, pet. It's just—'

'I know. Come on, let's sit down and try to get this sorted.'

'Have you checked Nicky's room?' Massey asked, once they were seated again. 'Perhaps he's left something in there, a note perhaps, or a phone number that might give us a clue to his whereabouts.'

'We've checked. Nothing.' Wragg pushed his hands through his hair then grabbed handfuls of the gingery grey thatch. 'He's a very tidy lad, is my Nicky. Keeps his room spotless.'

'Does he have a car?'

Nina nodded. 'A Yaris.' Her mouth twisted in distress as she spoke. 'That's not here either.'

Does he keep any belongings elsewhere? In the garage perhaps, or in a shed in the garden. Or maybe at his uncle's house?'

'What do you mean?' Wragg demanded. 'No. Nothing. Not that I know of, anyway. And what's this sudden obsession with Billy? What's he done?'

'We'll need a list of Nicky's friends.' Sparks said. 'And contact details.'

Looking thankful to have something to occupy her hands, Nina dashed off and returned a few moments later with a notepad and pen and proceeded to copy names and numbers from her phone's contact list. She handed the list to Sparks, who scanned the names.

'Stevie Grant isn't here.'

'Uncle Steven?' Nina said. 'Why would I put Uncle Steven down as one of Nicky's friends? They don't even know each other.'

'Stevie Grant is also your cousin, isn't he Mr Wragg?' Sparks said.

Ronnie lowered his head and nodded. 'He is. We don't have anything to do with him though. Haven't done for years.'

Nina's eyes had grown wide with astonishment. 'You mean, me and Nicky are already related?'

Ronnie Wragg looked uncomfortable. 'I'm sorry pet. I thought Nicky would have told you. Or your mother. Marie is my cousin too.'

'Nicky knows? And he didn't tell me? But how can I marry him if we're related?'

'You're only second cousins. And even first cousins can get married. I assumed you knew. Why has your mother never told you?'

'I have no idea, but I know what she meant now. The first time I took Nicky home. She said he looks just like Grandad Alan, my great grandad Alan. And I thought at the time, what a strange thing to say, why would she say my boyfriend looked like my great grandad? And she was probably thinking that I already... So that means—'

Ronnie drew her in close, like a grizzly cuddling a meerkat. He patted her back. 'That's right, pet. Your great grandad Alan was my Nicky's great grandad too, and my grandad.'

'Much as we'd like to stay and listen to you two reminiscing,' Sparks said. 'We have more immediate things to discuss. Do either of you have any idea where Billy Wragg might be?'

Ronnie Wragg turned a mutinous look on them. 'It's my Nicky I'm concerned about, not bloody Billy.'

'And we'll get onto that as soon as we have all the information we need,' Massey said. 'Now please answer the question.'

'I have no idea where Billy is. I am not my brother's keeper. He's probably out with that stupid cow who got my Sonia killed. He's been tomming around with her ever since the funeral.'

CHAPTER 71

'See Lou, if we'd left it another half an hour, we'd have missed food service.' Keegan placed a large glass of coke down in front of Portas. After a long day, they'd taken an hour out to grab a bite to eat at the Shiremoor House Farm, one of the closest food-serving pubs to Area Command.

At eight forty-five in the evening on a January weekday, with snow bleaching down outside, the place was quiet, so they had their pick of tables. They chose one in a dimly lit nook away from other customers so they could talk shop. Portas had insisted on no alcohol. Not if, as looked likely, they'd end up working through most of the night. She felt guilty enough taking an hour.

'How long, did they say?'

'I asked them to put a rush on it. It shouldn't take longer than fifteen minutes.'

Their food arrived after only ten minutes and they both tucked in, ravenous after having had nothing to eat since breakfast.

'Talking about food,' Keegan said eventually. 'Sarah keeps asking me to invite you over for dinner and I keep forgetting. Now you've moved over here, she wants to catch up on what's been happening with you. Like why no significant other in your life again yet. That sort of thing, you know. She's already measuring up all the single blokes she knows as potential candidates.'

Portas smiled. 'I have no wish to get involved in any sort of relationship just yet, but I'd love to come over for dinner. Tell her thank you and ask her to DM me some dates. It's ages since I saw her, or those girls of yours.'

No sooner had they finished eating than the waiter came to the table to collect their plates. Over to the left of his arm, Portas caught the swish of a long sleek curtain of dark hair as a couple walked to the door arm in arm, intent only on each other. She grabbed hold of Keegan's sleeve to warn him to stay silent and prayed for the waiter to continue masking them from view until the couple had left the pub.

'Did you see who that was?' she whispered once the door had closed, and the waiter had gone.

'Yeah, Ray bloody Flowers. Not too ill for work after all then. A bit brazen coming here though. You'd think it would be a little too close to HQ if he's playing a fast one.'

'I meant who he was with. Didn't you see?'

'I assumed it was his wife.'

Portas gaped at him, still in disbelief. 'No it bloody wasn't. That was Helen Massey.'

'What? You're kidding. Are you sure?'

'Absolutely. I just met her last week.'

'Jesus wept.'

They sat for a moment in silence, each contemplating what they'd just witnessed and the implications it could have at work.

'James does not get to hear about this from either of us, right?' Portas said. 'Especially not while we have all this going on with his mother. Deal?'

'Deal. Hold on.' He fished his ringing mobile out of his pocket. 'Bloody hell, it's Massey.'

Portas winced.

Keegan arranged his features into a neutral expression and tapped the screen. 'Flash,' he said, 'what's up?'

CHAPTER 72

Massey stood at the front of the MIT incident room that stank of stale coffee and someone's egg sarnies. The only people missing from the three teams now working as one were DCI Ray Flowers and DC Rob Laidler, who were both on sick leave; a couple of the civilian investigators who had childcare responsibilities, as well as Lonnie Burke and Robyn Moodie, who'd gone to talk to his mother's next door neighbour.

He clapped his hands to draw everyone's attention. 'Firstly, thank you all for continuing to work into the night, and especially to those who've come back in after believing they'd already escaped the madhouse.'

A flutter of comments and laughter rippled through the assembled teams before everyone settled down again, ready to get to work, each one of them conscious they were on the brink of something big.

'Okay then, here goes. We have three missing persons we need to trace as a matter of urgency, all involved in one way or another with the cases we're working on.' He tapped the first face on the big screen. 'Number one. Abigail Grant. She of the frozen party clothes. Abigail has not been seen since she left her home in Ashington on Sunday afternoon at around two thirty in the company of her father, Stevie Grant, and two of his crew, as reported by Superintendent Elsom and DCI Baker at this afternoon's briefing. At this time, we don't know if Abigail went with them willingly, although we do know she walked out of the house and got into her father's car under her own steam. However, to our knowledge she has not returned home since then, not even to feed her two cats, and we do not believe she would have deliberately left the animals to fend for themselves for this long.

'DS Brooks and DC Land have confirmed that none of her friends have heard from her nor seen any activity on her usual social media accounts since Saturday. Her mother, Patti Rose, says she hasn't seen her since Sunday morning and that Abigail told her nothing of what she had planned, although we do believe Patti has information she is unwilling to share, for fear of what Stevie Grant might do to her if he finds out she talked to us.

'We're treating Abigail as a vulnerable person. She has recently reported being raped. Although the crime happened three years ago, we do know that it continues to have a negative effect on her mental health. We know too that she has drawn the attention of a stalker. And on top of that, the fact she has not responded to any calls or texts to her mobile nor had any contact via social media since Saturday night has given us just cause to enter her home without a warrant in order to carry out a wellbeing check, in the event she had returned without our knowledge.' He looked towards Brooks. 'Kirsty, could you tell everyone what you found when you entered Abigail's house.'

Brooks nodded and looked down for a moment to the notebook she had open in front of her. 'We gained access to Abigail's house via her front door with the support of two uniformed officers. But in order to preserve any potential forensics, I was the only one who actually entered. I found no sign of Abigail in any of the rooms, and nothing to suggest there'd been any altercation in the house, although there was one thing I thought strange. A dining chair had been jammed under the handle of the back door and there was another matching chair next to the front door, as if that had been used for a similar purpose and then removed in order to open the door. Um… that's all, I think. Oh, except to say that I fed the cats while I was there.' Under her freckles, her cheeks turned pink. 'We're going to have to do something about the animals longer term though, sir. We can't just leave them trapped in the house.'

'I agree Kirsty. If we haven't found Abigail by then, could you call the RSPCA please first thing in the morning and ask if they could take them into temporary custody until we know what's happened to her.'

He tapped the middle photo. 'Number two. Nicholas Wragg. Reported missing this evening by his father, Ronnie Wragg, and by his fiancée, Nina Selby. Neither have seen him since late Saturday night. We know that this is the man who let himself into Abigail's house in the early hours of Sunday morning and then left again some hours later. He is now our main suspect in the serial rape inquiry and therefore most likely to also be the man who raped Abigail three years ago.

'We assume Abigail became aware at some point that he was in the house, and perhaps that was her reason for wedging the chairs under the door handles after he'd gone. We suspect this man of being her stalker. We believe he delivered the envelope of photos to her house and murdered Leon Robinson after having been spotted delivering it. We also know he is a person of interest over at Serious and Organised with regards their investigations into the activities of Stevie Grant, Abigail's father.

'And of course, if Nicky Wragg *is* the man who raped Abigail three years ago, then we're also looking for someone who shares a quarter of their DNA with him for the rape and murder of Julie Probert forty years ago. So, grandfather and grandson, uncle and nephew, or half-brothers. And there are only two people we know of who fall into any of those categories as far as Nicky Wragg is concerned.

'We now know that his mother, Sonia Wragg, who was killed on New Year's night – and, by the way, we'll be looking at that investigation again now too – had no siblings and her father died when she was still a child, and so he was no longer around in 1983. That leaves us with Nicky's paternal grandfather, Thomas Wragg and his father's brother, Billy Wragg, who as it happens is also on the missing list, along with number three here on the screen, Eleanor -Ellie – Morgan.' He blinked a couple of times but otherwise managed to keep his emotions in check. 'And now I need to hand over to DI Keegan. If you have any questions on what we've covered so far, I'd appreciate it if you keep them until after DI Keegan has finished.'

***

'Alright folks, listen up. And, before we go any further, for anyone among us who hasn't already heard the jungle drums, full disclosure, Ellie Morgan is the mother of our very own DCI James Massey and, under normal circumstances, he would be kept well away from such a potential conflict of interest. But these are not normal circumstances and we've already got half the force off sick. Things are moving fast and there is no time to parachute someone else in and bring them up to speed before things kick off big style. For those reasons, a decision has been taken at the highest level to allow DCI Massey to continue. Anyone who has a problem with that can take it up in the first instance with DSU Portas over there.'

Standing at the back of the room, Lou Portas raised a hand to acknowledge Keegan's words.

'Ellie,' Keegan continued, 'has not been heard from since Sunday morning just before nine thirty, when she had a brief conversation with her heavily pregnant daughter via her mobile phone to say she was going to stay with a friend for a few days. She did not say who with, or where. She has been out of contact now for over thirty-six hours, which is way out of character for her, particularly since her daughter is due to give birth any day now. The family feel Ellie would not deliberately be uncontactable at this time.

'You'll remember that Ellie was a witness to the death of Sonia Wragg on New Year's night three weeks ago since they were talking on the phone to each other at the time. What you may not know is that both Sonia and Ellie were interviewed following the rape and murder of Julie Probert on New Year's night forty years ago. In fact Julie was the third member of their little posse out on the town that night when they all finished up at a nightclub called JoJo's, which no longer exists – or not as a night club anyway. It's just around the corner from the back lane where Julie's body was discovered the following morning. So, the three of them, Ellie, Sonia and Julie, friends since primary school, were all out on the hoy for New Year.

'We know that Nicky Wragg's father, Ronnie, was interviewed in 1984 in connection with Julie's murder too, although we have no evidence to suggest that he and Sonia were an item at that time. However, as of less than an hour ago, we now know that his brother Billy – he of the twenty-five percent DNA match – was also at JoJo's that night.'

Keegan allowed the hubbub to die down before continuing.

'But here's the kicker folks. Ellie Morgan has been getting very pally with Billy Wragg since Sonia's funeral, to the point that we now believe him to be the person she is currently with, although we have no idea where they are.'

'Thank you DI Keegan.' Massey stood up again and moved to the front of the room. 'So there you have it. If you count Billy Wragg, that's four people missing, rather than just these three, and all four are connected to our investigations. Thoughts anyone?'

'Sir,' Kirsty Brooks spoke up. 'Are we thinking they could all be together? All four of them.'

'It's possible, but we can't make that assumption and ignore other avenues.'

'Maybe Stevie Grant snatched Nicky Wragg.' DI Poole said.

'Good call Adam. Use your liaison link with Serious and Organised and see if you can find out what they know. Any stonewalling, get back to me.'

'If he has,' Keegan said, 'the lad has a bargaining chip – if he knows about what his uncle did – since Julie was Grant's cousin too.'

'If it is definitely Billy Wragg we're looking for on that one,' Sparks said. 'It could still have been the grandfather, Thomas Wragg.'

'He's in a hospice,' Johnson said. 'Lung cancer.'

'Then he's going nowhere for the moment,' Massey said. 'We need to concentrate on Billy for now. He's out there somewhere and needs to be found.' Not least because, if they found Billy, they may find his mother too. 'What about properties? The Wraggs are builders. They could own several properties – individually and through the business – where Nicky or Billy could lie low. '

'I'm looking at the Land Registry now,' Johnson said.

'And vehicles. There are calls out on the Toyota Yaris and the Land Rover Discovery they were each last seen driving, but what about any other vehicles registered under their names. Or any others they might have access to. In Nicky's case for instance, what about Nina's car? Or his mother's car. Is that still around?'

Donaldson raised his hand. 'I'll get onto DVLA.'

'I'll call Ronnie Wragg,' Sparks said. 'On both. And we need someone to chase up phone records. We've got three warrants through now. For Ellie's and Abigail's phones as missing persons, and Nicky's as the suspect for the serial rapes. We don't have enough on Billy yet to be granted access.'

CHAPTER 73

Abigail turned her face to the window, trying to control the apprehensive quivering inside that she felt sure her father could feel through the huge meaty arm he'd placed protectively – possessively – around her shoulders. All she could see through the car window was a constant swirling whiteness. She had no idea where they were or where they were going except that they were driving west, which she'd gathered from the instructions her father had given to the driver to stick to the main A69 because of the snow. Nigs Bowen had argued that they could be more easily tracked on the main roads, but her father was having none of it. Not in snow this bad, he'd replied. And he wanted to get there in one piece, even if Nigs didn't. They had work to do tonight. Two birds, one stone.

Abigail ran her tongue around her parched mouth, trying to work up some saliva to ease the dryness. How had she ended up in the middle of all this?

'You should be pleased,' her father had told her. 'You'll get to watch the filthy pervert who raped you being relieved of his tackle. There aren't many victims of rape who can achieve that level of justice. And by the time the little bastard is found, if he survives the blood loss – which, to be fair Abbie girl, is unlikely – he's never going to be able to stick it where it shouldn't be ever again, because he won't have a prick any more to stick.'

He'd laughed at that. That same mad maniacal guffaw she remembered from when he'd knocked her mother right across the room with one swipe of his arm when she was a child; the reason she'd tried since her teenage years to remove herself from his orbit.

Right now she felt as far away from being pleased as it was possible to get. Appalled, disgusted, horrified. Yes, she felt all of those. Petrified too of what would become of her after this. Because how could she possibly return to the normal life she'd fought so hard for, as if nothing had happened, after being made to witness what they planned to do tonight?

She couldn't watch. She wouldn't watch.

But she knew there'd be no way she could block out the sounds. They were in her head already, before they'd become a reality.

She thought of that poor excuse for a man in the back of the van that followed behind them. She'd seen Nigs and another man load him in there. His arms and legs all tied together behind him. No blindfold, only a gag.

'So he can see every second of what's happening to him in glorious technicolour,' Nigs had told her.

But she'd seen his terrified eyes seek out hers, wordlessly pleading with her. 'Stop this,' he'd begged her. The man who'd ruined her life three years ago, someone she'd trusted because he was family, who must have been laughing behind her back every day for all that time, and who'd pushed his luck too far by breaking into her home on Sunday to turn her into a quivering wreck for a second time, had begged her to save him. But even if she wanted to, she couldn't hope to prevent the express train that was her father from taking his own revenge.

Now, all she felt for her rapist was pity.

CHAPTER 74

'Bad tempered cow,' Moodie said down the line.

'Sounds like someone you'd have a lot in common with then,' Keegan commented.

'Come on, I know it's a little late, but you'd think she'd be a bit more concerned about the fact we're treating her next door neighbour as a missing person.'

Burke's calm voice of reason butted in. 'She was fine,' he said, 'considering we did get her out of bed.'

'Who the hell goes to bed at nine o'clock?'

'Come on then,' Keegan said. 'We haven't got all night. What did she say?'

Burke cleared his throat. 'Mrs Glenda Hill. A widow, early seventies, lives on her own. Spends more time than the average person looking out of her window. Says she saw Mrs Morgan—'

'Ellie,' they heard Moodie say in clarification.

'—being driven off in a large beige-coloured vehicle at ten to nine on Sunday morning. We asked her if she could identify the make and model, but she could say only that it was one of those huge things that anyone over the age of sixty would need stepladders to get into.'

'And the driver?'

'A big man fitting the description we have of Billy Wragg.'

Keegan gave Massey a grimace. 'And is this man a frequent visitor to Ellie's house?'

'Says she definitely saw him there on Saturday at around twelve thirty, although on that occasion Mrs Morgan kept him talking on the doorstep and then, as soon as he'd left, she had another visitor. A woman with red spiky hair. I believe we know who that was.'

'We do.' Keegan nodded towards Sparks. 'Anything else?'

'Yes there is,' Moodie said, 'because once she'd got into her stride, the stupid woman wouldn't stop talking. She insisted on telling us about another night she'd been rudely woken up. Friday evening, she said, the same man arrived to pick Ellie up in a taxi – a Beardshaw black cab apparently. She says she didn't see them return because she was in bed, but she heard them. Around twenty to midnight. Another taxi, she said. Only one person got out and then she heard Ellie's front door open and close, and the taxi drove off again. How could she be so sure it was a taxi though, unless she was at that bedroom window twitching the net curtains? Nosy cow.'

Keegan laughed. 'And where would our jobs be without nosy cows?'

Massey felt his mobile vibrate and checked the screen, hoping to see his mother's number come up, but no. Not a number he recognised. He huffed a big sigh, rejected the call and shoved the phone back into his pocket.

***

'Sir,' DC Andrew Donaldson called out. 'According to the DVLA, Billy Wragg owns only the Land Rover Discovery. It's in Lantau Bronze, which looks a lot more beige than bronze to me, so that fits with what your mother's neighbour said. As far as I can see, he's not the registered keeper of any other vehicles, although I imagine he'll be insured to drive any of the Wragg company vehicles.'

'Hopefully, it's the Discovery he's still in then, and it's been picked up on an ANPR camera somewhere,' Keegan said.

'That's the vehicle I saw outside the house on Saturday,' Sparks said, her phone to her ear, still waiting for Ronnie Wragg to pick up.

With a nod, Massey acknowledged the long apologetic look she gave him. Although she had nothing to apologise for. He knew it would have been wrong of her to pass details from her interview with his mother to him. And, given her own home circumstances – which she'd told him about on the way back to Middle Engine Lane from Ronnie Wragg's home – she hadn't needed to be here tonight either, but she's insisted, and he appreciated her presence more than he could convey. Maybe once all this was over they could talk about it, and he'd be able to thank her properly.

He'd been shocked when she'd told him the reason for her absence earlier in the day. Her own mother, whose dementia he knew had been getting worse, had somehow managed to get through Sparks' security measures and left the house on her own in the middle of the night and had gone on a dementia walkabout, seemingly reliving a routine of her past, putting herself in danger and Sparks into a panic once she realised what had happened.

Eventually, she'd been found outside the gates of the primary school Sparks and her brother had attended as children, but not before wandering the streets alone in the freezing cold for hours, where anything could have happened to her.

Sparks told him the shock of it all had given her the push she needed to admit her brother was right and that it was time for their mother to move into a care home, where she'd be given the support she needed. Her brother had even taken a week's emergency leave from work to help with the arrangements, although Massey suspected it would take a lot longer than a week to sort something out. He couldn't imagine it would be as simple as finding a care home their mother would like and moving her in. There'd be assessments needed, applications to be made, waiting lists to navigate, and a lot of frustration and heartache involved too before they got her settled.

He didn't envy them. But at least they knew where their mother was now – her physical being anyway – whereas he had no idea where his own mother was.

Something shifted in his belly. The same recognition of evil as before. At the same moment, his mobile rang, the same unknown number. He was about to answer it when Donaldson spoke up, a note of urgency in his voice.

'Got something. A Toyota Yaris registered to Nicholas Wragg has been reported burnt out in West Sleekburn. No sign of anyone inside.'

'We need forensics on that car ASAP,' Massey said, rejecting the call and sliding his mobile back into his pocket. 'Nicky might well have dumped and burnt it out himself, but it's looking more like DI Poole could be right. Maybe Stevie Grant *has* snatched him. Which begs the question, if Abigail is still with her father, is she a part of what's going down? Could she be using her father to help her exact her own form of justice on the man she thinks raped her?'

'Nah,' Sparks said. 'Can't see it.'

Brooks looked up from her desk. 'I agree. Abigail hates everything her father stands for.'

With the older Wragg brother still not picking up, Sparks stabbed at her phone screen in frustration. 'West Sleekburn,' she said. 'That's close to Billy Wragg's address, isn't it?'

CHAPTER 75

By the time Sparks finally heard Ronnie Wragg's voice reverberate down the line, the receiver felt hot in her hand. Maybe landlines could fry your brain, the same as mobile phones. 'Mr Wragg. DS Christine Sparks here. I came to see you earlier with DCI Massey. I have a few more questions I hope you can help with.'

'Have you found Nicky yet?'

'Not yet.'

The man sounded frantic. If his son had done all the things they suspected him of, how could he possibly have no idea? And how could Nina not realise her fiancée didn't just know her Uncle Steven but worked for him too? Could they both really be so blithely unaware of Nicholas Wragg's true nature?

'Can you tell me if Nicky has access to any other vehicles besides the Toyota Yaris? Your late wife's car, perhaps, or Nina's car, if she has one.'

'Nina's car is in my garage here now. I sold my wife's car as soon as we got the funeral out of the way. It was no good to me and Nicky didn't want a bright red car.'

Of course he didn't.

A bit in-your-face noticeable for a rapist to drive around in.

'I told him it was in much better nick than that crappy Yaris he drives because his mother hardly used it, but he wouldn't listen. Said it would remind him too much of her. So I got rid.'

'And what about Billy? Have you ever seen him drive any vehicles other than his Land Rover Discovery?'

'Sod Billy. I want your minds on finding our Nicky.'

'And what if Nicky is with Billy?'

Wragg gave a big sigh. Sparks imagined him running a big hand through his hair and grabbing handfuls of it, as if to pull it from its roots.

'No. Billy doesn't have any other vehicles that I know of, not since he bought the Discovery, unless you count company vehicles, and he only drives those if he absolutely has to. Thinks he's too good for that, being a partner and all.'

'Do you keep track of all the company vehicles yourself? Could Billy have taken one without your knowledge? Or could Nicky have?'

'I wouldn't know who's got what vehicle at any given time. It's the office manager who deals with all that day to day crap and holds the keys. But no, not Nicky. He has no interest in the company.'

'I'd like you to contact the office manager to find out if either of them took one, and then get back to me.'

'What? I'm not calling her at this time of night.'

'Yes you are Mr Wragg, or you can give me her contact details and I'll call her.'

'And have her know about...' The man couldn't have sounded more exasperated. 'Yes, yes, alright, I'll call her and get back to you.'

'Good. Thank you. Do it straight away, and don't forget the details of all the properties the family owns, individually or through the business, that Billy or Nicky might have access to.'

***

It took almost an hour for Ronnie Wragg to get back to Sparks. On the vehicle front, she ended up no further forward since all of the company vehicles were accounted for. Neither Billy nor Nicky Wragg had taken any of them.

'And properties?' she asked.

'I have a list I can send you. I own this house outright now Sonia has gone, and I have a couple of rental properties in my name, but most of the rentals are in Nicky's name, technically anyway. So you could say he owns twelve properties. But all of them are rented out. We have nothing standing empty.'

They'd still need to check them all.

'Billy has the house at Choppington you say you've already checked but I've no idea how many other properties he owns, if any, or whether they're currently occupied. He could have dozens, or he could have none, that's his business – you'll have gathered by now that we're not the closest of brothers. I do know though that a few years ago he bought himself some ramshackle old place to renovate, out on the moors.'

'Where? Which moors?'

'No idea. If Nicky were here, he'd be able to tell you. He used to go up there with Billy some weekends when he was a teenager to help out, but not for the last couple of years as far as I know.'

CHAPTER 76

Ellie awoke with a pounding headache and a stabbing pain in her neck. Her eyelids felt as if they'd been glued together, and her tongue had stuck to the roof of her mouth. It took a few moments to register how cold she'd become, and it wasn't until she'd groped for a duvet to pull up around her shoulders that she realised she still wore her jeans and sweatshirt. She prised her eyes open, and only then did she grasp the fact that she wasn't in her own bed at home. She lay on a settee. And not even her own squashy settee in her own lovely kitchen, but a much more solid affair in front of an open fire that barely glowed in the darkness.

Billy's lodge.

But where was Billy? Had they both fallen asleep downstairs?

She tried to sit up, but pain exploded in her head, making her retch.

She tried again, gingerly this time, and eventually pulled herself into a sitting position.

No sign of Billy.

The effort had caused her whole body to shake. Sweat broke out along her hairline and her parched mouth cried out for a drink of water.

She had to get to the kitchen. Somehow.

***

The glass rattled against her teeth, but the water tasted like nectar. She drank it slowly, scared she'd bring it straight back up again if she took a big swallow.

What the hell had happened to get her into this state? It can't have been the drink. She couldn't have had much. Certainly not enough to make her feel this bad.

And where the hell was Billy? Had he gone to bed and left her down here? What a bloody rotten ungentlemanly thing to do. He hadn't even put a blanket over her.

It didn't matter how attractive a man was, or how blue his eyes, if he was an unthinking bastard inside. And a man with a nasty side, judging by what that poor woman from the pickup truck had said. And what she'd seen for herself. If he thought she was prepared to stay with him in this wilderness for a moment longer than first thing in the morning, after leaving her down here like this, he had another bloody think coming. This whole trip had been a huge mistake. How the hell could she have been so stupid?

Oh God, she so wanted to be home now. Safe in her own bed.

And what the hell time was it anyway? How long had he left her down here on her own to freeze?

With her legs still shaky, she made a grab for the worktop with her right hand so she could lift her left wrist to see the time. In doing so, her fingers nudged a sheet of paper and would have sent it fluttering to the floor had her hand not shot out automatically to catch it. But the sudden movement sent her head throbbing again, as if her brain were trying to pound its way out from the inside, and her vision was so skewed she couldn't make out the numerals on her wristwatch anyway.

What the hell was wrong with her?

Scrunching the paper between her fingers, she groaned and let the worktop take the full weight of her upper body until the pain subsided again. Once she thought she could bear it, she tried to rotate her neck to ease the crick in it. Automatically, her fingers began to straighten out the sheet of paper, which she felt sure hadn't been there when she'd washed the dishes and wiped down the worktops after they'd eaten, however long ago that was.

Had he left her a bloody note? What the hell for if he'd just gone to bed and left her down here? She'd already managed to figure that much out for herself, and she'd have words to say to him in the morning about it. Face to bloody face.

She might even end up using some of those precious fucks she'd been hoarding.

No two ways about it, if she wanted to read the note or see the time she would need to get some light on the matter, but she didn't think her eyes could stand the glare from the big ceiling light.

She moved closer to the wood burner, which still emanated a red glow marginally brighter than that from the open fire. At least it allowed her to see that something had been handwritten across the paper in landscape format, but she still couldn't read the words.

She screwed her eyes shut and flicked the switch.

Fuck!

The light hit her like a laser aimed directly at her eyeballs. Why the hell had Billy put a bulb of that strength into the fitting?

When the shock abated enough for her to reopen her eyes, and after a good few more seconds for her to focus them, she managed to make out Billy's spider writing.

> Sorry for abandoning you Ellie. Needed at home.
> Back soon.
> Billy

He'd what?

He'd gone and left her here on her own?

No. He couldn't have! No-one in their right mind would leave a woman stuck on her own in the middle of *fucking* nowhere, with no fucking transport. Not when he knew perfectly well her daughter was about to give birth and she needed to be home when that happened.

Fucking bastard.

Ellie staggered to the front door and threw it open.

Outside, heavy snow swirled and eddied.

In a panic, she stepped out into the maelstrom to look for Billy's Land Rover Discovery but saw only an expanse of white. Any tyre treads he might have left there had been obliterated by the snow that fell so thick and so fast now that he could have left hours ago or only in the last thirty minutes.

She felt a freezing cold sensation and looked down at her feet. Horrified, she realised she'd come out wearing only her slipper socks. Turning to go back inside, with snow bleaching into her face, she only just managed to catch the door before it slammed shut on her.

Fuck, fuck, fuck!

Back inside, quivering from the cold, with her back to the now closed door, Ellie slammed her fists against the wood behind her, giving in to tears of fury and frustration.

How could the *fucking* bastard have done this to her?

CHAPTER 77

'Maybe he bought the place in another name,' Massey said. 'A company name, maybe. Have we checked Companies House?'

'I'm on the website now,' Donaldson said, 'but if he's operating just as a sole trader, we're not going to find him on here. We'll have to contact HMRC.'

'Surely he'd be better off registering as a limited company for tax purposes.'

Keegan gave a harsh laugh. 'Maybe tax liability wasn't his primary concern when he bought the place.'

Massey stared at his phone, willing his mother to call. Then he remembered the unknown caller from earlier and his blood ran cold. What if that had been his mother trying to reach him from another phone? He was about to tap the call button when the device rang in his hand. The same unknown number. He accepted the call. 'James Massey. Who's this?'

A female voice he didn't recognise launched into a garbled explanation about how she came into possession of one of his business cards. It made no sense.

'Stop a moment. Now, take a breath and go back. Start at the beginning. First off, who are you?'

Sensing a breakthrough, the whole room had fallen silent.

'Mary. Hello Mary. Yes, this is DI James Massey speaking.' No point in confusing the poor woman any further by saying he was now Acting DCI Massey. 'First of all, Mary, can you tell me where you are? Brampton, really? That's in Cumbria, isn't it?'

He glanced around. Half of his colleagues had silently moved towards him. Like Dr Who's Weeping Angels. Only moving when his back was turned. If he looked away and looked back again, they'd be upon him. He switched his phone to loudspeaker. 'So a woman left my card on a table in your café this afternoon? Did she say anything to you?'

'No. I found both cards after they'd gone.'

'They? She was with someone. Can you tell me what they looked like?'

He listened while Mary described his mother and Billy Wragg to a tee.

She explained that the man had spent some of the time standing outside the café on his phone, while the woman appeared to be struggling to get her own phone to work inside. When he returned to the table, she'd heard him telling the woman that her phone mustn't work because reception in Brampton was sketchy and maybe her network was worse than his.

'But that's not the case at all,' she said, 'so there must have been something wrong with her phone. And I'll tell you something else for nothing. She looked like she didn't want him to see her leave the cards on the table, which made me think that she expected me to do something with them, and at first I thought it's none of my business what others get up to. If she wanted me to call you, she should have asked while he was outside. But then I thought about what they were talking about at the town meeting. About that *Ask for Angela* thing. But she didn't ask for Angela, so I thought she must be alright. I mean, well, you must know what I mean, you being a policeman and such.'

It took a moment for him to register what the woman was talking about, but eventually he got there.

The *Ask for Angela* campaign, which aimed to keep people safe from sexual assault by telling them to ask for Angela at the bar or counter of any establishment as a codeword for seeking help if they felt threatened or in danger.

'Did you hear anything else they said? Like where they were staying perhaps?'

'No, they didn't speak much at all, but when I asked Jess what she'd said to her—'

'Just a moment. Jess? Who's Jess?'

'She lives up past the Gilsland Spa turn off. Has her own little business. Well, not so little these days really. She collects orders for folk from all the local shops and drops them off at home for them. It means lots of people can still shop local without having heavy bags to lump around with them. She does very well.'

'And why should Jess have spoken to the woman who left my card on your table?'

'It was while the man was outside. She came to the back door, like she usually does. But this time she asked me to take a message to the woman. She wanted her to come to the kitchen door. Had something to say to her. But I didn't know what any of that was about. Not then.'

'And now?'

'Yes well, I worried about that for hours, about what the woman meant by leaving these business cards on the table, especially when I saw one was a policeman's card. So I thought I should give Jess a ring...'

Why the hell hadn't she called the number on the card straight away?

'And that's when Jess told me it was about her sister. The man, you see, was the same one who went out with Lucy—'

'Jess's sister?'

'That's right. And Jess didn't want the same thing to happen to another woman that had happened to Lucy. But then she told me that she'd been looking out of her window earlier and saw his car leaving with only him inside. Well, then the snow started coming down heavy, and Jess got to worrying about the woman out there on her own. She told me I should call the number of the card—'

'Where's "out there"?'

'The old hunting lodge. It's miles out on the moor north of Gilsland, and the road across there is treacherous in this weather. It's poor at the best of times. And I tried calling you, like she said, but you didn't pick up. So I tried calling Jess back, but she's not picking up neither now, and I'm worried she's gone out there on her own to see if the woman is alright and turned the truck over off the road, and I couldn't go to bed thinking something terrible might have happened, and—'

'I need you to give me Jess's number and her address.' He gestured to Donaldson to take note. 'And I need to know exactly where this old hunting lodge is.'

***

'I've got it up on here, sir,' Johnson said, pointing to a detailed Ordnance Survey map he'd brought up on the big screen, and then to a blown up satellite view on his laptop. 'It's just over the border into Cumbria. And I mean just over. It's adjacent to the RAF Spadeadam firing range.

That's where they do all the electronic warfare training, isn't it? Massey said.

A ringtone blasted a tune like something from an old silent comedy film. DI Adam Poole reached into his pocket, looked at the screen of his mobile and had a short conversation with the caller.

'That was my contact on Serious and Organised,' he announced. 'A vehicle belonging to Stevie Grant was clocked twice earlier tonight heading west on the A69. And on both occasions it was being followed closely by a Ford Transit van reported missing earlier today.'

'Shit' Massey said. 'How long ago.'

'First clocked just after 9 pm, he said.'

Massey looked at the wall clock. Almost a quarter to midnight. 'And it's taken them this long to inform us when they know we're looking for Abigail?'

Superintendent Portas held up a hand to stay any more pointless gripes. 'Then we need conversations with Serious and Organised as well as with Cumbria Police. And the RAF too, in case we have to stray onto Ministry of Defence land. They might even be able to offer a bit of assistance.'

Massey drew his hands down his face. 'Looks like you might have been correct, Adam. Why else would Grant be travelling west on a night like this with a stolen van in tow, if it's not to visit family?'

CHAPTER 78

Keegan looked up from his laptop screen. 'RAF Spadeadam. A Wing Commander Geoff Brayfield is in charge. He's got enough letters after his name to form his own sodding alphabet. Bachelor of Science, Master of Science, Master of Arts, and what the bloody hell does MRes mean?'

'Master of Research,' Portas said.

'Jesus wept. When the hell does he manage to fit work in?'

'I know him. Good bloke.'

Keegan laughed. 'Of course you do. Will he help, if necessary?'

'I'm sure he will if he can. Actually, he could be very useful.'

She scrolled through her contacts.

'You mean you've even got his number saved to your phone?'

Portas gave a smug smile. 'His personal mobile number, no less.'

'Did a bit of night flying on his joystick when you worked over there, did you?'

'At least you didn't say on my broomstick.'

Massey listened to their banter. He understood that it helped in stressful situations, but he didn't feel capable of joining in. Stevie Grant would have had ample time by now, even in poor conditions, to reach the lodge where it looked like his mother was staying with Billy Wragg. If that's where he was headed. Grant himself was a lunatic, but he never went anywhere without his giant sidekick Nigs Bowen, who by all accounts was twice as vicious as his boss. And there was no telling how many other henchmen they'd taken with them – plenty of room in a 4x4 and a transit van. And if Grant really did have Nicky Wragg and Abigail with him...

Jesus, a drug lord and his pet psychopath, a rapist and a murderer, with possibly a terrified girl. And his mother. He felt sick.

***

Portas finished her call to the Wing Commander, but had no time to update them before her phone rang again. 'Sir.' Portas listened to the voice at the other end for less than a minute. 'Thank you sir, that's brilliant. I will, sir. Thanks.'

'Well?' Keegan said.

'That was Chief Superintendent Crowder. We have a trained crisis negotiator on the way in. Inspector Gary Dunn. Has substantial experience in hostage situations apparently. Oh, and Superintendent Elsom has a team already on the road. Thinks he's going to get there before us. But he's got no chance.' She grinned.

The possibility his mother could be used as a hostage had passed through Massey's mind more than once in the past hour, but now the words had been spoken aloud it felt suddenly real. And horrifying.

'Cumbria's DCI Dave Graham is mobilising a team,' Portas continued. 'Another good man. They'll stand by in Gilsland until we get there.'

'What about RAF Spadeadam,' Keegan asked.

'Just getting to that. Geoff said his lads are bored and would love a bimble over the moors in the snow. He's sending a cab to meet us at the airport. So you see, we'll be there—'

'He's what?'

'They'd love a stroll across the moors,' Massey said, 'and he's sending a helicopter to pick us up. I grew up with an RAF man for a stepfather.'

'Why not NPAS?' Keegan asked.

'Grounded for an overdue service, apparently.'

The National Police Air Service provide a 24/7 air support response to forces across England and Wales. Their Newcastle base covered the whole of the North East and Cumbria.

'Thank Christ for your Wing Commander then,' Keegan said. 'How many can we take? We need to get going. And someone needs to get onto that negotiator and reroute him to the airport.'

'Room for six. Us three and the negotiator plus another two. Who do you want?'

'Lonnie,' Keegan said. 'He should be in at the end.'

'And Christine,' Massey said.

CHAPTER 79

Ellie forced herself to think through her dilemma. It took a while because her brain might as well have been encased in bubble wrap since it crackled with every step she took and every move of her eyes.

Her watch told her the time was a quarter to midnight, but she hadn't managed to work out yet how long she must have been asleep.

In Brampton, they'd bought food they could just shove in the microwave, and they'd prepared and eaten it as soon as they got back to the lodge. She could vaguely remember sitting down in front of the fire after finishing the washing up while Billy poured some drinks, and it must have been around five or half five by then. But not a thing after that until she woke up with a mouth like sandpaper, her eyes glued shut and her neck jammed against the arm of the settee.

She'd lost around six hours of her life.

How could that be?

She shivered in her wet sweatshirt. Right now, it didn't matter how any of that had happened because the very first thing she needed to do was to get warm and dry. And that meant getting the wood burner going again, because then she'd have central heating right through the lodge again. At least there were plenty of dry logs next to it, and a bag of kindling.

Moving slowly to lessen the pain in her head as she bent down, she opened the front of the burner and arranged a few sticks of kindling over the fading embers, adding a few more once she was sure they'd caught, and then eventually the smallest logs she could find so she didn't smother the precious flames.

Once she felt confident the burner could be left to its own devices for a while, she made her way upstairs, each upward step heaping more pressure onto her aching head until she felt she'd buckle under the strain.

In the room she'd slept in just once, she changed into a thick woollen jumper and dry socks. Then she located the pack of paracetamol she always travelled with, shoved it into her back pocket, and packed all her remaining belongings into her travel bag to take downstairs with her. She'd leave the bag ready by the front door, so that as soon as Billy showed his face again, she could insist he get right back into the car and drive her home. No matter what time it was.

But before returning downstairs, having never explored further up here than the landing and the room she'd been allotted, she decided to check all the rooms. Just in case. Although in case of what, she had no idea.

She crept silently into Billy's room first and peered towards the bed, a small part of her still convinced she'd find him asleep under the duvet and that everything she'd gone through since waking up on the settee had been part of either an elaborate hoax or a horrifying dream. But Billy's room was deserted, and the bed looked like it had never even been slept in. He'd put a wardrobe in here, unlike her room next door, but she found it bare. The drawers in the bedside cabinet were empty too, and not so much as a towel was out of place in the en suite. The man had left nothing behind. No toothbrush, no shaving gel, nothing. The place looked like a hotel room awaiting a new guest, not a middle aged man's weekend retreat. What if he had no intention of coming back for her at all, despite what the note said?

Stop. Don't even think that.

She moved back onto the landing. Apart from Billy's own room and the one she'd occupied, there were three other rooms up here. None had light bulbs in the fittings, although the white of the snow at the uncurtained windows allowed her to at least see they were all at various stages of being boarded out and plastered, and that the first room she came across must be intended as a bathroom because she could see a bath in the middle of the floor, still wrapped in polythene and cardboard. She assumed he intended the other rooms to be bedrooms. And he'd used the smallest room as a repository for his work tools.

It was while examining the tools that Ellie thought she caught a flash of light outside. There one second and gone the next. She stepped over a black plastic bucket containing a plastering float to get to the window, and realised that this room looked out towards the old, ruined outbuildings. Had the light come from there? Or from the plantation of pine trees beyond the boundary fence, where the single track road continued past the turn off to the lodge?

Or had it been a figment of her imagination?

She watched for a while but saw nothing but swirling white.

On the way out of the room, she paused and returned to the bucket. Was that a knife? Yes, it was. A Stanley knife. A retractable one, with a lockable blade, like those she used regularly when preparing a canvas for painting.

On an impulse, she tucked it into her back pocket alongside the paracetamol.

***

Back downstairs, she dumped her travel bag by the door, with her coat on top, and put on her boots. She intended to be ready to go as soon as Billy showed his face, so that all she'd need to do would be to grab her coat and her bag and she'd be ready.

If he showed his face.

No. When he did.

The wood burner blazed nicely now, so she knelt by the open fire and got that going too, before returning to the burner and adding more logs. Already, the lodge felt warmer.

The headache wasn't budging though.

She felt her back pocket. The paracetamols would do no good in there. With blood pounding in her temples, she pushed a couple into her hand, the last two in that strip, although she still had another whole strip in the pack. She refilled the glass with water, slugged the caplets back and kept drinking. When the glass was empty, she refilled it and forced herself to drink another glassful, slower this time, in an effort to rehydrate herself.

She flipped the lid of the bin to dispose of the empty strip. Closing it again, she paused. Something strange inside had caught her eye. Tiny plastic objects had caught on the wrapping from the dinner she'd shared with Billy before he'd abandoned her here. She bent closer and squinted.

Four halves of two capsules. Two blue and two white. The sort that prescription medication might come in. What the hell?

And then suddenly it all made sense.

Billy had drugged her!

Ellie felt the blood drain from her face and had to grab the worktop to stop herself from falling.

The fucking... bastard!

That's why she felt so weird, and had no memory at all of anything from sitting down with him in front of the fire after finishing the dishes until she woke up on the settee with a raging hangover.

But why? And what the hell was she supposed to do now?

Then, through the haze, she remembered her phone. If her suspicion was correct, that Billy had messed with the settings so it had no mobile reception, then perhaps she could reverse his actions and get the damned thing working again. She might be able to get through to James.

She rummaged in her handbag. No phone. She checked her coat pockets and felt down the back and sides of the settee she'd woken up on. Nothing. She swept her hands across the black kitchen worktops to make sure she hadn't just failed to see it there because her eyesight was still a bit dodgy. In a panic, she went back upstairs to check in the bedroom, even though she knew without a doubt that she'd checked everywhere in there only moments before to make sure she wasn't leaving anything behind.

Fresh tears sprang to her eyes. Billy must have taken her phone with him.

He'd *fucking* drugged her and he'd *fucking* taken her phone.

And when he came back, what else could he be capable of?

Her hand moved to the Stanley knife in her back pocket, feeling glad of its presence.

Billy would not expect her to have a weapon.

If he came back.

CHAPTER 80

Tuesday 23rd January 2024

Ellie had no idea how long Billy intended to abandon her here. It could be hours, or even days. Or he could walk in the door at any minute.

And, when he did, what would he do?

She had no idea.

But then, she'd had no idea that the man she'd assumed him to be could stoop so low as to drug her into unconsciousness.

And for what purpose?

He hadn't raped her or otherwise interfered with her while she'd been incapacitated. All he'd done, as far as she knew, was to leave her unconscious on the settee and drive home, even though he couldn't fail to have known she'd prefer to go home too. So why hadn't he taken her back with him and dropped her off? He could easily have rid himself of the inconvenience of having her around if that was what she'd become?

Or perhaps it wasn't home he was going to, and he'd drugged her so that he didn't have to have that discussion with her.

Or because he had some other reason for keeping her here?

Something tugged at her brain. Some stray thought that kept eluding her. A niggle she'd suppressed more than once over the past few weeks because she hadn't wanted to give it oxygen. She scrunched her eyes closed and tried to winkle the thought out from its hiding place, but it kept being overlaid by her current dilemma.

If Billy had been prepared to drug her, what else was he capable of?

With no answer being generated by her befuddled brain, that same question kept turning over and over again, banishing all other thoughts.

What else was he capable of?

One thing was for sure. No way was she prepared to sit here passively waiting for him to come back in order to find out.

But she stood no chance out there in the snow on her own with no transport. Certainly none of the few clothes she had with her were suitable for going walkabout in deep snow and freezing conditions, in the middle of nowhere, at night, with a dangerous Royal Air Force firing range so close by.

So what options did she have?

None, bar staying in the lodge until Billy chose to return, in the hope she'd be able to talk him into driving her home.

At least in here she could stay warm. She had food and fresh water. The fact that staying made her a sitting duck for whatever else he had planned for her was immaterial because, logically, she was one hundred percent certain to freeze to death if she took the only other option, which was to go out into the snow. In here, when Billy returned, she stood at least a small chance of being able to talk her way out of whatever he intended to do to her.

Or she could stick him with a knife.

Although she wasn't about to stick him very deep with a Stanley knife.

She took the knife out of her pocket and played with the mechanism a few times to make sure it worked properly. The short blade could do some damage if she slashed with it rather than stabbed, but it was hardly likely to put a man the size of Billy out of action for long. Not unless she struck lucky and hit one of the main arteries on her first go.

She needed a bigger knife.

She gave a harsh laugh. Never before in her entire life, had she ever had to seriously contemplate the most efficient ways of harming a man.

Overreaction?

No it bloody wasn't.

She jumped to her feet, then regretted it when pain seared through her head again and made her crumple back down into the chair. How long ago since she'd taken those paracetamol? She looked at her watch. Not even an hour ago.

No, she told herself. In no way was it unreasonable for her to be planning ways to defend herself. Billy had brought her out here under false pretences. He'd disabled her phone, drugged her and abandoned her here. When it came down to it, he'd risked killing her, since he had no way of knowing how her body would react to whatever drug he'd given her. So it was perfectly reasonable for her to suspect he might have worse things planned for her when he returned. And if that were the case, she needed to prepare herself as much as possible for any eventuality.

And a Stanley knife was not the answer.

Or at least it wasn't the only answer.

***

The kitchen drawers held a full set of chef's knives, every one of them sharp enough to do some damage if necessary. And there was the corkscrew; a basic t-shaped one where the handle fits into the palm of the hand and the spike sticks out between the fingers. She held it now and remembered Billy using it earlier to uncork the bottle of wine they'd bought in Brampton. They'd shared the bottle over dinner and then he'd poured out the last glass for her while she moved over to the fire, and got a whisky for himself.

He'd probably put the drug into that last bloody glass of wine.

And she hadn't noticed a thing.

Her body shook with anger. How fucking dare he?

She made a sharp jabbing motion with the corkscrew spike and imagined driving it into one of his dazzling blue eyes. Then she grabbed a sheet of kitchen paper and returned to the bin to retrieve the broken capsules. Wrapping them carefully, she stowed the little twist of paper in her pocket so that if she ever got out of here, she had evidence of what he'd done to her.

Her plan, if she could call it that, was simple. She'd keep the Stanley knife and the corkscrew in her back pockets, partly because they were the only makeshift weapons she'd managed to gather that were small enough to hide in there. But also because she'd be less likely to do herself damage with them than she would with a big unsheathed kitchen knife in her pocket.

When Billy returned, if she felt even the least bit threatened, she'd attack with the corkscrew first, going for the neck, and keep the Stanley knife as back up.

But she had no illusions about Billy's ability to disarm her easily enough if she failed to do enough damage immediately, and so she hid the kitchen knives out of sight around the downstairs of the lodge, where he'd be unlikely to spot them, but she'd be able to grab them to defend herself. If necessary.

If she got the chance.

It was only once she'd finished the task that she thought to check the doors.

Why on earth hadn't she thought of it before? If there were internal bolts, she could engage them, then Billy's keys would be useless. He wouldn't be able to get in. Except that all he'd need to do then would be to break the door down, or smash one of the windows and climb in. But it should at least slow him down.

The front door had substantial bolts top and bottom that looked almost as old as the building itself. It took some effort, but eventually she managed to shoot them both home.

She moved to the back door. Only one bolt here. A much flimsier modern affair. Hopefully, it would hold. If it came down to it.

It was only as she passed the big picture window – the one she'd noticed as soon as she walked in the lodge door on Sunday – that she saw the snow has stopped falling. She could even see stars peeping through, so the clouds must be breaking up.

And in the distance, she saw headlights approaching up the narrow road.

Moving slow. But definitely coming this way.

Billy had come back.

He was almost here.

Ellie's guts turned icy cold. Something buzzed in her head and her knees almost failed her. If she hadn't grabbed hold of the window sill, she'd have fallen to the floor.

***

Fight or flight. But Ellie had nowhere to flee to. She had no choice but to fight. One thing for sure, she could not afford to freeze. .

Staring out of the window, she could feel her heart pounding in her chest. Miraculously, her headache had disappeared, her vision cleared.

Fight it was.

She needed to move.

She ran upstairs to the unfinished room that looked out towards the ruined outbuildings and the turn off from the road. Nothing yet but a dancing phosphorescence, like nymphs flitting across the snowy moor as the headlights approached.

But then the vehicle slowly moved into her vision.

Not Billy's car at all.

A snow plough.

But that didn't mean Billy wasn't behind the wheel.

Breathing hard, she watched the truck take the right turn onto the track that led to the front of the lodge, and then lost sight of it for a moment as it took another bend to the right around the outbuildings.

As it turned again, the truck's headlights seared her retinas

CHAPTER 81

From the front window she saw the snow plough perform a wide pirouette, snow flying in an arc from the edge of the blade, until it faced the way it had come. Not an actual snow plough after all, but a pickup truck, like the one she'd seen yesterday, with a snow blade attached to the front.

The driver blasted the horn. But, with the passenger side now closest to her, Ellie couldn't see who was driving. She had to assume it was Billy. Who else would come all the way out here? Who else would even know there was anyone here?

Full of indecision, she waited. Had Billy had a change of heart when he saw how bad the snow was and decided to come back to rescue her?

With a different vehicle?

But surely, knowing he'd given her enough of whatever drug he'd used to knock her out cold, he wouldn't just assume she'd respond to a blast of a horn and come tappy lappy out of the lodge like an obedient dog.

But if not Billy, then who?

And then the driver emerged from round the back of the vehicle. It was the woman Billy had threatened yesterday. The one from the café.

What on earth was she doing all the way out here?

But all that mattered was that the woman *had* come. It meant she'd be able to get away from the lodge before Billy came back.

She ran to the door and tried to pull back the bolts. She slid the bottom one open easy enough, but the top one had stuck fast. She gave the door a push then tried again, snagging the skin of her knuckle, making it bleed.

The truck driver pounded on the door and called her name.

'I'm here,' Ellie grunted. 'I'm just trying to... open the... door.'

But it was no use.

In shooting the bolts, she'd trapped herself inside.

She clenched her fists and tried to concentrate her still fuddled mind. There was still the back door. She assumed that opened okay, but it would mean a hard trek with her bag through the snow that lay in drifts against the back wall to get back round to the front.

Then she had a brainwave. She ran to the kitchen and flung open the cupboard doors. She'd seen a bottle of rapeseed oil cooking spray in here somewhere. Yes. There.

She grabbed the bottle, ran back to the door and sprayed oil liberally on the bolt.

The pickup driver hammered on the window.

Ellie stood back for a moment, so she could be seen, sticking her thumbs up so the driver would know she'd been heard. Then she returned to her task, working the handle of the bolt, moving it up and down, allowing the oil to work its way into every crevice before trying to pull it across.

She gave it another wiggle, her hands slipping on the oiled metal, then tried again. This time, the bolt shot open, taking her by surprise and catching another sliver of skin.

She unlocked the latch and flung open the door.

***

'Thank God!' The woman looked close to tears. 'I thought he'd done something awful to you too.'

'He did,' Ellie said, trying to control her own tears of relief to be getting away from this place. 'He drugged me. Left me unconscious on the settee. I didn't know what... what he would do when he... when he came back.'

'Don't worry, we're not hanging around to find out. Is that your bag?'

Ellie turned. Saw her travel bag sitting on the floor just inside the door. Her coat and handbag on top. She'd forgotten she'd left it there.

And then the whole ridiculous contradiction of it all hit her like a smack in the face. Packing her things and leaving her bag by the door so Billy wouldn't have a chance to refuse to take her home when he got back. Planning how best to injure him when he did return. And then bolting the doors so he couldn't get in anyway.

But none of that mattered. She was going home. Or at least she was getting away from the lodge to somewhere she could call James and ask him to pick her up.

She put on her coat and slung her handbag over her head and across her body while the delivery driver grabbed her travel bag and stowed it on the back seat of the pickup.

'In you get, Ellie. My name is Jess, by the way.'

'Good to see you again, Jess. I can't tell you how grateful I am you came to get me.'

***

Hunched over the wheel, tension radiating from her as she concentrated on navigating the driveway around the old outbuildings, Jess followed the pickup's own tyre tracks slowly back out onto the narrow road. She couldn't have noticed the glint of a reflection as their headlights swept the stone ruined outbuildings, but Ellie did. She remembered the flash of light she thought she'd spotted from the lodge's upstairs window and wondered what it was.

But she'd never know now, for she was on her way home. To safety.

Wide-eyed, she took in the deadly beauty of the snow covered moor and thanked her ingrained common sense that had prevented her from venturing out here on her own earlier in her drug-addled stupor. The snow might have disguised them, but she knew the ground beneath was full of dips and gullies. She could have easily fallen into one of them, broken her ankle and died of exposure out here.

'What made you come all the way over here in the snow to find me?' she asked.

'I saw the bastard leave. Driving like a bat out of hell. Only him in that car, and it looked... ominous, somehow. I can't explain. And then the snow started, and I kept looking for him coming back, but he didn't, not that I saw anyway, and I live just on the road above Gilsland Spa, so I see most things that go past. No sign of his Discovery. And I thought maybe he'd done something to you and left you there. And then I thought... Well, never mind what I thought. But I'd never have forgiven myself if he'd done something to you too. So I strapped the plough onto the beast.' She patted the pickup's dashboard affectionately. 'And here I am.'

'I can't tell you how relieved I felt when I saw it was you and not Billy.'

'Yes well, when it comes to bastards like him, us women need to stick together.'

They stayed silent for a while then, until Ellie's curiosity got the better of her. 'How did you negotiate this road coming the other way with no tyre tracks to follow?'

'I've lived here all my life. I know this road and the moors like the back of my hand. But actually, I was surprised, because there *were* still tracks to follow. Faint traces anyway. The bastard must have bloody good winter tyres on that Discovery for them still to have been visible.'

Already driving conservatively, Jess slowed down even more as she descended the dip down to the little bridge. On the other side, the road kinked and then rose to a blind summit. The same spot where Billy had taken the bend too quickly and almost crashed into Jess. Less than twenty-four hours ago, yet it felt like a lifetime.

Was Jess thinking the same thing?

The pickup truck bounced a little as the tyres sought a grip on the impacted snow. Jess patted the dash again and murmured encouragement to her steed, urging the vehicle up and round the bend at the top of the slope.

Before either of them had time to register its presence, something big shot out of the passing place over the brow and smashed into the driver's door. The truck slewed across the road and slid to a halt. Jess grunted once in pain, then fell silent.

Ellie heard a vehicle door opening and the crump of footsteps on snow. Only one person it could be, but Jess's motionless bulk blocked her view. Crump, crump, around the back of the pickup. She held her breath, wishing she'd kept track of the distance view and left Jess to concentrate on the road immediately in front of them. Then she might have spotted a hint of Billy's headlights. Crump, crump; closer now. Then the passenger door flew open. A large figure reached across and unbuckled her seat belt. Strong hands grabbed the collar of her coat. Dragged her out onto the snow.

'Fancy meeting you here, Ellie.' Billy said.

CHAPTER 82

Billy gripped Ellie's left arm above the elbow and forced her round to the other side of the truck. He threw her against the side of the Land Rover Discovery, bouncing her head off the door post. She tasted blood from a split lip as he wrenched open the door and pushed her inside, fastening the seat belt across her arms, trapping them at her sides.

'Don't fucking move.'

Through the windscreen, she could see the Discovery's bonnet still embedded in the driver's side of the truck, and Jess hunched forward over the steering wheel, still unconscious, or possibly worse. Ellie knew Billy had no intention of helping her. He was going to leave her out here in the snow, where she'd freeze to death without help.

If it hadn't been for her, Jess would still be safe at home.

Climbing into the driver's seat, Billy slid the car into reverse and revved the engine. The wheels spun, but the Discovery didn't move. It was stuck fast.

He thrust the gears into drive, jolting the pickup half off the road. Jess's body slid away from the steering wheel and out of view. Ellie sat forward, trying to see her, but Billy's arm shot out and pushed her back.

'I told you not to move.'

With a high-pitched shriek of metal, he managed to free the Discovery from the side of the pickup and swung it round in a semi-circle. They shot down into the dip and back up onto straight road on the other side, staying in the tyre tracks Jess had left only minutes before, heading for the lodge.

Beside her, Billy breathed hard. 'How are you even awake now, Ellie? You should have slept until morning.'

Her whole body vibrated with fury. 'How *fucking dare* you drug me?'

He laughed at her indignation. 'Language, Ellie. But really, just one cap put you out for the whole night on Sunday. So how come two didn't do it this time?'

Horrified, Ellie remembered how odd her head had felt, and her surprise at having slept right through on their first night in the lodge. And now he was saying he'd drugged her then too?

The fucking... fuck-head.

'Why did you bring me here?'

'For a bit of fun.'

'You find it funny to drug women?'

He shrugged. 'And to find out how much you really know.'

What was he talking about? 'How much I know about what?'

'Haven't you figured it out yet? What Sonia was trying to tell you that night before her little accident?'

Ellie's blood ran cold. Only now did that stray niggling thought work its way out into the open. It must have been Billy who'd said something different that night at Sonia's New Year's party to what he'd always said before. He was the reason her friend had felt impelled to go out in the cold and dark to make a phone call.

'She looked so stupid out there in that red coat, you know. Skidding around on the ice, legs everywhere, like fucking Bambi.'

'Oh God! You killed her?'

'I didn't know she was already on the phone to you at the time though. I've thought about it a lot since then, you know. I should have just spiked her drink, then made sure she didn't wake up again. It wouldn't have been difficult. I was supposed to be staying the night after the party. I could have slipped into her room after Ronnie had put her to bed and finished her off quietly. Made it look like she'd choked herself to death on her own vomit. She always overdid the drink anyway. Raging alcoholic, so no surprise to anyone. Odds on, if I'd done it that way, she wouldn't have been found until morning. But I panicked, slipped out the back when I saw her go out the front.

'I'd had to park up the street. Not this beauty, you understand. I was driving a little anonymous runaround I use sometimes, because I knew there wouldn't be any room on the drive by the time I got there, and I wasn't about to leave this on such a narrow road with drunken idiot drivers around. It's in the garage at home now.'

He chewed his lip for a moment before continuing.

'Did you know they hadn't slept in the same room for years? It wouldn't have been the first time I'd slipped in to see her. Only it was usually to give her a good seeing to. For which she was always pathetically grateful, by the way. Started on their wedding day. While she was still in her wedding dress for fuck's sake. Payback for Ronnie stiffing me on a deal. In fact that son of hers is more likely mine than his. She told me Ronnie hasn't been able to get it up for a long time. Did she tell you that too? I bet that saint of a husband of yours hadn't been able to get it up for a long time either. What was his name? David?'

Ellie's rage bubbled in her throat. 'Don't you dare even say his name.'

Billy roared with laughter. 'You must be so fucking desperate for a shag by now Ellie. Christ, you should have seen your face as soon as I suggested it. You'd have had me there and then over the table in that little café if I'd let you. But don't worry, I'll still see you right. I'm no old man like Ronnie or David. I'm still as big and hard today as I was as a teenager.'

Ellie felt every muscle in her body curl up in disgust at his words.

That she could ever have fallen for the things he'd said…

'I intended to screw you stupid tonight when I got back. I was going to carry you upstairs to my room, do the business while you were still out for the count and tell you that you'd crept into my bed in the middle of the night, begging for it. You'd have bought it. I know you would. You've bought everything else for fuck's sake.'

Ellie's hands itched to reach into her back pocket for the corkscrew and stick it in his heart, but her arms were still trapped at her sides by the seatbelt. And anyway, it probably wouldn't even penetrate his jacket, let alone the clothes he wore beneath. Her best chance was back at the lodge, where she'd hidden the knives.

'You said you expected me to be out cold until morning,' she said.

'I did. I'm buggered if I can understand how you're not still comatose. You drank the wine. I washed your empty glass.' He gave a short laugh and shook his head. 'Anyway, nearly there now. We can still get it on when we get back, can't we? Although I have to say, you're not my usual type. I prefer my women younger and with a bit of flesh. Not so much an old bag of bones, you know? But I've put a lot of effort into you now. I deserve something back for that.'

'Why the hell did you even chat me up?'

'I needed to know what Sonia had said to you on the phone. At first it was a relief when you said she'd made no sense, but then you kept trying to work it out—'

'You kept prompting me to remember.'

He shrugged. 'To check you hadn't. But I knew that one day you would. Anyway, it's not like chatting you up was difficult. Soon as I saw you I thought, there's a woman begging for a good seeing to. So, before this night is over Ellie, I'm going to give you the ride of your life. Show you what it feels like to have a real man for once.'

The conceited bastard.

'If you think I'm going to...' She could hardly speak for the anger in her throat.

Billy put his head back and roared with laughter again. 'You still think I'm giving you a choice? Really? That's hilarious.'

Ellie closed her eyes and thought again about the corkscrew and the Stanley knife in the back pockets of her jeans, and the kitchen knives she'd stashed around the lodge.

She still didn't get it though. The drugs in her system must still be hindering her brain because it wouldn't make the leap. Why did whatever he'd finally admitted to Sonia matter so much?

'Tell me one thing,' she said, in as calm a voice as she could muster. 'Why did you leave a note if you thought you'd be back before I woke up?'

He shrugged. 'Just covering my bases. There was a possibility I might have had to stay a little longer than intended at home.'

A cloud settled over his face, and he fell silent after that, steering the Land Rover along the pickup's tracks at way too fast a pace for the snowy conditions. Eyes dead ahead, Ellie prayed they'd stay on the road while at the same time running through possible scenarios in her head on how she could defend herself back at the lodge. She had no illusions now. She knew without a doubt that her life was at stake here. From the moment Billy had admitted killing Sonia she knew he intended to kill her too.

And it wouldn't be only her own life at stake. Jess could still be alive in that truck, but she couldn't survive long out there in the snow on her own, injured. The poor woman deserved none of this. She'd only wanted to warn Ellie of the danger she was in. She'd even come all the way out here in treacherous conditions as soon as she thought something worse might have happened to her.

Somehow, Ellie had to put Billy out of action long enough to steal the fob for the Land Rover. If she could do that, then both she and Jess might still survive this.

Ellie prayed that when it came down to it, she'd have the courage to stick a knife into human flesh.

'How do you know Jess,' she demanded, as he slowed down to take the exit onto the lodge drive.

Billy gave a snort of derision but said nothing for a moment while he negotiated the bend around the side of the ruined outbuildings.

Ellie searched for that mysterious glint of light again but saw nothing.

'Had a thing with her little sister last year,' he said eventually. 'Just a bit of fun, you know, but the stupid cow went and topped herself over it.'

Oh God. In the café yesterday, when Jess had told her he'd ruined her friend's life, she'd been talking about her sister, who'd ended up committing suicide because she couldn't live with whatever Billy had done to her. Had he drugged her too?

Ellie imagined a young woman with wild dark hair like Jess's, sitting in front of the fire at the lodge, where she'd sat herself, sipping a drink she had no idea had been spiked, like she had herself. Is that what did it for him, defiling women while they were unconscious and therefore unable to say no or to defend themselves? How could she not have seen the evil in him as soon as she'd stared into those astonishing blue eyes?

'I didn't dope her the first time,' he said, as if he'd read her thoughts. 'I wouldn't normally. What's the point if they can't appreciate what they're getting?'

Ellie felt sick.

'But she was so fucking... needy.' His lips curled with distaste. 'The stupid cow came back for more, gagging for a repeat performance. And

I couldn't be arsed with having to keep telling her how beautiful she was, over and over again, when she was nothing of the sort. So I spiked her drink.' He laughed. 'First time I'd ever done it. And I discovered it's so much easier when they're asleep.'

'So now you do it to *any* woman you sleep with?'

Facing the lodge now, Billy slammed on the brakes. The Discovery slid a few inches in the snow before coming to a halt.

'Jesus, Ellie. You left the lights blazing and the fucking front door open.'

Ellie stared at the door, pulled to, but not closed properly, light leaking out at the sides. She might not have turned the lamps off – saving energy had hardly been uppermost in her mind – but she was as certain as she could be that she'd closed the front door properly behind her.

CHAPTER 83

Billy frogmarched Ellie towards the front door, muttering about the waste of energy and of money she'd caused by leaving the lodge like this. 'What if I hadn't come back Ellie, huh? The lodge would have stood like this for a week or more. Christ knows what fucking wildlife could have found its way inside and wrecked everything. You know how long it took me to renovate the place? Do you, Ellie?'

She planted her heels hard in the snow. 'You think I give a shit about that? Or about the money it costs you, after what you've done to me, and to Jess and her sister, and – oh God, to Sonia? And don't think I don't know what you plan to do to me, you bastard. I'm warning you. I won't go without a fight.'

'Oh Ellie,' He grinned that demonic grin again. 'Keep talking. You're making me hard. Maybe I'll kill you while we're doing it. How about that? It's a long time since I've seen the light go out in a woman's eyes while I'm fucking her. Maybe tonight's the night for a rerun, eh? Christ, that takes me back a bit.'

What? Ellie felt something cold twist in her guts.

She had no time to think about it. They'd reached the door of the lodge now. Billy reached over her shoulder and pushed the door fully open, so it banged against the wall.

'In you go.'

Moving across the threshold in front of him, Ellie saw it first. Something so incongruous, it took a moment for her to realise she was looking at a naked man. Arms and legs stretched out and lashed to the exposed upright timbers. A much younger, more slender version of Billy, his pale torso heaving with laboured breaths and adorned with fist-sized bruises, all at varying stages of development. The poor man must have been used as a punchbag over a period of hours, days even. His head hung forward, so Ellie couldn't see his face fully, but she thought she recognised him from the funeral. Nicky. Sonia's son. His chin rested on his hairless chest, bloody drool dripping from his swollen mouth and down onto his genitals, devoid of pubic hair, which hung shrivelled and pathetic between his wide open legs.

Then Billy saw it too.

'Fu-u-ck.'

He turned to run. Straight into the chest of the biggest man Ellie had seen in her life.

'Good evening, folks. Nice of you to join us.' The voice came not from the man in the doorway, but from inside the lodge, from another man silhouetted against the light from the open fire that flickered brightly, as if it had been fed with fresh logs since Ellie had left here with Jess. 'Come in, come in.' Laughter rumbled in the man's barrel chest. 'Of course, excuse me. Where are my manners? Am I allowed to welcome my cousin into his own house? Long time no see Billy boy.'

The huge man pushed Billy forward, buckling Ellie's knees and throwing her into the side of the kitchen island. The Stanley knife in her back pocket thunked against the wood and she froze, instinctively covering the sound by rubbing her elbow.

But no-one so much as glanced at her.

For a moment, she'd been forgotten. And the front door still stood open.

If she could ease herself along the floor...

She made it just a few inches before a pair of snowy wellington boots planted themselves in front of her, blocking her way. A third intruder. Younger and nowhere near as large as the other two, but still big from this angle.

The man got down on his honkers and grinned at her. 'Where do you think you're going? Dad, do you know we've got a woman over here trying to crawl her way outside?'

'You hum it son, and I'll play it.' The man by the fire guffawed at his own little joke. 'No? Did you not like that one, Billy boy? Shall we bring your lady friend over here? Explain to her why she should have stayed away from scum like you?' He laughed again. 'And put the big light on while you're at it, son. Can't see a bloody thing with just these poncey lamps on.'

The third man gripped Ellie's left arm above the elbow and dragged her to her feet. He looked around him at the walls for a light switch.

'Over there,' she said.

'Thanks.' His polite response sounded incongruous, given the situation.

The man flicked the switch, bringing the glaring overhead light to life, bleaching out everyone's eyesight for a moment. Expecting the brilliance of the light, Ellie had screwed her eyes shut to protect them, and took the opportunity to reach her right hand into her back pocket for the corkscrew and secrete it up her sleeve.

Just in time.

The man holding her arm shook his head to clear his sight and dragged her so close to the injured hanging man that her wrist brushed his thigh. She'd thought he must be unconscious, and yet he flinched and hissed in shock at her touch, his head lifting momentarily so she got a better look at his face. Despite the black and swollen nose and eye sockets and the bloody mouth, she knew for a fact now that this was Sonia's son, Nicky. And, if Billy could be believed, his son too rather than his brother Ronnie's.

As the third man dragged her past and shoved her towards the lounge area, she wondered what the boy could possibly have done to deserve this.

Her captor pushed her down onto the settee, but she reared back in shock when she almost sat on a young woman, the back of her head connecting with his nose. He grunted and lashed out an arm, knocking Ellie to the floor. The corkscrew flew from her sleeve, skittering out of reach under the settee, and her hand landed on a cold wet patch on the dark rug.

An image flashed across her brain and then repeated itself again and again, like a social media meme. She saw herself leaning forward to place a half-full glass of wine on the floor, but it toppled over, spilling the contents onto the rug. Already woozy, she'd groped for the glass to stand it back up but made no attempt to mop up the spilled liquid.

That was why she hadn't blacked out for longer. She'd only drank a small amount of the drug.

Where had Billy been when that happened?

Surely he'd have noticed.

But he couldn't have, because he thought she'd drunk it all when he'd found the glass empty and washed it. He mustn't have noticed the wet patch on the dark rug.

But, having already drunk some of the wine, she'd slid down into the uncomfortable position she woke up in, and if her neck hadn't been bent so awkwardly, she'd probably have slept the night away like that. It was probably the discomfort in her neck that had woken her up.

'Bunk along, Abbie pet,' the man in charge said – nowhere near as tall as his giant henchman but equally as wide, his dark hair cropped close to his scalp 'Let the lady sit down.'

The young woman on the settee sniffed and gulped hard, as if she'd been crying, but she did as he'd asked, and Ellie climbed up from the floor to take the vacated place.

'I've no idea who you are love, but you can call me Stevie, and this here is my daughter Abbie. Abigail she prefers to be called, but she'll always be Abbie to her old dad. Isn't that right, pet?'

The dark-haired young woman sniffed again and dragged a sleeve across her tear-swollen face. She gave a terrified nod. She might be the man's daughter, but it was clear that all this was alien to her, that she'd been brought here against her will too.

The man called Stevie drew closer to Ellie and looked down upon her. For the first time, she noticed the gun in his hand. Small, black and deadly.

But at least he didn't point it in her direction.

'This here is family business,' he said, 'and I'm sorry you've been caught up in it. As you might have already guessed, given what you've seen, I can't let you leave here alive, and I'm sorry for that too. You look like a nice lady, and I don't like having to kill people who've never done me any harm, but I promise I'll make it quick.'

Ellie stared at him, struggling to take in his words, thinking instead how ineffectual the Stanley knife still in her back pocket, and the kitchen knife she'd hidden down the side of the very cushion she sat on, would be against a gun.

The man called Stevie turned to glare down at Billy, now on his knees on the floor, breathing fast, his arms pulled back and wrenched upwards by the man-mountain towering above him.

'And that brings me back to this piece of shit here, because he's the reason you can't be allowed to survive this night.'

For the first time since they'd re-entered the lodge, Ellie looked Billy in the face. Those electric blue eyes that had so beguiled her, stared back, burning inky black in impotent rage and humiliation.

Never in her wildest nightmares could she ever have imagined she'd end up with two men determined to kill her – in one night.

CHAPTER 84

They made it to the airport and boarded the helicopter by just after half past one. Keegan asked the pilot how long the flight would take.

'No problems with visibility now, so probably less than fifteen minutes once we're in the air. There's transport waiting at the other end for you.'

'Good old Geoff,' Keegan said, with a grin towards Portas.

'As long as we beat Elsom's lot there,' she replied.

The pilot was true to his word. As soon as they touched down and the rotors slowed, the door was wrenched open from outside to reveal a stocky man with a sandy-haired military cut and a liveliness about him that made Massey feel the weight of every one of the eighteen hours he'd been on duty.

'LouLou,' the man cried.

Keegan tried to hide a chuckle by stroking his beard.

Portas closed her eyes and wrinkled her face. 'Geoff. Thanks for the assistance. You could literally be a lifesaver.'

'Always ready to serve and all that. Good to see you, LouLou. Who have you brought with you?

***

Their small party, bolstered by half a dozen RAF personnel, climbed aboard twin Land Rover Defenders, the dull matte camouflage livery looking light years removed from the smart Lantau Bronze of the Land Rover Discovery they knew Billy Wragg must be driving.

At the turn-off onto the moor, they liaised with a firearms unit from the Cumbria force in two marked 4x4 Toyota hard top double cabs. Portas gave a salute and a wide smile to a dark officer around Massey's age in the first vehicle – who he assumed to be the same DCI Dave Graham who Portas used to work with – and got a wink back. He wondered if she'd engaged in inappropriate relationships with colleagues in Cumbria too before she moved over to the east coast.

The Wing Commander had noticed too. 'Arrow to the heart, LouLou,' he said, with a wry grin and a fist to his chest.

Portas nudged him in the ribs as their vehicle took the lead up onto the single track road.

Once over a cattle grid, the convoy passed through a plantation of snow-laden pine trees. Miniaturised, any one of them could grace a Christmas cake. As the trees thinned and the vehicles rattled over another cattle grid, they could see the narrow road stretching out in front of them, like an alabaster snake slithering across the desolate moor, where snow-covered hassocks of vegetation gleamed like scattered pearls in their headlights.

'There's been a plough along here recently,' their driver said, pointing to the piled snow that edged either side of the road, 'and at least one other vehicle since then.'

They knew they'd leapfrogged the Serious and Organised convoy on the way here, so this must be Stevie Grant and his gang. Massey felt his anxiety over his mother's safety rise another notch. What the hell had possessed her to get herself mixed up in all of this?

To the left of the road, at regular intervals, they passed snow spattered signposts, some flanked by an empty flagpole.

'Military bombing range warnings,' the Wing Commander said in response to Keegan's question. 'We fly red flags during exercises.'

Massey cocked his head. 'Hear that?'

Above the sound of the Defender's engine and the squeaking of seat springs, he thought he'd detected a keening sound.

Their driver stopped the vehicle. The convoy behind came to a halt too. They listened.

'There. That's it. Can you hear?'

They did.

'Is it a car horn?'

'Let's find out,' the Wing Commander said. 'Easy does it though.'

Climbing a rise, Massey was the first to spot a flickering glow of light over the next hump in the road. They all registered together that the flickering had a pattern to it. Three short flicks, three long and three more short, then a pause, and repeat.

Morse code. SOS.

***

A pickup truck with a snow plough blade attachment perched at a forty five degree angle, its nearside wheels sinking into the boggy moor, with the corner of its plough blade wedged into the road surface, preventing it from toppling further.

Even before their Defender had drawn to a stop, the only female member of the RAF team in the leading Defender needed no prompting from her Wing Commander. She grabbed a medical kit from under a seat and used the threshold of the Defender to lever herself over to the driver's side window of the stricken truck, speaking calmly to a casualty inside. 'You're alright,' Massey heard her say. 'We've got you now.'

The offside of the truck canted upwards from the road, it's tyres clearing the surface and its door panels caved inward, although there was nothing around it that could have caused such damage.

It could only have been deliberately hit by another vehicle coming straight at it from the passing place, maybe lying in wait for the truck to emerge from the dip.

Tyre treads in the snow confirmed the theory, and the way the bend in the road angled downwards, Massey reckoned anyone driving up the slope towards the passing place wouldn't have been able to see anything parked up here until they were already upon it. And it was upon them.

Female, although thankfully not his mother, the injured driver was conscious, but only just.

Blood from a head wound covered half of her face and she appeared to be trapped in her seat, slumped sideways into an awkward position, suspended from her seat belt, with the fingers of one hand clamped tight to her vehicle's headlight control and the other hand still pressed down hard on the horn, despite their arrival.

How long had she been out here alone trying to raise help?

If they hadn't come along when they did, she'd most likely have died.

'You... have to... help her.' With the seat belt constricting her breathing, the woman struggled to get the words out.

'Someone was with you?' The medic turned to raise her eyebrows towards her team, who spread out to train powerful torch beams over the moor surrounding them.

Nothing. But Massey had noticed the bag on the rear seat and felt sure he recognised it as his mother's.

'I'm Donna,' the medic said, her concentration returning to the injured driver. 'What's your name?'

'Jess... Jess Tyler. You need... She... she needs help.'

'Who, Jess? Who needs help?'

'He... took her.'

Determined to stay conscious until she got them to understand, the woman's words came out in painful gasps. She'd been carrying a woman called Ellie to safety, she told them, when her truck was rammed. Ellie had been dragged out and taken away.

'Who did this?' Massey said, struggling to keep his voice calm and controlled.

'Billy... Think he... took her back to... to the lodge.'

Massey thanked her and told her he was Ellie's son. She grabbed his hand and squeezed it harder than he'd have thought possible, given the state of her.

'Save her,' she croaked, 'before it's too late.'

Portas had a quick confab with DCI Graham, and they all climbed back into the vehicles.

'Corporal,' Brayfield said to the medic. 'Stay here with the casualty. Help is on its way.'

'Sir.'

CHAPTER 85

'Look at him,' the man called Stevie said. 'He knows this is the end for him. And he knows Nigs here could squash him like a fly if he so much as moves a nut. But I want him to know why I've come for him instead of just offing his disgusting toad of a nephew and being done with it. And I think that you deserve to know the reasons why I have to kill you too. Would you like that?'

Oh God, anything to draw out the time while hoping for a miracle. 'Yes please,' she managed to say.

The man shoved the gun into the pocket of his jacket. 'That's good. We're all on the same page then. So, the first thing you need to know is that Billy here and me, we're related because our mothers were sisters. That makes him and his brother my first cousins. And the little scrote hanging up over there – Nicky is his name – he's my first cousin once removed because he's the son of Billy's brother, Ronnie. He's also a rapist, by the way. He even dared to defile my little girl Abbie here, who is his second cousin. And, for that, he has to die. But you already know that don't you? You look like an intelligent woman, so you'll appreciate that you knowing that is another reason I have to take care of you too.'

He uttered the words in such a matter of fact way that if it wasn't for the bloodied and beaten man lashed to the uprights and Billy forced to his knees in front of her, Ellie might have believed he meant it in a caring way. But, given the context, she knew he meant he'd have to kill her, and she couldn't keep the horror from showing in her face.

'Now, don't go looking at me like that, all prissy-like. You'll agree once I tell you who he really is – the name the press have given him anyway – that he needs to be exterminated. You see, believe it or not, that snivelling, pathetic piece of shite hanging up over there is the infamous Musk Man, who the police have been chasing him for the past year. Can you believe that? And my little Abbie is not the only poor lass he's defiled and terrified. Not by a long chalk. In fact my sister's youngest is one of them too. Nicole, she's called. And the worst thing about that part is that the little scrote is actually engaged to Nicole's sister, Nina. So you see, I'll be doing the world a favour by putting him down like the rabid mongrel he is. Don't you agree?'

Ellie nodded. What else could she do? And besides, she knew all about the horror of being raped. A horror she'd thought she was about to be forced to relive tonight after Billy's little speech on the way back here. And yet, thinking about her current situation, with four of the five men present no doubt prepared to kill her at the drop of a hat, wouldn't rape be preferable if she were then allowed to walk away?

But Billy hadn't intend to allow her to walk away either, had he?

She reached out and took hold of Abigail's hand; an instinctive gesture driven by a shared trauma. She thought the girl would pull away, but she didn't. Instead, she squeezed Ellie's hand in return and held on tight, while her father watched closely with an odd look in his eyes.

'So anyway,' he said, dismissing whatever thought had crossed his mind and walking over to look up at the man/boy fastened tight to the upright timbers. 'Young Nicky here used to work for me. The little bastard got above his station a couple of times but, you know, family and all that, you make allowances, don't you? Of course that was way before I knew what he'd done to my little Abbie, and to Nicole. And it showed a degree of ambition, I thought. Which I liked. At the time. But then he got too cocky by half. He started skimming, you see. Not much. Just enough to keep it under the radar of most people. But not Nigs. You see Nigs here has a gift when it comes to figures. He spotted the blips in the accounts, and he came to me about it. So we were already planning to have a little chat with Nicky boy by the time I heard about what he'd done to my Abbie.'

He shot a hurt look of injured pride to the young girl sat next to Ellie.

'Even though it took three years for me to find out. You know, she never said a word about it to me, her own father, in all that time. Until just the other day that is, when young master Wragg here decided on a repeat visit. Only this time she recognised him. And even then she only told me because her mother got in first.'

Abigail's fingers gripped Ellie's so hard it hurt.

The man called Stevie nodded his head towards the bruised and battered body in front of him. 'As you can see, we've already had a bit of fun with him, but that's nothing compared to what's going to happen. Because this little pervert is about to lose his tackle. That's why we've fastened him up here, see, so that Nigs has plenty of space in which to work. Like an artist, you know?'

If she ever got out of here alive, those would be the words she thought of every time she picked up a paintbrush.

'We did think about lashing him across this nice piece of wood here.' He stroked his hand across the surface of the dining table Billy had told her he'd built himself. 'But we're saving it for Billy boy. See, we're going to pin him down on his back, lash his arms and legs to the table legs and take him apart, bit by bit, one little piece at a time. See how far we can get before he stops squealing like a stuck pig. But not before he watches what Nigs is going to do to his precious nephew.'

Ellie could hear Billy's panicked panting now, over her shoulder.

'And do you know why?'

Ellie hadn't a clue. But she did know that turning her head so far over her shoulder in order to keep the man called Stevie in sight was aggravating the pain in her neck she still had from lying so long scrunched up in the corner of this same settee, unconscious. She didn't think she could shake her head without crying out in pain.

'No,' she croaked. 'I don't.'

'Well you need to know. You've been staying with him here after all. Sharing his bed. And yet you don't know what he is.'

'No, I haven't.' She sat up straight and squared her shoulder. 'We didn't... I couldn't...'

'What?' The man looked at her in amazement. 'Is this true? You're telling me that you've never let the great Billy Wragg into your knickers?' He guffawed with laughter again and returned to stand in front of Billy, looking down at him and laughing in his face.

Billy snorted like a bull and struggled to get free, but the immense and silent Nigs easily subdued him by forcing his tethered arms upwards behind him.

'You must be losing your touch Billy boy. You've brought this lovely lady...' He turned to her and clicked his fingers. 'What's your name, pet?'

'Ellie,' she said, rubbing her sore neck.

'Is that right Billy boy? You've brought the lovely Ellie all the way out to your love shack on the moors for a little romantic rumpy pumpy, and she's kicked you into touch? A spelk of a lass like her has had the guts to say no to you. That's precious, that is. That has to be a first.'

He wheeled round to face her. 'You know he thinks he's God's gift? Thinks all women should worship at the altar of his dick. But I can't believe it's as fabulous as he claims, can you? Shall we see? Nigs, if you could do the honours. Son, give him a hand.'

It took just two minutes for Billy to be divested of his clothes. When it was done and he was once more on his knees, with his arms wrenched up behind him, Ellie stared at his powerfully muscled body, at the taut sinews beneath the tanned skin, the whorls of golden hair spreading across the heaving chest and down over his tight belly in a line towards his genitals. And despite everything he'd said and done to her, she could still feel a lust for him in the pit of her belly.

'You see that, Ellie? That shrivelled cheesy Wotsit between his legs that he's so freaking proud of? I'd like to bet you've had way better than that in your time, eh?'

Ellie tore her eyes upwards from Billy's groin to his face, feeling his raging fury burn into her soul.

'See, Ellie,' the man called Stevie said. 'Here's the thing. While we were having our cosy little chat with young Nicky, after I'd told him exactly what I was going to allow Nigs to do to him, he got it into his head that he could still save himself by telling me a story. Now, of course, he was never going to be able to save himself. You understand that don't you? Not after what he'd done to my precious daughter and my niece. But I do like a good story. So I allowed him to think he could still live. If what he told me was worth the price. And it was. Almost.'

CHAPTER 86

The man called Stevie seized the poker and riddled the ashes in the grate before adding another log from the stack on the hearth. He watched it burn for a moment, seemingly mesmerised by the spitting flames that provided the only sound in the room, although Ellie imagined she could hear a clock ticking, counting down the time she had left on this earth, until this intimidating square man brought the gun back out of his pocket, placed the cold muzzle on her forehead and pulled the trigger.

She wondered what the time was, but didn't dare look at her watch. It felt like there'd been time enough to fit two whole 24-hour days into this one long night, and yet she probably hadn't been back in the lodge for much more than an hour.

In the warmth of the fire, despite the danger on all sides, her eyes began to cross and her mind drift, the drug still in her system attempting to reassert itself against the rapidly depleting adrenaline that had carried her through so far, threatening to leave her drained and lethargic and defenceless.

But she couldn't afford for that to happen. Jess still lay injured out there. She had to do something to get help for her before it was too late.

But what?

Carefully, she eased her hand down the side of the cushion, feeling for the kitchen knife she'd left there, finding the handle in just the right place to grasp it securely. But what use was a kitchen knife against three strapping men, at least one of whom had a gun? And even in the impossibly ludicrous event she might somehow manage to defeat all three, there would still be Billy to contend with, and a far more incensed and unpredictable Billy than before. The image she'd been holding onto of herself as a knife-wielding dervish shrivelled and died there and then. If it had been Billy alone, as she'd imagined when she'd hidden the knives, then perhaps she'd have stood a chance. If she caught him unawares. But—

Abigail gave her hand a squeeze and shot her a warning look with her eyes.

She noticed the girl's other hand down the side of her own cushion. She must have found the knife Ellie had hidden down that side, and was warning her against using them.

She replied with a reassuring squeeze and a miniscule nod.

Pulling out a knife now would be the last living thing she'd ever do. And with every moment she remained alive, she still had a chance. There was an injured woman out there on the moors who needed her help. She had a new grandchild on the way. And she needed to apologise to James. She couldn't afford to do anything so stupid.

And besides, she wanted to hear the end of the story.

With a sudden shake of his shoulders, the man called Stevie roused himself. 'Where was I? Oh yes. Now Ellie, I need to bore you with some more family stuff first before I can explain the rest of it. You see, while Billy boy here may be my cousin on my mother's side because my mother's sister was his mother, my father had a sister too. My Auntie Sheila if you're interested. And she had a daughter, my only cousin on my father's side. Her name was Julie, and she was raped and murdered forty years ago, almost to the day. And, according to young Nicky over there, it was this snivelling turd you see here on his knees in front of you who killed her.'

Ellie felt her jaw drop. Her brain flooded with images of the three of them together. Herself, Sonia and Julie as small children in primary school. Then in the first year of secondary school, when they'd all gone on a school trip to Spain and began calling themselves the three amigas. Then the birth of their nicknames, Ells Bells, Sonic and Jools during their punk period, hair like porcupines. Then Sonia as a pale-faced goth, dressed all in black, while she and Jools embraced the glorious colour of the New Romantic movement, both with bleached blonde hair backcombed into huge elaborate haloes around their heads, adorned with feathers and lace.

Then Jools on that New Year's night, her last night on earth, telling them about the crush she had on the tall strutting peacock on the other side of the dance floor, the strobe lights catching the colour of his red hair, changing it to blue, to green, and back to red again. She heard Jools saying something about the peacock's fabulous blue eyes.

Like Billy's eyes.

And she remembered Sonia's words on the phone, just before Billy mowed her down and killed her. 'He said he was there,' she'd said, 'where before he'd always said he—'

Sonia hadn't been able to finish the sentence, but now Ellie knew exactly what her old friend had been trying to tell her. The night Sonia died came forty years to the day after Julie had been killed. She must have mentioned the anniversary at the party.

She did. She'd told her so on the phone.

And Billy must have said something then that had contradicted what he'd always claimed. For the first time, he must have admitted to being there at JoJo's on that New Year's night, when he must always have previously claimed to be nowhere near.

CHAPTER 87

Only Billy Wragg's Discovery was parked in front of the lodge. They found the Transit van and Stevie Grant's vehicle concealed along an access track to a conifer plantation that bordered the lodge grounds on two sides.

Approaching out of sight through the plantation, three Cumbria firearms officers took up positions at points along the tree line facing the front of the lodge itself, a small snowy field sloping down in front of them towards the brightly lit windows. Two others peeled off to seek out vantage points to cover the back of the building.

The Northumbria officers and RAF personnel gathered behind the ruined outbuildings, along with Cumbria's DCI Dave Graham. From there, they had only an oblique view of the lodge and would need to rely on reports from the firearms officers with clear sight lines to get an accurate picture of what was happening inside. But at least there were no curtains or blinds pulled over the windows to obstruct their view.

At least there were no curtains or blinds pulled over the windows to obstruct their view.

A voice crackled through their radios. 'Four two five to control. Four two five to control. You receiving?'

DCI Graham lifted his radio. 'Control to four two five. Yes, yes. Go ahead.'

'Four two five to control. In position. Ground floor window, second left, two IC1 males in view. Both standing. Repeat, two IC1 males standing. Assume others not in view. So far.'

'Control to four two five. Two IC1 in view. Understood. Carry on. Over.'

'Four two five to control. One IC1 male is a big bugger. Six foot six, at least. Over.'

'Nigs Bowen,' Keegan said.

'Three five seven to control. Receiving?'

'Control. Receiving, three five seven. Go ahead. Over.'

'Three five seven to control. Better view. Three standing. All male. Repeat, three males standing. Two are IC1. Third unknown. At least two others, looks like they're seated, possibly female. Over.'

DCI Graham's eyes scanned the tree line to the right of where he'd been focusing before. 'Understood three five seven. Reading back. Three males standing. Two confirmed IC1. At least two seated. Could be females. Over.'

Massey shuffled his feet. One had to be his mother. The other probably Abigail Grant. And the three men standing were likely to be Stevie Grant, Nigs Bowen and whoever had driven the Transit van. They could have brought more men with them, of course, who could now be watching the police activity. Although, if that was the case, they'd have warned those inside. The windows would have been covered, or the three men in there would have moved out of view. 'So where the hell are the Wraggs?'

'Three five seven to control.'

'Control to three five seven. Go ahead.'

'Not one hundred percent on what I'm seeing gov. Looks like a fourth male tied to posts in there. Over.'

CHAPTER 88

'Julie's death devastated our family.' The voice of the man called Stevie seethed with emotion as he faced Billy. A stark contrast to the matter of fact nature of everything else he'd said. 'And finally. After all these years...' He took the gun from his pocket and jammed the barrel into Billy's forehead.

Billy jerked his head away from it, but the big man behind him was prepared and yanked his arms hard upwards. Billy screamed in pain.

The man called Stevie gave a high-pitched laugh. 'After all these years, I've found the degenerate sicko who did it. Isn't that right Billy boy? "Vengeance is mine", the bible says. "A dish best served cold". Someone else said that. No idea who, but I think forty years is cold enough, don't you, Ellie?'

'I was with Julie that night,' Ellie said, her voice tremulous, terrified of the effect her words might have on him, but unable to stay quiet if it could help stop the situation descending any further.

'What?' The man called Stevie wheeled around to face her, turning the full power of his intimidating presence in her direction. 'What did you say?'

'Julie was one of my best friends. We were Ells Bells, Sonic and Jools. The three amigas.' Lay it on thick, she told herself. If she could prick the man's conscience enough, maybe he'd have second thoughts about having to kill her too. Then maybe...

'You're telling me you were one of Julie's little gang?'

'Yes, since primary school.'

'Well now.' He rubbed a hand over his close-cropped mat of hair. 'That's a turn up for the books, eh Nigs? Quite the coincidence.'

Nigs remained silent, knowing his boss well enough to realise the question was a rhetorical one. The third man, who Stevie had called 'son', shuffled his feet and cleared his throat, as if this was a lesson he was still only learning.

Stevie himself, head down now and chin in hand, paced the floor in front of the fire, the gun hanging loose at his side.

'She was a lovely little girl, Julie was. And she used to dote on me, you know, because I was her big cousin Steven. And you're telling me you were one of her friends back then? Well blow me down. I remember seeing her and her friends playing hopscotch on the pavement outside Auntie Sheila's. And you were one of them?'

He paced again.

No-one spoke, until a deep groan from Nicky broke the silence as he sagged further against the ropes that bound him to the uprights.

Abigail gripped Ellie's hand harder. She could feel the girl's trembling through her fingers and attempted in her answering squeeze to convey a reassurance she didn't herself feel.

'So, let me get this straight,' the girl's father said. 'Are you saying you were out with Julie on the night she died?'

Ellie flinched.

This could go either way. What if he thought she was equally at fault for not having protected Julie.

'I was, yes. All three of us went out together.'

'Who was the third girl?'

What? Ellie had assumed he'd know. Sonia would have been family to him too in a way, his cousin's wife. Cousin-in-law? Was that a thing?

'It was Sonic. Sonia Wragg. Ronnie Wragg's wife and Nicky's mother. She was Sonia Chambers then. Billy killed her too, not even a month ago. He admitted it to me tonight.'

'He did, did he?'

'He was going to kill me too, after raping me. He spiked my drink earlier. He... he thought I'd still be out for the count when he got back, but—'

Stop gabbling.

'I'd knocked my drink over, you see. So I hardly drank any of it. So I wasn't, you know... comatose, like he expected.' It wasn't even remotely a lie. And anything to pull another heart string – if there was a heart anywhere inside that big square chest. Anything at all that might persuade him to change his mind about killing her.

'And then that woman came for you, right?' he said. 'The one with the snow plough truck.'

They'd been watching? At least that made sense of the reflective light she'd seen twice from the old outbuildings. They must have been hiding there, waiting for Billy to come back, and then, when they'd seen her leave too they'd decided to move inside into the warmth to wait for him.

'Yes, that's right. That was Jess. Her sister killed herself because of Billy, so she came to save me, because she thought he was going to do something to me too. And she was right all along. But Billy hurt her. He drove into the side of the truck. And now she's lying unconscious in the snow out there. She needs help.'

The man called Stevie began pacing again, back and forwards in front of her, his chin once more in one hand, the gun swinging by his side in his other.

Reconsidering?

Perhaps.

She hoped.

Then he stopped in front of her, the belligerent mask back on his face.

'Well I'm sorry pet, but that's not my concern.' He gave a harsh laugh. 'All said and done, it really hasn't been your night, has it?'

Understatement of the fucking century!

He raised the gun to her forehead, just as a disembodied voice shouted from outside.

'Steven Grant. Nigel Bowen. William Wragg. This is Northumbria Police...'

***

The man called Stevie ducked below the level of the sill. Nigs Bowen turned to yank a curtain across the window.

Taking advantage of the loosened hold on his arms, Billy reared up and smashed the back of his head into Nigs' face. The big man crumpled to his knees and Billy drove his elbow down into the huge arm that still clung to his, the crack of breaking bone reverberating around the room. Grant levelled his gun, about to shoot, but Billy kicked it out of his hand. The weapon fired before skittering across the floor towards him.

Ellie screamed as she felt the bullet's heat singe her ear and the cordite sting her eyes.

She heard a thump from behind her.

Billy grabbed the gun and pulled the trigger. The man called Stevie grunted and clutched his shoulder, falling against Abigail.

Her face a mask of horror, Abigail pushed her injured father away, shrinking as far away from his cursing form as she could, her head shaking uncontrollably as she muttered the same word over and over. 'No, no, no, no...'

For a moment, everything seemed to pause, and then restarted in slow motion with the sound turned down too low, muting the throb of something heavy beating against the front door that Ellie couldn't remember anyone having closed.

She saw the big man rise up from the floor like a monster from the depths, one arm hanging loosely by his side, the other locking itself around Billy's neck, bulging muscles squeezing hard.

She watched the girl grope down the side of the cushion, then heard her muffled scream as she launched herself across the room at the man who'd shot her father.

With the giant's arm still clamped around his neck, Ellie saw Billy's glorious naked body tense, the muscles of his flank rippling in momentary expectation of the knife Abigail carried sliding deep into his flesh. Yet still his eyes flashed in surprise as the girl collided with him, knocking him and the big man backwards, all three writhing on the floor like a nest of hissing snakes.

In the midst of it all, Ellie's eyes met Billy's. She saw the shock bloom in their deep blue depths. She watched him lay one hand on his bare chest, then lift it to see his own blood drip from his fingers. She flinched as the gun fell from his grip, expecting it to go off again, to be hit squarely this time by another stray bullet. But the only sound was a solid clunk. And only then did she realise she'd instinctively covered her head with her hands and curled up as small as she could get.

As she lifted her head, time ramped up and Ellie's vision sharpened. Abigail sobbed, trying to free herself, and Ellie knelt down beside her, pulling her away from Billy's scrabbling feet as Nigs continued to choke the remaining life out of him, those blue eyes rolled now to the back of his head.

And above the high pitched buzz in her head, Ellie heard the front door splinter and crash against the wall, the thump of feet on the floor as black clad figures charged in, firearms levelled in front of them.

'On the floor, stay down,' they shouted, over and over.

Or at least that was what she thought they'd said before the blackness claimed her.

CHAPTER 89

'I thought you were dead,' Massey cried as he gathered his mother into his arms, trying to make out her mumbled words, shocked when he identified the one word she repeated over and over.

'Fuck, fuck, fuck...'

He laughed out loud. He couldn't help it. He'd never heard her utter the word before. 'Damn' and 'blast' were the worst she'd normally come out with, salted with the occasional 'buggeration'.

He gazed down at the woman who'd given him life, who felt so small and fragile now in his arms, her face all puckered and her eyes still screwed tightly closed as if she didn't dare open them, and the depth of his love for her almost overwhelmed him.

'Christ's sake, Mam, I thought you were dead.'

'I'm not *fucking* dead yet,' she muttered into his stab vest.

CHAPTER 90

They watched the injured Stevie Grant and Nigs Bowen being loaded into the helicopter with an armed police escort, on their way to hospital. Nicky Wragg had been prioritised and airlifted separately. They had two fatalities to deal with. Nigs Bowen had succeeded in throttling Billy Wragg to death, an outcome Massey knew his mother would be processing for some time to come. And the man she'd told them Stevie Grant had called 'son' had been killed outright by the stray bullet that had singed her ear before burying itself in his brain.

'Sorry we dragged you all the way over here,' Massey said to Police Inspector Gary Dunn, the trained negotiator whose skills had become superfluous as soon as shots were fired inside the lodge.

'No problem,' he replied. 'Something different to do on a snowy January night. Better than watching crap on TV.'

'You don't need to hang around you know,' Keegan said. 'You could travel back to RAF Spadeadam with the two women in one of the Defenders and be helicoptered back from there. Or Flash here could take you all over in the Discovery. Much more luxurious in that thing. And it has to be shifted from here one way or another.'

Ellie glared at the bearded detective. 'Not on your life,' she told him. 'I will never get into a Land Rover Discovery ever again. And more than likely, not even any car of a similar colour.'

Massey knew she was serious about the colour at least and made a mental note never to buy any kind of beigey bronze coloured car, ever, but he wasn't convinced she'd know a Land Rover Discovery from any other make or model. Cars had never been her strong point.

'You should go too,' Portas told him. 'Be with your mother. But not in the Discovery.'

'I'm staying, ma'am.'

He wanted to. Despite Portas' senior presence and the fact he was supposed to have nothing to do with anything his mother was involved in, technically at least he was still SIO. Still in charge of Operation Bryony and of the MIT.

Sparks stepped forward. 'I'll go with them. If that's okay, ma'am.'

'Thanks, Christine,' Ellie said, then patted her son's arm. 'Don't worry about me, James. I'm fine.'

And he knew she would be, especially now she knew Megan had not given birth in her absence and had been assured her mother was safe, with likely nothing worse than a headache and a burnt ear.

***

'Just as well Ellie did say no to Wragg's Discovery,' Portas said as the Defender engine sprang to life, and it rattled away from the lodge. 'Or I'd have had to overrule you. Forensics need to go over that car.'

'What do you expect them to find? There'll be nothing in it. It's not like he had the car back in 1983.'

'He murdered once. We have no idea yet what else he might have got up to since then.'

Lonnie Burke gave a big sigh. 'And now he's not going to face a court of law and pay for what he's done.'

Keegan patted Burke's shoulder. 'Still a kind of justice for Julie though. And it must be good to be in at the end, after all these years. Eh, Lonnie?'

'Aye, it is that. It's bloody marvellous, in fact.'

'Is that a lifetime of TV sport I can hear calling?'

Burke laughed. 'Already got my retirement resignation letter written. Just need to put in the date.'

Portas looked at Massey. 'It'll be interesting to hear what Nicky Wragg has to say. He'd obviously taken lessons from his uncle.'

'If he pulls through,' Massey said. 'No guarantee of that by the looks of him. But it's good to know he won't be able to wriggle out of it when he does recover. Cocky bastard should never have kept his rape kit in a metal box in that Yaris.'

'Donaldson says it's survived the flames pretty much intact,' Keegan said. 'Complete with an ancient bottle of Jovan Musk aftershave.'

'I got a Jovan Musk gift set for Christmas one year,' Lonnie said. 'Not long after I got married. Had to stop wearing it though. The wife said it was either her or it. I had no idea what the fuss was all about. Couldn't smell a thing. And then she went and left me anyway.'

They all laughed. Hands in pockets, Keegan turned to Portas. 'One thing I want to know.'

'What's that?'

'What the hell happened to Elsom's lot?'

Portas grinned. 'An articulated wagon jack-knifed across both lanes on a contraflow section of the A69. They're probably still stuck there.

***

It was sometime after 11 am on Tuesday morning before Massey made it home. He pulled his car onto the drive. No sign of Helen's car. She must have recovered enough to go back to work. He was glad. He didn't feel ready to even look at her again yet. He felt so bone tired he could easily just lay his head back and fall asleep out here behind the wheel, but he forced himself to make a move before his eyes closed. He didn't even have the energy to pour himself a drink to celebrate the news he'd received on getting back to Area Command, where a letter awaited him, confirming his permanent promotion to the rank of Detective Chief Inspector in charge of the MIT, to Keegan's old job.

He had no idea how long he'd slept by the time Helen's hand slid over his hip and up onto his chest, but it must be at least six o'clock if she was home from work. He felt her snuggle against his back and kiss his shoulder as she gently ran her fingernails down to his belly and back up to his chest.

He pushed away the residual rage from the last words they'd spoken to each other. She wanted to make up and, his defences lowered, he was all for that. No use pursuing pointless anger. And certainly not while she rubbed herself against him like that, making it perfectly clear what she wanted.

Who was he to say no, when he still felt so unbelievably grateful after all these years that she was his and no-one else's.

CHAPTER 91

Sunday 18th February 2024

Today was a good day. Two months to the day since David died, and four weeks exactly since Billy had taken her to his lodge out in the wilderness where she'd come so close to death herself. Neither of which should be anything at all to celebrate, and yet they were. She still felt glad that David was dead since the only alternative had been for him to live on in agonising pain.

And of course, obviously, she was overjoyed that her own life had not ended out there in Billy's old hunting lodge on the moors.

But there were two other huge reasons why today was a good day.

Firstly, today was for family, because not only was her new grandson, Davey, three weeks old today, but her youngest son, Alex had suddenly decided to spend a whole week up here, away from his job in London – although Ellie suspected that had more to do with his new girlfriend, who also hailed from the North East, than a wish to see much of his own family.

She'd already laid the big kitchen table for eight and she could smell the huge joint of pork roasting in the oven. For dinner this afternoon, besides herself, there'd be Alex and his new love, whose name he'd yet to tell her, Megan and Mark and the two children, although little Davey didn't yet require a place at the table. And James of course, but not Helen, for which she felt quietly grateful. There was something going on there. James wasn't ready to tell her, but she'd find out in time. And the eighth place at the table had been set for Christine Sparks, because today was the first weekend since her mother had moved into a care home. It wouldn't have been right for her to be sat at home on her own.

Ellie had wondered whether to invite Jess too, but she understood it was a long way to come at the best of times, never mind with a damaged leg and the lingering effects of concussion. She knew they'd always stay in touch now though. The poor woman had almost died that night in an effort to save her, so in a way they were now bound together.

She wished she knew what was happening with Abigail, and whether she was alright, but James had told her it wasn't appropriate for her to contact the girl until everything had been settled, which could take a long time yet. In the Land Rover back across the moors to RAF Spadeadam, she'd tried hard to impress upon Abigail the importance of having some sort of counselling after everything she'd been through. She hoped she'd taken the suggestion onboard and that someone was supporting her in that.

The second reason today was such a good day lay in the fact that this was the first day in those four weeks in which she'd been able to pick up a paintbrush and actually paint.

Ever since she'd been forced to listen to Stevie Grant telling her that the reason they'd lashed young Nicky Wragg's pathetic broken body to the upright beams was so that Nigs Bowen had room to castrate him like an artist at work, she had struggled to rid herself of the memory whenever she entered her studio.

Yet in the time since then, her profile as an artist had reached an all-time high. Mostly, that was down to the publicity surrounding her involvement in the solving of a forty year old rape and murder cold case, the hit and run death of her friend, and the unmasking of the serial rapist, who the press had named Musk Man, not to mention the bringing down of the infamous drug lord Stevie Grant and his main man Nigs Bowen. Her paintings had been selling like hotcakes, and the majority of her time had been taken up with making sales, packaging and sending paintings by courier to her new customers, and fighting off enquiries from all the galleries wanting to feature her work and all the people offering her commissions.

But this morning, with a watercolour sun gracing the garden with premature spring colour, she'd made a good start on a new portrait in oils, the inspiration for which had branded itself on her subconscious mind in the midst of those last horrifying moments in the lodge, before the police had broken down the door. The idea had crystallised since then, each day becoming a little clearer, until she woke up this morning and had no choice but to get straight out of bed and into her studio to express her vision in paint.

She stood back now and tilted her head to study the canvas before her.

Billy Wragg, naked and magnificent in the very moment Nigs Bowen had loosened his hold, allowing Billy to rise up from the floor, his lips fixed in a snarl, just as his head began to snap back. His arms still pinned behind him, but his powerful legs driving him upwards. Every muscle and every sinew straining. Those sensuous whorls of golden body hair glinting in the stark overhead light. And those startling blue eyes filled with fire and fury.

His eyes would be the very last thing she'd paint on this canvas, and she had to get them exactly right before she could judge the portrait finished.

It was because of those eyes that she'd acted like a stupid lovestruck teenager over a man who, despite the beauty, was evil personified. She was almost sixty years old for goodness sake. She'd known and lost a love far greater than most people ever got the chance to know.

How could she possibly have lusted after a man who oozed such insincere... *flattery,* while concealing such wickedness?

Yet if even one small event had changed, she might never have met him. If David's funeral had been a day earlier or a day later and Sonia had not spotted her at the crematorium. Or if her old friend had never signed her own death warrant by mentioning the anniversary of Julie's murder at that New Year's Eve party. If she herself had not then gone to Sonia's funeral.

Or if she'd had more self-restraint and gone home straight afterwards instead of succumbing to the allure of those electric blue eyes...

If, if, if ...

Sonia had called their bumping into each other after so many years serendipity, a happy coincidence, but it had been nothing of the sort.

Sonia's death and everything that had happened since then, right up to that terrible night out on the moors, had its roots in the evil Billy had wrought on that New Year's night forty years ago.

An old evil roused from sleep by the clashing together of a series of events that were anything but serendipitous.

Completely the opposite, in fact.

Looking back now, she could see the inevitability, the zemblanity of everything that had happened.

When this new portrait was finished, and the oil paint had dried, Ellie intended to arrange a little ceremony in the garden that only she would attend, and she would set fire to this canvas and watch the flames devour the beauty and the evil of the man who'd caused her so much pain, who'd murdered her two old friends exactly forty years apart, and had almost taken her life too.

And while he burned, she'd drink a toast to Sonic and Jools.

THE END

COMING SOON

What could an ancient Northumberland pele tower,
a charity rugby match, William Shakespeare
and an arsonist have in common?

Find out in this next unputdownable
Massey and Sparks crime thriller.

Sign up for all the latest news at www.jacquelineauld.com

f: JacquelineAuldAuthor

A FEW WORDS

I loved writing *An Old Evil*. My first novel, *The Children of Gaia*, took me all of twelve years to write and publish, while this story virtually fell out of my head fully formed. Perhaps it had been there all along, percolating away in my subconscious mind, ready to unfold as soon as I gave it enough head space to flex its wings.

For a small part of the story I have reused the fictional town of Hartington – which I invented for my first novel – as one of my settings, more for reasons of continuity than anything else. Also entirely fictional is the Filcher Estate in Ashington where Abigail Grant lives. A couple of other settings are based on real locations that have featured in my own life and of which I generally have very fond memories.

JoJo's nightclub for instance, is based on Scamps nightclub in Newcastle upon Tyne, where I used to go in my own youth. The fight I describe happening outside JoJo's actually did happen outside Scamps one night when I was there. Although the real incident wasn't quite as big, it was certainly vicious. Like Ellie, my friend and I were interviewed by the police as witnesses. I too was only nineteen at the time, and I'll never forget the looks on the faces of my parents when police officers turned up at our door the following day to take my statement.

Billy's lodge, out on the moors near Spadeadam, is based on my memories of a cottage my family actually did rent from the Forestry Commission when I was young. It lay a few miles further along the same desolate road I describe here, and was one half of an old hunting lodge that has now been renovated as a single dwelling. The ruined outbuildings I describe also really did exist, although are now rebuilt as a bothy the owners rent out as a holiday let. As kids, we balanced old tins on the ruined walls and used them for air rifle target practice.

There really was a herd of highland cattle grazing on the moors back then too, although I saw none on my research trip in 2023.

RAF Spadeadam, was known then as Spadeadam Rocket Research Centre and I imagined British rockets being flown to the moon, like those of the USA. But now I know the place tested Blue Streak ballistic missiles then, and later had a role in our Cold War nuclear weapons programme, so nothing lunar going on there at all. Today, the 9,600 acre site is used by the RAF as an Electronic Warfare Tactics facility where aircrews from NATO countries practise manoeuvres against the sort of threats and targets they'd face in real contemporary warfare situations.

The RAF Spadeadam characters who feature in this novel, however, are wholly from my imagination.

The King's Arms in Seaton Sluice, where the family go after David's funeral and Massey and Sparks later discuss the case, and the Snowy Owl near Cramlington, where Massey meets up with Guy Keegan, are real pubs that also made appearances in *The Children of Gaia*. The Woodhorn Grange in Ashington, the Jolly Bowman in Wallsend, the Brockwell Seam in Cramlington, the Shiremoor House Farm in North Shields and Three Mile in Gosforth are all real places too. And only now, writing this, have I realised just how many pubs I've included in this book! But then I did work for almost thirty years in the pub trade, and I actually managed three of those pubs mentioned above at one time or another.

The Café Des Amis in Morpeth, where Ellie meets Billy for their first date is real too, and heartily recommended if you're ever in Morpeth. It's a lovely friendly little place on Newgate Street where I occasionally meet up with a group of fellow retired colleagues from my last job before I became a serious author, although I have never overheard the sort of risqué conversation in there that Ellie and Billy have.

ACKNOWLEDGEMENTS

First of all, my utmost thanks to you for taking the time to read this novel. I hope you've enjoyed it. If so, please do tell all your friends, family, work colleagues, fellow dogwalkers, hairdresser, and slightest of acquaintances about it, and even any random strangers you might happen to strike up a conversation with.

I would be most grateful if you would also consider leaving a review on the platform where you bought the book, or on Goodreads to help other readers find it.

Thank you to the booksellers and buyers who find precious space for this book on their shelves. And thank you to my structural editor Cressida Downing, who pulled me up on all the instances I'd originally made Ellie sound too old to be only fifty-nine, who helped the story flow better and who has boosted my confidence as an author.

Thanks also to my early readers: my mother Shirley, my friend Jacqueline, and my brothers Geoff and David, each of whom brought a different kind of critical eye to my manuscript.

And not forgetting all the rest of my family and friends who have believed in me and rooted for me as I've struggled to learn the ropes as a self-published author. In particular, my husband Kevin for being so patient whenever I need a companion on a research trip and for continuing to come out with such off-the-cuff corkers, some of which inevitably find their way into my writing.

ABOUT THE AUTHOR

Jacqueline is the author of the Massey and Sparks crime thriller series, set primarily in the North East of England, and winner of the Lindisfarne Prize for Crime Fiction in 2022 for the opening of her debut novel, *The Children of Gaia.*

Writing crime fiction is something Jacqueline took up seriously only relatively recently after retirement from employed work, having spent three decades working in the pub trade and two in the charity sector.

Born and brought up in Low Fell, Gateshead, Jacqueline now lives in the south-east corner of Northumberland with her husband Kevin, the source of many of the off-the-cuff comments she includes in her writing.

Jacqueline draws inspiration from the countless beautiful settings, and grittier locations, around her in the North East of England, and from her years spent observing human nature and the complicated social entanglements of her regulars from her time working behind bars in pubs, hotels and nightclubs, although she has no idea if any of her regulars actually did commit the sort of murders she writes about.

FOR BOOK CLUBS

Is your Book Club looking for its next read?

This Book Club Kit Companion is currently available to all to download from my website:
www.jacquelineauld.com/An-Old-Evil/
The Companion contains: a welcome letter, an author bio, a collection of ready-to-go discussion points, a Q&A with me - mostly about the book, and information on locations featured in the book.

I love chatting to my readers, so please don't hesitate to contact me via the online form if you'd like to arrange an in-person discussion at your Book Club meeting:
www.jacquelineauld.com/Contact/

Printed in Great Britain
by Amazon